Praise for *Sister Stardust*

"Jane Green has outdone herself with this mesmerizing and delicious story of a young girl trying to find her way—and losing control—in the Swinging Sixties in London. Jet-setting, glamorous, intoxicating, and a tad bit dangerous, *Sister Stardust* transports you to the very center of the glitterati and under the spell of Talitha Getty. A wild ride."

—Taylor Jenkins Reid

"A sumptuous feast for the senses."

—Elin Hilderbrand

"Smart and sexy."

—Lauren Weisberger

"Jane Green's best novel yet!"
—Christina Baker Kline, #1 *New York Times* bestselling author

"An unforgettable, spectacular read."
—Adriana Trigiani, bestselling author of *The Good Left Undone*

"Wonderful and big-hearted, expansive and page-turning."
—Laura Dave, #1 *New York Times* bestselling author of *The Last Thing He Told Me*

"An absolute must-read."
—Liv Constantine, internationally bestselling author of *The Last Mrs. Parrish*

"The most luscious book you'll read this year."
—Jenna Blum, *New York Times* bestselling author of *The Lost Family*

"Glamorous."

—*Parade*

"Dreamlike… A rich and sensual read."

—*PopSugar*

SISTER STARDUST

Also by Jane Green

SISTER STARDUST

a novel

JANE GREEN

HANOVER
SQUARE
PRESS

HANOVER
SQUARE
PRESS™

Recycling programs
for this product may
not exist in your area.

ISBN-13: 978-1-335-44958-0

Sister Stardust

First published in 2022. This edition published in 2023.

Copyright © 2022 by Jane Green

"Haschich Fudge" from The Alice B. Toklas Cook Book by Alice B.Toklas. Copyright © 1954 by Alice B.Toklas. Copyright renewed 1982 by Edward M. Burns. Foreword copyright © 1984 by M.F.K.Fisher. Publisher's Note copyright © 1984 by Simon Michael Bessie. Used by permission of HarperCollins Publishers.

Hanover Square Press
22 Adelaide St. West, 41st Floor
Toronto, Ontario M5H 4E3, Canada
HanoverSqPress.com
BookClubbish.com

Printed and bound by CPI Group (UK) Ltd, Croydon, CR0 4YY

SISTER
STARDUST

TALITHA GETTY

October 18, 1940–July 11, 1971

"I knew the generation of the 60s: Talitha and Paul Getty lying under a roof of stars in Marrakesh, beautiful and damned, and a whole generation assembled as if for eternity where the curtain of the past seemed to rise on an extraordinary future."

—YVES SAINT LAURENT

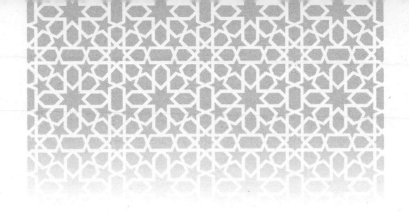

PROLOGUE
CLAIRE, OCTOBER 2020

It wasn't until my husband was in hospital that I finally allowed myself to cast my mind back. I knew he wasn't coming home, my protector, my best friend, my rescuer. The phone would ring every day, a doctor keeping me updated, and I am thankful for that, for the compassion he showed, the unendurable shock of not being able to visit my husband, to sit with him and stroke his hands, hands that used to be so strong, hands that could fix anything, including me.

I woke up at 2:13 a.m., my dream still vibrant and alive in my head. In it my husband was kissing my forehead, as he was always wont to do, looking into my eyes with tremendous love. It wasn't my husband as he is now, at eighty, but my husband as he was when he was young, his hair that bright ginger, his nose covered with freckles, his grin lighting up his face like sunshine. "You will be fine," he said. "I will always look after you." I woke up, and knew he was gone.

Six months later, and I am fine, if still adjusting. I am not sentimental. I sent all his clothes off to the charity shop. What on earth would be the point in keeping those closets filled? I gathered his shirts, his ties, his beautiful suits, and took them myself. I couldn't ask Tally; my daughter would have been horrified.

Since he died, I have started working again. Coiled pots and vases, some sculpture, but small, simple, not like the large ones I did twenty years ago, the ones with which I made my name. I have arthritis now and my hands don't have the dexterity they used to, so I keep the sculptures manageable. I take daily walks through Hampstead village and photograph scenes that might inspire me; the windows of the little shops that line Flask Walk, the people sitting outside the Spaniards Inn, the ducks on Whitestone Pond. I come back and sketch ideas for sculptures and pots at the kitchen table.

I have not been able to go into the attic, to sort through the detritus of a shared life. I have not been willing to revisit the past, but my husband has been dead for six months, and as I sit, this morning, I know that it is time. I need to move forward, I think, looking out the window, admiring the garden.

The shrubs are bursting into color as spring becomes summer, the profusion of cherry blossoms now dropping as the leaves burst into green, and the alliums and tulips start to droop, their time now over.

The kitchen soothes me, with its pale gray cabinets and open shelving, white plates and bowls stacked on the shelves. There is little color anywhere, save for cookbooks, and of course paintings that we collected over the course of our marriage, paintings that tell the story of our lives, that cover all the walls.

The television is on low as I decide to try to map out some new ideas today. I have an idea for an abstract duck sculpture, but first, I will paint it and see if I can make sense of it on the page. I dip my brush into water and swirl it around the cadmium yellow on a white china plate, diluting it until it is sufficiently watery, as I start to paint the outline of my duck. In the background, the murmurs from the television help me relax. I'm not really listening, until the music starts, when I catch my breath and drop the paintbrush.

It is *Madama Butterfly*. *Un bel dì, vedremo*. Maria Callas at her height. That voice. I would know that voice anywhere.

Un bel dì, vedremo
levarsi un fil di fumo sull'estremo
confin del mare.
E poi la nave appare.
Poi la nave bianca
entra nel porto, romba il suo saluto.

I have heard this over the years, of course. It is the most popular aria in the opera, filled with longing and a hint of the tragedy that follows. I remember exactly where I was when I first heard it. Morocco. I was perched on the edge of a divan, the colorful kilim cushions piled up behind me, as Paul carefully moved the needle on the record player. He explained the story of *Madama Butterfly* to me, and what this aria was saying. He would pause to sing parts of it, softly, as if in a reverie. Of course he spoke beautiful Italian, understood every word as he translated it to my willing ears. I knew nothing about opera. I knew nothing about anything. I had never heard anything so beautiful in my life.

"She sings bel canto," Paul said, when I opened my eyes. I had to close them, to shut everything out so I could lose myself in the music, and when I opened them there were tears trickling down my face. Paul was delighted, moving an ottoman close to me and sitting down. "It's beautiful, isn't it. Callas. There is no one like her. She had such rigorous train-

ing in the kind of singing that hasn't been fashionable for decades. Can you hear how light her voice is? Most of the bel
canto singers in the last century were taught by castrati, even
though there were few of them left."

I had never heard the word *castrati*. He saw my confusion,
and explained that castrati were male singers who were cas-
trated before puberty in order to keep their beautiful voices
intact. Women were not allowed to sing in churches, so in the
eighteenth century, castrati were often all you heard, many
of whom had been sold to singing schools by impoverished
parents, hoping their child would become rich and famous.
He explained that the castration stopped the production of
testosterone; the lack of it kept their bones soft, so they were
often very tall, with large rib cages. Their breathing capacity
was huge. They could hold notes for an inordinately long period of time, with a higher pitch than was thought humanly
possible. "They were the voice of angels," he said, once he
had recovered from a fit of laughter at the horrified expression on my face.

This was act 2, Paul explained, putting the aria on again.
"It's the perfect opera for the beginner. You love it, don't you."
The smile spread across his face as I nodded, and he explained
that Cio-Cio San is Butterfly, awaiting the return of her husband, an American naval officer, three years after their marriage. Butterfly imagines a glorious reunion, unaware that her
husband has married another woman. The opera culminates
with a distraught Butterfly taking her own life.

Paul taught me about opera, starting with the light ones,
Donizetti, Rossini, Bellini, moving on to Verdi and Wagner.
He would escape the hordes of people sprawled out on the
daybeds beneath fur blankets and retire to his room, playing
music, drinking whiskey, smoking opium. I would join him

there, some of the time, as his willing pupil. It was his sanctuary. And it became my sanctuary, too.

I am so lost in memories, the paintbrush having skittered across the floor once I had dropped it, I don't hear the doorbell ring, and suddenly Tally is there in the kitchen, her eyes wide with fear.

"Oh, thank *God!*" She claps her hand onto her chest, presumably to quell the heart attack that may or may not have been coming. "I thought I'd find you on the floor."

I am lucky, so very lucky, to have a daughter who lives a few streets away, who cares. Since her father died, she has worried about me unnecessarily, insisting I give her a key, insisting I check in with her on a daily basis.

"Darling, I know you're worried about me, but I'm fine. I was focused on painting." I follow her eyes to the red sable paintbrush on the floor next to me and lean down to pick it up.

"Are you sure you're feeling okay?" She looks at me suspiciously, her red hair so like her father's, streaks of gray running through the temples now.

I catch sight of myself in the metal around the wall oven. My hair is now completely white. I had always hoped it would go silver, a steel gray, something imposing and dramatic, but it went white, and I have accepted it, knowing that we always want what we cannot have.

And sometimes, when we get what we want, we discover it is not the thing that we wanted after all.

"Mum?" I look up, about to dive into the rabbit hole of memories again. "Can I go into the attic? I think there's a chair up there that would be perfect for Lizzy's room. She's tossed out everything from her childhood and wants mosquito nets around her bed and twinkly lights." She rolls her eyes at my granddaughter's antics. "Remember the gray chair that used to be in Dad's office in the old house? Is it okay if I take it?"

"Of course."

Tally's phone buzzes. She looks down at the screen and sighs.

"Everything okay?" I worry about my daughter. I have always worried about my daughter. She is a good girl, a kind girl, a girl who has spent her life thinking of others. I wasn't quite so keen on her husband. He was rather...dull. Or so we thought. None of us had any idea he was fooling around with his office assistant.

Tally only found out when she stumbled upon a pile of receipts in his desk drawer at home. Not just any old receipts, but receipts for regular dinners at The Ivy, Hakkasan, Ottolenghi. All restaurants Tally had never visited.

Alan could have got away with it had there just been receipts for smart restaurants, but there was so much more. There were countless expensive hotels. When he was supposed to have been on a work trip in Birmingham, he was, in fact, at Whatley Manor in the Cotswolds.

There were receipts from Gucci, and Chloé, and Chanel. Which was perhaps the worst thing of all. My beloved Tally is not interested in clothes. If she splurges, she'll buy one of those utterly shapeless but wonderfully comfortable dresses from TOAST, and pair them with her gardening clogs. She doesn't care. She is an incredibly talented artist (I like to think she got a little of that talent from her mother), who never fulfilled her potential because she found that her most favorite thing in the whole world, far better even than painting her days away, was being a wife and mother.

She did everything for Alan. Created a beautiful home filled with books and paintings, and cozy sofas piled with squashy cushions that beckoned you to kick off your shoes and curl up the minute you walked into the house. She cooked delicious dinners every night, and toward the end, when he was always working late, she would leave them in the fridge, tired of waiting up for him, watching the clock tick past midnight.

The receipts told a story of a man who was obsessed with a woman half his age. How tiresome, my husband and I thought, to become such a cliché. Of course we were horrified; everyone was horrified, but I was also, if I am completely honest, the tiniest bit impressed. Who would have thought Alan had it in him? Alan, who was so quiet, so disengaged from Tally, her art, her passions; Alan, who only seemed to be interested in working at the bank and very occasionally going to the opera, mostly when work had provided a box and his boss was going to be there.

My lovely Tally deserved better. Six months after he left to live with Mandy, Mandy found someone younger and more exciting. Alan attempted to come back with his tail between his legs, but—thank God—Tally said no. It was the only time I was happy to hear her saying no. Usually, she says no because she has lost her joie de vivre, is content, she says, being home, pottering in the conservatory that is now an art studio, listening to Radio 4.

Tally taps on her phone. "Sorry, Mum. A girl from my art class is trying to get me to join them in Ibiza. I keep saying I can't go, but she won't take no for an answer."

"Darling, why on earth wouldn't you go? Ibiza? Sunshine? Friends? You must."

"Mum. You know I can't stand travel. Look at my skin. If I so much as look at Mediterranean sun I turn into one giant freckle. Plus, Ibiza? Do I look like a twentysomething? I'm not the slightest bit interested in dancing all night and taking drugs."

Oh my, I think. If only she knew how much fun that can be.

"It's a big *no thank you* from me," she says finally, and I stop pushing. She is old enough to make up her own mind. So much of her life was devoted to others—to her husband, her children—I simply want her to seize life and squeeze out every last drop. She has no idea what she has no idea about. Ibiza is exactly where she should be. And if it includes dancing all night and taking drugs, so much the better. But I have pushed her far enough and know to keep quiet.

"Right. Shall we go into the attic?"

We head into the hallway and Tally pulls down the cord and ladder. She insists I go up first so she can catch me if I fall. I find my footing on each rung before I put any weight on it. I am quite proud of myself, of my newfound agility, as I stand up in the attic and flick on the light.

"My God," says Tally, coming up behind me, surveying the floor-to-ceiling piles, the furniture, the things I had forgotten about. "There's a whole other house stashed up here. How in the hell did you get everything up here?"

"The movers did it." I push a chair out of the way, hiding my own surprise, for I too hadn't realized quite how much there is up here.

The space is stuffed to the rafters with furniture and knick-knacks we had collected over the years, much of which has no place in this pretty but small Georgian cottage, the house we bought in the midnineties, once Tally was firmly settled and moved out, with a place of her own. I have loved it here, this flat-roofed gracious white stucco dwelling in the heart of Hampstead village. I love the floor-to-ceiling windows and the way the light pours into the living room. I love the pale tiled floors in the kitchen, and the grays and browns that are soothing to my soul.

Most of all I love the simplicity. And yet, when my husband was in hospital, for the first time in years I found my mind drifting elsewhere. To brass lanterns and markets filled with colorful spices. To soft-soled babouche shoes that slipped on like silk, shoes that kept my feet warm on mosaic stone floors that held on to the cold, no matter the temperature outside.

Tally is oohing and aahing over everything in the attic—
Victorian stationery boxes she remembers from her childhood,
sofas that would be perfect in her office. She finds an empty
box and starts packing it with knickknacks, calling over to
ask if it's okay, but I hardly hear her.

I had no idea quite how many things we had accumulated
up here. Tray tables, chairs, paintings from the very first flat
we bought when we returned from honeymoon, rails filled
with clothing not worn in years.

I spot a box filled with old paperbacks. My God. Why
are these even up here? A sense of dread washes over me as I
think of all the useless things that are contained in the boxes
up here, things that should have been given away or thrown
out years ago.

I flick through some of the books, seeing how I had made
occasional notes in the margins. The pages are now brittle and
yellow, the covers in both English and French. I had forgotten
that I used to read in French, that once upon a time French
came almost as naturally to me as English.

Truman Capote's *In Cold Blood*. *The Valley of the Dolls* by
Jacqueline Susann, and *The Adventurers* by Harold Robbins.
I remember buying *Valley of the Dolls* at Better Books. I'd
taken the bus to Charing Cross Road, desperate to visit this
bookstore, knowing that Allen Ginsberg had given readings
there, wanting to be part of something exciting, something
bigger than my sleepy Dorset past. I bought *Reality Sandwiches*
by Ginsberg, but never got through it, although I pretended.
I would go to parties and tell everyone how fantastic it was,
although I only read "Love Poem on Theme by Whitman,"
which was the most erotic thing I had ever read. I could see
how I grew in people's eyes as I casually explained the poem
to them, as if I were the kind of bohemian hip chick I was so
desperate to be.

Being able to quote lines from Ginsberg made me feel intelligent and worldly. I did not confess that I'd also grabbed *Valley of the Dolls* on the way home, which was much more my speed. I tucked myself in bed in our little room at the youth hostel and gasped at Neely O'Hara's behavior, mesmerized by the glamor of the world within those pages, hoping that my boring old life—being a shopgirl, sharing a tiny room with a bunch of other girls—would somehow transform into a life filled with glamour, excitement and handsome men. I wanted my world to be bigger than my job in a department store in the West End, bigger than my room in the hostel for unmarried women in Gower Street.

I wanted *more*.

"What's in there?" Tally comes over and looks at the book. "Ugh." The shudders. "I'm not sure a charity shop would even take those. They're all yellow." She flinches as I drop the book back on the pile.

I feel the boxes before I see them, pulling me as if by some invisible thread. They are at the very back of the attic, and although I have spent my entire life trying not to think about them, surely it is no coincidence that I heard *Madama Butterfly* this morning. This is a sign from the universe, I think, although I have not thought about signs from the universe in decades. Not since, I realize, leaving Morocco.

I see it, a box double wrapped in tape. I ask Tally for a key and saw it back and forth. Together we tug the box open.

My treasures from Morocco.

I shake my head as I pull out a clay ashtray and turn it over, the words *Hotel Mamounia, Marrakech* painted around its edges.

Ashtrays, I think. They used to be everywhere. We had crystal ones and china ones, ashtrays on every table. How funny, that everyone smoked back then. On planes, trains and automobiles. On television shows. In offices. In the bath. In bed. From the minute we awoke to the minute we went to sleep or, as happened far more often, passed out in a haze, the cigarette slowly burning in our fingers. Many was the time we would wake up with a shout, our fingers burned.

I remember the night I got this ashtray. Our whole gang was at La Mamounia for drinks. Bill Willis was there, rangy and so handsome with dark hair and sparkling green eyes, a true dandy in his flocked velvet jacket, a silk scarf around his neck, his large square Saint Laurent sunglasses—a gift from Yves, of course—never leaving his face, even though it was so dark inside the bar you could hardly see anyone.

He liked me, Bill, thank God. He could be vicious to those he didn't. I was beautiful then, and Bill liked beautiful things. Our whole little gang was at the bar at La Mamounia for drinks. He was already three sheets to the wind, high on life, or more likely the cocaine he had just snorted in the bathroom. He noticed me admiring the ashtray.

"Chérie?" His Memphis accent was unchanged, even when he spoke French. "If you want the ashtray, you shall have the ashtray." And he immediately pocketed it. The bartender was watching, but who would stand up to Bill Willis, one of the greatest decorators of all time?

"What even is that?" Tally's voice brings me back to the present as she takes the brown clay object from me and turns it over in her hands. "Is that an ashtray? You smoked?" She is horrified, as I laugh. Oh, if only she knew.

Tally helps me pull out the contents of the box, all those items I shipped back to London when I first arrived, drunk on the beauty and glamor, wanting, intending, to recreate the magic when and if I ever got back home, thinking I could transform wherever I ended up into a slice of Morocco.

I never unpacked those boxes.

All those items I spent fortunes on to send home—punched

brass lanterns that lit up the stalls in Djemaa El Fna at night, the candles inside casting dotted patterns over the canvas fabric draped across the stall.

The memories come flooding back as we keep pulling things out of boxes, Tally exclaiming over the beauty of it all. I say nothing, too busy remembering where I was when I bought each item, remembering what it all meant.

The rug Tally is now unfolding? I remember being swept into a tiny stall in the souk, a small glass of mint tea in my hand as I tried to explain I didn't want to buy a rug. By the time I had finished my tea, two young boys emerged from the back room. They grinned at me, carrying the rug I had admired when I first came in, not because I wanted to buy it, but because I was polite, did not know what else to say when the owner pointed it out and asked what I thought. Unbeknownst to me, as I was sipping tea and marveling at the warmth and welcome this lovely shopkeeper was giving to a young English girl, that rug was then wrapped in brown paper and tied with string, as the owner cheerfully informed me they would carry it back to my riad for me to make my life easier. Being the well brought-up girl I was, I had no choice but to buy it. I didn't know then that I overpaid enormously. I had no idea that haggling was what everyone did. The idea of offering less than asking price filled me with a shudder of mortification.

Tally keeps pulling things out.

"These are stunning, Mum! So much color! It's so unlike you!" There are pillows covered in rich embroidered antique fabrics, floor-length velvet kaftans with embroidered bibs and deep sleeves, slippers in the softest of leather, together with some of the clothes I had brought over from London. Tally gasps as she goes through the clothes.

"Mum! I had no idea you had all this hiding up here. Oh, my God! Look at this! This is Biba! And Ossie Clark! This is

probably worth a fortune. I would wear these kaftans now."
She shakes one out and we both stare at the tiny item word-
lessly, both of us knowing it would never fit my beautiful Tally.
I was sixties skinny thanks to a yogurt diet when I moved
to London and realized I would have to get rid of my country podge if I had any shot at all of being discovered, which
is why any of us moved to London back then, hoping to be
rich and famous, hoping a modeling agent would screech his
Rolls-Royce to a halt on the King's Road and jump out, telling us we were the next Twiggy, another Jean Shrimpton, the
new Celia Hammond.

"Mum?" Tally is standing there with a satinwood box in
one hand, a sheaf of letters in the other, a frown on her face.
"Mum? Who on earth is T?"

She hands me the letter as my cheeks flame up and my heart
pounds. This is what I didn't want to revisit. This is why those
boxes have stayed in the attic, untouched. My heart does a
flutter as I remember her sparkling eyes, her tiny hands and
feet. I remember the way she made me feel, and I am aware
that every fiber of my body is trembling.

*I miss you every second of every minute of every day. I long to
be back in London so I can see you again. I love you. T.*

"Oh, my darling." I look down to my shaking right hand,
to the gold serpent snake with the ruby eyes that I have not
removed in over fifty years, the ring my daughters loved rubbing when they were small, the ring that hides a story I have
never told. My eyes take on a faraway look as I wonder if now
is the time to revisit the past, if now is the time to forgive
myself, to get over the guilt and pain that I have carried with
me all these years.

"Oh, Tally. There is so much you do not know."

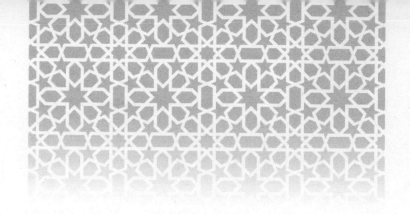

ONE

DORSET, 1966

I knew where Linda hid the biscuit tins. My stepmother thought she had gotten clever, putting the Tunnock's caramel wafers somewhere else, thinking I wouldn't know. She liked to hoard things, just in case someone came for tea, she would say. No one ever came for tea. I'd seen that red-and-gold foil packaging at the bottom of the shopping bag. I knew she would keep them for herself.

I felt around in the cupboard over the oven. Nothing. The biscuit tins contained dried Garibaldi biscuits and Rich Tea. She had stopped buying Lemon Puff Creams and Bourbons, because she knew I liked them. She'd started buying biscuits I wouldn't eat, but she couldn't resist the Tunnock's for herself.

I moved around the kitchen, wondering where I would hide them if I was my stepmother. I found them, eventually, in the tin box by the back door that held my father's shoe cleaning kit. I pried open the lid to see the wrappers glinting, and felt a swell of satisfaction that I had outsmarted Linda.

I didn't care about her finding out. I stood there in the kitchen and ate four Tunnock's at once. The first bite was delicious, the rest, I didn't taste. It was only later, much later, that I realized I wasn't eating because I was hungry; I was eating to fill an emptiness, to numb myself to my dull, pointless life.

As soon as I had finished, I felt sick. And guilty. And filled with shame. I took the wrappers and rolled them into tiny balls, folded them in tinfoil and stuffed them in the bin, all the way at the bottom, underneath the damp tea bags and chicken bones. I wondered, as I made my way up to my bedroom, how long it would take her to discover they were gone.

The woman people so often presumed was my mum was not actually my mother. I didn't think of her as Mum, I never did. I had always thought of her as Linda, my mum's best friend, and have never forgiven her for stepping in "to take care of" Dad, right after Mum died.

I was five and my brother, Robbie, was seven. It was a car accident. Mum was riding a bike from our house in Evershot to Holywell, and was run over by a bus. No one was drinking, no one was doing anything wrong, but the bus driver didn't see my delicate mother on her delicate bicycle until it was too late.

I was so young I didn't fully understand what had happened. I remember Linda collecting me from the village school, sobbing as she picked me up and hugged me. I remember thinking it was all so strange, that Linda was crying, that she was hugging me so tightly. Linda hadn't ever been married and I remember my mother once saying that Linda didn't like children very much, so perhaps try to leave the two of them alone when she came over.

I didn't remember my mother nearly as well as I would like. The few memories I did have were unclear. I had a memory of her holding me in the garden, swinging me round and laughing. Of her tucking me up in bed and covering me with kisses. I always felt safe with her, and we knew we were loved. She was beautiful, my mum, young, fun loving.

When she died, something died in my dad, as well. The fun, said my brother and I, when we were older, when we would huddle together in the garden, sneaking cigarettes and discussing my dad's marriage to Linda and why it felt so very wrong.

After my mother's death, my dad seemed to age instantly. He was bewildered in those early days, with absolutely no idea how to take care of two young children, which of course gave Linda ample opportunity to move in. Suddenly, she was picking us up from school, or we would come home and find her in the kitchen making tea. When my dad got home from work, she'd have a drink waiting for him, a whiskey in a crystal glass. She'd serve it on a tray along with a small bowl of nuts, the paper neatly folded next to it, his slippers drawn up to his chair.

"Why are you doing that?" Robbie had asked Linda, never having seen a setup like this before.

"Every man deserves to have comfy slippers and a nice drink waiting for him when he gets home from work."

"Mum never did that."

Linda sniffed. I didn't know what that meant, but it didn't feel good, that sniff filled with unsaid words, judgments about our mum. "Yes, well. Your mother and I didn't always agree on how to treat a man."

Later, much later, when Robbie reminded me of this, I felt a wave of fury. What did Linda know, I thought. Linda, who had never been married, who didn't have a boyfriend, who didn't like children. Linda who always seemed to have a sour expression on her face, unless Dad was around, when suddenly she was all smiles. Linda, who was not a patch on our mum, but who somehow managed to insinuate her way into our family.

Then one night our dad called us into the living room, announcing that he had some wonderful news to share. He was sitting in his chair, Linda standing next to him, a hand on his shoulder, looking—for once—like the cat that got the cream.

"Linda and I have decided to get married," he said. I noticed that he wasn't able to look Robbie or me in the eyes. "Obviously, no one can ever replace your mum, but I think Linda is a welcome addition to the family, and I'd like to think your mother is looking down on us all and is happy. This is what she would have wanted."

No she wouldn't, I thought, noting that I had never seen Linda smile in the way she was smiling that day. This was indeed the pinnacle of everything she had ever wanted in life.

"I think as well, now that Linda is going to be my wife, you ought to call her mum."

"But we already have a mum," said Robbie. I didn't say anything, and swallowed hard to try and get rid of the lump in my throat.

My father cleared his throat as Linda's smile faltered. "Yes, your mum will always be your mum, but now you have another mum. This is a mark of respect to Linda as my wife and as your new mother."

I held back the tears until later, alone in bed, crying into my pillow.

By the time I was eighteen, it felt like nothing good had ever happened to me. My brother had moved away, and now I was on my own, standing at the bus stop every day to catch the bus to my job at Denners, the department store in Yeovil, trying to stay in Yeovil as late as possible so I didn't have to see my stepmother.

★ ★ ★

I had made a friend, Dorothy, known to all as Dottie, who lived in Yeovil with her parents and worked in the underwear department at Denners. I was in ladies' clothing, but we tried to coordinate our breaks so we could sit together in the canteen and share a cup of tea and a cigarette.

I sometimes spent the night at Dottie's, loving the fact that her parents always made me feel welcomed. If we were lying on Dottie's bed, gossiping, her mother would bring us a pot of tea and a plate filled with cakes. There was no judgment there, no frowning if we asked for more or denying us seconds. It helped that Dottie's parents were as round as she was. Sunday lunch was the best. Enormous piles of mashed potatoes and roast beef, boiled cabbage and Yorkshire pudding swimming in gravy. I'd polish off at least two helpings, and somehow always found room for the steamed pudding and custard.

Dottie's house was fun, completely different to mine. Sometimes, on a Friday night, we'd come downstairs to watch *Ready Steady Go!*, her parents letting us take over the sitting room so we could turn the music up and dance around, doing our best to emulate the dancers on the telly as we bumped around the room.

Our dream was to go to London, but we weren't quite sure how to turn that dream into a reality, so we spent hours planning what we would do, where we would live, how we would decorate our London rooms. Naturally, our plans involved boyfriends, in my case not just any old boyfriend, but Dave Boland, lead singer of the Wide-Eyed Boys. Why Dave Boland would be the slightest bit interested in a chubby, round-faced, wavy-haired eighteen-year-old from Dorset was beside the point. In my fantasies, I had miraculously morphed into Twiggy, my hair turning into a silken sheath. My calves, which couldn't fit into any of the suede knee-high boots I longed for, were suddenly as slim as a reed, encased in the perfect Biba boots.

I sat on the floor of my bedroom, leaning back against the bed, overcome with guilt at the food I had just eaten. *It will be okay*, I told myself, staring at a poster of Twiggy on the wall. Tomorrow I'll only eat lettuce. I'll never eat chocolate again. One day I will look just like Twiggy, and I'm going to have an amazing life.

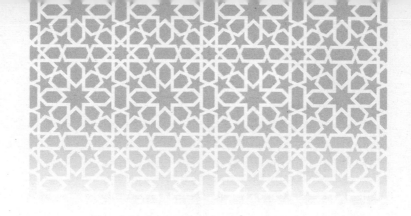

TWO

It was Saturday afternoon, and I was over at Dottie's house. I propped a magazine up on the dressing table and tried to copy the makeup, ringing both our eyes with dark kohl, making a big mess of the fake eyelashes we'd bought at Boots. There was glue everywhere, which I covered up with black eye shadow until we were suitably smoky.

Robbie had said he'd be late. He was bringing his best mate Benji to see a band at the Assembly Rooms in Yeovil, and we were going to meet them there. This gave us the whole day to prepare, including much daydreaming by me of how Benji was finally going to realize I was the woman of his dreams. Benji was growing into a fine-looking man, a freckled redhead with broad shoulders and an easy way about him, although I felt anything but easy around him. Still, he always made time for me, teasing me, but gently, in a way that made me feel important, made me feel seen.

That Saturday, Dottie and I both finished work at Denners around lunchtime, then came home to get ready for the evening. I was determined to finally iron my hair flat, which both Mr. and Mrs. Connell found hilarious. They stood in the doorway of the kitchen, laughing at me as I lay my head on the ironing board and Dottie carefully ironed it until my hair was pin straight.

When we were finally ready, Dottie's dad dropped us off in town. With a few hours to kill before the Assembly Rooms opened at eight, we wandered around the record shop, asking the assistant to play 45s of Petula Clark's "Downtown," "Stop! In the Name of Love" by the Supremes and "What's New, Pussycat" by Tom Jones. Dottie and I squeezed into a booth, sharing the headphones, bopping our heads, impressing each other with how well we already knew all the words, including synchronized hand movements for the Supremes.

We sat for coffees in Finley's the tobacconist, then went to the Blackbird for egg and chips, ignoring the bikers who wolf whistled every time girls came in.

Dottie had been to the Assembly Rooms before and seen the band who was playing that night, The Tornadoes, but I had never been. The prospect of seeing an actual band live was almost as thrilling as seeing Benji. To me back then, life in Yeovil seemed as sophisticated as you could get, certainly a lot more sophisticated than my tiny home village of Evershot.

By the time we arrived, there were groups of people waiting outside the Assembly Rooms. A boy Dottie knew from school, Tom, was there with a group of friends and a hip flask filled with Scotch stolen from his parents. We all passed it round outside, taking big swigs and trying not to cough, swarming the door as soon as they opened it.

We stood around, chatting with Tom's friends, waiting for the band to start and, in my case, waiting for Robbie and Benji to arrive. I kept checking my watch, worrying they wouldn't come, but once the band started, we started dancing, and soon all was forgotten.

I felt someone put their arms around my waist from behind and whipped my head round.

"Robbie! You made it!" I gave him a huge hug. Benji stood next to him.

"Where's my hug, Bean?" he said cheekily. I hugged him quickly, mostly so he wouldn't see that my cheeks had turned bright red. He had always called me Bean, as in, little bean, as in, annoying younger sister. But I was eighteen now. I worried the teasing quality of our relationship would never change.

"You're looking rather sharp." He stood back and looked me up and down admiringly.

He might have been teasing me. He probably was teasing me, but I couldn't hide my delight.

"How about a drink?" Benji said. "Lord knows, I need one. What can I get you? Glass of wine? You are eighteen now, aren't you?"

"Glass of wine would be lovely," I lied, not having yet grown accustomed to wine. I would have been perfectly happy with a glass of lemonade, but I didn't want to appear childish.

"Coming right up." He went off to the bar with Robbie.

The wine went straight to my head. As did the glass afterward, particularly after the beer and Scotch I'd already had. I can't say I was completely drunk, but I was definitely less inhibited than I would have otherwise been. I flung myself around the dance floor with abandon, shaking my straight hair and gyrating with the best of them. Robbie and Benji both danced with us, and when they started playing the slow songs, when they played "What the World Needs Now," Benji took me in his arms and I honestly thought I might throw up with nerves.

He pulled me so close I could feel his breath on my neck, and we shuffled around the floor as my heart pounded.

"Can I ask you something?" he whispered, after a bit. I pulled back so I could look him in the eye, get ready for my first kiss. I nodded, in what I hoped was a sexy way, and tilted my head a bit, unsure of whether or not I should close my eyes.

"There's this girl I really like in London," he said. "She reminds me a bit of you. She's gorgeous, a model and trying to be an actress, and I've phoned her three times this week, but she hasn't called me back. You're a girl. You understand how these things work. What should I do? Should I call again?"

I stared at him in horror as a sob made its way into my throat, and before I had a chance to think about what I was doing, I had shoved Benji away and was running out of the Assembly Rooms in floods of tears.

Benji already liked someone. She lived in London. She was thin, and gorgeous.

There was only one thing for it.

I would have to become the sort of girl Benji liked.

THREE

I refused to tell Dottie what had happened. Her father picked us up, and when we got home, Mrs. O'Connell came in with a pot of tea and an arctic roll cut into huge slices. I declined and, as shameful as it is to admit, watching Dottie polish off three slices, not having any myself made me feel good.

I found the yogurt diet in a magazine I was reading on one of our breaks at work. Looking back, I'm mortified. I suppose I thought that thinness equaled happiness, that the only way I could get the things I wanted—a boy, a job, a dream, even revenge—was to look a certain way. Forgive me for my superficiality. As I say, times were different then.

"Look, Dottie!" I pushed the magazine excitedly over to her, pointing out the before and after picture. "She lost two stone!"

"Goodness. She looks like a completely different person!"

Dottie scooped a forkful of Victoria sponge as I sipped my coffee. I had read somewhere that coffee sped up the metabolism, as long as you drank it black and without sugar. I was training myself to drink black coffee, and even though the taste was vile, I swear I felt thinner already. I definitely felt more sophisticated, sipping black coffee, refusing cake.

"We should do it!" I said. "It says the yogurt diet may burn fat and boost your metabolism!"

Dottie looked dubious. "When you say *may*, what does that mean?"

"Look at that before and after. It means losing two stone, that's what it means. If you're not going to do it with me, I'll do it alone."

"No, I'll do it." Dottie was always eager to join in. "What do we have to do?"

I quickly skimmed through the directions. It said yogurt for three days could lead to over half a stone weight loss. I could eat yogurt for more than three days, I was certain of it. The girl in the picture had added steak and vegetables, but for three days every week she had nothing but yogurt.

"Let's do this!" I imagined going off to London, going to parties, meeting rock stars.

"When shall we start?" Dottie said, standing up. "Are you sure you don't want any cake? It's very good. One last blowout before the diet?"

"No, thank you, Dottie. There's no time like the present. I'm going to start right now. I'm going to stop off on the way home and buy the yogurt."

Dottie nodded enthusiastically. I knew she didn't truly want to try the diet, but I loved her for joining anyway; I loved her feigned enthusiasm, and for ensuring I was never on my own.

We didn't own scales, but by the time the following weekend came around, it felt like I had definitely lost half a stone.

My waistbands, which had been squeezed tight only a week before, were suddenly gaping so much I had to borrow Dottie's mother's sewing kit to take in the seams.

My round face, the face that could be "*so* pretty if I lost weight," was definitely slimmer, and I thought—could it be possible?—I could see the hint of actual cheekbones.

Dottie's mother was skeptical, not least because Dottie and I were turning down all her delicious food.

"I don't think it's good for you young girls to eat nothing but yogurt." Mrs. O'Connell frowned over her huge plate of Lancashire hot pot. "Young girls need to eat."

I said nothing. Dottie accepted a small plate of the Lancashire hot pot and boiled cabbage. "I'll go back on the diet tomorrow," she whispered, when her mother was out of earshot.

By Sunday night when I was back home at my dad's, back home with Linda, I cracked.

She'd bought Tunnock's again. A replacement pack for the packet I had eaten the other day. I wasn't looking for them this time, was determined to carry on losing weight, to stick to the diet, but I opened a drawer in the kitchen looking for scissors, and there was a familiar flash of red and gold.

I shut the drawer with a bang and went upstairs to my bedroom, but all I could think about was biting into those chocolate wafers, that familiar sweetness and deliciousness making its way into my stomach and making me feel, for just a few moments, absolutely nothing.

I tried to fight it. I tried to bury myself in a book, but the words swam on the page. I could taste the chocolate, feel the chocolate, and I couldn't think about anything else.

I raced downstairs, grabbed the Tunnock's and took them up to my bedroom, guilt, fear and excitement making my heart pound.

I didn't want to eat them, didn't want to break my diet, but even as I thought that, I was tearing open the wrappers, cramming one after another, after another, into my mouth. It stopped me feeling inadequate, stopped me hating Linda, stopped my lovesickness over Benji. For those few minutes of eating, I felt absolutely nothing. I didn't understand then that I was using food as a drug, numbing myself from pain, that no amount of numbness would stave off the crushing guilt and shame that would sweep over me the minute I finished eating, the minute that chocolate was all gone. I knew I had to finish them. If I saved one bar, it would call to me, whisper from the corners of my room, from underneath the bed, and I could have no peace until it was all gone. Tomorrow, I told myself, I would start again.

I was up in my bedroom, reading *Black Sheep* by Georgette Heyer, the perfect way to escape my life, when I heard Linda call up the stairs.

"Claire? Claire? Come down here right now."

Oh, God. I knew that tone of voice. She'd once again discovered the missing chocolate. Why hadn't I gone out to the corner shop and replaced them?

I decided to brave it out.

Linda was standing at the bottom of the stairs, her lips pursed.

"Where are they?"

I shrugged. "Where are what?"

"You know what. There was a brand-new packet of Tunnock's in the drawer yesterday. The packet I bought to replace the packet you stole before. Where are they?"

"Yesterday? I didn't touch anything yesterday." That, at least, was true.

"I don't care whether you touched them yesterday or today, where are they?"

"Why do you always blame me? I don't know."

"Who else is there, *Claire*? Robbie's moved out. You're the only person who could have eaten them." Linda rolled her eyes.

For a minute, I wished we had a dog.

"Maybe it was Dad."

"Your father doesn't like them."

"Maybe you're confused. I haven't seen them. Maybe you didn't buy them. I don't know. Either way, it wasn't me." I sounded appropriately outraged at her accusation. If I were her, I thought, I might be starting to doubt myself right about now.

"Do you think I'm stupid?"

Oh, Linda, I thought. Do you really want to know the answer to that? Yes, I thought she was stupid. And cold. And a gold digger. And selfish. She was the diametric opposite of my mother.

I said nothing.

Linda sighed. "Do you know what the real pity is? It's that if you stopped stuffing your face, you'd actually be quite pretty. You'll never get a boyfriend looking like that. Is that what you want?"

My face darkened as I felt tears springing behind my eyes. But I wouldn't cry in front of her. That would be letting her win.

"You think boys like fat cheeks and a double chin?" she continued, glee in her eyes, knowing that she was hitting me at my weakest spot. "You think Benji would ever even notice you, looking the way you do? Why do you think I gave away your mother's clothes? No point in keeping them when they'd never fit you."

I exploded. All these years of my walking away, refusing to

take the bait, saying nothing, and this, finally, was too much. I had no idea she had given away my mother's clothes. I thought they were boxed up and in the attic, waiting until I was old enough, or thin enough, to wear them.

"Fuck off!" I screamed, shocked and exhilarated at the volume, the sound of my voice reverberating around the small staircase, the shock on Linda's face. "How dare you give my mother's things away. Who bloody asked you anything. As for what boys like, you have no idea what boys like. You just tricked my father into marrying you, you witch. You think he loves you? He doesn't love you like he loved our mother. You have no idea what love is, but I do, because I saw the way my father looked at my mother, I saw the way he treated her. You're a cruel, bitter woman who will always be second best."

There. I'd said it, all the things I'd always felt, the things I'd been too terrified to say, knowing that once said, they could never be unsaid. I stood, frozen, feeling at once strong and terrified as I watched Linda turn red, her eyes wide with shock.

"Get out," she said, through gritted teeth. "Pack your things, and get out."

Usually, when we fought, she would say, *Wait until your father gets home*, or, *Wait until I tell your father*, both of which filled me with shame. I didn't want to test my father. I didn't want to give him the opportunity to side with Linda; it was easier to stay out of trouble, to never put my father in a position where he had to make a choice.

We had never discussed Linda, but I felt sure that he sided with her only because he had no other option. He never said as much, but when Linda's aunt died and she went to Wales to stay with her cousin, my father ever so slightly rolled his eyes when Robbie made a joke about her controlling ways.

"Go on," Linda spat, from the bottom of the stairs. "I've had enough, and your father's had enough. Get out."

I pushed past her, pulled a suitcase from the cupboard under the stairs and bumped it up to my bedroom, not caring if I chipped the wallpaper. I didn't need to be told again.

My heart was pounding, and it felt surreal that I had finally dared to swear at her, to let out those pent-up feelings. I had no idea where I would go, given that Dottie and her family were away for the week, but I suddenly felt strong. Maybe this was what I needed to finally get my life started.

I'd go to London. London, where the streets were paved with miniskirts and go-go boots; London, where I'd get to have the life I'd always dreamed of living.

London.

I had ten pounds in my pocket, a couple of weeks' wages, but I was sure it was enough. Excitement overcame the trepidation.

I was on my way.

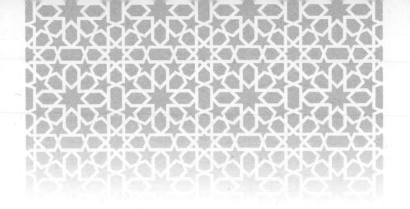

FOUR

Waterloo station was filled with people, more people than I'd ever seen anywhere. Walking along the platform, lugging my suitcase behind me and with no idea where I'd go, I felt exhilarated. A girl passed me in a cubist minidress, her hair in a slick bob. I wanted to look exactly like her.

In the main concourse, I stopped outside a recording booth, stunned to find something so glamorous in a railway station. "Make your own record in 3 minutes," it said. Two shillings and sixpence.

I didn't have enough money to do it, not if I wanted to find a hotel, so I waited until a giggling couple appeared, just to see how it worked. They squeezed themselves into the booth, slid the door closed, and I heard snatches of singing and lots of laughter. After a little while, they emerged, holding a proper vinyl seven-inch disc.

The girl saw me hanging around outside. "Go on," she said. "You should do it. It's so much fun."

"Another time," I said, thinking of the fiver in my pocket and wishing I had saved more back in Dorset. "Do you by any chance know of any cheap hotels around here?"

"Sorry, love," said the man. "We're not from here. We were just up to see a band at the Marquee last night."

"Oh!" My eyes widened. "How was it?"

"Fantastic!" said the girl. "It was a new band called Cream. So good. You should go."

"I will." She smiled at me, and for the first time in my life I didn't feel like an outsider looking in. I felt like I was at the center of the action. Even though I'd had moments of anxiety on the train, this was a sign that I had made the right decision. Now I just needed to find somewhere to stay.

I didn't know anyone in London. I had enough money, I thought, for a hostel or a cheap hotel until I found a job, which would surely only take a day or so. There was an information desk in the station, but no one was there. I took a leaflet that listed some of the hotels, and a map, and set off, my suitcase growing heavier with every step.

I lugged it up the steps of the first run-down hotel on the list, pausing before pushing the door open so I could catch my breath. The woman behind the desk didn't even look up, as I panted over toward her. "No rooms available." Her voice was a flat monotone.

I bumped the suitcase down the steps, telling myself it would be fine, that the next hotel would definitely have a room, maybe even a front desk attendant who would smile at me, who would make me feel something other than an invisible country bumpkin.

"Fully booked," said the second, who looked at me but didn't smile.

The door was locked at the third, and no one ever showed up to answer it.

There was one hotel, much nicer than the others. The carpet was red and plush, and I made my way to the front desk.

"Do you have any rooms available?"

"Certainly, madam," said the man, with a smile as my shoulders relaxed. I was so relieved I felt tears prick at the back of my eyes.

"We have one queen-size room left."

"Queen-size!" I immediately thought of a plush large bed, of disappearing into clean sheets and sleeping the sleep of the dead. "Lovely!"

"It's five pounds, ten shillings per night," he said. "How many nights will you be staying with us, madam?"

I stared at him.

"Do you have anything…less?" I swallowed hard, willing myself not to cry.

"I'm so sorry, madam. That's the last room available."

I stood in front of him, a lump in my throat and tears threatening to fall, praying he might take pity on me, but I wasn't the sort of girl that could work that kind of magic. I thought of the girl in the station, with the cubist dress and endless legs. He probably would have found a way to let her have the room for less.

An awkward silence fell. He cleared his throat, then disappeared through a door behind him. I heard whispers before another man came out.

"I'm sorry, madam," said this one. "If you're not going to be taking a room here, we're going to have to ask you to leave the premises."

It was dark, then. Suddenly London didn't seem paved with

miniskirts and go-go boots, or with glamorous men who only wanted to bring out my star potential.

"I'll give you a place to sleep tonight, love," called a man who staggered out of a pub in a blue-and-white Everton scarf. His friends, all similarly attired in blue and white, laughed and jeered at me as my ears burned and I quickened my step to get away from them.

I walked and walked, until I had ticked off all the hotels. It was the weekend of the FA Cup Final, between Everton and Sheffield, and all of England seemed to have the same idea as me—to find a cheap hotel room in London.

I was cold, hungry and beginning to regret my impetuous decision. Why hadn't I called Robbie and gone to stay with him? Why hadn't I phoned Dottie? Why had I been so set on London?

I walked around in circles until I was so tired I couldn't walk anymore. I found myself back at the station, underneath the viaducts. It was quiet under there, and protected from the wind. It wouldn't be so bad, I thought, to spend one night here, tucked away in the arches. Tomorrow would be a new day, tomorrow I would find myself a job. Tomorrow I would feel better about everything.

I felt the ground with my hand, and it was cold and damp. I couldn't do it. I couldn't bed down here, no matter how tired I was.

"Want some cardboard?" A woman's voice echoed out from one of the arches. "You can't sleep on the pavement. It'll chill you to your bones. I've got some spare cardboard if you want."

A face emerged from the darkness, weathered and wizened, but probably not that old, perhaps the same age as Linda.

"Thank you. That's so kind, but..."

"It's alright, darlin'. Shit happens to the best of us. I don't sleep much anymore so I'll keep an eye on you, make sure your stuff is safe."

I could tell she was kind, but I couldn't do it. I couldn't lie down on a sheet of dirty cardboard under a dark, damp viaduct in Waterloo, even with a kindly hobo godmother looking out for me.

"Have it your own way," she said, when I shook my head. "You won't find any place cozier. And be careful."

The streets of London were not so appealing at night. Waterloo station was quiet, and there were benches outside. In the end, I sat on a bench, my arm protectively around the suitcase next to me, should anyone try to steal it. I was awake for most of the night. Occasionally I'd nod off to sleep, but my head falling to one side would wake me up with a jolt before I'd fall asleep again.

One of those jolts snapped me out of a dream in which a huge caveman was squeezing my leg, deciding whether or not I was meaty enough to throw on the fire. I awoke, terrified, more so to find a man sitting squeezed up next to me, his hand on my leg, moving up my thigh.

I stood up quickly, my heart pounding. The man was roughly my father's age, his eyes clouded over with an expression that years later I recognized as lust. Even then, with this strange man's hands on me, I had been brought up to be polite, to never talk back, to have respect for your elders.

He grinned then, stood up and leered over me as I stood, shaking with fear, before we both turned at the sound of a loud hiss.

"Get your hands off her." A blade from a small penknife was held against his neck, by the old woman.

"Alright, alright, grandma." He backed down and stepped away. "I wasn't up to nothing."

"Not much you weren't. Filthy scum." She stepped toward

him, waving the knife, hissing in his face. He turned and walked quickly away.

I have replayed that scene over and over during the years, and in every reenactment I shout at him, or swear, or ask what the hell he thought he was doing, but at the time, I said nothing, was too shocked and stunned to find the right words. I hate to think what might have happened had the old lady not stepped in.

"Told you," she said triumphantly. "You'll want that cardboard now, won't you?"

I nodded meekly and followed her under the arches, sitting far enough away that the smell of her wouldn't knock me out.

"I don't know how to thank you," I said.

"I warned you," she grumbled, before rolling onto her side, and in a matter of seconds she was snoring.

I didn't try to sleep after that. I sat and listened to her snores, and when the sun finally came up, I left the arches to walk around the station, avoiding dark corners, waiting for the world to open up, terrified by the unknown, wishing I could hop back on a train and go home, even as I reminded myself home was no safe shelter for me, not with Linda there.

I had never been more grateful for daylight, for the small coffee shop on the corner that opened its doors at six o'clock, allowing me to stash my suitcase and wash my face in the tiny loo, waiting for eggs, beans and toast, and a cup of hot tea to see me through the day. I asked for an extra roll, and slid the egg and half the beans into the roll, and wrapped it in a paper napkin, putting it carefully in my bag.

I left with the roll, and a cup of tea in a cardboard cup. Under the arches, my friend was still fast asleep, snoring, a tatty blanket now over her head to keep the daylight out. I didn't wake her. I slid the roll and the tea next to her, and hoped it might somehow save her day, a small thank-you for the way she saved mine.

FIVE

Daylight washed away the fears from the previous night, along with the hopes, dreams and possibilities that had filled my silly head on the train. How naive, I thought, that I expected to be pulled out from the crowd at Waterloo Station, that I would find the streets paved with dance auditions and modeling gigs, that I would step straight into an exciting life.

Instead, tramping up and down Oxford Street, my feet were sore and I could feel blisters forming as I limped, pausing every few minutes to change hands, my suitcase growing heavier and heavier, bumping against my legs as I walked, going into every shop I could find to ask if there was a job available.

In the phone booths there were cards stuck on the windows advertising bedsits. I slipped each one into my purse.

There was nothing at any of the department stores, not at

House of Fraser, Debenhams, nor Peter Jones. I approached woman after woman, occasionally filled out forms, but no one had granted me an interview.

I ended up in Selfridges, exhausted from carting that suitcase up and down Oxford Street. In the makeup department I asked a woman who tried to sell me lipstick whether there were any jobs available, cringing in shame when she looked me up and down and visibly recoiled.

"A job in the makeup department?" she asked. "Looking like that? You can't be serious, dear?"

I couldn't help it. The tears started, and as they trickled down my cheek, they became proper sobs, my shoulders heaving with the strain of trying to keep them inside. The woman who had tried to sell me lipstick softened, her face crumpling with concern as she rushed out from behind her counter and threw an arm around my shoulders, ignoring the suitcase next to me.

"There, there," she soothed. "Look, my lovely, I know I sounded harsh, but you're never going to get a job looking like that. Why don't we get you fixed up and looking smart? I know Bourne & Hollingsworth are looking for a girl in the millinery department. I'll give you a bit of makeup and I'll phone my friend Sharon who works there and tell her to look out for you. How's about that?"

I sniffled, pulling a ratty old tissue from my sleeve and blowing my nose. "Thank you," I managed. "I'm so sorry. I didn't mean to turn into a blubbering idiot."

"Don't you worry," she said. "I've got a daughter not much younger than you. I understand. I've got some lovely Yardley Face Slickers that will give you a glow, and we'll cover up those bags under your eyes. Look at you, what a pretty face you've got. I know how to turn you into a Bourne & Hollingsworth girl. Lose a bit of weight, and you might make it up to women's clothing!"

I felt a hot burst of shame, but it disappeared as she started to apply makeup, chatting away. Soon I felt as if I had landed in the lap of the gods, perched on a stool as Jane Hazel Ward (she told me her full name) gently instructed me to open my eyes, close them, turn this way and that. She applied lashes, and lipstick, and when she had finished with my makeup, went to fetch her handbag and used her own brush and headband to tame my unruly locks into a sleek ponytail.

"Perfect," she said, standing back to admire me, then passing me a hand mirror to admire myself. I looked quite unlike myself. She had shaded my cheeks to give the illusion of cheekbones, and used eyeliner to make my eyes almond shaped and exotic.

I couldn't believe it was me.

"I don't know what to say. I don't know how to thank you."

"When you get your first paycheck, come and buy a lipstick from me." She winked. "And I'll tell you what. Leave that big suitcase here. You can come and get it later. You can't go showing up for a job interview with your life's possessions by your side."

Wishing me luck, she sent me off to Bourne & Hollingsworth.

The makeup did wonders for my self-confidence. I walked through women's clothing, looking at the skinny shopgirls, wishing I could look like them, wishing I could get a job in women's clothing, but the millinery department delighted me, with its polished wooden stands of various heights displaying all manner of gorgeous hats.

"Hello," said a smiling young woman. "You're not Claire, by any chance, are you?"

I nodded.

"I'm Sharon. I just picked up a message from my friend. She told me to look out for you. It's perfect timing. We've found someone in millinery, but the girl in ribbons was fired this morning, and they're desperate. Would that be alright?" She walked as she talked, and I followed her, through haberdashery, through millinery, to the ribbon department.

"Miss Smythson!" She led me to the manageress, who looked perturbed. "I have saved the ribbon department! This is Claire. She's ready, willing and able to start work immediately."

"Thank the Lord!" Miss Smythson gave a quick prayer up to the heavens. "You'll be known as 406. I shall call you over the loudspeaker if I need you. In the meantime..." She pulled an apron from behind a counter and handed it to me.

"Sharon? Will you show her the locker room and put her coat away? We'll need you on the floor immediately."

I scuttled after Sharon to the locker room, placing my coat and bag in a locker.

"Does this mean I've got the job?" There had been no interview, no filling out of forms, nothing I had to do. I couldn't believe my luck had turned.

"Trial by fire." She grinned at me. "If you work hard and you're efficient, Miss Smythson will keep you forever."

I returned the smile without telling her what I was thinking. I didn't want Miss Smythson to keep me forever. I didn't want ribbons.

I wanted to work in women's clothing.

I wanted to work at Biba's.

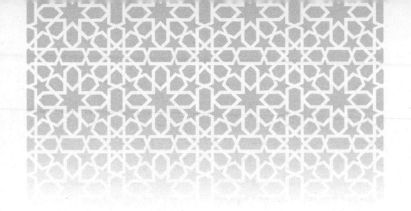

SIX

Biba had opened almost three years earlier in Abingdon Road in Kensington and immediately became the coolest shop in London. It was, I imagined, chock-full of rock stars and models, a shop where going to work felt like going to a nightclub every day.

I had made my pilgrimage to Biba and hadn't dared go in. I wouldn't step inside until I was certain I looked like I belonged.

I was grateful to have found a job, to have finally escaped Dorset, to be in London, but for those first few weeks, I was utterly unmoored. I didn't miss Linda, but I missed my routine. I missed Dottie. As much as I wanted to move to London, I missed the safety that came from living in the same village in which I had grown up, a village where I knew everyone.

Now, I had taken a room in the women's hostel in Gower Street, Warwickshire House. I was surrounded by women my own age, but they all seemed to know one another, all seemed to have already made friends, and as the newcomer I had never felt quite so alone.

I thought I had been desperate to get away, but standing in line for the bath every morning as clouds of steam billowed through the hallways, girls refusing to hurry up, the constant strain of worrying I would be late for work, the ever-present loneliness, made me homesick.

How could I be lonely, I kept thinking to myself. I was surrounded by women. But they weren't friends and the constant swarm made me oh so aware that I wasn't one of them, that I didn't fit in.

I had been assigned a roommate, Suzy, whose previous roommate was—oh, the scandal!—asked to leave when her ever-growing stomach turned out to contain something other than treacle tart. She, it seems, had been the perfect roommate.

"Oh, we had such fun!" trilled Suzy. "We went to all the best places together!"

"I could come with you," I said hopefully, shrinking, as Suzy vaguely sneered in my direction before going back to her magazine with a sigh.

Every morning I would be woken up by the sounds of Suzy's bedside Teasmade. There were two cups and saucers in the cupboard, but not once did she offer me one. She was from Surrey, and mocked my faint Dorset accent, which I swiftly decided to change, practicing how to sound like a Londoner under my breath.

"Go on," she'd say, while we were waiting for the bathroom. "Tell Monica where you're from."

"Dorrrrset," I'd purr, lingering on the *r*, as everyone I knew did, before I realized they were sniggering at those rolling *r*'s and soft *t*'s, before I started pronouncing it like a hardened Londoner. Where was I from?

"*Daw*-sitt," I replied, relieved that they never asked me to repeat it.

I stood in line by the pay phone next to the staff staircase and asked the operator to put me through to Dottie's phone number.

"Dottie! It's me! I've got a job at Bourne & Hollingsworth in London! No, no, I'm in the ribbon department, but still! London! The store has a women's hostel for unmarried female employees and I moved in two weeks ago. It's called War-wickshire House and it's like a five-star hotel! It has a ball-room and a swimming pool! I want you to come! You would love it, and it would be much more fun if you were here. I've spoken to them and they could give you an interview if you could come up. Oh, please say you'll come up! They need one more girl in haberdashery and I've already mentioned that I might have a friend. Miss Smythson is the manageress and she's a bit of a dragon but she likes me."

"It sounds wonderful!" she said. "Have you met anyone fa mous yet? I'll die if you've seen the Beatles!"

By the time I put the phone down, I was excited by life again. Hearing Dottie's breathless enthusiasm reminded me of the possibility, and as my stomach rumbled, I started to think that it would get better.

I hadn't eaten that day and had an apple in my bag. My stomach was rumbling. I stared at the menu, smelling chips, and salt, and vinegar, imagining eating a huge burger, but no. I couldn't do it. I ordered a coffee, with nothing to eat.

Women's clothing, I told myself. If I lost more weight I might have a chance at women's clothing, and women's cloth-ing was the next step in getting where I wanted to be. And where was that? Oh, foolish girl that I was, I wanted nothing other than frippery—to wear pretty clothes, to be famous, to have some fun, to meet interesting people, before getting married and having a couple of children. I had no ambitions then beyond becoming someone's wife and mother.

Suzy worked in women's clothing. Even though we weren't friends, she would bring other girlfriends back to our room, and they'd sit on her bed gossiping while I pretended to be reading a book, all the while listening to what they were saying.

"She's a terrible commission-swiper," Suzy said to Deborah one night. I perked up, careful to keep my eyes glued to my book, to not let on that I was listening.

"Every time I get approached by a customer that looks rich, Miss Maple appears from nowhere and takes over. I can't bear it. I know exactly what she's doing. I could have made so much money from that fur coat today, but she swiped the customer just as she always does."

"Someone should move the old bag to ribbons," said her friend. "She's much too old to be in women's clothing." I looked up to see Suzy shoot her friend a warning look, tipping her head toward me, before they both started giggling.

Suzy and Monica went to the Marquee on Friday night. I stayed at the hostel, ate by myself, and was up in the room by eight. Suzy, who was horribly untidy, had a ton of clothes draped over the back of her chair. I couldn't relax with the room that untidy, but before I hung everything up in the wardrobe, I tried a few things on. Her furry coat with the balloon sleeves that made me feel oh so glamorous, her black bouclé jacket with the gold buttons that almost…almost…did up. If I sucked in my stomach and turned to the side, I could nearly pass.

My door was shut, but I could hear the excited chatter of the girls on my floor leaving, dressed up for dinner dates, or off to see a band, or sit in the window of a coffee shop, making two cappuccinos last for four hours.

I sat on the bed with the book on my nightstand. I didn't understand how I could be so lonely. If anyone talked to me, it was small talk, and it hadn't led to any friendships, and certainly not with my roommate, who I abhorred.

I didn't even care about Biba, or going on the telly, or meeting a rock star. Finding a single friend would have been enough.

Three weeks later, just as I was thinking I had made a terrible mistake, might have to chuck it all in and go back to Dorset with my tail between my legs, Dottie phoned.

"I didn't want to tell you in case it went wrong, but I'm coming to London!"

"What? How? When?" My words jumbled up in my excitement.

"I came up for an interview last week, but I wanted to wait to hear whether or not I got the job before I surprised you!"

My mouth dropped open, a faint chink of light suddenly appearing at the end of the tunnel. Dottie was my secret weapon. On my own, this was too hard, too overwhelming, but with Dottie by my side, I knew that London would work.

Dottie arrived the following Saturday. My diet, such as it was, was working. It wasn't actually a diet, more of a starvation. I had an apple a day, lots of yogurt, and very occasionally a slice of toast, but that was all. For the first time in my life my desire to be thin had overtaken my desire to eat.

Oh what misery, I think now, looking back at young me. I was perfect just as I was. Why did we think that being thin was the answer to everything? How did we buy into such a ridiculous thing?

"Claire," Dottie's mother looked at me with concern when she stepped out of the car. "You're disappearing! Are you unwell?"

"No, it's a new diet." I tried to hide my delight.

"Well, don't lose too much weight," said Dottie's father, his hands resting on his stomach. "You'll disappear completely. Come on, then," he said, looking up at the imposing front door of the women's hostel. "Let's see what this place is all about."

I had spoken to Miss Nicholl, who had agreed to let me move rooms to share with Dottie. Suzy was delighted, and Monica had been bringing things to our room for days. It was as if I had already left.

Dottie collapsed on her bed, dizzy with excitement.

"This isn't a *hostel*!" She hugged herself tight. "You were right! It's a dream come true! Maid service for our evening meals! A snack room!"

"I'm not snacking," I said sternly, flicking the pages of yet another magazine I had bought that week which focused on women's weight.

"A ballroom!" Dottie kept talking. "Do they hold dances? I want to go and see some bands, Claire. When can we go out? Where shall we go? And Carnaby Street! When can we go shopping?"

Her excitement and delight were contagious, and within minutes we were chattering away, making plans for our glamorous futures.

It was as if I had never left, and it felt wonderful having my friend by my side.

I had received an envelope from my father, sent to Dottie's house. Inside, was a card that just said "love, Dad" and a five pound note. I knew he couldn't do anything else or Linda would never let him hear the end of it, but this was enough; this showed me he cared, it showed me he was sorry and that he loved me, whatever Linda might think.

"When shall we start?" Dottie said, standing up.

I had a plan. Robbie was about to turn twenty-one, and there was going to be a party back home in Dorset. I may have been kicked out of my own home, but nothing would stop me from being at my brother's party, and the sweetest revenge would be to have transformed myself into someone Linda could never hope to be.

"Robbie's party's happening in a few weeks. By then I plan to be the same size as Twiggy."

Dottie's eyes widened. "Ooh! I'd forgotten all about that! What are you going to wear?"

"I haven't decided yet." I was trying to be cool, trying not to show how excited I was at my imminent reinvention, my imminent revenge; how excited I was to step into a life that I was sure would be waiting for me once I did everything the magazines told me to do.

I didn't know then what I know now. Back then, I felt that my life would only begin if I transformed myself into the look of the moment.

If only I had known how dangerous it would be

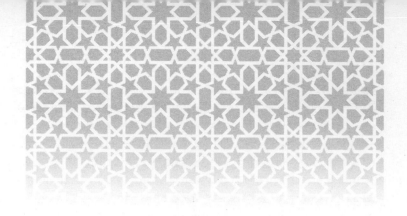

SEVEN

LONDON, 1967

I was fast asleep, an eye mask on, when I felt myself being shaken awake.

"Claire! Wake up! Claire!" I pushed the satin mask off my face to see the light had been turned on and Dottie was standing over me, shaking me.

"What's going on? What time is it?" For a minute, I had a horror that I had overslept and would be late for work. I was still at Bourne & Hollingsworth, having finally made it to women's clothing, but Miss Selfridge had just opened, and suddenly B & H felt old and stuffy, a huge old department store where we were never called by our names, only by our numbers or occasionally our surnames. I was sick and tired of Miss Poole, the fashion floor manageress, singing out across the floor, "Four oh si–ix?" her voice a singsong lilt, and I would have to sing back, "Yes, Miss Poole?" to see what she wanted.

When Miss Selfridge opened, everyone was talking about it, how the mannequins were based on Twiggy, how they were selling paper dresses that you could just throw away after one wear. Dottie and I went to see what all the fuss was about, and the manageress immediately came over and offered me a job.

I had finally achieved the right look, you see, and in doing so, had found my confidence rising tenfold. I finally felt like I belonged. The yogurt diet had worked, and my teenage pudge, at nineteen, had disappeared, leaving me with proper cheekbones, a flat stomach and slim legs that looked perfect in a miniskirt. Not that we had been allowed to wear miniskirts at Bourne & Hollingsworth. We would leave the building after work and roll our waistbands over and over until our skirts were short enough. Dottie had a friend who worked in the rag trade over on Great Portland Street, who manufactured miniskirts and matching knickers, which was a life changer. It meant you could walk up to the top of a doubledecker without worrying.

I asked the manageress if I could let her know, worried I would have to leave the hostel, which was only for shopgirls of B & H, or so I thought. As we were walking out, we heard, "Claire!" and turned to see a girl who lived on the floor below us in the hostel.

"Hello!" She came over to us with a big smile. "I don't think we've ever met properly. I'm Celia. I live in Warwickshire House on the floor below you. I've seen you both in the snack room."

"How do you do," Dottie said primly, and we all shook hands.

"I saw you speaking to Miss Caruthers. Are you coming to work here?"

"*Can* you work here and still live at Warwickshire House?"

"Oh, yes. There are a few of us here who live there."

"I should have realized." I turned to Dottie. "Isn't that Mary down the hall training to be an actress at RADA?"

"Yes. And the girls upstairs are all nurses at University College Hospital."

"So I could come and work here and stay at the hostel?"

"Oh, yes. You ought to. It's enormous fun and everyone's been coming in." She leaned forward conspiratorially. "Pattie Boyd was in yesterday. She bought eight paper dresses and was so pretty and so kind. I was ever so jealous of her before I met her, because George Harrison is my dream man, but now I just adore her."

"Did you talk to her?" Dottie's eyes were wide as Celia's chest puffed up with pride.

"I helped her and she asked me which of the dresses she should get, and she bought all the ones I chose."

"You know Pattie Boyd!" whispered Dottie in amazement. "You're practically best friends!"

I pretended to be blasé, but this was why I moved here, this was what I dreamed of—to rub shoulders with Pattie and Jenny Boyd, to be *discovered*, to become rich and famous, even though at nineteen I had no discernible talent, but I was blonde, and newly thin, and convinced that thanks to my recently bought and long-saved-for over-the-knee Biba suede boots, it was only a matter of time before I was spotted walking along the street by a film producer in a Rolls-Royce. The fact that Miss Caruthers had spotted me across the crowded floor of Miss Selfridge and made a beeline to offer me a job was, I presumed, only the beginning.

I took the job and loved it, which is why I was lying in bed, my satin mask pushed up, rubbing the sleep from my eyes, confused and terrified that I had overslept and would be losing the chance to meet George, or Paul, or Mick, or Keith.

"Jean just came back. It's two a.m. She bribed Mr. Harding with jelly babies so he won't tell on her." We had a curfew of midnight, and woe betide anyone who got caught, although often Mr. Harding was not at the desk, or at least not by the time we got back, and we would sneak back to the hostel in the early hours and sign the book, pretending we had come home at eleven the night before, that he must have been off in the loo and hadn't noticed us coming back.

"And?" I was starting to get grumpy. I loved Dottie, but why was she waking me up at this ungodly hour?

"And she says there's a party at a flat in Montagu Mews North and Mick Jagger and Marianne Faithfull are supposed to be there."

My grogginess left me in one fell swoop. I leaped out of bed, my heart pounding. "Are you sure?" We would hear these sorts of things all the time. There was a pub that Mia Farrow was supposed to have visited regularly, and we hung out there but never saw her. Henekey's on Portobello Road was rumored to be filled with tons of famous people on a Saturday morning, but I was usually working. If ever we did manage to show up to, say, Bar Italia, thinking that Gerry Marsden was there, thanks to a breathless phone call, we'd show up and they would have just left.

"I'm absolutely sure. Apparently it's their manager or something."

Half an hour later I was in my Biba suede boots, a mini-dress from Miss Selfridge, and a feather boa I had bought at Portobello market, sneaking down the back stairs on our way to the unknown. Whatever it was, it was bound to be more exciting than spending the rest of the night in bed in Warwickshire House.

★ ★ ★

In 1967, London was suddenly filled with color, and excitement. All anyone could talk about was *Sgt. Pepper's Lonely Hearts Club Band*. We had pages from magazines stuck up with Sellotape all over our room, models we admired, fashion we lusted after, pop stars we dreamed of, lives we longed to be leading. Everything felt like it was moving from black and white to Technicolor, and *Sgt. Pepper* gave way to feathers and fur and brocade.

Dottie and I couldn't afford Carnaby Street, but that didn't stop us going there to window-shop. Everywhere you turned, it was an explosion of flowing scarves and floppy-brimmed hats, the men in candy-striped blazers and striped trousers. It was glorious. We'd wander up and down Carnaby Street drooling over the windows of Lady Jane, stopping at Gear to admire the Union Jacks surrounding their windows. There was Lady Jane, and Pop, and Carnaby Girl, and we watched the windows change, psychedelic fashions taking over the mod-ish fashion that had come before.

I had never known women who shopped. No one had ever shopped. It's hard to understand now, but Britain took so long to recover from the war, and those years were gray and depressing. Suddenly England won the World Cup, and the future wasn't just bright, it was here and it was ours. We all wanted to look good, to wear the latest fashions, to listen to the latest music, even when we couldn't afford it.

Every now and then Dottie could get hold of a "cabbage," an extra dress that a good cutter would be able to get out of the fabric, selling it on the side and on the cheap. They'd make their way to the markets, these dresses made of sewing garbage, but Dottie's old boyfriend would often offer it to her, and she would frequently offer it to me.

"Can you imagine if Charlie is there?" Dottie had a crush

on Charlie Watts of the Rolling Stones, but I was far more interested in the Wide-Eyed Boys. Dave Boland, the deliciously cute lead singer with his long blond curls and big blue eyes, was my future husband. Of course, I would have settled for Paul McCartney, but Dave Boland was my number one.

"If Mick's there, maybe they'll all be there. Can you imagine? Perhaps they'll ask us to star in a film." We all knew that's how Pattie Boyd had been discovered by George Harrison—she was playing a schoolgirl in *A Hard Day's Night*, and reader! She married him! If it could happen to anyone, it could surely happen to us.

We were on the top deck of the number 3 bus, looking out at the shops on Oxford Street. We were both so young, I was about to turn nineteen, and Dottie was seventeen, and we still thought it was cool to sit in the very back row. Every time the bus stopped we would turn to see if any good-looking young men had got on, and we had just passed Debenhams when three boys stomped upstairs.

"Well hello," said the most handsome one, swinging into the seat in front of us. "Do you have a spare fag?"

I happened to have a brand-new pack of Benson & Hedges Pure Gold. I'd switched from Rothmans because the packaging of these was so beautiful. I felt sophisticated, opening up a packet of Pure Gold, the crinkle of the plastic, the gold paper inside. The royal seal lent the cigarettes a class and elegance that we would find shocking today, but when he asked for a cigarette, I felt proud that I was drawing out Pure Gold.

I offered them to everyone, and they all took one, the boy pulling out a lighter and lighting it for us.

He paused before lighting his own, then looked up at me. "What do you keep in reserve for special occasions?"

I couldn't resist. The ad was playing all the time. "Why, Pure Gold from Benson & Hedges, of course."

He laughed. "Where are you two lovely girls going in the middle of the night?"

"We're off to a party," said Dottie. "Off Baker Street."

"A party? At this time?"

"Can we come?" said one of the other boys.

It did occur to me then that this was perhaps slightly bonkers, getting a bus in the middle of the night to a party where we knew no one other than a friend of a friend, but nothing felt dangerous back then. I had no street sense, and the world was there to be explored, common sense be damned!

"I wish we could invite you," I said quickly, seeing that Dottie was making eyes at the biggest of the three boys, who seemed rather taken with her as well, "but it's a friend of a friend and we don't really know them. I don't know that we can turn up with other people, especially people we don't know."

"Oh, come on," said the first boy, the confident one. "I'm John. Now you know me."

"I'm Andrew," said the biggest one.

"Jimmy," said the other.

"I'm Dorothy but all my friends call me Dottie, and this is Claire."

"Claire?" John laid his chin on his hand, stretched across the back seat and looked at me. His hair was growing out, the ends just touching his shirt collar, and the sleeves of his jacket were embroidered. He was actually rather handsome, even though I found his confidence slightly annoying. "You don't look like a Claire."

"Oh no?" I couldn't help the flirtatious lilt in my voice. "What does a Claire look like?"

"Claires are sensible and boring. They work in accounting offices and always go to bed before eleven. Claires are definitely not sitting on the bus in a feather boa on their way to a party. I'm going to rename you." He closed his eyes and thought for a few seconds. "You're a Cece."

I started laughing. What kind of a name was that? He pronounced it *See-See*. "Cece? That's a ridiculous name. I sound like an American housewife."

"I beg to differ," he said, sitting back and watching me. "Cece is a girl who knows what she wants. She's the kind of girl who's going to be famous. Cece could be a model, or an actress, or a singer. Cece is just the kind of girl who'd look excellent on John's arm."

I raised an eyebrow. "John Lennon? Hmm. I'll have to consider it."

"Not John Lennon," he grumbled. "John McKenna. Who would be me."

"Nice to meet you, John McKenna," I said, warming to him but still dubious.

"I have a little something else," John McKenna said, as the bus trundled along, producing a fat joint from his inner pocket. "Shall we?"

I had smoked pot before, but not much, and I'd never really understood what all the fuss was about. This time I took the proffered joint, which was about the size and shape of a tampon, which made me want to laugh without even taking a hit.

My Lord, it was strong stuff. Within minutes, we were all giggling hysterically, so much so that the conductor came storming up the stairs.

"What are you lot up to up here," he said gruffly, pausing to smell the sweet, undeniable aroma of cannabis. "You're smoking drugs, aren'tcha? Get off my bus. Go on. The lot of you. Off."

I tried to protest, but I was laughing too hard, and the five of us stumbled off the bus as the conductor muttered darkly. We found ourselves on Baker Street, with not a soul around.

"What do we do now?" John was clearly the leader of this particular pack.

"Oh, just come with us to the party," I said. I didn't have the strength or mental acuity to suggest anything else.

We found Montagu Mews North, which seemed to take an age. By the time we got there I was feeling less giggly and far more normal, but there didn't seem to be any party. It was a tiny mews bathed in darkness, but at the end there seemed to be a dim light flickering in one of the windows.

It's funny to look back and think how different times were then. We thought nothing of knocking on a stranger's door in the middle of the night. I was the one who knocked, John standing next to me, the others hanging back, Dottie and Andrew standing shoulder to shoulder, a beatific smile on her face which was either because the boy she liked clearly liked her, too, or because she was stoned. I couldn't tell which it was.

It took a while, but eventually a young man wearing an untucked cotton shirt and beaded necklace came to the door.

"Hello," I said politely. "We're here for the party. We're friends of…" I paused. I had forgotten the name of the friend of the friend.

"Hey, man!" He stepped back, gesturing for us all to come inside, and I felt relief wash over me. I was such a good girl, I realized, so worried about offending or doing the wrong thing, and I so desperately wanted to be different. I wanted to be the kind of girl who showed up to parties in the middle of the night, stoned.

We could hear low music coming from upstairs and a strong smell of cannabis, which got stronger as we climbed the spiral staircase to the floor above, finding ourselves in one large room, windows at both ends, lit only by lanterns filled with flickering candles. The floor was covered with large pillows, and bodies were everywhere, some sleeping, some smoking joints, a low murmur of conversation, with the faint sounds of "Strawberry Fields Forever" coming to a close. As it ended, someone got up and moved the needle back to the beginning of the song, and hands were raised to lazily greet us as we stood, looking for a space to sit.

I felt a bubble of excitement. I couldn't see anyone famous although it was hard to make people out in the dim light, but there was a sophistication about this crowd. They seemed to have the kind of cool I craved. The air smelled of cannabis and incense, a cloying, sweet smell that made it hard to breathe when you first walked in but which you quickly acclimated to. On the walls were framed posters of art I had never seen before, swirling colors and fields of poppies. A beaded curtain, now held back by purple velvet ribbons, separated the room into two.

The host, who turned out to be Nigel, pulled a hookah over and offered it to me.

"We were talking about Redlands," says a girl with long dark hair and huge lashes that I coveted. One of the girls down the hall had just bought Loads of Lash from Mary Quant, which was the most brilliant thing I had ever seen, false eyelashes on a sort of tape, that you cut to whatever size you needed. I had my regular eyelashes on, but hers were so amazing I couldn't stop staring at her.

"What do you think?" continued the girl. "Were the Stones set up?"

Thank God. The Redlands bust. I had no idea what she was talking about until then, but as soon as she said the Stones, I knew. It had been in the headlines for weeks: Stones Arrested; Nude Girl and Teapot!

I remembered the story well. Keith Richards, Mick Jagger, Marianne Faithfull, Michael Cooper, Christopher Gibbs and Robert Fraser all went to Keith Richards's country house for an acid trip and got busted. Robert Fraser, an old Etonian art dealer friend of theirs, was the only one found with hard drugs, a bunch of pills that turned out to be heroin. They didn't find anything on the others, but arrested them anyway.

I didn't have particularly strong feelings about it either way, but my favorite part of the story was that Marianne Faithfull came downstairs naked but for a fur rug.

I wanted to be the naked girl under the fur rug.

"Did you hear about the Mars Bar?" said someone else. Of course I had heard the story about the Mars Bar, but it seemed ridiculous. Mick Jagger was supposed to have been caught eating a Mars Bar from between Marianne Faithfull's legs, but it made no sense to me. It didn't sound the least bit erotic, and far too sticky and messy to be true, especially about Marianne Faithfull, who seemed too classy to be doing that sort of thing.

"I don't believe it for a second," I spoke up, once I had exhaled a long, thick stream of smoke. "Marianne would never do something like that."

"A friend of my friend was one of the coppers and he told me."

I started laughing. "Those stories are always passed on by someone who knew someone who knew someone who was there. I still don't believe it."

The girl with the lashes looked at me admiringly. "I like you," she said. "What did you say your name was?"

I paused before answering. "Cece," I said, for in an instant that's who I had become.

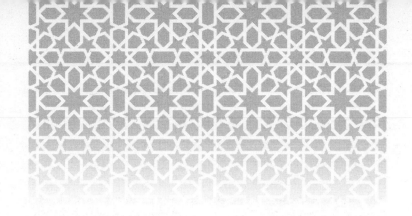

EIGHT

Four days later, John took me to the Scotch of St. James.

I had heard about the famed private club, of course, and knew it was somewhere behind Fortnum & Mason, but had no idea how I could possibly get in there. Dottie and I had been to the Ad Lib once, right before it closed, to hear The Moody Blues and we'd been to the Bag O'Nails just off Carnaby Street, but the Scotch of St. James was, by its very name, out of our league. Or so I had always thought.

It had opened in July 1965, and, according to the papers, which I pored over the next day, three Beatles were there, four Rolling Stones, The Who, The Kinks, The Animals and The Hollies. It was in a small cobbled street that Dottie and I had walked down after treating ourselves to chocolate milkshakes one day. Next to the Scotch of St. James was the Indica Gallery and Bookshop, and we had gone in there, ostensibly to look for books but in fact hoping that we might see Paul McCartney's girlfriend Jane Asher, whose brother was one of the owners, or perhaps Marianne Faithfull, who was married to John Dunbar, one of the other owners. Of course, the only people we saw were other giggling girls our age, all clearly there for the same reason. I had picked up a number of books, but they were pretty far-out, and I couldn't get much beyond the first couple of paragraphs, although I had to buy something. I ended up with *The Psychedelic Experience* by Timothy Leary.

I had no idea how prescient that purchase was. Today everyone knows he was the man that brought LSD into the mainstream, the founder, if you like, of psychedelic drugs, but back then he was a psychologist, a director of the Center for Personality Research at Harvard, investigating the effects of legal hallucinogens, including LSD, believing them to be an excellent alternative treatment for alcoholism and schizophrenia.

John knew about psychedelic drugs. He knew about everything. He was twenty-three, it turned out. He worked as a manager for a band called The Bended Grass, who he said were going to be the next big thing. He was living in a flat in St. John's Wood with Jimmy and Andrew, and even though nothing about his friends seemed glamorous to me, the fact that John was in the music business, that he knew Brian Epstein, that he had once stood next to Paul McCartney at the Ad Lib, with whom he chatted about seeing The Yardbirds the week before, made him at least three times more attractive to me than he already was.

I fancied him that night we met. He kissed me at the party in Montagu Mews North and wanted to find a bedroom to make love, but I wasn't quite ready for that. You can take the girl out of Dorset, but it seems I wasn't ready for someone to take the last bit of Dorset out of the girl.

Dottie was almost as excited as me, even though she wasn't coming. We spent ages in our little shared room, me trying on outfits, half the girls on our hallway stopping by to give their opinion. Everything I had now felt a little...ordinary. This was—I hoped—the hippest club there had ever been. I couldn't wear Miss Selfridge, or a cabbage. I wanted to look and feel extraordinary.

Celia downstairs saved the day. She heard about the Scotch of St. James night and phoned her older sister, who agreed to lend me some clothes. There was a knock on the door and Celia walked in with two large plastic bags.

"My sister says don't spill anything on it or she'll murder you," she grinned, pulling a long, flowing multicolored gown from one of the bags.

Dottie and I both gasped at the same time. It was the most beautiful item of clothing I had ever seen, a long, flowing velvet robe, the back covered in an appliqué of a woman in a psychedelic field of flowers, in every color imaginable.

"It's like Joseph's coat of many colors!" sighed Dottie.

"Where on earth did she get this?" I slipped it on over my white minidress and it instantly transformed me.

"It's from Granny Takes a Trip," she said, handing over the other bag, laughing at my confusion. "The shop? In Chelsea?"

"Oh!" I lied. "Of course." I had never heard of it.

"I don't know what shoe size you are, but she got these from Chelsea Cobbler and that's what she wears with the coat." I pulled out a pair of snakeskin boots in a size seven. A little big, but I stuffed the toes with tights, and they fit well enough that you'd never know they weren't my size.

"Oh, Claire!" Dottie clasped her hands together. "You look like Paulene Stone."

"Do I?" I was delighted as I turned my head to look at the torn-out page of Paulene Stone on my wall. I finished my makeup, a very pale pan stick on my lips that made my eyes look enormous. "Oh, and I'm not Claire any longer, remember? I'm Cece."

"I love the name Cece," said Celia, who popped her head out the doorway to respond to someone who was calling for me. "Apparently your beau is downstairs," she said. "He's chatting up Miss Nicholl."

"He's hardly my beau," I said, but I was secretly delighted that anyone thought I had a beau.

I groaned, not wanting Miss Nicholl to see me tonight. Our warden could be kind, but she was a stickler for ladies being ladies, and a lady being a lady did not include a miniskirt, a multicolored velvet robe, and snakeskin boots. She would not approve, and I had very much hoped I could sneak out without being seen.

The last time we had spoken had been about two weeks ago, when she reprimanded me for washing my underwear and hanging it over the radiator to dry. "We are ladies," she had said, sniffing at the sight of my tights draped over the old cast-iron radiator. "Not savages. We treat you like ladies. We expect you to behave like ladies, and ladies do not dry their smalls in their bedroom."

"Sorry, Miss Nicholl." I gathered up the underwear and gave a surreptitious wink to Dottie, who was terrified of Miss Nicholl. "Won't happen again." But of course it would. I had no intention of going all the way down to the laundry room when I could wash everything in the bathroom sink at night and have it dry the next day. I vowed to be more careful in future about leaving the door open.

When I got downstairs, I found Miss Nicholl to be positively giddy, talking to John. He was very charming, I saw in that instant, remembering his confidence the other night when he sat in front of us on the bus. Well-spoken and comfortable in his skin. I knew so little about him, but he seemed worldly. Miss Nicholl thought so, too. She was actually giggling as they spoke, which I found astounding. Not only had I never known her to giggle, I wouldn't have thought it was something one would ever see her do.

"You look beautiful." John saw me approaching and kissed me on the cheek. I saw Miss Nicholl look me up and down, and I knew she disapproved, but what could she say with John standing there.

"Don't forget to be back by midnight, Miss Collins," she said, her eyes flickering down to the snakeskin boots.

"I shall have her home on the dot," assured John. "No turning into pumpkins on my watch."

Miss Nicholl laughed, her shoulders relaxing, and John took my arm to steer me out the building. I was glad to see he had dressed up for me, in a very smart high-collared shirt and a large kipper tie.

"I thought we'd have supper first," he said. "We have a table at Buzzy's Bistro. It's a lovely night but it's Chelsea. Okay to get a cab?"

"I'd love to," I said, with no idea what Buzzy's Bistro was, but I was game.

"I wanted to take you to Mrs Beaton's Tent but they didn't have a table. You'll love it. It's close, in Soho. I'll take you there next time."

"Is it a seedy sex shop?" I joked, for that was what much of Soho was. Sex shops and brothels, and dirty old men going into stores filled with porno magazines. Every phone booth in the area was plastered with bits of paper offering phone numbers for paid sex. When I'd worked at Bourne & Hollingsworth, I'd sometimes have to run through Soho to pick up an order that hadn't been delivered by the rag trade, and

I always kept my eyes down, making sure I didn't make eye contact with anyone.

"Do I look like the sort of man who'd take you to a seedy sex shop?"

"I don't know. I haven't decided what kind of a man you are yet."

"But you agreed to come out with me? I must have something special."

"Oh, no." I shook my head vigorously. "It's the only offer I've had all week." And then I burst out laughing.

It didn't feel like I was being taken anywhere particularly salubrious. We were dropped off at the end of a small, dark alley, and right before the dustbins was a door to the basement that was Buzzy's Bistro.

It wasn't smart—red-and-white-checked tablecloths and wine bottles with candles stuck in them, inches of dripped wax coating each bottle, but the people were beautiful. Thank goodness I'm wearing this coat, I thought, walking in. I had spent my whole life feeling out of place, and suddenly, in the spectacular coat, I could see the girls in the restaurant giving me admiring glances.

"Hello, John!" A couple of people waved at him, and John waved back, continuing to follow our waiter to the table.

"So what exactly is it that you do that everyone knows you? I thought you were the manager of an unknown band?"

John laughs. "You're not scared of a direct question, are you?"

I shake my head. "Go on, then. Answer the question."

"I am the manager of a band that is about to be huge. I was the manager of Gerry and the Pacemakers, for about a minute. I got them their first record deal, and then they dumped me, so I'm not really on good terms with them now. But I do know a lot of people in the business, it's true."

"Gosh, I don't know that I'm exciting enough for you."

"Trust me, you're more than exciting. Tell me about you, Cece Collins. I like that your warden revealed your surname. It made me even more sure of calling you Cece. Cece Collins is perfect, although frankly, now that you're Cece, I don't think you need a surname. There's only going to be one Cece. Can you sing? I meant to ask you that the other night, because we could very easily turn you into a star."

My heart did a little flip before I remembered that I had no voice whatsoever. "I'm a ghastly singer, I'm afraid. Entirely tone deaf."

"Act?" he said hopefully, as I shook my head. "What *are* you good at?"

I thought for a few seconds. "I'm very tidy and organized, and I'm very good at problem-solving. I think I'm quite a good sales assistant, but I haven't been at Miss Selfridge very long."

"Being a shopgirl isn't something you're good at," he said. "It's something you do until you find what you're good at. So what do you want out of life?" he asked.

I knew what was expected of me, because girls like me were often asked that question, and the answer we were supposed to give, the answer that was supposed, the answer that seemed to make everyone happy, particularly prospective suitors who were currently sitting opposite you in a nice restaurant, was to get married and have children.

I didn't want that. It was the last thing I wanted. When I thought of marriage and children, I wanted to think of my mother, but the few memories I had were fading fast. Instead, I thought of my father's marriage to my stepmother, the only real experience I had of marriage. I thought of Linda's hair covered in a hairnet for working around the house, rolled up in curlers and sprayed into a helmet if she joined my father down at the pub. I thought of the way my father called my stepmother "Mother" if he wanted something answered. He didn't call her Linda, her name. In fact, I'm not sure he'd ever called her by her name, but instead, "Mother? Do you know where my green shirt is?" Oh, what irony that she had never been a mother. Not to us, nor to anyone else.

They slept in separate beds in the same bedroom. Perhaps at one time those single beds had been pushed together, but now they were far apart, each covered in a green candlewick bedspread. Of course they must have had sex at some point, but it was very hard to imagine it now, and I'm quite certain there was no fun or enjoyment in it. I imagine it was duty, Linda fulfilling her role as a wife.

They had always seemed to be content enough, without ever being truly happy. Their lives have seemed separate. And dull. *So* dull. I didn't recall them ever having conversation about anything meaningful, and certainly didn't recall them ever laughing together. Their marriage has always felt more like a business arrangement. He married her so we, Robbie and I, could have a mother, and she married him because she wanted to be a married woman.

I may not have known exactly what I wanted, but I was very clear as to what I didn't want. Marriage, children, country life.

"I want to live," I said. "I mean really live. I want to have adventures. I want excitement. I want to travel and see other countries, maybe even *live* in other countries. I want to stay up all night, dancing, and then sit on a sandy beach somewhere hot to watch the sun come up."

John raised an eyebrow. "Have you ever been to any hot countries?"

Of course I hadn't. Our holidays were a caravan near Bournemouth, which rarely seemed hot, even in the height of the British summer.

"Have you?" I asked, by way of not responding.

"I was in Spain this past summer. Marbella Beach Club. Lovely."

"I've heard," I said, although I hadn't. Gosh, it sounded appealing though. It made me think of oranges and handsome men, of swimming pools and brightly colored cocktails.

"Maybe one day I'll take you there." He grinned.

"You should be so lucky." I had no idea where my new-found confidence came from, presumably from my magic colorful coat, but I was liking the new Claire or, rather, Cece. She was bold and fearless. Cece was definitely the kind of woman who wouldn't think twice about jumping on an airplane with a man she hardly knew and jetting off to the Marbella Beach Club.

"Lucky is my middle name." He took the menu off the waiter and asked if he could order for me. I didn't mind. I gave a cursory look but hadn't ever eaten anywhere like this. Back then, the girls and I didn't think to go to a restaurant and sit down for dinner in the way everyone does now. Then, everything was about music, and all these fantastic bands that had sprung up. It was about going to clubs and listening to live bands, and dancing.

Britain took a long time to recover from the war. In the early sixties, when I was a young teenager, we were listening to Motown, and all this wonderful music from America, because we didn't have any of our own. Suddenly we had our own music, and you could go and see the actual bands live. Sometimes, if you were a pretty enough face in the crowd, or if you hung around outside long enough, you'd get to meet them. And in London, it wasn't just local bands like it was in

Somerset; you might see the Beatles, or Herman's Hermits. You might see Dusty Springfield.

So this, sitting in a restaurant off the King's Road, filled with the kinds of people I sometimes served in the shop, but never mixed with, was new to me. I wanted to be myself, but I didn't want John to think I was the country hick that I knew myself to be, so I let him order for me, hoping he wouldn't order fish because, other than fish and chips, I didn't have the stomach for fish.

He ordered me a prawn cocktail, and a steak, well done. And all of it was delicious. Even the prawns.

John knocked at the door of the Scotch of St. James (already I had ascertained that those in the know referred to it simply as the Scotch), and we heard the vague sound of scraping wood as someone looked at us through a peephole before opening the door and welcoming us in.

They knew John at the Scotch of St. James, welcomed him like an old friend. I felt like a movie star, walking in beside him, down the twisty staircase into a dark basement, the walls covered with a red tartan, with a full-size stagecoach on one side, complete with luggage on the top, a man climbing out of it as we walked in.

I saw him first. His blond hair, those full lips. It was a beautiful face, almost androgynous, perfect in its symmetry, but for the slightly puffy pouches under his eyes. Although he looked tired, he was brown, as if he'd been in the sun.

John and I made our way to a dark corner, sitting down and immediately lighting up cigarettes and, in John's case, a joint. John pulled on it hard and passed it to me before looking at the staircase at who had just come in, his eyes lighting up.

"Brian!" John waved at the man I had seen as my heart pounded. It was one thing to play it cool when Brian Jones walked into the club you were in, but quite another having to play it cool when you'd have to speak to him. Judging from the way he turned his head and the smile that lit up his face, we were going to be speaking to him.

I couldn't believe it. Not just a member of the Rolling Stones, but *the* member of the Rolling Stones. The pretty-boy founder who played all the instruments. Yes, Mick Jagger was the lead singer, but Brian Jones was the one everyone fell in love with at the beginning, until the drugs took hold, and Mick Jagger and Keith Richards started writing their own music.

"Hey, man." He came over to greet John.

"Looking good, Brian. Where's this suntan from, then?"

"I've been in Morocco. Got stuck there and the rest of the band pissed off. I just got back, but found some great music there. Pipes, man. These old men playing these pipes in Jou-jouka. I recorded them, and I'm telling you, they're going to be huge."

"That's great, Brian. If you want any help with the record, I'm managing The Bended Grass, but I've always got time for you. Oh, this is Cece."

This wasn't Brian Jones the rebel, for that was how I thought of all the Rolling Stones, particularly after the drug bust, and his subsequent arrest (he hadn't been at Redlands, but if it wasn't for Brian, at least according to John, none of it would have happened). He was the first to wear the big hats with floppy brims, the feathers and furs, the embroidered shirts; he was the first to perfect the androgynous look, with appliquéd flowers, long beaded necklaces that you'd only see on women.

Standing in the Scotch, in an Afghani vest and velvet flared trousers, one leg purple, one leg blue (and not very well sewn, they looked like he'd sewn them himself), he seemed less rock star and more quiet, respectable young man (although, and I wouldn't admit this for years, the vest smelled like an old yak. Put it like this. If it was anyone other than Brian Jones, you wouldn't have wanted to get too close).

"How do you do," he said, as I gazed into his eyes and found myself, unusually, at a loss for words. "Great coat, Cece," he said, reaching out and stroking the velvet on the shoulder. I vowed never to wash the coat again, before remembering that I had to return it the next day. I would tell Celia's sister that the coat had now been sprinkled with rock star fairy dust and that she should never wash it.

I found my voice. "Thank you. Was Morocco fantastic?"

"Insane," he said. "Part of it was fantastic, and part of it was hell. I got ill, and the rest of the gang left me while they went on to Marrakech, and God knows where else. Still. I wouldn't have recorded the pipes if they hadn't left me, so maybe it's a good thing."

"Where's Anita? Is she here?" John had no idea the impact his words would have. Not just on Brian, but on me. I knew immediately he was asking about Anita Pallenberg, model, actress, muse, and long-term girlfriend of Brian Jones.

At least, that's what we thought.

Brian's face hardened. "She's with Keith. Fucking Keith. We had him practically living with us for months at Court-field Road after he split up with Linda." He shook his head. "We went to Morocco to get away from all the shit that was happening in England. Our lawyers thought they could get the whole thing dropped. It was meant to be this amazing trip, with Christopher Gibbs, and Cooper snapping pictures, and Robert there for the fun, and it all went to shit. Anita left me for Keith, and they left me in Morocco with the bill." He shook his head, disgusted. "I fucking understand now what Mick and Keith are doing," he spit. "They want to prove that they're better than I am. I've got to work on doing more things by myself or they really will finish me off."

John's face fell, neither of us knowing what to say as an awkward silence descended. Brian ran his hands through his hair and sighed deeply.

"So the pipes, man," John said eventually. "That's a great project to do yourself."

"Yeah." Brian didn't sound hopeful. "I need something to take my mind off it. Got anything?" He looked hopefully at John, who shook his head. He didn't bother looking at me, much to my relief.

"I'm going to see if I can score something. Something to put me in a better mood. Nice to meet you." He flashed a smile at me, and I saw, suddenly, how his spirit rose out of the darkness just for a few seconds, making him irresistible. I understood how women threw themselves all over him.

When he'd gone, I turned to John. "How on earth do you know Brian Jones?"

"We had a mutual friend, Tara Browne. He was killed in a car crash last December. Terrible tragedy. We all went to his twenty-first birthday party in Ireland. A bunch of people stayed at Luggala, the family estate, but I went off to Leixlip Castle with a couple of others. Brian and I spent hours talking about music, and I went back to his pad when we got back. You should see it. It's the most amazing place I've ever been. It has a minstrel's gallery, tapestries hanging from every wall, cushions all over the floor. It's fantastic."

"You mentioned Anita. What's she like?" I found Anita Pallenberg to be compelling. She wasn't traditionally beautiful, not in the way Marianne was, but she was sexy, and mischievous. She looked tough, not a girl you would want to mess with. Frankly, I found her a bit terrifying, although when I thought about new clothes I wanted to buy, a picture of Anita often made its way into my head.

"I think she's a witch. I'm telling you. She and Brian used to hold séances at Courtfield Road."

"How do you know?"

"I was there one night and Anita got out the Ouija board. I don't like any of that stuff. It spooked me and I got out quick."

"She's into Ouija boards?"

"Darling, she's into all of that stuff. Never goes anywhere without her tarot cards."

I had heard many things about her, but not this. I leaned forward, fascinated. "Did they contact anyone?"

"According to the Ouija board, they were speaking to Leopold von Sacher-Masoch, who turns out to be one of Marianne's relatives. Sadomasochism was named after him." He paused. "Not my scene."

I was wide-eyed. "Do you believe it was really him?"

"I didn't stay long enough to find out. Look, I like Brian. I think he's a brilliant musician, and the Stones wouldn't be where they are without him, but there's a side of him I don't like at all." He shook his head.

"What do you mean?"

He sighed, looked off in the distance as if he was thinking about whether or not to tell me, but I knew he would. He turned back to me. "He'd get rough with Anita. I only saw it once, because most of the time the two of them were off their faces, high as kites, but I didn't like it. You don't touch a woman like that. Ever."

I was breathless, not only at what I was learning, but at the very fact that we were discussing people like Brian Jones and Anita Pallenberg as if they were my friends, as if we were talking about Dottie or Celia rather than the hippest, coolest actress, and a member of one of the biggest bands in the country.

Later, of course, we all found out what happened in Morocco. That Keith, Brian and Anita were driven there in Keith's Limited Edition Bentley. The back was filled with scarlet fur rugs, velvet pillows and dirty magazines. To avoid customs and any danger of the car being searched, they hid drugs in secret compartments drilled into the walnut interior and sent more by shuttle service. Once they were out of England, all bets were off. They picked up Anita's friend Deborah in Paris and flew down the motorways, determined to have a great time in Morocco.

But Brian was on the brink, his usual paranoia and jealousy heightened by being in a small car. He had asthma, which wasn't helped by the cloud of hashish and tobacco, and by the time they got to France, he had developed a frightening cough.

It got so bad, he checked into a hospital where they found pneumonia, and blood in his lungs. He assured the others he would be fine and told them to carry on to Tangier without him, that he would meet them there.

He had no idea, or perhaps he did, that Anita and Keith were falling madly in love.

Brian and Anita's relationship finally ended when he lost his shit at her refusing to take part in an orgy with two prostitutes he had picked up and brought back to their hotel. The fight escalated with Brian throwing a tray of cold cuts at Anita, before beating her. She escaped to Keith's room, who was horrified and whisked her straight back to London, leaving Brian to collapse in the lobby of their hotel, a mess in every way, a mess that was only going to get worse.

But we knew none of that at the Scotch of St. James. Only that their Moroccan trip had been documented, and that Brian looked tanned, healthy and tired, with a fragility to him that I hadn't expected. I was doing my best to play it cool, but all I could think about was telling the other girls back at the hostel. I wasn't sure they'd even believe me. Brian Jones! It was extraordinary! Everything that I was moving toward seemed to be encapsulated by that night, by sitting in the hottest club in London, with an actual member of the Rolling Stones. It couldn't get better, surely.

"I lied." John leaned toward me and put his lips close to my ear, so close they brushed my ear, and I shuddered, feeling something deep down that I hadn't felt before.

"Lied about what?"

"About this." He reached into his pocket and withdrew his hand, now in a fist. Slowly, keeping his eyes locked on my face, he unfurled his hand to reveal two small sugar cubes.

"This? What? Sugar?"

"It's acid. LSD. This is what Brian was looking for, but I only have enough for me and you."

Me and you, I thought. Interesting. I stared at the sugar cubes in his palm, thinking about everything I had read about drugs. I thought about the book I'd picked up in Indica, the scientific experiments Dr. Timothy Leary was doing, and how incredible it was supposed to be. I thought about how I had only read the first few pages, but the first sentence stuck in my mind: "When in doubt, relax, turn off your mind, float downstream."

I didn't think about it more than that. I opened my mouth and popped in the sugar cube.

Even now, all these years later, you hear the same thing about acid. That it swirls and twirls, that walls start melting, that colors smash into each other, that inanimate objects become animate. That wasn't what it was like for me, that first time, at least, not after the beginning.

What it was like, other than a completely heightened sense of being, was the sudden dawning on me that I knew absolutely everything in life that was going to happen, right before it happened.

I looked at the stairs at the Scotch, and knew that in five seconds three people would walk in, two men and a woman, and the woman would be wearing a white fur coat and brown leather boots. I knew that in exactly two seconds, a woman would cross the room looking for the lavatory, and she wouldn't know where it was, and would stop and ask me. I knew which song was going to play next. I knew exactly how everything in the world was going to play out, but to this day, I wonder why I didn't project beyond that night. Why, for example, I didn't envision Brian Jones dying two years later. Think of all the things I might have stopped. I have thought about that for many, many years.

My acid trip didn't make sense. I didn't try and explain it to anyone. I felt as if I was momentarily gifted with a superpower. And superpowers are best kept secret.

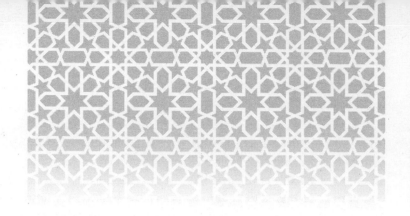

NINE

I woke up the next morning in John's bed. The first to open my eyes, it took me a while to orient myself. I was on a queen-size mattress on the floor, John's arm flung over my naked body. There were slatted blinds on the window through which a dim light was filtering. I wasn't sure what to do, whether to wake John, whether to look for a bathroom, or whether to wait.

I remembered everything. How the red tartan walls of the Scotch started pulsing, the walls moving back and forth in rhythm, as if I was sitting inside a giant plaid heart, and how I found I had my miraculous superpower. I waited, my eyes open, to see if I still had it, if I could tell what was about to happen, but no. It was gone.

John woke up and reached over for a cigarette, lighting two

at the same time and rolling back to the middle of the bed to pass one to me.

"How are you feeling?" He leaned forward to plump up the pillows behind our heads, before stretching luxuriously and leaning back against the wall that had a giant print of a woman's head, her hair fanning out like a sea of medusa-like waves.

"Pretty far-out. Last night was truly the grooviest night I've ever had."

John grinned. "I'll take that as a compliment, shall I?"

"I wasn't talking about that!" Although, the truth was, I wasn't sure we had done anything. I remembered taking off my clothes, but don't remember much after that.

"Did we...?" I wished I could remember, but I just couldn't.

John smiled. "I don't remember. I'm sure we had fun though."

I felt simultaneously relieved and disappointed. My virginity, something I had never considered in Dorset, surely was something of an encumbrance now. And yet, I wanted to be present for it. To know what it was I was losing. And gaining.

"What time is it?" I presumed it was around six or seven. I needed to be at work by ten. As for the hostel, I didn't know what I would tell Miss Nicholl. Oh, God. If I said I forgot to sign in, would she believe me? I had never slipped up before, other than my underwear drying on the radiator, and I knew that she had given other girls a free pass, but they were girls she liked.

John reached over to the bedside table and felt around for his watch. "It's almost twelve."

"What?" I shrieked. If I wasn't stark naked, I would have jumped out of bed, but, despite having spent the night with John a few hours earlier (I presume), in the cold light of day, now that the effects of the acid had worn off, I wasn't ready to be naked in front of him. "Are you serious?"

"Yes. Why wouldn't I be serious?"

"Work! I'm supposed to be at work at ten. Oh, God." Nakedness be damned. I threw off the sheets and started scrambling to get dressed. "They're going to fire me. I can't believe I did this. I may get thrown out of the hostel, as well."

"Relax," John said, completely unperturbed. "If you lose your job we'll find you another one. I saw Nigel last week and he's looking for shopgirls that look just like you."

"Who's Nigel?" I hooked my bra together.

"He's one of the owners of a clothes shop in Chelsea. Granny Takes a Trip."

I think my mouth may have fallen open. "Are you serious?"

John started laughing. "There you go again."

"That's my dream job."

"Don't worry. I promise you, you'll be absolutely fine."

I trusted him. What choice did I have?

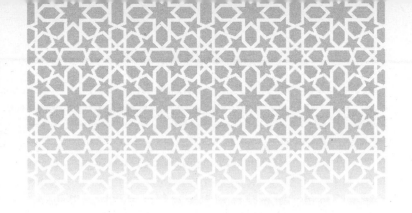

TEN

John was wrong. I wasn't absolutely fine. Dottie was in floods of tears as I packed up my things.

"I can't believe they're not letting you stay. It's just so un-fair. Tons of people have stayed out all night and got away with it. Where are you going to go?"

"I don't know. I'll figure something out. Look, I'm supposed to be at home this weekend anyway. It's Robbie's twenty-first."

"You're staying with your parents?" Dottie's eyes were wide with horror.

"Thankfully, no. Robbie's friends are staying at one of his friends' houses, and there's room for me."

Dottie peered at me closely. "Will you see your dad?"

I wanted to. I had been mentally preparing myself to see Linda. I looked the part, in my trendy clothes with my new shapely calves, but I had to perfect an air of insouciance; I didn't want to show her that I cared. I was going to be polite but detached. I was going to show Linda that she would never be able to hurt me again.

"I'll definitely see my dad at the party. Don't worry about me, Dottie. I'll be back in no time. John says he can get me a job at Granny Takes a Trip. As soon as I get that, I'll figure out a flat somewhere. Maybe you could leave the store and come with me."

"I don't belong there," she said, with an air that was more resigned than sad, before perking up. "But you do. And maybe you'll end up marrying someone rich and famous, and I can come and live in the spare wing of your mansion."

I laughed, then sat down on the bed and put an arm around her. "You and I will always be friends, Dottie. Why don't we find a flat together when I'm back? You're eighteen now. You could move out of the hostel and still keep your job."

"The hostel is for unmarried women," she reminded me.

"Or for ladies who are not yet eighteen. Now that you are, you could leave."

"That would be lovely," she said. "When you get back from Dorset can we really start looking for a flat?"

"As soon as I get myself a new job, whether it's at Granny or somewhere else, then we'll find somewhere really groovy to live. Promise."

"Swear on your life?" She held out a finger, and I hooked mine around hers as we shook up and down.

"Swear on my life."

The English countryside flashed past the train window, fields green and lush from the constant drizzle as I made my way home, and back to my past. London was so vibrant and alive, but as soon as we left Waterloo Station, as soon as we got into the suburbs, everything felt exactly as it had always been, mile after mile of back gardens, of dirty redbrick terraced houses, ragged gaps where bombs had hit during the war, with no one having the money to rebuild. Washing lines were strung through gardens covered in weeds. It was everything I had moved away from; it was everything I wanted to escape.

I was mortified at returning, although it gave me some small amount of pleasure that I had fulfilled a little of my dream, at least in how I had reinvented myself. I would be showing Linda, finally, that she was wrong about me.

I could picture her clearly, standing at the kitchen sink with yellow Marigold gloves on, turning as I walked in. "Hello, dear," she would say, coldly, perhaps extending her cheek for a kiss, possibly looking me up and down, but not saying anything. She wouldn't need to say anything for me to know she disapproved of my miniskirt, my boots, my fur-trimmed suede coat and my Mary Quant lipstick. She wouldn't need to say anything for me to feel great about how different I looked.

For a tiny village of only a couple of hundred, we had the essentials, and even our very own stately home, Melbury House, whose owner, Lady Theresa Agnew, was restoring Melbury Park, the gardens designed by Capability Brown. We had a village shop, a post office, a bakery, a village school and even a church with its clock by E. B. Dennison, the designer of Big Ben. But were it not for the fact that I adored Robbie, I would have no wish to go back home for anything.

The train pulled in to Yeovil station, and I hauled my small suitcase out. I had left a lot of my things with Dottie, in a large box that we pushed under her bed far enough that hopefully Miss Nicholl wouldn't notice. I left all the clothes I had brought with me to London that I no longer wore; in other words, everything I had owned when I moved. I kept a Fair isle cardigan my mother had knitted, and a full skirt she had run up for herself on her sewing machine. Neither of them were my style, but they reminded me of my mum, and I would keep them forever.

I heard Robbie before I saw him. I was waiting outside the station, sitting on my suitcase, thinking how pretty it was for a train station, how I had never once noticed how charming Dorset was when I lived here, but suddenly it was all I noticed. Even the huge Blake & Fox glove factory that loomed over the tracks as the train pulled in couldn't detract from the appeal of the red brick of the station, its stone trim, the gables and chimneys stretching to the sky.

A few people walked past and looked me up and down. I liked to think they were surprised to see such a hip chick in their little town. I felt proud that I no longer looked like I belonged.

I hadn't seen Robbie since I left. I hadn't heard about his move to Brighton, his new job with an estate agent. I couldn't wait to see him, but I didn't expect him to roar up in the passenger seat of a red Frog-Eyed Sprite, a cool little Austin, with a familiar redheaded man driving. They screeched to a halt as Robbie leaped out of the car, flinging his arms around me, squeezing me tight and lifting me up as I laughed. In the car, Benji, as handsome and familiar as ever, grinned and waved.

And yet, this time, my heart didn't stop. Our slow dance the last time I saw him, my embarrassment at thinking Benji was going to kiss me, then running out so he didn't see my tears, felt like a lifetime ago, as if it had happened to someone else.

I was hoping he didn't remember, ready for both of us to box up that memory and store it away somewhere safe. Yes, Benji had been my first crush. I had watched him grow from a cheeky little boy with a big grin and a mop of ginger hair, to a tall young man with hair that was still ginger but less fiery, blue eyes, freckles everywhere and a smile that didn't melt my heart in the way it did, even a couple of months ago, but instead gave me a jolt of sweet nostalgia, reminding me of a time when I thought everything he did and said was perfection, showing me how much London had changed me already.

"Hey, Bean." He was back to calling me Bean. "You're looking pretty groovy. You look like you just stepped off of Carnaby Street."

"What do you know about Carnaby Street?" I joked. "Do you even know where that is?" I tossed my hair, now almost to my waist and fashionably straight, giving him a teasing look.

"Where do you think these are from?" He opened the car door to show off his pink trousers as Benji put my suitcase in the boot. "Actually, that's a bit of a lie. I got them at Hem and Fringe," he said sheepishly. "Moreton Street."

"You were so close! Why didn't you come and see me while you were in London?"

"I had to do a little bit of this and a little bit of that," he said, which made me laugh. Benji was still trying hard to pull off the cockney charm of Michael Caine, but was far more Roger Moore, if Roger Moore had been a redhead. He did, however, still have a way with people. Whatever his accent, he had always been charming, and knew how to get things done. Put it like this, if ever I were in trouble, I'd turn to Benji.

"Anyway, I did come and see you. Or at any rate, I tried. I popped into Bourne & Hollingsworth, but they said you'd left."

"I've been working at Miss Selfridge."

"Selfridges?"

"Well, yes, but Miss Selfridge is the new young bit. It's great. I loved it."

He cocked his head as Robbie got into the back seat, letting me sit in the front beside Benji. "Loved? Past tense?"

I blushed. "I lost my job, but it's fine. I was thinking about doing something else anyway."

Benji peered at me. "Now what does a lovely young girl like you do in order to lose her job?"

I so wanted to tell him about my night at the Scotch. I wanted to prove that I was not the same quiet Dorset girl, that I had grown into the sophisticated Londoner; that I was living the kind of life most people dream of, but my brother was sitting in the back, and honestly, I wasn't sure how I felt about losing my virginity to John McKenna, if indeed that had happened. I wished I could remember. What I could remember about the night was very little. Yes, LSD was definitely wonderful and I very much hoped my superpower would return someday. But then again, I didn't want anyone thinking I was some kind of hippie.

"All-night party," I said, somewhat lamely. He held my gaze a little longer, until I looked away, cheeks reddening. I am certain he knew I was lying.

"I like this whole look." He waved a lazy arm at me. "You've grown up."

"It had to happen sometime."

"Met anyone exciting in the Big Smoke?"

I shrugged. "A few people. You know how it is."

"Dave Boland?" my brother piped from the back as I turned to face him.

"Sadly not—" I grinned "—yet. Are you excited about your party? I can't believe you're twenty-one."

"Well, we've got big plans for it," Robbie said. "We've got a marquee in the garden and we're bringing in The Yardbirds."

For a moment I thought he might be serious, then he continued. "I'm kidding. Linda insisted on organizing it, so it's probably going to be cheap wine and a few canapés in the village hall. All the old gang will be there though, so maybe it will be fun. Benji's bringing a record player with all his vinyl. I'm hoping we might end up dancing."

I groaned. "God. Linda isn't exactly who I'd trust with organizing a party for me. You did say village hall, didn't you?"

"Exactly." He rolled his eyes. "But we've got twenty-four hours to plan something else if you have anything in mind."

"Drugs?"

Benji let out a bark of laughter. "You *have* grown up. Got anything with you?"

I shook my head. "Nothing, I'm afraid."

"Going to be a great party." Benji rolled his eyes, and I couldn't help but let out a snort. With Linda organizing, this was hardly going to be festive. I could have, *should* have, asked John to get me some hash, something, anything other than cheap white wine to liven things up.

I turned my head as we drove, experiencing a wave of nostalgia as we pulled into the village of Evershot. There was the street corner where I fell and scraped my knee when I was small. There was the gazebo, where I had my first awkward kiss with Michael Armitage. Up Fore Street, past the village, narrow streets winding their way through golden stone cottages with thick thatched roofs, clusters of green ivy snaking their way up the houses.

"I've just got to run in and grab some clothes," said Robbie, as we pulled up to our house. "Want to come in and see Dad?"

"I'll protect you from the wicked stepmother," he added, and I found myself climbing out of the car before I could think of a good reason to say no. Robbie opened the door, and Benji walked into me when I stopped just inside the hallway and inhaled deeply. The smell was exactly the same. Home. Not necessarily bad, but neither was it good. Just familiar to every fiber of my being.

"Hello?" I didn't hear Linda's voice from the kitchen, and

my heart lifted a bit. She must be out. I took a deep breath, telling myself to calm down. I was a different person today than the girl I was when she kicked me out. I was a hip chick now, I had grown up, and I had been practicing. However Linda behaved, I was going to be distant but polite; I was going to act like the adult. God knows, one of us had to.

It didn't occur to me then that she probably never had a chance with me. Maybe things would have been different if she had been warmer to us, but I had spent my life longing for someone else, resenting her for sweeping in and replacing a woman who was irreplaceable.

On the table in the hall there had always been photographs, including my mum and dad's wedding photograph. It wasn't much of a surprise to see that my mum and dad's photograph had disappeared.

"Cuppa tea?" called Robbie from the kitchen.

"Yes, please." I walked in, glad that the kitchen was still the same: linoleum floors and white Formica tops, sliding doors to the small garden, shelves by the round table in the corner, filled with cookbooks, cups, plates and knickknacks.

Benji was already making himself at home, the biscuit tin open on the table in front of him as he grabbed a handful of custard creams.

"Don't let Linda see." I declined one for myself, passing the tin straight over to Robbie. Even before the Tunnock's incident, Linda considered the kitchen to be hers and had always hated any of us helping ourselves to what she considered her food.

"Where's Dad?"

"Still at work. I forgot he doesn't get home until later."

"And Linda?"

"She left a note to say she's gone out to get more wine. Apparently she didn't realize how many of my friends were coming, and is now panicking she doesn't have enough."

"Do you have lots of friends coming?"

"Not as many as hers. I think she thought this was really about her friends. She's invited all her friends, and thought I would just have a handful." He rolled his eyes.

"Does she have any friends?"

"That's what I asked. It's everyone from church. Her idea of a friend is someone in the village whose name she knows."

"That's awful. It's *your* birthday."

"I know. But you know Linda, it's always all about her." Robbie slid mugs of tea in front of me and Benji.

"How many are staying at the Briggses' house?"

"Five, including you. Anyone else who's come from elsewhere is booked in at The Strangways Arms. I'm sure the others will either drive home or sleep in their cars."

"Drive home?" Benji looks horrified. "Are you not expecting much of a party, then?"

"I told you. Linda's arranged this. It's in the village hall. Wine and canapés. Chicken vol-au-vents, deviled eggs, cheese and pineapple on cocktail sticks, chipolatas and devils on horseback."

I took a custard cream and ate it slowly, savoring it because I wouldn't allow myself more than one. "Mmm. That makes me hungry."

Robbie looked glum. "The food sounds good, but I can't imagine it's going to be much of a party."

"We'll make it a party. What's the music?"

"Linda thinks Gerry's going to play the piano for everyone, but Benji brought his record player."

"And a stack of vinyl," Benji added. "Yardbirds. Gerry and the Pacemakers, Manfred Mann, Rolling Stones, the Beatles, Herman's Hermits. I've got it all."

"What would we do without you, Benji?" I was so grateful that I was able to say something like that without turning red, that thanks to John, I was able to finally be friends with Benji, without wishing that he would secretly fall in love with me.

Benji shrugged. "We'd have a very dull night indeed."

The front door opened, and Linda walked in. I realize now that London, you see, had been overtaken by the young. Everyone was fresh-faced and glamorous, so in that moment Linda looked much older than I remembered her, older than her forty-five years, but perhaps everyone did back then. Forty was firmly middle-aged, which was easy to believe, looking at Linda in her midlength skirt and sensible shoes.

She untied the scarf that was holding the rollers tight to her head, shrugged off her beige coat to reveal a gray plaid sleeveless dress, knee-length, which she immediately covered up with a floral housecoat that was hanging on the hook by the front door.

She had new glasses, cat's-eye shaped, which did her round face no favors. Oh, I was so wicked in my criticism of her, in the hint of pleasure I got at seeing her look so unattractive.

"Hello," she said, looking me up and down and sniffing slightly, which made me smile inside.

She stepped back. "You're looking very... London." Her gaze lingered on my short skirt as she pursed her lips disapprovingly.

I smiled sweetly. "You should see what I'm wearing for the party!" The color slid from Linda's cheeks, leaving me somewhat gratified. I no longer lived under her roof. She had no say in what I wore or what I did. Her face pinched into a scowl.

My mother had the kind of beauty that would have seen her grow more beautiful as she aged. Linda hadn't had beauty to begin with, and now? She looked like an unhappy woman, the edges of her mouth turned down, no light in her eyes.

Linda had spent years doing everything for my father, but we knew she resented it. I have overheard her tell people she always wanted to be a wife and mother, which I knew to be untrue. I suspect she wanted to be a wife because of the status she thought it conveyed, and it is true, back then, in the sixties, it can't have been much fun to have been encumbered with being a spinster.

"Hello, Mrs. M!" Benji called from the kitchen, and I watched, fascinated, as Linda's face transformed.

"Benji! I didn't know you were here!" She had always liked Benji, although Robbie and I, cynical children that we were, always thought that was as much to do with the fact that his father was an earl, than anything else. You see, Benji's full name was The Honorable Michael George Benedict Longsworth. He had changed it himself to Benji when he was five, even though his father tried to explain that one of his middle names was Benedict, not Benjamin, but he didn't care. There was a prefect at school called Benji, and that's what he decided to be called.

It was one of the things that had always made me laugh about Benji. He grew up in a Jacobean manor house that had been in his family for generations, that made ours look like a staff cottage, and not a senior member of staff, but a lowly maid. He despised being a member of the upper class.

"You're looking very lovely, Mrs. M. I like the new hairstyle."

Linda patted her hair and blushed. "Oh, thank you, Benji. I worry it makes me look a little old."

"You? Old? Never!"

Linda chuckled as Robbie and I made funny faces at each other out of her sight. As soon as she bustled over to the fridge to put the food away, Benji winked at me. I shook my head. He was incorrigible, and he knew it.

There was something comforting in seeing how nothing had changed at home. As always, Linda prepared a bowl of nuts and my dad's drink, putting his slippers by his chair.

"I'd like a drink myself," whispered Robbie.

"Shall we go down to the Acorn for drinks and maybe supper?" I was learning to call tea "supper" or, if it was formal, "dinner." I had only ever called our evening meal "tea," but I had learned this was not the done thing in London, at least not in Warwickshire House.

"Tea is what we have at four o'clock," said Miss Nicholl one day, overhearing one of the girls say she was starving for her tea. "It is a cup of tea with biscuits, or perhaps scones, and tea sandwiches. Our evening meal is supper, or, if it is formal, dinner."

I took note, and hadn't called it tea since.

"Do you mean tea?" said Benji, who, unless he was around his parents, had always called it tea in a bid to come off as working class.

I laughed with him, both of us getting the unspoken joke, and then my dad walked in.

My dad poured a sherry for each of us, and we sat in the lounge (henceforth referred to as a living room, on John's instructions) with him as he had his drink.

"You look very groovy," he said, taking me in. Robbie and I both burst out laughing.

"*Groovy?* Since when do you use the word *groovy*?"

"Since I'm looking at my daughter in her groovy clothes."

"Dad! I never knew you were so hip."

"I never knew my daughter was so hip. Wait a minute…" He put down his drink and peered at me. "Are you actually my daughter?"

I turned my head to the side. "See that chin? I think you'll find that's your chin, so yes, I am very definitely your daughter."

"Ah, yes. My chin. But you have your mother's eyes. It's ironic, how much you suddenly look like her." His eyes twinkled as he took me in. "Just like her when we met. Same heart-shaped face. It's very nice to have you both home. Linda's excited about the party tomorrow. Twenty-one, eh?" He looked at Robbie. "How does it feel to be turning twenty-one?"

"I'll tell you in the morning."

"Fair enough. How about you, missy? How's your job? How's life in the Big Smoke?"

"Not smoky at all. I'm about to get another job, which is very exciting." I decided to bluff. "I'm going to be working at a very cool clothing store. It's going to be great."

"Well, that is good news. Will you stay at the hostel?"

I couldn't possibly tell him I had been asked to leave. Seeing disappointment in his eyes would be too much for me to bear.

"I'm not sure yet," I lied. "I may look into getting a flat with friends. Remember Dottie, who I worked with at Denners?" He nodded. "She's in London, too, and she's eighteen now, so she doesn't have to stay at the hostel. We're going to get a flat together, maybe with a couple of other girls."

"That sounds like fun," he said.

Conversation petered out a bit after that. I loved my father, of course, but we had never been particularly close, nor had we ever had real conversations. "How's school? How's work? You alright, love?" seemed to be the extent of it.

When I thought of him, I thought of him sitting right here, drink in hand, reading the paper. In the evenings he and Linda would sit together on the sofa, a large space between them, watching the television. He wasn't much one for conversation, my dad, but I always felt loved by him. I blamed Linda for getting in the way of his love for us, certain that had my mother lived, we would have been the happy, joyous family we had been (if the photographs are to be believed) before my mother died. In hindsight, perhaps that wasn't fair, perhaps my father was the sort of man who wasn't able to express love, whoever he was married to. He loved us quietly. I could tell in the way his eyes softened when he looked at me. The way he pressed five pounds into my hand when we told him we were going to the pub.

"You're stopping with us, aren't you?" he asked hopefully.

I was about to answer when Linda walked in. My guess is that she had been at the door, listening. "Oh no," she said. "I don't have enough for tea. I wish I'd known you'd be staying. I would have bought extra mince."

"But you'll stop here for the weekend?" my dad asked again.

"If you're sure," I said, knowing that I would be fine, that Linda didn't have power over me anymore, that I didn't have to run scared.

"I'm quite sure," he said, without looking at Linda. "What will you do for your tea?"

"We'll grab something out. I've missed scampi and chips anyway."

"You're not eating scampi and chips with that figure," Benji said as he walked in. "You must be surviving on lettuce."

Yogurt, I wanted to correct him.

I had scampi and chips (three pieces of scampi and four french fries), two-and-a-half glasses of white wine, and much laughter and gentle ribbing. I loved Dottie, and John, and all the new friends I had made in London, but being with my brother and Benji, tucked into a cozy corner at the pub I had been coming to almost all my life (and certainly long before I was old enough to be allowed to drink in the pub), felt, finally, like home.

By the time we got back, the house was dark, Linda and my father already in bed. She had made the spare room up for Benji, but there were no towels. I grabbed a set of towels from the airing cupboard for him and knocked on his bedroom door.

He opened it shirtless, which was embarrassing, and fascinating. It wasn't as if I hadn't seen him shirtless before—we'd had many a day trip to Weymouth growing up. I remember being fifteen, and Benji being the first to get his driving license, all of us packing into his first car, the little Rover, driving off and parking near the main town beach.

We had brought bottles of pop and sandwiches, and after we parked the car, jumping out of the way as the boat train came steaming through the street, right next to the harbor, bell ringing to warn unsuspecting beachgoers like us to get out of the way. We hadn't even noticed the tracks on the road.

Robbie and Benji and their other friends were all seventeen and seemed so grown-up, but as soon as we were on the sand, they busied themselves for hours building a huge, complicated sand castle, complete with different levels, draw bridge and moat.

We would eat our sandwiches, covered in sand, which I'm sure made them more delicious, and afterward would make our way through the crowds—on hot days there were always crowds—past families sitting on deck chairs, men with their jackets hanging on the back of the deck chair, their shirt sleeves and trouser legs rolled up, on our way to the kiosk for orange squash in pint glass milk bottles with green foil caps.

So yes, I had seen Benji shirtless, his shirt tied over his shoulders to try to avoid sunburn, which he never avoided. He would start the day as pale as cream, and by the end his shoulders, back and neck would be bright scarlet, the freckles on his face joining up to form what he always laughingly called an alternative tan.

Seeing him shirtless on a crowded beach, his shirt tied over his shoulders, was very different to seeing him shirtless in the doorway of the spare bedroom. He had matured, I noticed, or rather his body had matured. Gosh, I thought to myself, as the vestigial memories of my old crush washed over me. He's so attractive.

"See anything you like?" His voice was low.

It was my turn to blush. I handed him the towels and went to turn away, but he put a hand on my arm. I paused and looked up at him.

"You're not entitled to secret thoughts," he said, a direct quote from the film *Alfie*.

"Everyone's entitled to secret thoughts," I said, which was exactly how Annie responded in the film.

Benji half smiled. "You liked *Alfie*, too?"

"Who didn't?" I had not met anyone who hadn't seen the Michael Caine film, although Benji had taken it to heart in a way I hadn't encountered before. There were times when he sounded more like Alfie than Alfie himself.

His face turned serious. "May I have the first dance tomorrow night?"

"If there's any dancing to be done, the first one is yours," I said, with a flicker of excitement that I refused to think about. After all, I was, I think, dating John. I was definitely sleeping with him, or at least, *probably* sleeping with him. I wish I knew for certain. I didn't want to spoil anything in my life, least of all the potential of working at one of the hippest boutiques in town. But a dance wouldn't hurt.

I turned at the top of the stairs to see Benji still framed in the doorway, still looking at me. I went back downstairs, surprised to find my heart fluttering still.

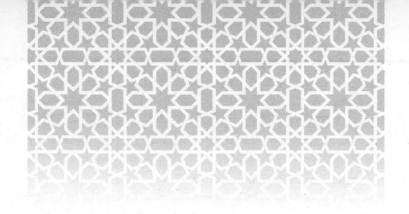

ELEVEN

"You look like a London dolly bird." Benji's voice was pure East End cockney.

"Am I supposed to take that as a compliment?"

Benji could see that as flattered as I was, I was also annoyed. A dolly bird implied, at least to me, beauty but no brains. I may have been a nineteen year old shopgirl, but a dolly bird I was not. His face immediately fell, as did his cockney accent, and his next statement came out as pure lord of the manor.

"Oh my gosh, Claire. I didn't mean to offend. I'm so sorry."

"Don't worry, Benji. Thank you for the compliment, even if it was slightly backhanded. I think I know what you meant."

I was wearing a purple-and-gold Biba minidress, with the over-the-knee suede boots and, in a fit of I'm not sure what, a hot pink feather boa around my neck, a perfect match to the hot pink beads in my hair.

I felt beautiful and sophisticated, and but for my brilliant idea, it would have all gone to waste in the village hall in Evershot.

I couldn't bear for Robbie's party to be taken over by Linda. I had to do something, and the thing that I thought of doing would not only give Robbie a party he would always remember, it would—oh, the heaven of this!—infuriate Linda.

I made my way to the pay phone in the village and dialed John.

"Did you make it safely?"

"I did, but my stepmother has taken over poor Robbie's party, and I have an idea to make it more fun."

"I like to make things more fun."

"I'd noticed. I was thinking you could come, and bring some groovy friends."

"When you say groovy friends, did you have anyone in mind?"

"Dave Boland?" I laughed. "I'm kidding. Well, not really, but people who are fun and famous and fabulous would drive Linda insane."

"Hang on. Let me write down the details. Leave it with me."

I put the phone down feeling smug, hoping against hope that John would come through with the goods. Talk about killing two birds with one stone in the most spectacular fashion—models and London types showing up to Robbie's party would make his day, and ruin Linda's. I couldn't stop smiling.

Robbie, Benji and I spent the day ferrying food back and forth, picking up more wine and begging posters off various local friends to try and decorate the hall. We ended up with

Union Jack bunting, which wasn't perfect but was better than nothing, and a couple of big posters of the Beatles and Manfred Mann.

Benji disappeared for a while, returning with a disco ball and pink spotlight, which was hard to see in daylight, but we were pretty sure it would look fantastic come nightfall.

Yes, there would be piano playing when people first arrived, and yes, it would undoubtedly be a staid party in the beginning, with Linda and my dad, and a bunch of their friends; with people standing around drinking warm beer and room temperature white wine. At some point we were going to put on the music, and the dancing would begin. I had promised Robbie we would make this a party to remember but wasn't sure I would be able to deliver. This was now in John's hands. Benji whispered to me that he was off to score some drugs in the afternoon, so that would help, but it wouldn't piss Linda off as much as losing control of the party.

"Did you get hold of anything?"

He brought out a tin from his pocket and opened it to reveal a slab of black hashish. At some point he would stick a few cigarette papers together, usually five, and lick the side of a cigarette, tearing a strip of the paper up and rolling the cigarette back and forth between his finger and thumb, until tobacco rained down onto the cigarette papers waiting to be rolled. Then, he would crumble the hashish on top, and roll the joint together, inserting a rolled-up piece of cardboard at one end as a makeshift filter, twisting the other end. I had seen pictures of Americans smoking cannabis, and it looked completely different. Their joints were thin and dainty. Ours were enormous, and I never understood why. Still. Benji was the man who knew how to make it, and I was impressed he had found something to make the evening more fun.

"Want to share some with me now?"

I looked at the clock hanging in the village hall. "Give me half an hour. I want to try and be straight while the old people arrive. But come and find me in half an hour. Promise?"

He put his hand on his heart. "Swear on my life."

The old people arrived on the dot, the men in overcoats and hats, the women dressed up in twinsets and chunky costume necklaces. They all felt like they were from another generation, like they would have no idea how this one operated. I greeted my father's old friends, and was polite and charming to Linda's. After a short while, Robbie's friends started to file in. Everyone stood around politely, chatting to one another with a glass of wine in hand, as Gerry the piano player played big band music from the forties. He eventually went into the theme from *Dr. No*, and the entire room cheered, but he went from that to "Rock Around the Clock," which—at least in my head—elicited silent groans. This was not how anyone should celebrate their twenty-first, I thought, turning my head and seeing the record player sitting quietly on the side, waiting. I would give it until eight, and then perhaps we would let Gerry take a break. Maybe we'd manage to get rid of the old people so we could get some real music on, dim the lights, turn this party into what it should have always been.

An hour later, Robbie tapped me on the shoulder and leaned in to whisper in my ear. "Good Lord, this is awful. This isn't my party. This is Linda's. Benji has cannabis. I'm going outside for a smoke. Coming?"

I followed him, my shoulders slumped, dejected. John seemed to be a man who could make anything happen, but clearly he hadn't been able to come through for tonight.

"I could pull the fire alarm," Benji said, pulling hard on the joint and passing it to me as we stood by the side of the village hall, the grass still wet from that afternoon's rain, the cold and wet getting through to my toes and creeping up my legs. I shivered.

"We could get rid of all the old people and have a proper party," said Robbie.

"How on earth would we get rid of all of them?" I let out a sigh. "We could all leave. Start a party somewhere else."

Robbie looked glum as he took the joint from me. "It's fine," he said. "This was never my idea to have a party anyway. I would have been just as happy with my friends down at the pub." His face lit up. "Why don't we all leave and go to the pub anyway?"

I was thinking what a good idea that was, wondering how quickly we could get away, when we saw headlights in the distance, and heard bass thumping from a car that was roaring toward us.

The three of us turned, standing stock-still as a silver car roared to a halt in front of the village hall, the windows blacked out, a huge distinctive grill on the front, a *B* with wings attached on top of the grill.

"Jesus," Robbie whistled. "Is that a Bentley S3 Continental?"

"It would seem so," said Benji, who was, obviously, not as impressed, given that his father drove a Lotus Elan, but still seemed bemused as to seeing this kind of car in our sleepy little village.

The music inside the car was turned off, the passenger door opened, and out stepped John, slick in a dark suit with a huge grin on his face. He extended his arms. "Happy Birthday!"

I couldn't wipe the smile off my face. Benji and Robbie stared at me, and when I turned, Robbie's mouth was hanging agape. He knew I was having a great time in London, but he didn't know that great time extended to having friends who traveled in silver Bentleys.

Nor, it has to be said, did I.

"John!" I didn't do a good job of pretending to be surprised. "What are you doing here?"

He stepped toward me and leaned forward to kiss me on the lips, but I felt self-conscious and turned my head, giving him, at the last minute, my cheek. "I took a chance," he improvised, giving me a look. "You said you would be in Evershot and I thought it was such a small village, I'd just ask someone. Turns out, we didn't need to ask anyone. We saw the lights, and here you are!"

I mouthed the words *thank you* at him, making sure no one else could see. I was so busy being impressed at his discretion, not to mention the Bentley, I forgot myself and my manners. "This is Robbie, my brother, and this is Benji, his best friend."

They shook hands before John turned back to the car. "I've brought some friends. I hope that's okay."

The back door opened and I saw first a dark blue velvet cape trimmed in ermine, then a shock of shaggy blond hair as Lissy Ellery emerged from the back seat, smoothing her leopard fur skirt as she grinned at us and spoke in her signature husky tones.

"Hey. I'm Lissy."

Our mouths fell open. Of course we knew who she was. Everyone knew who she was, the hottest, hippest, coolest, most beautiful, most famous woman in the music business. When I say in the music business, that isn't strictly true, for as far as I knew, she had never played an instrument or sung in her life. What she was, more than anything, was a famous groupie. She had dated Donovan and Eric Clapton, before finally landing Dave Boland.

My chest was so tight I could hardly breathe. Lissy Ellery had accompanied the Wide-Eyed Boys on their recent tour to America, and there were pictures of her striding down Madison Avenue with Dave Boland, thousands of screaming girls held back by policemen as they walked, huge sunglasses on both their faces, Lissy laughing at the camera, as if she knew exactly what kind of chaos they would cause, Lissy in a crocheted dress through which her nipples were visible, clear as day. She had a bag over her shoulder, with a bottle of Jack Daniel's sticking out.

"Jesus, I need to pee after that car ride." She strode off into the bushes before we had a chance to tell her where the loo was inside the village hall. Robbie looked like he'd either fallen in love or was too shocked to speak, as Benji turned back to the car, his mouth opening and closing like a fish.

Out climbed Dave Boland, yawning and stretching, running his fingers through his blond curls, his cheekbones even sharper than in the pictures, his eyes softer. My only disappointment, if I have to confess to a disappointment, was how short he was. Even in his Cuban-heeled boots, he can't have been more than five feet seven inches. But he was beautiful. And, more to the point, he was Dave Boland. Standing outside my brother's twenty-first birthday party in Evershot. I pinched myself to make sure I hadn't inadvertently drunk some fruit punch spiked with acid. No. I was as sober as a judge. I resisted the urge to scream, instead composing my features into something I hope resembled coolness. *Hey,* I tried to convey. *Dave Boland. That's no big deal.*

But it was. It was the biggest deal of my life, and my insides felt like they were going to burst.

"Bloody hell," said Dave Boland, to no one in particular. "That was a good nap. I needed that."

"Too much bloody smoking," said Eddie Allbright, the lead guitarist, who emerged from the front seat with a huge floppy hat and high-collared silk shirt, a big floppy bow around the neck. Next was Kevin Jennings, their drummer. Quiet and meek, he looked vaguely embarrassed at showing up to gate-crash a party in Dorset. Either that, or he was completely stoned. And finally, another blonde woman clutching a small leather box, who introduced herself, in the poshest voice I had ever heard, as Minty, short for Araminta. She was very pretty and, Benji realized, very familiar.

"Minty?" he peered at her. "Is that you?"

She looked at him with tiny pupils, and I wondered whether she had taken something. From the way she weaved toward Benji, it seemed like she had. I wondered what she had taken, and whether there was more in that little leather box and what it would take to get some.

"Benji?" she said, before falling into his arms and hugging him. "Oh, my God! I haven't seen you in years!" She didn't pronounce it "years," she pronounced it "yars," and I will admit to feeling the vaguest hint of jealousy as she flung her arms around Benji.

Finally, the chauffeur got out. His name was Jimmy, and he was huge and menacing. He leaned back against the car and lit up a cigarette. It was like watching a clown car, except instead of clowns, the people that kept emerging were some of the biggest rock stars in the UK. They were the people I moved down to London hoping to meet. And here they were, in my tiny little Dorset village, like some kind of psychedelic trip imagined by Dr. Timothy Leary.

At least, that's how it felt.

"What. The. Fuck. Is. Happening. Right. Now?" Benji spoke very slowly, thoroughly confused.

"I brought the gang," said John, shooting me a look. "We were hanging out at Dave's house and Lissy wanted to do something different, so I thought we'd come out and gate-crash the party. We even brought our own booze." John leaned back into the car and brought out a box containing several bottles of Jack Daniel's, some champagne and a small wooden box that almost certainly contained something far stronger.

Lissy made her way back from the shadows, pulling her skirt down, her hair mussed from the branches, which only served to make her look cooler. In anyone else, it would have looked ridiculous. In Lissy, it looked like she had just had incredible sex for hours.

"That's better," she said, her voice singsong, traces of her native Sweden still audible. "So where is this groovy party then?"

No one answered. What could we say?

Oh, how I wish I had had a camera. How I wish I could have filmed what happened when we walked back into the village hall with the Wide-Eyed Boys, all three of us with stunned looks on our faces, with this multicolored glamorous group of people. How I wish I could have captured Linda's expression on camera, so I could enjoy it for the rest of my life.

You know those old cowboy movies where the hero rides into town and pushes open the shutters to the saloon, and the music stops, everyone stops speaking, a silence falling on the room? That's what it was like walking back into the village hall with Dave Boland, Lissy Ellery and Eddie Allbright. Even Gerry stopped playing the piano as the whole room went dead quiet. I heard at least three glasses crash to the floor. *Oh, shit*, I thought, at the same time thinking that I had to stay in this moment, cherish it, remember everything about it, for it was entirely possible that I would never be this cool again in my life.

A silence, three dropped glasses, and then the screaming started. I can't blame them. We were all young, all excitable, all in shock, but I at least had been living in London, I at least had learned to contain my hysteria. Not so, the women in the village hall.

Dave and Eddie were—and I wouldn't have expected this—

brilliant with the attention, with the women on the verge of madness. They spent ten minutes signing scraps of paper, indulging all the local girls by doing the rock star thing, and then went back to the car and pulled guitars out the boot. Within minutes they were back inside, plugging guitars into amps, as Robbie's friends shook their heads in disbelief at what was happening. John started exploring the back room, and found a riser, used to put on plays by the students at the village school, which was swiftly brought out and put at one end of the hall, forming a stage. The three of them—Dave, Eddie and Kevin—jumped on the riser, Kevin grabbing from the car drumsticks and a small wooden box that he started drumming. Later, I discovered it was called a cajon. Eddie started to play, the distinctive opening bars of their biggest hit, "Blue-eyed girl," and the crowd went wild.

Live, the Wide-Eyed Boys, were incredible. I hadn't realized how unbelievably sexy Dave Boland was. I stood at the back with Lissy—Lissy!—both of us leaning against the wall, smoking the filterless Gitanes she offered me, watching coolly as Dave strutted around the tiny riser as if he were playing the Hammersmith Odeon. He held and caressed the microphone, swiveling his hips as the girls started screaming again.

I accepted the bottle of Jack Daniel's Lissy passed me, put it to my lips and took a hefty swig. It was only when I handed it back to her that I saw Linda across the hall, watching me, arms crossed, her downturned lips unable to hide her displeasure. This was not the party she had envisaged, and I was delighted. This wasn't about her, for once. This was about Robbie. This was the party he was always supposed to have had.

I knew she would blame me for being upstaged, and I didn't give a damn. I was the reason one of the biggest rock bands in the country was now playing the village hall in Evershot, but I didn't care. I looked at Robbie, dancing, shaking his head, losing himself in the music, and knew he would be talking about his twenty-first birthday party until the day he died. It had nothing to do with me, in that I hadn't known this was going to happen, but I also couldn't help but take credit for it: John was here because of me, and John's being here made this a night to remember.

I watched as my father appeared, helping Linda into her sensible double-breasted coat, as all of their friends started heading to the door.

"The twinsets are leaving!" laughed Lissy. My father waved at me, and I wandered over to say goodbye, although Linda was already out the door by the time I reached him. He leaned over and kissed me on the cheek. "It's time for the old people to go. You make sure everyone enjoys themselves."

"Goodbye, Linda," I said, unable to hide my joy. I had won this particular fight. She knew it, I knew it, and the strangest thing was, I no longer cared. My resentments against Linda seemed to disappear, and I knew she would never be able to hurt me again; I just didn't care enough. There were far more important things on which to focus.

I went over to the trestle table that was serving as a bar and poured Jack Daniel's into two glasses, taking one over to Lissy, who looked me up and down appraisingly, and nodded.

"You're cool," she said, as my heart threatened to burst with happiness. She downed the whole thing in one, so I did the same.

"What do you think of this skirt?" she said, immediately afterward, looking down at the leopard print.

I looked at her skirt, which fell to just above the knees.

"I think it's gorgeous," I said. "I love the leopard print. But I think it should be about six inches shorter."

She grinned then. "I think that, too. But no one is honest

with me. Thank you for being honest with me." She chinked glasses with me. "Cheers."

"Cheers." A warm flush spread inside me which felt like Jack Daniel's but was undoubtedly something else. If Lissy Ellery and I were not yet friends, it was surely only a matter of time. And if nothing else happened to me for the rest of my life, this would be enough. I could dine out on this forever and ever, and I would be happy.

Lissy reached into her bag and brought out a small glass contraption unlike anything I had seen before. I didn't want to be uncool, and said nothing when she handed it to me while she dug around in her bag for a lighter, before walking over to retrieve something from the small wooden box I had brought in earlier.

"This will be a treat for you," she said, taking out hashish and pushing it into what I realized was a bong. I had been up and down the Edgware Road, seen the Middle Eastern men sitting outside the cafés with their giant hookahs and water pipes. I had never seen one this small before.

There was water in the bottom of the glass bowl, and when she lit the hashish and put her mouth to the pipe, the water bubbled in a way I found hypnotic and exciting. She inhaled deeply before passing it to me. It was not the same smell as the hashish I had smoked before, presumably because this was not your regular street stuff. I took the bong as Lissy held the lighter to the tube, and copied her, pulling the drug deep into my lungs as the water bubbled and vapors escaped, and a wave of warmth and peace instantly washed over me, unlike anything I had felt before. I felt weightless, almost as if I was floating but at the same time aware of everything around me. Any worries I had drifted away. I had never felt so fantastic in my life. Whatever this was, it was glorious. And I wanted more.

I passed the pipe back to Lissy, who inhaled, then slipped it back to me with her signature naughty grin.

"Shall we go outside and look at the stars?" I exhaled the smoke, completely at peace with the world. We moved outside, where the sky was blacker and more velvety than I had ever seen, the grass greener, everything unfeasibly beautiful. Lissy stopped on the grass verge, melting down onto the grass. I lay next to her and she took my hand, entwining our fingers as she moved our hands up to the sky.

The night was clear, and there were thousands of stars. I had never seen a night sky more beautiful, nor the way our hands moved together, as if we had melted into each other. Lissy pointed out the constellations, the faint hint of what she swore was the Milky Way.

I was aware of movement and turned my head, as if in slow motion, to see that Benji had come outside with Minty. He moved so beautifully, I was entranced. How had I never noticed before how beautifully Benji moved? He sat next to us, his legs crossed. "What are you two doing?"

"Lying here admiring the sky."

"Are you stoned out of your mind?"

"I don't know." I felt myself smiling. "All I can tell you is I've never felt so wonderful in my life."

"Here." Lissy rolled onto her side and pulled the bong out of her bag again, passing it to Benji, who declined, then Minty, who inhaled when Lissy pressed her lighter to the pipe. Soon, she was lying next to me on the grass.

Benji sniffed. "What is that you're smoking?"

"Opium, darling. Isn't it wonderful?"

I sighed as I lay, one hand holding Lissy's hand, the other now holding Minty's. "It's glorious."

I remember thinking I should probably care that I had just smoked opium rather than hashish, that this was altogether a much bigger deal, but I didn't. I didn't care about anything. I didn't care about Benji's horrified reaction.

"What the fuck?" he said to Minty.

"Relax, darling," said Minty. "Have some. It feels fantastic."

"I'm not taking *opium*." His face was screwed up with disapproval. "I'm not a drug addict."

"Neither are we, darling," said Lissy, holding her other hand out to him. I could see him hesitate. This wasn't just anyone inviting him to lie down on the grass with us. This was Lissy Ellery. What man could refuse?

This man could refuse. "I hope you know what you're doing," he said to me with a slight shake of his head. Under different circumstances, his disapproval would have upset me, but tonight, this beautiful, beautiful night, it rolled right over me like a faint breeze.

I was vaguely aware of Benji scribbling something down on a piece of paper and handing it to Jimmy. "Just in case," I heard him say.

John came out. "I hear you're corrupting Cece," he said to Lissy, taking the bong she handed to him and inhaling deeply, sitting down next to me. "You are awful," he said to Lissy with a grin. He leaned down then and kissed her on the lips, which I watched, wondering why the man I appeared to be involved with was kissing another woman, wondering if I should be jealous, except I couldn't remember what jealousy felt like. All I felt, lying under the velvet sky, was a kind of euphoric laziness.

I was aware that there appeared to be more cars on this sleepy road, and the cars were stopping. Suddenly there were headlights, and noise, and lots of excitable teenagers who were swarming around us, heading to the town hall.

I have no idea how the news spread so quickly, but I could see Benji acting as bouncer, stopping the kids from coming in, the crowd growing larger and larger outside the hall, people borrowing their parents' cars to see if it could possibly be true that the Wide-Eyed Boys were playing a party at the village hall in Evershot.

We lay outside for a while listening to the music, and when the music stopped, John came running out, followed closely by Dave, Eddie and Kevin, as their chauffeur, who, I was beginning to realize, was probably more of a minder than a chauffeur, attempted to hold back the girls outside, all of whom started screaming and crying as soon as the band appeared.

"I love you, Dave!"

"Eddie! Will you marry me?"

"Aaaargh!" The screams were deafening.

"Let's go!" shouted Eddie, as someone grabbed the hat off his head. He paused but was pushed forward by Kevin.

"Let's get out of here," shouted Jimmy the chauffeur, as a few of the girls surged toward us. He shielded the boys as they tumbled into the back seat, Eddie taking the front. "Get a bleedin' move on!" he shouted at us. Lissy was laughing as she and Minty stood up, and before I knew it, they'd grabbed my hand and dragged me into the car, pulling me on top of them as Jimmy shut the door firmly, running round to the driver's seat. Before we knew it, the crowds parted like the Red Sea as Jimmy swung the Bentley round and took off down the road.

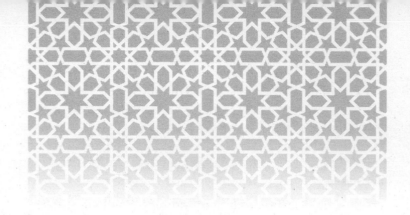

TWELVE

The interior of the car was red, like a large, luxurious womb. Seats of red leather, red fur on the floor, there was a record player built in to the walnut dashboard, and as we pulled away, Eddie pulled a bunch of 45s from the door and put on something I had never heard before, "Purple Haze" by Jimi Hendrix.

I was pulled over everyone's laps, lying on my back, my head on Lissy's lap, my feet in John's. Everything was blissful as we roared along, the engine purring, the music blaring, without a care in the world. My eyes were closed, and when I opened them, Lissy and Dave were kissing, which struck me then as the most beautiful thing I had ever seen. I was right at the center of the world.

I knew Robbie would forgive me for leaving. I had, without planning or intention, provided him with a twenty-first birthday party to end all birthday parties; he would remember this for the rest of his life. As would I.

"Where are we going?" I asked, after a while.

"I don't know." Eddie turned and shouted over the music, "Where do you think we should go?"

"Darling, why don't we go to Morocco?" Lissy peeled herself away from Dave. "We could go and see the Gettys at their palace. They have room for us."

"The who?" I asked.

"Old friends of mine," said Lissy. "Paul is J. Paul Getty Jr., son of the American oilman who lives over here at Sutton Place. Paul recently married this fabulous ball of fire, Talitha. She's an actress, Dutch, but they met in London."

I look back at this time, still, the way we made spontaneous, crazy plans like this, then carried them out without a second thought, with huge affection. I couldn't imagine anyone doing that now, certainly not the way young people work these days. But back then, we were just discovering that it was possible to have a crazy whim, then act upon it. We didn't worry about responsibilities or plans we had made. We just did it. The world had burst into a technicolor feast, and we were going to savor every last bite.

"How did the Gettys meet?" asked John, who always wanted to know everything about everyone and everything.

"At a dinner party," Lissy said. "She was supposed to be sitting next to Rudolf Nureyev, who was said to be in love with her, but he didn't show. Paul was there, instead. They fell madly in love instantly. He showed up the next day with arms filled with flowers, and took her to meet the old man in Sutton Place that afternoon. I ran into them both at the Robert Fraser Gallery a week later, and already they were inseparable." She shook her head. "Every man in London is mourning, *especially*, I hear, Desmond FitzGerald."

"Don't you mean the Knight of Glin?" said Dave, putting on a posh accent.

"The Knighty Knight," teased Lissy, nudging him. "Don't pretend you don't love it. You take the piss out of them, but we all know you love rubbing shoulders with the Hooray Henrys."

"The Hooray Henrys!" Eddie cracked up in peals of laughter, changing the 45 on the record player to the Beatles' "All You Need is Love." The entire car, save for Jimmy, stopped talking to sing along to the chorus: *da-da-da-da-da*.

Hooray Henrys. I had never heard the term before. I researched it later, and discovered that it was a term coined by Damon Runyon in 1936 in his short story "Tight Shoes." By the fifties it had become part of common usage, referring mostly to the raucous upper-class fans of jazz trumpeter Humphrey Lyttelton, who would shout "Hoorah!" between each musical piece he played at the 100 Club in London.

I didn't know that it was starting to be used by the general population to sneer at the upper classes and their privileged upbringing. It was only used by people who were not from that class, and class, as everyone in Britain knows, is something that cannot be changed.

Years later, I have tried to explain this to American friends. It doesn't matter how much money you make, you will never transcend the class into which you are born. I was firmly lower middle class, and it didn't matter that the man I would eventually marry was well-off. I was born into the lower middle class, and there I would stay, no matter how much I thought I had moved up in the world, no matter how glamorous my life.

"What's Talitha like?" I asked, liking the sound of her name. That was the first time I'd said it out loud. Talitha. Pronounced correctly, with or without Lissy's lovely accent, Tal-

ee-ta. It made me think of Tabitha Twitchit, feline mother of Moppet, Mittens and Tom Kitten. Except that's pronounced *Ta*-bitha, which is quite different to Talitha. *Taleeta*. What a mysterious name for the woman who stole the heart of the son of the richest man in the world, a woman who lived in a palace in Morocco.

Not Talitha, but Talita. I mouthed it again and again as I lay across their laps, liking how the name sounded in my mouth, in my head.

"They are both fabulous in every way. He's a sweetheart, can be quite serious, but likes to drink, and she brings out the best in him. She is gorgeous, just a spectacular woman. She's got more life and fire in her than anyone I've met."

Eddie turned in the front seat to look back at Lissy, raising a sardonic eyebrow. "More than you?"

Lissy broke into a peal of laughter. "She's my negative. Where I'm blonde, she's dark. And petite. She's always laughing, which we know, is definitely not me. She's got this beautiful, compact little body, with funny little hands and feet. She's truly gorgeous, inside and out. They're restoring a palace in Marrakech. Dave? You remember the New Year's Eve party we went to, yes?"

Dave shook his head. "Sweetheart, I don't remember anything about that New Year's Eve party. I remember Tangier, but once we went to Marrakech I don't remember a fucking thing. Spectacular palace, and then, out of it. All I remember is being flat on my back with John Lennon flat on his back on one side, and Paul McCartney on the other. None of us could get off the floor, let alone talk."

"That was the wildest party I've ever been to." Lissy's eyes shone at the memory. "I've never seen so many people out of control. That's Talitha. She's dangerous." She clapped her

hands, and you could see how much she loved it, how much
she was dying to do it all over again.

"Dangerous?" I asked.

"She doesn't know when to stop," said Lissy. "She's this
wild creature who burns so brightly. She seems tough, but
she's not. She's fragile as hell, and I worry about her."

"Don't say that," said Eddie. "That's tempting bad juju,
that is."

"No, it's not. It's just how it is. I think Mick and Marianne
are out there now?" She changed the subject. "I spoke to Marianne just before they were leaving. Let's go and see them!"

"How do we get there?" It was Minty's turn to speak.

"Let's drive!" said Lissy, who may not have been in the band
but was clearly the ringleader. "Jimmy?" She leaned forward
and tapped him on the shoulder. "Can we drive to Morocco?"

I had the sense Jimmy didn't much like her. Before he answered, he looked at Eddie, who gave him the slightest of
nods, as if giving him permission to answer Lissy, to treat her
not only like a member of the band but an equal. I suspected
that Lissy called the shots.

"We could drive across to France and go from there." Jimmy's voice was flat, with no enthusiasm whatsoever.

"That's what Keith did." Dave's voice rang with excitement.

"No! For God's sake!" said Lissy. "We don't have to copy
everything Keith Richards does. Carve your own path, darling. Let's do things differently. I haven't got the patience for
a long road trip. I'll ring my travel agent and have her book
us all on a flight."

"What about the you-know-what?" Dave looked panicked.

"Jimmy can meet us in Marrakech!" she exclaimed with
excitement. "They'll never look for the drugs if we're not in
the car. Jimmy, everything's well hidden, isn't it?"

Jimmy caught her eye in the rearview mirror and gave the

faintest of nods as Lissy clapped her hands, either not knowing, or not caring, that he didn't seem to like her at all. "Everyone got their passports?" she said.

"No!" I said dreamily, not really caring what was going
to happen.

"Where is it?" asked Minty as I shrugged.

"Wait!" As sleepy as I suddenly was, I managed to hoist
myself up, and pulled my velvet tote bag into my lap, rum-
maging through the contents until I found my purse. There
it was. My passport. I had put it in my purse for safekeeping
when I left Warwickshire House, and had forgotten all about
it. I only had a passport because Dottie and I had dreamed of
going to France, and we'd both got them, just in case. Already
that life felt a million miles away.

I pulled my passport out with a flourish, as everyone in
the car cheered.

The fact that all my earthly possessions were in a suitcase
at my parents' house, that I had no clothes with me, no job,
nowhere to be, meant nothing. The fact that I was supposed
to be going back to London to look for a flat to share with
Dottie was suddenly unimportant.

This is what I wanted, I thought. An adventure. And this
was what the universe was presenting to me. I was going to
grab the opportunity with both hands, one of which was
clutching onto my passport as I sank back onto the laps of my
new friends, knowing that finally, after all these years, life
was finally going my way.

THIRTEEN

I missed most of the drive to the airport, too comfortable, too drowsy lying across laps, my eyes fluttering closed. I only realized we had arrived when car doors started opening and closing, and I had to rouse myself.

We dropped Kevin the drummer off at a tube station. He had to get home to a wife and young baby, and seemed perfectly happy to jump on the tube. John had a series of meetings lined up that week with record companies, so he couldn't come, either. I got out the car to kiss him goodbye, and wondered if I should have made an excuse and left. John was, after all, the sole reason I was there.

"I think maybe I shouldn't go." *Please say I should. Please say I should. Please say I should.*

"You absolutely must go." John gave me a kiss. "And then tell me all about it when you get back."

I couldn't have wiped the smile off my face even if I'd wanted to. I climbed back in the car, and everyone cheered.

I still don't know who paid, only that someone had passed a Diners Card at the ticketing counter, and the next thing you know we were being escorted through the airport as people stopped and stared, some digging Polaroid cameras out their bags, taking pictures of the band. A few took a picture of me, which was funny. I was glad I wouldn't be around to witness their disappointment when they realized I was no one at all.

"How come Lissy's the only one with luggage?" I whispered to Minty, turning to see a trail of pink feathers in her wake, like crumbs of bread leading to the gingerbread house.

"She takes it everywhere." Minty laughed. "She always says you never know when you might need something. Jimmy hates it."

I paused. "What are *we* going to do about clothes."

She lit up a cigarette and blew a puff of smoke in my face. "We're going to Marrakech. We'll shop." I decided not to tell her that although I had been saving my somewhat meager earnings, I wasn't equipped to splurge in the way she seemed to think was normal.

In the first-class lounge (the first-class lounge!), our tickets in hand, drinking free champagne (free!), we heard a voice shout from across the room. "Minty! Darling!"

A group of people came over, a beautifully dressed man, handsome despite a receding hairline, with impossibly perfect white teeth, an Italian accent, and his equally glamorous French wife. There were others with them, all just as elegant, and Minty introduced us.

Dado was his name, his wife Nancy. "Well, hello, Cece."

His eyes looked me up and down, a spark of interest in them. "Why haven't we run into *you* before?"

"She's our newest best friend," Minty trilled. "We've all come from a little village hall in Dorset for a party. So sweet. We picked Cece up and we're dragging her off to Morocco."

He turned then, alert. "Morocco? Are you going to see my darling Talitha and Paul?"

"We are!"

"Damn. We ought to come. We're on our way to Saint-Tropez. Why don't you come to Saint-Tropez first? Sasha's going to be there." He winked at Minty. "I know how well you got on last time."

I had no idea people did this, but after squealing with excitement, Minty called someone over and arranged to change her flights, kissing all of us goodbye as she took off to board the plane to Nice.

"Dado Ruspoli's an Italian prince." Lissy leaned over to me. "And so very naughty." She shook her head, smiling to herself at memories I wasn't meant to access.

"Naughty?"

"There is a reason they call him the Playboy Prince. When you're with Dado, the party quickly becomes an orgy." She chuckled and I wanted to ask more, but I was too tired.

Despite the adrenaline that had been coursing through my body, I was now coming down, and I fell asleep quickly, waking up to a stewardess gently shaking my shoulder and requesting I put my seat back up. Lissy and Dave were canoodling on the other side of the aisle, and Eddie, who was next to me, was staring at them. I realized suddenly that Eddie, who had famously broken up with a model a couple of months ago, might have had a bit of a thing for Lissy. I didn't blame him. She was not only spirited and beautiful, she had an edge of danger that I could see would make her irresistible to some.

I was thrilled to be in her orbit but recognized, I think, even then, that I shouldn't get too close, that she had the capacity to lead me into adventures that might be much more treacherous than an opium bong.

Eddie, on the other hand, was smitten with her. One look at his face and I could tell. I reached over for his hand and gave it a squeeze, not in a suggestive way but in a way that hopefully conveyed I was on his side, I understood, I had empathy for his pain.

"You alright?" He looked down at our hands, clasped together now, then up at my face, confused.

"I'm alright. Are you?"

"I don't like flying much," he said. "I'd much rather have driven."

"Why didn't you just drive with Jimmy and meet us there?"

His eyes flickered back to Lissy, and I knew why. He came up with an excuse that was probably true, even though it clearly wasn't the only reason.

"It's probably better for us not to be in the car when it crosses the border. They're looking out for us now."

Ah, yes. Dave had a reputation for drugs. He had never been caught, but even me, innocent little shopgirl, knew of the rumors.

"Lissy asked if the drugs were hidden. Are you worried?"

Eddie shook his head and grinned, leaning forward and lowering his voice. "We had the car customized. Secret compartments all over the place."

My eyes widened. "Like where? Tell me!"

"I could." He paused, looking at me thoughtfully, stroking his chin in an exaggerated way. "But if we got caught and they tortured you, you'd give it up in a second."

I burst out laughing. "Will you be my friend, Eddie Allbright?" I couldn't believe I had the temerity to ask a rock star if he would be friends with a nobody like me, but then again I couldn't believe I was sitting in first class with new friends who were arguably the most famous people in England.

This time it was Eddie's turn to take my hand and give it a squeeze. "I'll tell you what, Cece. I already am."

There was a huge jolt in the plane, and my stomach dropped to my knees. I turned to Eddie, all the color draining from my face.

"What was that?" I imagined bits falling off the plane, of spiraling into the sea, knowing we were all going to die, and not being able to do anything. I was terrified.

Eddie squeezed my hand. "Don't worry. That was the landing gear. We're about to land. It's normal. Is this—" he peered at me in disbelief "—your first time on a plane?"

I said nothing, just looked out the window feeling ashamed at my naivete. Next time, I would play it much more cool.

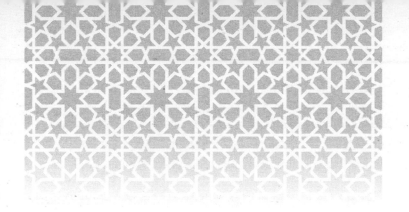

FOURTEEN

The heat hit as soon as we stepped off the plane. We made our way down the steps onto the tarmac as a scalding wind whipped my hair.

A car was waiting, and after we piled in, it careened through unfamiliar streets, wide and lined with concrete buildings, dropping us, finally, inside the gates of Marrakech. We stumbled out, bleary-eyed, into bright sunshine, which was surprisingly cold in the shadow of the wall, as the driver jumped out, calling to a man with a cart and donkey, who loaded all Lissy's bags on top as we climbed out the car. From here on, we were to walk alongside our cart. I was instantly hit with the smell, unlike anything I had ever experienced. Orange blossom hung heavy in the air, mixed with warm spices and what I presumed to be an animal odor, both fur and dung.

More than anything, it smelled like life; if it were possible for a smell to be alive, this was completely alive.

I felt a fizzing inside my body, an excitement so palpable I thought it was going to burst out. I wrapped my arms tightly around myself, and had a smile I couldn't wipe off. Of course I had seen films set in foreign countries, but I had never traveled abroad, and the magic and energy and newness was intoxicating.

We must have looked out of place because the locals started pushing and shoving to get close to us. I caught snippets of French, Spanish, English, offers of guided tours shouted in our direction. It felt dreamlike. Our driver tried to wave the men away, but they kept coming, swarming us as we set off through the streets. I don't think anyone knew who we were specifically. The Wide-Eyed Boys didn't have an international reach back then. But we were immediately clocked as tourists.

I looked to Eddie, who was entirely unfazed, and felt myself relax. Dave's energy was more brittle, and not just because he was physically less imposing. Eddie just seemed more confident. He seemed like someone you could rely on to get you out of trouble.

Not that it felt like trouble. It felt like excitement, and possibility, and heat, and spice, and lust. Not that I even knew what lust was. Not then. But I knew this was what I had been waiting for. I wasn't scared or intimidated or overwhelmed. I wanted to grasp Morocco and swallow it whole. I wanted it to become part of me.

"Oh, fuck," Eddie muttered under his breath, pushing through the men that surrounded us. "I wish Jimmy was fucking here."

"How long will it take for him to get here?" I clung to the back of his jacket, clutching the fabric tightly in my hand, as if letting go would whisk me into the dark unknown.

"Dunno. I think about two days. He'd get rid of these men in a heartbeat."

I didn't ask how he would get rid of them. I thought it was probably best that I didn't know. "Do you know where we're going?"

He shook his head, setting off again to make sure he didn't lose Lissy and Dave. "Lissy knows. She always knows."

"You like her."

He didn't hear me. Or perhaps he did and pretended not to. For that, I was grateful.

"Tell me about Talitha," I asked, as we wound our way from the airport, and into the old city, through an area called Sidi Mimoun. Already I loved saying her name, was fascinated by this mysterious woman who lived in a palace and had managed to seduce the son of the richest man in the world. Would she intimidate me? Frighten me? Would she be superior and cold, or welcome me as one of the gang? I was filled with a mix of nerves and excitement, all the while her name echoing in my brain.

Around us, cows and goats wandered in the middle of the road, men in full-length djellabas occasionally hitting them with sticks to move them out the way, carts piled high with oranges and spices. The cars veered from one side of the road to the other in controlled chaos.

"Talitha is a spirit unlike any other," said Eddie. "She isn't everyone's taste. Much of Paul's family, especially his father, is extremely suspicious of her. But she casts something of a spell. It's quite possible you will fall madly in love with her."

"I'm not that way inclined," I said.

"You haven't met Talitha," said Eddie.

I kept a tight grip on to Eddie's shirt, periodically shutting my eyes, convinced I was about to see a crowd of people plowed down. We were just inside the city walls, red sandstone, giving it the nickname the Red City. We turned down a narrow street when a donkey-pulled cart almost knocked us over. Finally we turned into a small alley, dark and crooked, a stray cat sitting in a doorway. In front of us were huge wooden doors at least sixteen feet high, and our strange little group gathered outside. I wondered where the palace was that we were supposed to be visiting.

"What are we doing here?" asked Dave.

"This is the palace, darling!" said Lissy, as Eddie started sniggering. This was far away from the high stone house on a hill I had presumed to be our destination. I looked around at the rubbish scattered on the dark cobbled street, and Lissy must have registered my surprise.

"It's a series of riads," she said. "You can laugh now, but wait until they open the doors."

The word *riad*, I later discovered, comes from the Arabic word for garden. There is always a central interior, usually with a fountain, and trees. Riads were, historically, built for wealthier families, like courtiers and tradesmen, built upward in a medina, the old walled center, of Moroccan cities.

Islamic architecture is typically modest on the outside, wealth and riches hidden behind nondescript stone walls, so as not to inspire jealousy. Tiled courtyards and fountains, hand-carved painted wooden ceilings, the scent of orange trees, rosemary and jacaranda—gardens of Eden blooming behind austere exteriors. But none were like the Palais de la Zahia, which consisted of numerous riads strung together to form a palace you would never have known about from the outside.

Lissy rang three times, to silence. Eventually she banged on those huge doors, as I stepped back, worried we would offend even before we had arrived. Finally we heard locks being pulled back, and before us stood a wizened old man whose face exploded in a smile when he saw Lissy. She flung her arms around him in a hug, before introducing him as Si Mo-hammed, the gatekeeper. He was delighted to see her, to see us, as he ushered us in through the gates, into an enormous courtyard that, to this day, I can only describe as Paradise. A bewitching, magical land that no one would have believed existed from the outside. I gasped, my mouth falling open as I looked around.

We were standing on the edge of a large garden with a fountain in the middle. The garden was being adorned with emerald green tiles, parts of it were still bare concrete. There were men crouching down, carefully cementing and placing each tile, finishing it off. Everywhere you looked, elephant ear plants exploded from the ground. There were patches of blue sky in between heavy jacaranda branches that twisted overhead, dripping with leaves and lavender-colored blos-soms, the petals falling, even as we stood, covering the tiles in an explosion of pale purple. Palm trees surrounded every-thing, and as we stood, three peacocks appeared and strutted across the tiles, one of them fanning its tail out when it saw us, as Lissy laughed and I smelled the jacaranda, almost like honey, filling the air.

"Alright, Eddie?" A man appeared with long hair, his lithe, slim body in cigarette pants, his pout even more beautiful than I could have imagined. I recognized him immediately—and felt myself swooning, my heart pounding with adrenaline as I willed myself not to faint. Or scream.

"I'm Mick," he said, as my mouth opened and closed like a fish. Mick Jagger. No one would believe me about this back home, I thought. I could barely believe it myself.

"I'm Cece. How do you do." I shook his hand and turned as Marianne Faithfull appeared from a passageway, her hair caught back in a clip, huge sunglasses covering half her face, doing nothing to disguise her ethereal, aristocratic beauty.

"Come on, darling." Mick turned to Marianne. "We'll miss the flight."

"You're leaving?" Lissy pouted. "You can't leave. We've only just got here."

"We have to leave," Mick said. "We're in the studio next week and I've got to get some rest."

"You're such an old man." Marianne leaned her head on his shoulder. "Can't we stay one more night with our friends?"

"You know what that means here. A lost week, if not more."

Eddie leaned over to me, his voice low. "And that," he said, "is why the Rolling Stones are going to be around forever."

I turned and frowned. "Because Mick's the boss?"

"No. Because Mick's a grown-up. While we're getting high and listening to music, he's having a cup of tea and an early night."

I watched them leave, disappointed that I wouldn't get to know them better, before glimpsing a mysterious figure in an upstairs window looking down at us. Dark hair, huge eyes, fabric billowing as she turned to look at us, to look at me. I felt my heart flutter with mystery and magic as I looked up, knowing this had to be her. *Talitha*. She moved back into the darkness as I stood still staring up at where she had just been, a strange sort of emptiness overcoming me when she disappeared from view.

We walked through the courtyard with its mosaic floors and fires being lit by men who nodded at us. I peered into small alcoves and regal rooms, oversize multicolored glass lanterns casting a magical glow over everything as dusk fell. The hand-carved benches and chairs invited you to take a seat. I had never seen anything, nor been anywhere, as magical in all my life.

Out of the corner of my eye, something moved. I turned to see her wafting down a grand marble staircase, the robes of an embroidered kimono floating as she walked, an ethereal beauty, petite, with a shoulder-length mane of dark auburn hair, and curiously wide-set eyes filled with life and laughter beneath a heavy fringe. Her smile seemed to wash over all of us as we stood, dirty, tired, entranced.

She was the most beautiful creature I had ever seen.

"I'm Talitha," she said to me, hugging each of us, hugging me.

She wrapped her arms around my waist as she pulled me in, and I sensed both her fragility and her strength. I knew then that I would go to the ends of the earth to protect her.

And I knew my life was never going to be the same.

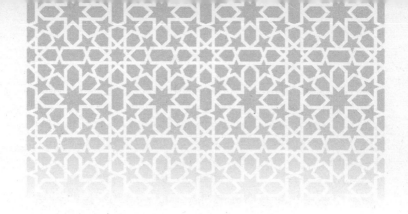

FIFTEEN

My room was off another courtyard, a second garden with a tiny star-shaped fountain in the middle but, much to my disappointment, no peacocks. The walls were coral waxed plaster, and a fire roared in the fireplace. Lanterns sat on either side, and the scent of mint and rosemary filled the room, mixing with the delicious smells of the orange wood burning.

A four-poster bed with intricately carved posts was hung with lavish tapestries of green velvet embroidered with gold. Ancient Amazigh rugs covered the stone floor. The bathroom had rich royal blue plaster on the walls, a plaster called tadelakt, a traditional lime-based technique that had been used in Morocco for thousands of years. The floor and bath were covered in zellige, a mosaic of tiny tiles, in blues, greens, yellows and reds. As I lay back on the bed, turning my head to look out the window, I caught the shadow of the Atlas Mountains in the distance.

I was drifting into sleep when there was a knock on the door. I managed to rouse myself, my hair mussed, and opened it to find a man standing there, his arms filled with clothes.

"Pour vous," he said, as I stepped aside to let him in. I presumed either Lissy or Talitha had sent them, knowing I had nothing to wear. Once he had left, when I laid them on the bed, I knew they were from Talitha.

There were midnight blue velvet robes embroidered in reds, yellows, blues and golds; beaded kaftans that swept to the floor, harem pants, silks and velvets and beads. And among the traditional Moroccan clothes were Yves Saint Laurent couture dresses, elaborately patterned fabrics with high beaded collars, lavish silk fringe encircling the skirts, down to the floor.

I had never handled clothes more beautiful, and was far too terrified to wear the Saint Laurent. I had never understood before this moment why people spent fortunes on clothes. I thought you could wear Miss Selfridge and make it look expensive, but I now understood that wasn't true; these weren't just clothes, they were art. Which is how I knew they were Talitha's.

Just as I was holding up one of the Saint Laurent dresses, noting the beaded corset, the bedroom door opened. There, in the doorway, with the sunlight shimmering behind her like a halo, stood Talitha.

"Oh! Look how perfect that is! That's exactly the one I was hoping you'd pick! Lissy said you hadn't brought anything. I hope you don't mind my sending down some clothes. Aren't Yves's clothes the most beautiful?"

I wondered if she was wearing Yves now, in a richly embroidered short dress with bell sleeves, strappy gladiator sandals climbing up her calves. I looked at the dress I was holding and sighed.

"I can't wear this! It must have cost a fortune. I'd be terrified of spilling something on it."

Her eyes danced with delight. "Darling, it was a gift from Yves. If you spill anything on it, I'll get another. Try it on."

I couldn't resist, as self-conscious as I felt, stripping down to my bra and knickers, while Talitha sat down at a small table and tipped out a white powder. Soon she was chopping it into lines, and by the time she had finished, I was in the Yves Saint Laurent dress.

"You look stunning," she said, offering me a line of cocaine. I hadn't done it before, but this was not my real life and I had already decided, unconsciously, that I was going to say yes to new experiences, I was going to say yes to everything. My God, in the space of a few weeks I had gone from being a girl who had never tried drugs, to a girl who had smoked pot, done LSD and opium, and was now about to try cocaine. I thought, fleetingly, of Miss Nicholl at Warwickshire House. Already I felt I had traveled light-years away from the girl who shared a room with Dottie, who tried not to break the rules other than hanging underwear over the radiator.

Talitha saw, I think, that I didn't know what to do with the cocaine, so she went first, holding a thin silver straw to one nostril as she held the other shut, gliding smoothly down the line until it was all gone. Then the other nostril, before she handed the straw to me, and I bent my head and did the same with the two lines that remained. I felt an acrid taste in the back of my mouth and sour drops down my throat, but before I had time to think about it, I was, instantly, awake.

I laughed with delight at how the sleepiness had completely left me. I was suddenly more alive than I had ever been, and filled with thoughts, wanting to tell Talitha everything that was going on in my head, but it was interrupted by a shout from outside. Talitha and I both went to the window. A man was striding across the courtyard, shouting.

Talitha rolled her eyes with a smile. "My husband. Paul. He's freaking out again. You'll meet him later. He's absolutely wonderful, but finding it a little hard to cope with all the building work. He likes peace and quiet." She let out a peal of laughter. "He's the opposite of me! I adore nothing more than being surrounded by people. Give me music, and dancing, and life! My poor husband. Every time he thinks we're almost finished with the noise and the mess, Bill finds more to do."

"Bill?"

"Bill Willis. Our decorator and builder. And, fortunately for us, our friend. He's the reason we're here. My darling husband is freaking out because Bill keeps finding new things to tile." She laughed. "He never stops. We keep thinking that each time we come back it will be finished, but each time we come back, Bill's found more things to do. Paul keeps telling me to stop that man, but he doesn't seem to realize that Bill thinks of him as his patron. Every time he tries to stop Bill, Bill points out how much more work has to be done. Thank heavens he's so talented. He's bringing back all these lost arts that they usually only do in mosques, or palaces. Hang on." She leaned over the edge of the window and called out.

"Paul! Darling! Don't worry. Bill says it's going to be finished next week." The man below stopped and turned, looking up at us. He was scowling until he saw Talitha, when his face instantly relaxed. I had never seen someone's face light up with love before now, and I thought to myself that when I fall in love, I want it to be like this; I want to see someone's face light up in just this way when they look at me.

Paul Getty, Talitha's husband, was less handsome than he was appealing. There was something cute and boyish about his dark red hair, the way his smile transformed his features.

"Come and meet Cece!" Talitha called. "She's a sweetheart. You will adore her." With a grin, he waved at me. "Meet us on the roof for drinks. Bill? Come and join us."

"Yes, sugar," called a Southern voice from behind a pillar. I couldn't see him, but I could hear him. "Your wish is my command."

Talitha and I stepped back from the window. Her voice was accented, and I couldn't remember where Lissy said she was from.

"Are you German?"

"Dutch," she said. "But I lived in London for ages before I met Paul. My father and stepmother are in Paddington. Chilworth Street. Do you know it?"

I was embarrassed that I didn't. I wanted to be the sort of Londoner who knew every street, like the cabbies who had to master the city layout before being allowed to drive taxis; I wanted to be in the know.

I shook my head.

"I'm a strange blend. My parents were both Dutch, I was born in Java, and my stepmother is English."

I thought of Linda, then, my own stepmother. Her pursed lips and resentment of Robbie and me. "How do you get on with your stepmother?"

"Poppet? I adore her! She's not my mother, obviously, and I will miss my mother forever, but I'm lucky. Poppet has always been wonderful to me."

I stopped and stared at her. "Is your mother dead?"

She nodded. "Tragically, yes. In the internment camp in Java my mother and I used to talk to each other through the wire fence. Can you imagine? I was terribly young, but my mother suffered enormously. After we were released I think it was all too much for her. She died very soon after we left."

She went silent then. I recognized what she was doing, how

she had carefully practiced telling the story without emotion, hiding the pain, making sure no one saw the hurt. I knew nothing about internment camps, couldn't imagine how she got there, what that experience must have been like, the damage that must have been wrought. But I did know about mothers dying. All too well. I felt a stab of pain, together with sweetness, the recognition that I was looking at someone with a hole in her heart the exact size and shape as mine.

I hadn't been aware of having a protective instinct before that moment. I had never sought to rescue people, or jumped in to solve other people's problems. If anything, I was used to being on the sidelines. But there was something about Talitha, about her honesty, the unselfconscious revelation of her story, that made me want to throw my arms around her and stop anything bad from happening to her ever again.

"My mother died, too. It was a car accident. Unfortunately I don't have a good relationship with my stepmother, but…" I trailed off. "I try not to dwell on it."

Talitha narrowed her eyes and nodded. "Things have always been good with Poppet, but I know what it's like to lose your mother." She gazed at me as I looked into her eyes, aware of being completely understood in that moment, completely seen.

"Do you know what is strange?" she continued. "I knew it. The minute I saw you through the window I knew we had a special bond. I felt this strong connection to you, and now I know why. Motherless daughters. You and me. You can't understand what it's like unless it's happened to you."

I swallowed the lump in my throat as I nodded. I'm not sure I had ever felt quite so understood as I felt for those few seconds, Talitha's large brown eyes, filled with compassion and understanding, gazing into mine.

Pull yourself together, I thought. Don't cry. Not here and not now. My brain scurried to change the subject, to find something anodyne to ask, something that would put an end to the emptiness that had suddenly opened up inside me, the emptiness that always opened up when I allowed myself to think about my mother.

I turned my head and blinked quickly to make sure tears didn't emerge. "How did you find this place? It's magnificent."

"It's okay," Talitha whispered, as she leaned forward and kissed me on the forehead. "I understand."

I felt a wave of love and relief rise up. Ridiculous, I thought, suddenly remembering what Eddie had said. I wasn't falling in love with her, but it did feel as if I had found a sister, a soul sister.

Then, her voice at a normal level, she continued speaking. "Bill found it for us. We live mostly in Rome when we're not here, and Bill had the most fabulous antiques shop around the corner from our apartment, near the Spanish Steps. He suggested we come to Marrakech for our honeymoon, and offered to be our guide. He clearly knew we'd fall in love, and brought us here immediately. By the end of the day, we had bought it."

"How could you do anything else. It's the most beautiful place I've ever been in my life."

"It is now, but it was completely dilapidated when we first saw it. It was built in the late nineteenth century for El Glaoui, the great Pasha of Marrakech. Can you believe it hasn't even been here for that long?" She laughed. "A fake countess from Casablanca had been living here, and she'd painted everything pink, red, blue and yellow. It was all crumbling away, but we saw the courtyards and how beautiful it could be. You know there are six riads put together? Six! Isn't that ridiculous? Bill had so many ideas, he helped us see it, too, and I do love it. It's my fantasy. My pleasure palace."

It was my turn to laugh. "Is that what it's called? The Pleasure Palace?"

"Not officially. Officially it's le Palais de la Zahia, but of course I had to rename it. Now it's Le Palais des Plaisirs, although we usually just call it Sidi Mimoun after the area it's in." She took my hand then and pulled me behind her, running out the room and turning to laugh. "Come on, darling. We're going up to the roof to get the pleasure started. Come and meet the others."

Others? Beyond our little group? I didn't know then that meals were rarely for less than fifteen, that Talitha collected people, was happiest when there were scores of guests for dinner every night, for picnic lunches in the Atlas Mountains, for spirited excursions around Marrakech. Talitha needed a crowd. She was never as good when she was on her own, but around people, a light came on, she fizzed with energy and liveliness.

We ran down the narrow winding stairs to the guest courtyard, both of us giggling as we passed construction workers carrying baskets of cement, pallets of tiles, trying desperately, I assume, to finish off this enormous job. Then we raced through a dark corridor to the main courtyard and up more stairs. I was out of breath by the time we burst onto the roof, but not Talitha. No amount of running could dampen that fire.

The roof was unlike any roof I had ever seen. There were rugs layered on rugs, white cushions on plaster divans built into the roof, kilim cushions piled on top. Low brass tables held carafes of wine, bottles of vodka and Scotch, plates dripping with nuts, figs and sweetmeats. Lanterns and fires were lit, as Talitha pulled me to where Eddie was sitting and nursing a cocktail, looking out at the Koutoubia Mosque, just as the sound of desert horns blew out across the sky, and the muezzin's voice sung out over the city, calling the faithful to prayer.

Eddie heard us approaching and turned, his face softening. "It's beautiful, innit?" I had to stifle the urge to laugh. He reminded me of Benji, trying to be something he was not, in his case, trying to be a hard man, a cockney, when one look in his eyes told you what a softie he was.

"I've never seen anything like it." I sank down on a pile of floor cushions and accepted the joint Talitha handed to me, happy that this, at least, I knew how to do. I passed the joint to Eddie as Talitha put a vodka drink in my hand and held out a tray of sticky, dark balls, encouraging me to try one.

As I bit in, I realized how hungry I was. It had been hours since I'd last eaten.

"This is delicious!" I reached for another, my mouth still full of gooey sweetness and spice. "What is it?"

"Mahjoun. Our chef makes it himself. It's chocolate, honey, butter, dried fruits, nuts and spices. And, of course, an awful lot of kif."

"Kif?"

"Hashish! That's what it's called here. Don't have too many. We need to ease you in slowly!" She helped herself to a ball, popping one in Eddie's willing mouth.

"Where are Lissy and Dave?" I asked.

"They're either making love, or they're fighting," said Eddie. "Or, more likely, some combination of both."

"Fighting? Do you mean actual, physical fighting?"

Eddie paused, as if he was considering how much to tell me, before nodding. "They have a very…passionate relationship. Dave can be a bit of an arse with women. He knocks them about a bit. And Lissy? Well, there's no one more passionate than Lissy. God knows, she gives as good as she gets. Dave slugs her, which is a fucking nightmare, but at least she slugs him back just as hard."

I was stunned. Dave Boland slugs Lissy Ellery? Everything

I had understood about the world up until that point shattered into tiny pieces. Dave Boland had been my hero, my longtime crush, my secret rock god. Up until I met him and realized that—oh, the shock—he was a mere human, he could, in my mind, do no wrong. Yet here he was, hitting his girlfriend. I was horrified. I didn't know how I'd ever be able to look him in the eye. How was I going to sit at a table with him and pretend I didn't know?

"Don't worry about them." Eddie could see my discomfort. "She'll be alright, Lissy. She's very strong."

"Don't you ever try and stop them?"

"I don't want to get involved. If I were to get involved, well…" He went quiet, staring into his drink. "I might just kill him."

"Don't let's get heavy!" Talitha ordered, jumping up and going over to a tape recorder that was on a table, a long cord leading to the door. "I slug Paul all the time when I get jealous. It's a terrible habit. I'm just too insecure. But listen! I have a surprise! Mick and Marianne left tapes of the new music here! Shall we listen?"

Eddie started laughing. "Mick would fucking kill you if he knew you were playing us their new music."

"Shh! I won't tell if you won't." She pressed Play, and the music started. I closed my eyes and took a hit of the pipe that was passed to me, losing myself in the heat, the spices drifting up from the street, the electric energy in the air. That was the first time I heard "Wild Horses," and when I opened my eyes Eddie and Talitha seemed to jump apart. I didn't see anything, but I could have sworn they were kissing.

So many people joined us that night. Lissy and Dave emerged from their room, giggly and all over each other. It was hard to believe those hands that stroked her cheek as she was talking were the same hands that knocked her about, hard to believe that these two, who were all over each other, had ever fought in their lives. Their relationship seemed, at least to the outside world, to be perfect. He was, in fact, so sweet with Lissy, I found myself wondering if Eddie was lying, if perhaps his jealousy had slithered into the gaps of misunderstanding, and created a story he needed to be told.

Bill Willis was there, drinking Jack Daniel's all night, openly snorting lines of coke from a big pile that sat on the center table. Arndt Krupp had his wife next to him at the table, a great big blonde German woman, the Countess Henriette von Bohlen, who everyone called Princess Hetti. A princess! And next to her sat la Comtesse Cignac, who was quite old and impossibly chic, as thin as a whippet, with the kind of silvery white hair that only very beautiful, or very rich women seem to get when they age, a slash of scarlet lipstick on her thin lips, immaculately dressed in head-to-toe Yves Saint Laurent.

"She owns the Villa Schiff," Talitha whispered to me. "We'll go there this week. She's done wonders with the gardens. Her son brings us the best drugs."

Talitha laughed again. She was always laughing. I tried to look as if I was used to mixing with countesses whose children were drug dealers, as if I was as much a woman of the world as she, but I kept thinking, *If only Dottie or Robbie or Benji could see me now.*

Music played all night. The whole table was treated to the new Rolling Stones songs, not just "Wild Horses," but "Brown Sugar," and then we listened to Marianne's "Sister Morphine" and Bob Dylan's "Wigwam." Talitha's favorite, unexpectedly, was Dolly Parton. She played "Coat of Many Colors" and "Yellow Roses," over and over until the band arrived, a group of musicians who played traditional Gnawa music on the roof, as people got more stoned, more relaxed, higher, drunker.

Later in the night, she moved around the table, mingling with other groups, making sure everyone had everything they needed. Every time I felt adrift, or insecure, or like I didn't belong, I would look across the table, and Talitha was there, smiling at me, or winking, or sticking her tongue out at me with a giggle, and instantly, I felt less alone.

MAHJOUN RECIPE
(Kif Optional!)

INGREDIENTS:

2 tablespoons butter or ghee

1 teaspoon ground nutmeg

1 teaspoon anise seed

1 teaspoon ground ginger

½ cup honey

¼ cup dark chocolate

½ cup water

1 cup dried dates, pitted and chopped

½ cup raisins

½ cup pistachios, plus extra chopped to roll balls in at the end

¼ oz dried cannabis flower (optional)

METHOD:

In a large pan, melt the butter on low. Chop the cannabis flower finely and gently stir into the butter until butter starts to brown slightly and/or the aroma is released. Add nutmeg, ginger and anise and stir well. Add honey, chocolate and water, mix well, add raisins, dates and pistachios and mix, cooking on low heat for around 20 to 30 minutes, until soft.

Pulse a few times in a blender so there is still texture. Cool and keep in fridge. When ready to serve, roll in cool damp hands to form balls, about 1" diameter. Roll in chopped nuts. Serve.

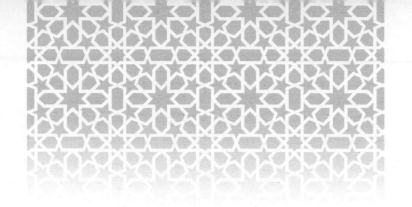

SIXTEEN

I woke up sometime around noon. From outside my window, I could hear the sounds of builders calling out to each other, the scraping of concrete as they continued laying on tile. I heard birds chirping, and pots and pans from somewhere, but otherwise no sign of life. I wasn't surprised. I had gone to bed before dawn, but only just. The sky was turning orange as I started yawning. Even the drugs couldn't keep me awake. Around me people were stretched out on the cushions, falling asleep. Lissy was still wide-awake, smoking endless cigarettes and chatting with Talitha, as I made my way back to my room.

It took a while to find it. I got lost a few times, turning into the wrong corridor, going up the same stairs twice, expecting to find myself somewhere else, but I kept emerging into new courtyards, ones I didn't recognize.

Eventually Eddie found me. He was as lost as I was, and the two of us burst out laughing. Together, we finally managed to find our courtyard. Eddie walked me to my room and I spontaneously hugged him goodbye. I recognized Eddie was attractive, but I didn't feel any attraction for him personally. It never occurred to me that he would have made a pass at me; even though we hardly knew each other, already he seemed like a brother, a protector, not someone to get involved with.

And then, for the first time since landing in Morocco, I thought back to John in London. Not that I knew what exactly I had with John, nor where it was going, but I didn't want to confuse things. And even if I had wished to confuse things, it wouldn't have been with Eddie Allbright.

After I woke up, I pulled on the same clothes as the day before. I'd have to go to the souk today. I couldn't possibly wear Talitha's glorious clothes by daylight, and needed something else, something simple, to wear.

Fresh coffee had been placed on a little table outside my room, and I drank a cup quickly as a delicious and distinctly familiar smell wafted through the courtyard. I couldn't help myself. I followed my nose, following the smell until I found myself in the kitchen courtyard, and then up a flight of stairs to where I found Eddie, standing by the stove, cooking up some sausages in a dented old frying pan. On the other side of the kitchen was a very old cook, rolling out dough for ghoriba, a Moroccan shortbread cookie that he was making later.

"Morning!" Eddie turned, sunglasses on.

"Is it too bright for you in here?" I teased.

He bent his head and looked at me over the top of his sunglasses. "Haven't you ever heard of a hangover?"

"How can you eat sausages if you're hungover?"

"Best cure there is," he said. "Bangers cure everything.

You've got to start the day off with a good breakfast. One egg or two?"

I asked for one, but ended up with two. We ate in the courtyard, the cook arriving with freshly sliced oranges, a pitcher of fresh orange juice, yogurt, and a basket filled with croissants and a Moroccan bread called khobz. In the end, I had to have a taste of everything. By the time we had finished, I was so full, I could quite happily have crawled back into bed.

Talitha appeared, clapping her hands with delight at seeing how we had fed ourselves, and were full and happy. I stood up to kiss her good morning, and she slipped a hand through my arm.

"Let's go to the souk this morning." She shot Eddie a look. "Just us. Girls' shopping trip." She looked me up and down, taking in the fringed miniskirt I had borrowed from Lissy. "You'll want to cover up out of respect for the locals. I forget every now and then, and quickly regret it. I'll lend you a scarf to cover your head. Go and put some harem pants on, and I'll see you by the main staircase in a few."

Down the dirty alley, arm in arm, we went, down cobbled streets lined with tiny shops, rugs hanging from the roof, lines of pointed babouche slippers in every color of the rainbow, punched brass lanterns, straw handbags, bolts of fabrics, bright yellow cones of turmeric and cumin. Dead chickens hung upside down, swinging in the breeze outside meat stalls, with whole lambs' heads that were both gruesome and compelling. Even in death, everything felt alive.

If nothing ever happens to me again for the rest of my life, I thought, I shall die happy. This little church mouse from Dorset, navigating her way through these dark cobbled streets, flashes of color punctuating every step. The more we walked, the more comfortable I felt, the more I wanted to see, to drink it all in.

Shopkeepers smiled and called out to us, trying to tempt us in. We kept on moving, going only into the vendors Talitha knew.

She refused to let me buy anything. I was embarrassed, but her will was stronger than mine. I didn't understand the currency, but she passed money over for cotton kaftans, simple shirts, robes that would keep me cool.

On we wound, arm in arm, chatting and giggling, until we emerged into the main square, Djemaa El Fna, where a snake charmer stood, his cheeks puffed out from playing a flute-like instrument, long and thin, with a ball in the middle, like a snake that had swallowed a beach ball.

I stood, mesmerized as a huge cobra bobbed and weaved, the crowd standing around bursting into laughter and stepping back. I had read about snake charmers, of course, but had never seen one, had never realized how hypnotic it was to watch the snake dance and dip, seemingly in thrall to the music. What a cliché, I might have thought today, but then, in the sixties, it was the most unimaginable thing, to stumble upon this while walking in the street.

"The instrument's called a pungi." Talitha leaned into me, her lips close to my ear so I could hear above the noise. "It's made from a gourd. The snake can't hear the music, it's watching the snake charmer's hands, knowing it's a threat. That's why it bobs and weaves."

I watched, fascinated. We moved through the crowds in the square, past cages of lizards and monkeys. Magicians, musicians, jugglers and dancers parted the crowd, creating spaces in which they could perform, afterward holding an outstretched fez, hoping for coins. Each time we stopped, Talitha put her mouth to my ear, whispering something about the act, something I hadn't known, weaving her web of magic as we walked.

"Come and play for us tonight!" Talitha said to the best

performers. "Palais de la Zahia," she'd say. "Sidi Mimoun. El Glaoui house, yes? Come at eight!"

I had no idea whether they would come, but I believed they would, for who could resist Talitha's charms? I watched them soften as she spoke to them, sloughing off their resistance under Talitha's gaze. They all smiled, they all nodded, they all seemed to fall for her, just as Eddie said.

We walked through the square to the spice market, where a young man jumped out from behind his stall and held out his palm, on which sat outstretched crystals.

"Look, look," he said, as I shrank back, Talitha laughing at me. "Smell! Smell!"

"Go on," she encouraged. He put the crystal in a tiny glass bowl and added a trickle of water, handing the bowl to me. As I inhaled, a spicy, strong scent hit my sinuses and cleansed everything out instantly. It felt like my brain had been spring-cleaned.

"It's pure eucalyptus." Talitha laughed, shaking her head when the man insisted we buy some. "I have tons at home. I'll give you some. It's wonderful for colds and pick-me-ups."

We arrived home, our arms laden with baskets of clothes, food, and some kif we had bought from a man Talitha knew.

"We'll picnic tonight," Talitha said as we walked back in, rousing Si Mohammed from his study of the Koran. "I'm having the cook make a tagine for all of us, and we'll take it into the mountains. You'll love it."

Of course I would love it. There was nothing to do here but fall in love.

The shouting woke me up. If tonight was going to be like last night, and I had a feeling it was, I was worried I didn't have the stamina. Then again, I had never felt so alive as I did with Talitha. She saw I had been flagging, and when we got back to the house, back to the courtyard, she reached into the folds of her robes and withdrew a small, white pill, putting it in my hand and closing my fingers around it.

"This will help you sleep during the day," she said with a wink. "You'll wake up refreshed and ready for a magical night."

"Will you take one, too?" I stared at the pill in my hand.

"I don't need it."

I took the pill and went to my room, where I snuggled into the canopied bed, asleep within minutes. I don't know how long I slept, but I woke up groggy, realizing my dreams had been filled with strange people shouting at me. As I swam up to consciousness, I realized the shouting was real, and coming from Lissy and Dave's room.

I grabbed a robe and ran out when I heard something crash and shatter.

"You fucking idiot!" screamed Lissy, who howled in what sounded like pain.

"Fuck off, you witch," shouted Dave, as something else crashed to the floor. "You're a slag. Who have you been screwing? Who? Was it Paul? Who were you with?"

I didn't know what to do, but footsteps came running, and soon Eddie was pounding on the door.

"Jesus Christ. Let me in. It's Eddie. Let me in."

The door was opened and Eddie went inside, emerging almost immediately, pulling Dave with him. Dave was half-naked, barefoot, clad only in tight velvet trousers, blood streaming from a cut above his eye, as Eddie dragged him away. He looked over at me, and even though he didn't tell me what to do, I knew what was expected.

I ran into the room and found Lissy, her right eye already swollen and bruised, her cheek blowing up to twice its usual size. "Oh, God." I ran over to her. "Are you okay?"

"That fucker," she spit. "I fucking hate him."

"Ice," I said. "We need to get you ice. Wait here." As if she would go anywhere else.

I ran through the riad to the kitchen. There was a block of ice in the cold room, and I chipped away furiously until I had enough. I wrapped it in a dishcloth and ran back to Lissy.

"Here." I held the ice to her eye, now dark purple, as I sat on the bed next to her. The fight had gone out of her. She seemed defeated, diminished. "Hold this on your eye."

"I don't know why I put up with it," she said. "That's the last time."

"Why *do* you put up with it?" She was strong-willed and gorgeous. She had intelligence, beauty and strength. It made no sense to me that she would allow herself to be treated like this.

"I love him," she said simply, but her eyes hardened. "I don't know. I used to love him, but I really don't know anymore. I think he may have slugged the love out of me. Maybe I stay because of habit. Maybe I like the lifestyle."

I snorted. "You don't need him for the lifestyle. You would have that anyway. You don't need anyone who treats you like that."

The bedroom door burst open, and we both jumped, startled and anxious. It wasn't Dave, it was Eddie.

"I've sent him to the Es Saadi hotel," he said. "I told him that if he comes back, I'll fucking kill him. And I'm not joking."

Lissy walked over to Eddie and folded herself into his outstretched arms. He rested his cheek on the top of her head and closed his eyes.

It was time for me to leave.

They didn't join us for drinks under the glass sunroom on the roof. But by the time we went downstairs, ready to head into the mountains for our night picnic, they had emerged,

Lissy's eye swollen and purple. Other than that, you would never have known anything had been wrong.

Now, when I think about abused women I have known—and I have, in my time, known a few—I think of how, before I knew they were abused, they were completely different people when their husbands were around. On their own they were sparkly and outgoing, but with their husbands, they were cowed, quiet, walking on eggshells.

Lissy was never like that. She never seemed to be frightened of Dave, and she often dished it back. But she did share some similarities with the other women I have known in the same plight: she kept going back. All those times when she could have left him, could have walked away, something kept bringing them back together.

We were assigned cars to drive out to the mountains. I was with Eddie, Lissy and Talitha. Dave was still, presumably, at his hotel. There were a group of others forming a convoy as we drove out of Marrakech and into the mountains.

"Be careful of the monkeys," warned Talitha. "They'll steal anything shiny. The last time we came they stole Yves's necklace."

"Yves?"

"Saint Laurent."

I was grateful I had read all the magazines, including, thankfully, *Vogue*, because Yves Saint Laurent was joining us for the picnic. What would Linda say, I thought to myself, with a private chuckle. The chances were that Linda would have no idea who he was.

Thinking of the monkeys, I started to laugh as I looked down at the gold link belt Talitha had loaned me for the evening. "Does that mean my skirt will be down by my ankles by the time I come home?"

"One can only hope," said Eddie, as I laughed. And blushed.

"Stop flirting with Cece," said Lissy. "She's an innocent. Don't corrupt her."

Talitha pouted. "Where's the fun in not corrupting her?"

"No, you're right. She is an innocent. That's why we need her in our merry little group. She'll keep us on the straight and narrow," Eddie said.

I was horrified. "I'm not an innocent! I'm here to live! How can I possibly experience all that life has to offer if you lot are protecting me?"

"Darling, it's not an insult. It's a compliment! We need a grown-up to keep us all in line. Who knows what we'd get up to if you weren't here?" Talitha was resting her chin on her hand as she turned round in the front seat.

"Oh, *I* know exactly what we'd be getting up to!" Lissy said, staring at Talitha with a raised eyebrow as they both shared what felt like a secret laugh. Eddie didn't laugh. Neither did I. I wasn't entirely sure what they meant, but it felt sexual even to an innocent like me. Then again, everything felt sexual that night. There was a chemistry crackling between Talitha, Lissy and Eddie. Lissy, even with her black eye, was more vibrant than I had ever seen her.

"Now, now," Talitha warned. "Behave."

Eddie shook his head. "I don't know what the two of you are up to, but leave us out of it." I liked that he looked at me when he said "us." I liked that he was looking out for me.

"Darling," Lissy purred, stroking his arms. "Are you quite sure you want to be left out of it? We were thinking of having you in the middle."

Eddie shook his head and let out a snort. "I've had my fair share of that. That's not what I'm looking for anymore."

Were they suggesting a threesome? It seemed that way, and I was suddenly grateful they weren't looking at me. There were many things I was willing to try, but as much as I hated them calling me an innocent, I realized I wasn't as worldly, nor as able to jump into the free love, free sex movement.

"That's not what Dave told me. The scene after the concert in Paris sounded…wild."

Eddie shrugged. "I'm a rock star. What do you want from me?"

Lissy cocked her head. "What do you think I want from you?"

"Be careful what you wish for," said Eddie.

"Promises, promises." Lissy laughed. "You're all mouth and no trousers."

"Apparently not in Paris," Eddie reminded her.

"Look at the two of you!" Talitha said. "Why don't you just fuck and get it over with?"

Lissy threw her head back and laughed. "Can you imagine what Dave would do if Eddie and I got together? Jesus. There are many things I would do, but that would kill him. Truly. He'd never recover."

I watched Eddie as she said that, and saw the flash of dismay, disappointment, maybe even grief, in his eyes. Did she know, I wonder, that Eddie was infatuated with her? The more I watched them, watched how he looked at her, the more sure I was. She knew he fancied her, everyone knew that, but I wondered if she knew how her flirting, her leading him on was messing with his head. This wasn't innocent banter for him, I could see that, and I wondered whether someone ought to make her see what a dangerous game she was playing.

"Maybe it would stop him bashing the next girl," Talitha said. I couldn't help but agree with her. "Now, what do we do about Cece? Who can we find for Cece to fall in love with?"

"I don't need anyone!" I protested. Not because of John, but because I truly didn't need anyone. I was already in love, with this new life, this new world.

Talitha's face, lit by the moonlight as we drove, turned thoughtful. "Cece, if you don't have anyone, and no job, why don't you come and work here?"

My heart leaped. "Here? In Marrakech?"

"I mean, for us. It's not really work. It's more, I don't know, an assistant, organizer, housekeeper type of job. We need someone to organize everything. I try and do it when we're here, but it's hard to keep on top of things, and we're going back to Rome in a few days. If I knew someone sensible was here in the house, making sure the work was done, looking after everything, I'd feel so much happier."

I felt like I was going to explode with joy. "You're offering me a job?"

Talitha shrugged. "Yes. But you're still first and foremost our friend. I'll talk to Paul about a salary if you want to do it."

"Sure." I tried to sound nonchalant, as if it was completely normal for a recently unemployed shop assistant at Miss Selfridge, formerly of Bourne and Hollingsworth, to be offered a job looking after a palace in Marrakech. "That would be great."

I looked out the window then, even though I couldn't see anything in the darkness, because my smile was so wide I didn't want Talitha to see. I didn't want anyone to see how uncool I actually was.

The car pulled over and we got out. Another car had joined us, and a delicate, slight man in square glasses emerged, more beautiful than handsome, feminine, with slim hips and long hair, a shy smile on his face. He glided over and kissed Talitha hello before she introduced him to me. He seemed shy, and sweet, turning to me with exquisite poise.

"Bonsoir," he greeted with his French accent. "Good evening. I am Yves."

"How do you do," I replied, the very model of a well-brought-up girl, but inside, my heart was hammering. Still, he seemed shy and sweet, and I wished I could think of something to say to him to show him I wasn't intimidated, except… I was intimidated.

"This is Pierre," he said, as his partner stepped forward and shook my hand with a warm smile, helping me to relax.

They were with the Comtesse, who I had clearly not impressed the night before.

"Hello." I gave her a smile as she stared at me without a shred of recognition, barely acknowledging me before turning away. Before tonight, I would have been devastated by her curtness, would have felt like she'd seen through to my soul and knew I wasn't good enough. But Talitha had just offered me more than a job—she had offered me validation, offered to make me part of their world. If Talitha thought I was good enough, I was. I shook off the shame that threatened to engulf me.

We arrived to a lavish picnic laid out on antique Persian rugs brought from the palace. Not just rugs, ottomans, tables, and floor cushions, lanterns and huge brass trays with traditional clay tagines. Plates piled with couscous, and a huge b'stilla, layers of pigeon and egg in flaky pastry, dusted with icing sugar and cinnamon; there were salads and vegetables and zaalouk, an eggplant dish, and crusty bread. There was kaab el ghazal, crescent-shaped pastries filled with almond paste scented with orange flower water and cinnamon. There was more food than it would ever be possible to eat. All of the opulence and magic of Sidi Mimoun had been transferred to the Atlas Mountains. I don't know how she did it, or how many people it took, but I am quite sure that no one other than Talitha could have pulled this off.

"What do they do with the leftovers?" I whispered to Pierre, who was walking behind me.

He smiled in the darkness. "Don't worry, everything is sent home to the staff for their families to eat. Nothing goes to waste."

We sat on the rugs, cross-legged, passing a hookah back and forth, eating, talking. Across from me sat Lissy and Eddie, locked in conversation all night, breaking off occasionally, but it felt that they only had eyes for each other.

Peter Fonda was next to me, an American film star that I hadn't yet heard of, but whose presence was a cause for excitement. He was getting ready to film *Easy Rider*, which became a huge hit when it was released the next year. None of us knew how famous he was going to be, although I had heard of his sister, Jane.

"Where's the LSD?" asked Susie, a Frenchwoman who was staying with Yves and Pierre.

"What makes you think I have LSD?"

"*Chérie*, you think I haven't seen your film *The Trip*? I'm friends with David Crosby. He told me about what happened when you went to the house the Beatles were renting in LA."

"Ah, yes," said Fonda. "The infamous Mulholland Drive house."

"What happened? What happened?" everyone asked.

"If you don't tell us, I'll ask John," said Talitha. "He was at our New Year's Eve party and he'll tell us everything."

"I'm sure he will. John's never been known for his discretion." Peter laughed. "It wasn't John who was having a bad time though, it was George." I realized he was talking about John Lennon and George Harrison, and again, I wanted to pinch myself at the world in which I now found myself.

"We'd all done LSD," continued Peter, "and poor George thought he was dying. I told him there was nothing to be afraid of because I knew what it was like to be dead. When I was ten years old, I'd accidentally shot myself in the stomach and my heart stopped beating three times while I was on the operating table because I'd lost so much blood."

The table went silent.

"Is that true?" said Yves finally. "This is not something made-up?"

Peter shook his head. "You can't make up shit like this. John was passing me at the time and heard me saying 'I know what it's like to be dead.' He looked at me and said, 'You're making me feel like I've never been born. Who put all that in your head?'" He paused for dramatic effect. "And then he wrote a song about it. 'She Said She Said.'"

"I love it!" Talitha clapped. "I want someone to write a song about me!" Her eyes were dancing in the light of the lanterns, and I found it amazing that no one had written a song about her yet. She was so captivating, how had these visiting musicians not written about her?

"You're right," Eddie spoke up. "Someone *should* write a song about you. And I think that someone should be me. What shall we call it? Talitha's Troubles?"

"She doesn't have any troubles!" Susie shouted, gesturing at her. "Look at her! She's beautiful, fun, and married to the son of the richest man in the world. What troubles could she possibly have?"

A shadow passed over Talitha's face, and for a second the smile left it. "My life wasn't always like this," she said. "I know how it looks, but it didn't start off this way."

"Oh, pfft," said Susie, who I was beginning to dislike. "What do *you* know about troubles?"

Talitha looked momentarily upset then, like a little girl. I wanted to walk over and shove Susie to the ground. Hurt her in the way she had hurt Talitha. Paul, who had been sitting at the other end of the table, spoke. I was glad. I hadn't spent any time with him, his presence so eclipsed by his wife, but I was glad he stepped in to protect her. I decided in that instant that I liked him.

"I think that is enough talk of troubles. If there is a song written about my lovely wife, and I very much hope there is, it should be Tantalizing Talitha. Or Thrilling Talitha."

"Tiny Talitha!" I called out, because Talitha was so petite. The smile was back on her face as she stuck her tongue out at me.

The others joined in. "Talkative Talitha!" said Pierre.

"Tremendous Talitha!" said the Comtesse, who had been very quiet up to that point.

"Tantalizing Talitha!"

"Tasty Talitha!" Lissy called out. With a peal of laughter, Talitha blew her a kiss, any discomfort, any painful memories now forgotten.

"Or simply… Talitha," said Yves. "For there has never been, nor ever will there be, anyone quite like her." He raised his glass in adoration. "To Talitha. Our one and only." The table raised their glasses with him, and we drank.

There was LSD, of course. We all took it after dinner, before the performers arrived, driven here after they showed up at Sidi Mimoun. As we waited for the LSD to kick in, lounging on cushions watching acrobats and jugglers, we passed around hookahs and brass trays of ktefa, paper-thin pastry filled with chopped almonds and sugar, doused in an orange blossom custard, and chebakia, a honey-coated pastry sprinkled with sesame seeds.

Musicians played during each of these acts, and as each one finished, they swept the floor with deep bows, and we cheered.

A silence fell when the belly dancer emerged. A turquoise veil covered her face as she slithered out of the darkness, a chain around her hips, silks floating around her legs as she walked toward us, swaying to the music, the beat of the drum moving faster and faster as she approached the table, her hips keeping time. She stepped between us and onto the table.

I had never seen a belly dancer before. I leaned forward to help remove plates, glasses to make room for her, mesmerized by the way she was able to move her body, by a beauty and sensuality I'd never witnessed. Her stomach was bare, a large red jewel in her navel, a gold chain around her hips, but the rest of her body was covered, chiffon veils swirling around her legs, as she moved those hips to the music, weaving among us, a veil over her face.

I looked over at Paul, who was delighted by the dancer. He caught my eye and gestured for me to come and sit by him. I had had no time with him, had barely spoken to him, but I liked him. With that lovely smile, it was impossible not to like him.

He patted the cushion next to him, and I sank down, leaning toward him to hear him better when he spoke.

"She's doing a variation of a traditional Moroccan dance called shikhat," he explained. "She's combining it with traditional belly dancing, which originated in Egypt. In Morocco, shikhat is more common, but she's clever, she's combined the two. In Arabic shikha means 'the wise one,' and they say that shikhat are considered 'women of the world,' experienced women who are usually invited to perform in rituals and celebrations in Morocco."

"Is this a celebration?" I asked.

"Every night in Marrakech with Talitha is a celebration," he said. "In case you hadn't noticed, my wife is intensely gregarious. She loves nothing more than a party, as she has no doubt told you."

"And you?" I asked. "Are you the same? Do you love it?"

His smile seemed sad as he tilted his head. "I love my wife, and often I love this way of life…but there are times I crave quiet. I've found a way to manage it. I escape to my room, to my books, my art and opera. When I'm in the right mood, I love these gatherings, and I love many of these people." He gestured to Yves and Pierre. "But sometimes…often… it's too much for me. I prefer smaller gatherings, and conversation. It's often hard to hear yourself think amid all the fun and laughter."

"How do you cope?"

"I try and brace myself for Marrakech. It isn't always like this. In Rome I can find quiet times, and in London, of course. Our house in London is divine. Very quiet. I think it's my favorite of all."

"Where in London is it?"

"Chelsea. Cheyne Walk. It's the Rossetti house. The artist and poet, Rossetti?" He saw me look blank. "Dante Gabriel Rossetti?"

I thought of pretending to know what he was talking about, or who, but I knew I would have been found out. There would have been no point in pretending to be someone I wasn't, and I sensed that there was no judgment from him. I shook my head in apology.

"I'm just a country mouse," I said. "I'm not very worldly, I'm afraid. I don't really know anything about art or poetry."

"That's quite alright. There are enough boring old fogies like me who can't get enough of it. Rossetti lived in the most beautiful house in the world, with a menagerie in the garden, much to his neighbors' chagrin. He kept a bull, a white peacock, a kangaroo, a raccoon, and a wombat that had a penchant for ladies' hats." His eyes twinkled as he said this last bit, and I laughed out loud. "I have no doubt you will be visiting us there soon." His gaze swept past me. "Oh! Look! Talitha!" His gaze was beyond me, his eyes lit up, and I turned to see the belly dancer had reached out her hands to Talitha, who had allowed herself to be pulled up to the table.

Some people left while Talitha danced. Yves and Pierre. Bill Willis, who was drunk as a skunk, who staggered off to find a driver.

I turned my attention back to Talitha, dancing on the table. She mirrored the belly dancer exactly, lifting up her shirt to expose her tiny waist, tying it up and mimicking the dancer, as we all cheered and clapped. I was aware, suddenly, of everything becoming brighter. The lights swam, the drumbeat consumed me. I realized the LSD was beginning to take effect.

As I watched, Susie stepped onto the table, pulling Talitha toward her, moving her hips. She let go of Talitha's hands and pulled off her shirt, and underneath she was wearing nothing, her breasts high and pointed. She pulled Talitha toward her and started to kiss her, the two of them swaying on the table as she pulled off Talitha's shirt, too.

I turned to Paul, expecting him to stop them, to say something, do something, but he was captivated, a lazy smile on his face as he watched them. A young Italian man who I hadn't paid attention to now stood on the table, and soon the three of them were embracing and kissing, their hands moving all over one another's bodies, and quickly they were naked.

I could feel the pounding in my ears as I watched in disbelief. I looked around the table to see everyone smiling approvingly or starting to fondle whoever was closest. Somehow I was the only one who seemed shocked.

My God, I thought, stunned. This was an orgy or, at least, on its way to becoming an orgy, and I was simultaneously turned-on, fascinated and horrified.

I wanted no part in it.

Lissy was lying back on the cushions, her top off, a woman fondling her naked breasts on one side as a man on her other side kissed her, his tongue slipping in her mouth as he unbuttoned his jeans.

It was too much for me. As high as I might have been, I didn't want to be here for this. It was too intense, too far outside my scope of experience. I have thought about this night many, many times since. You must also understand that it was a different world, one that cannot be assessed by today's standards. We had all emerged from the intense repression of the fifties, a time when women were not supposed to enjoy sex, could only in fact have sex if they were married, when they were expected to fulfil their conjugal obligations, to "lie back and think of England." Sex had never been about pleasure, but about duty or producing offspring.

Then the world burst into color and a full-scale sexual revolution. We all discovered the pill, and suddenly sex was not about duty or fear of pregnancy; it was about discovery and adventure and pleasure, wherever and whenever it could be found.

My new friends were well on the journey of discovery. Their lives were about exploration and freedom, sensory pleasure in every way imaginable. I was too new to understand that, one foot in Sidi Mimoun, one foot still in Dorset. I wanted to be like them, wanted to be able to feel everything wonderful that life, and sex, had to offer, but I wasn't ready. The country church mouse was as shocked as she was excited, and I chose to walk away.

No one noticed when I stood up and left that table. Why would they notice, everyone entranced by the shedding of clothes, the intertwined limbs, the kissing and stroking and sighing. The music was still throbbing as I stumbled across the desert floor, walking until the sighs and moans were distant; walking until I felt safe.

I sat down, crossing my legs, breathing deeply, even as the silhouettes of trees danced and sighed, twisting themselves around each other. I didn't hear footsteps, didn't hear any-thing until a familiar voice.

"Are you alright?"

It was Eddie.

I thought of Lissy, writhing between two people, half-na-ked, about to be more so, and I thought of Eddie, of what it must have been like for him. It was one thing accepting that she belonged to Dave, that she and Dave had sex or fought or did whatever they did in private, but quite another, I would think, to see her having sex with other people, and in front of everyone, no less.

I turned, my eyes searching for his face in the darkness. "Are *you* alright?"

There was a silence. "No one ever asks if I'm alright," he said.

"*I'm* asking."

"You mean Lissy, don't you."

"What else is there?"

There was a snicker in the darkness. "I ask myself the same question every second of every minute of every hour of every day."

"You love her." My question came out as a statement.

There was silence.

"Why don't you tell her?"

"The band," he said simply. "The band has to come first. I can risk everything but the band. Without Dave, there is no band."

"No? Haven't other bands re-formed, survived without their lead singers?" I didn't want them to keep Dave, not since I'd discovered how he treated Lissy. How could they possibly keep him, knowing what they knew?

"Yeah. They have. But the Wide-Eyed Boys formed be-cause of Dave. He's not just the lead singer, he's our leader. I'm not sure what we'd be without him."

"So you'll sacrifice your own happiness for the sake of others? That's…admirable." I shook my head. I wanted to say that was silly.

"Or stupid. I don't know which."

"And…everything that's going on over there." I gestured my head back toward where we had been dining. "The…sex stuff. Are you okay with that?"

I couldn't see his face in the darkness, but I imagined him smiling. "I've been around. There's little I haven't seen or done. Maybe, probably, I've even done too much. That's why I don't need to do it now. But yeah, is it weird seeing Lissy getting off with other people? It's not the first time. It's what she's into. Pleasure. Freedom. Living life to the fullest. It's not like I didn't know what would happen here. Everyone knows what happens with this crowd."

"Really? They're known for this?"

"God, yes. They've thrown some crazy parties. There's usually some crazy climax with something nuts happening, everyone sleeping with everyone else. Talitha's very…sensual, but I think Paul's into it, too. It's not like I haven't done it, either, I just don't feel like it tonight."

"Me, neither."

"You shouldn't. Either you're into it, or you're not, and there's nothing wrong with not being into it. Are you going to take Talitha's offer of working here? There's not much escaping that way of life if you work here. You know that, right?"

On some level, of course I knew that, but although part of me wanted to experience that way of life, I just wasn't ready yet. "I do, and it's worth it. Who knows, maybe I'll even become part of it. I don't know what there is to go home for. I definitely don't want to go back to being a shopgirl living in the unmarried women's hostel in Gower Street."

Eddie laughed. "Why don't we see if we can get one of

those houseboys to drive us back to the house? No need for us to be sitting here in the middle of nowhere. I'd quite like to have a hot bath and get into bed."

I grinned. "That's the least rock star–ish thing I've ever heard. Did you not drop any acid earlier?"

"Half a tab. You?"

"Half a tab."

"Come on then." He stood up and extended a hand to help me up. "Let's go."

I felt very grateful to be back at the riad, tucked up in bed. The fire had been lit in my room, and it felt cozy and safe. That night had been a feast for the senses, but it had all been a little too much for me; there were some senses that weren't ready to be awakened.

I didn't want my enchantment with Talitha to be damaged. Eddie had said she was sensual, that this always happened. A part of me wished that wasn't true, as if it somehow sullied her, but perhaps I was jealous. I couldn't join in, I didn't want to join in. Yet. Perhaps it fed into my own fears of inadequacy.

What I wanted was to get to know Talitha, but now I know I also wanted to protect her. I wanted to find out what drove her, why she was the way she was, why she did the things she did. And I wanted to be there when she did them. I sensed that she attracted danger, that she was headed for something dark, something bad, and I wanted to be there to stop her when it came. Perhaps the best way of doing that was by accepting her offer and staying here to help out with whatever they needed.

Or, most things they needed.

There were some things I simply couldn't do.

Yet.

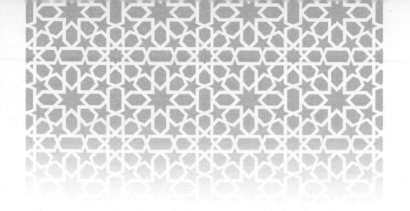

SEVENTEEN

The next morning I ran into Paul, crossing the courtyard and swearing at the peacocks as he stepped in what I presumed was peacock shit. I waved from my doorway, and he looked over, the scowl still on his face as he saw me, before beckoning me down.

"Young Cece! A postcard came for you. From your fancy man." Paul grinned, sliding the postcard out from a pocket and handing it to me.

I turned the postcard over, expecting it to be from John, wishing I felt more enthusiastic than I did.

Dearest C, are you having the most wonderful time? I would say wish you were here, except I don't. It has rained daily since you left. I hope you're behaving yourself or I shall have to come and fetch you. Yours ever, Benji.

A smile of delight broke out on my face. Benji! It made my heart swell as I read it over and over.

"Told you it was from your fancy man," said Paul. I didn't tell him I thought he had meant John.

He paused then, looked at me intently. "Was it too much for you last night?" he asked with concern.

"A little. I'm sorry."

"Don't apologize. Stay here long enough and you'll shed your innocence." He laughed at the expression of alarm on my face. "Or not. Either way it's fine. Do you want to come and see where I hide away from everyone?"

"You're not going to try and make me take all my clothes off when I'm there, are you?"

Paul gave a proper belly laugh at that. "I promise I won't. I'm going to show you a painting by Rossetti. Remember, we talked about him last night?"

"Dante Gabriel Rossetti," I repeated. "I remember."

"Good girl!" He was delighted. "Have I found myself a willing student?"

"It depends what it is you're wanting to teach me."

"I'm going to show you my favorite Rossetti painting. Come on. Follow me."

We went up to Paul's room. Whether it was his office, his bedroom, his study, I wasn't entirely sure. It was a little bit of everything. There was a large bed, sofas, a desk overflowing with papers and correspondence. The walls were covered in beautiful paintings, shelves bursting with rare books, and on the sideboard sat a record player, the shelves next to it crammed with records. I knew the upper classes lived differently to the rest of us. I had overheard the Comtesse, the other night at dinner, talk about how le comte always took to his room before the end of dinner.

"He hasn't visited her for years, honey," whispered Bill Willis that night.

"Visited her?"

"Marital relations," he said. "I think the last time they shared a bed may have been when Gerard was conceived."

"Gerard. The drug dealer son?"

Bill sat back in his chair. "Well, someone's been talking. We call him the Candyman. You'll meet him soon. He's absolutely divine. Just don't fall in love with him. And don't think you won't. He's the most beautiful man I've ever seen."

As if I would fall in love with a drug dealer, I thought.

Here I was, in Paul's room, and it looked as if the bed had been slept in. I thought, before Marrakech, that husbands and wives always slept in the same room, but now I wasn't sure. I turned my attention back to Paul's room.

On the sideboard, next to Paul's record player, was a small ceramic jar with a cloth over it, a glass spray bottle next to it.

"What's that?" I asked.

Paul walked over and picked up the spray bottle, spraying the cloth to keep it moist. "That's my opium," he explained, as if it were his tea bags or biscuits or something completely innocuous, something that every household would or should have. "Do you want some?"

"Oh, no, thank you." I was behaving like a country mouse again, I knew, but it was morning, for heaven's sake. I didn't mind indulging occasionally at night, but what on earth would I be doing smoking opium in the morning?

"You don't mind if I partake?" he asked, and I shook my head.

"Of course not."

Paul showed me the painting *Proserpine*, by Rossetti. Oh, it was so beautiful! I had never fallen in love with a painting the way I fell in love with that. A woman holding a pomegranate, in a luscious teal robe, her dark hair cascading down her back in rich, chestnut curls, her lips full and pouted in what I came to understand was the quintessential Pre-Raphaelite style.

"She's exquisite!" I whispered, noting the ivy climbing up the side, the gaze of the woman. "Who was she?"

Despite being stoned, lazy with opium, I could see how excited Paul was by my delight. He told me about the painting, how the model was Jane Morris, the wife of William Morris, how the story was based on Persephone, the Empress of Hades.

I sat on the sofa as Paul drew up his desk chair to tell me the story of Persephone. In Greek mythology she was the daughter of Demeter, the goddess of fertility. Demeter and Persephone lived in a world where everything bloomed and the sun always shone.

One day Persephone felt the ground rumbling and trembling, and a huge split formed, and Hades, god of the underworld, drove his chariot up through the split, snatched Persephone and took her back to the underworld with him. The split closed up, and all that was left of Persephone was a bunch of flowers on the ground.

Demeter searched and searched, but her beloved daughter was nowhere to be found. Her grief was so great that the earth began to grow cold, and everything that was green, and vibrant, and living and sweet, died. There was no food, and a terrible famine struck.

In the underworld, however, Persephone came to understand that Hades wasn't the terrifying god she had once thought. He had been so lonely, and he was so in love with her. He longed for her to stay by his side as his equal, the queen of the underworld; she started to fall in love with him.

And yet, she knew that if she ate or drank anything from

the underworld, she would be bound to stay there forever. Hades begged her to sip, to take a bite, but she didn't.

Above them, Demeter finally learned where Persephone was. She insisted her daughter be returned, and just before Hades reluctantly hitched his horses to his chariot, he offered her one last thing to eat: a ripe, bloodred pomegranate. Persephone took six seeds and ate them.

Up through the crack in the earth, Persephone threw herself into her mother's arms, overjoyed at being reunited. The earth again grew rich with flowers and fruit, and the sun shone once again.

But, because Persephone had eaten six pomegranate seeds, it was decided that for six months of each year she must return to the underworld with Hades, and winter would come to the world. And every year, in spring, she would once again return to her mother, allowing the earth to burst into bloom.

I was transfixed! Paul telling me this beautiful story as I drank in the painting, and then, seeing what a willing student I was, Paul reaching for *Madama Butterfly*, knowing, I am sure, that I was ripe for falling in love with art, with stories, with culture, with music.

And I did. I fell in love. With all of it. I had no idea that winter would soon set in.

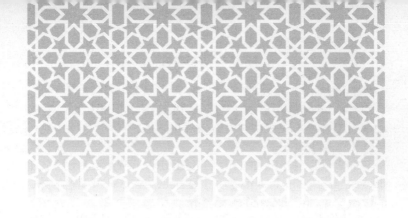

EIGHTEEN

I was nervous to see Talitha. I didn't know if I could look her in the eye. I buried myself in a book, sitting on the daybed outside my room, only moving when she came to find me that afternoon.

She walked in, her robes fluttering around her legs, and as soon as I looked up to see her impish expression, her omnipresent smile and sparkling eyes, I relaxed and smiled back.

"Oh, good!" She sank down next to me and kissed me on the cheek. "I was hoping someone would be awake. I have to go and get some food and I want company. Your company is actually the company I wanted. Will you come?" She was so natural, so unabashed at what had happened the night before, that my own embarrassment left me and I eagerly picked up my bag to join her.

"Where are we going?"

"I need fresh bread and I've decided to show you the gardens at La Mamounia. Would you like that?"

"I would love that."

We set off, Talitha in a full-length dress with embroidered sleeves, tiny coins hanging off the sleeves and a large, floppy felt hat with an embroidered trim.

"Wait——" she ran up to fetch a hat for me "——to protect your fair skin from the sun." She handed me a huge straw hat, colored pom-poms all over it. I didn't know whether to feel ridiculous or fabulous, but I was grateful for the protection.

Si Mohammed emerged from his little room to open the gates for us, and we stepped into the alleyway, out onto the bustling side street. Soon we were in Djemaa El Fna, crossing the square past jostling people, crowds gathering to watch the acrobats, this time a group of men all in white, who tumbled over and over each other as we paused to watch.

Bicycles whizzed past us, and I stopped, saddened, at an old metal box with six tiny monkeys chained to it.

"It's awful, darling. I know. But there's nothing we can do."

"How can you bear to see these animals being tortured? Don't you want to rescue all of them?"

"I rescued the cat. That's all I can handle right now. I wish someone would rescue the bloody peacocks from us. I can't stand the mess they make."

I thought of the peacocks, strutting around the courtyards, fanning their gorgeous feathers if we got too close. "But they're so beautiful! It's magical, having them around."

Talitha shuddered. "The mess. Argh. Come on. Let's go to La Vache Qui Rit."

"Qu'est ce que c'est?" It was about the only French phrase I knew.

Talitha laughed. "It's where to buy fresh baguettes. And

we'll have a glass of red wine while we wait." She mentioned nothing about the night before, was her usual effervescent self, so I let my residual awkwardness go. If Talitha was fine with it, I would be, too.

We sent a boy scurrying back to the house with the things we had bought and went to La Mamounia, the hotel right by the riad, to walk in the gardens.

"This was Winston Churchill's favorite spot," she said as we walked through the old colonial hotel, the fans slowly whirring overhead, all the heads turning at her eccentric elegance, her exquisite beauty. We walked through the long bar with its 1930s plump club chairs, to the gardens, almost twenty acres of serenity in the heart of Marrakech, luscious lawns framed by towering palm trees underplanted with bushes and shrubs and long, spiky cactus plants. It was a true oasis in the desert.

"May I ask you something?" We were walking side by side, in companionable silence, and I felt completely comfortable with her. She was always laughing, always fun, but now that it was just the two of us she was quieter. I felt I had the space to ask a real question, one that might elicit a real answer.

For I knew this couldn't be everything. I knew there had to be more to her than parties and exuberance. I could see it in her eyes; I saw it the other day when she talked about her mother dying. And I saw it last night, before the night devolved into a sea of sensuality.

"Anything." Her tone was light.

"Yesterday, at dinner, when that woman accused you of never having known trouble, you looked—" I searched for the right word "—stricken."

She stopped and looked at me. "Stricken?"

"Traumatized."

"Oh." She looked at the ground, quiet, before nodding. "Yes. I was… I am traumatized. It doesn't leave you, you know. The bad stuff. It shapes you into who you are, it becomes part of the fabric of your life, part of your soul. I am so grateful that I am who I am, that I have the life I have, but I can never forget. And…" She sighed. "People like that have no idea. They are the ones who are blessed, but they spend their time filled with resentment at others."

"You're talking about your mother dying?" I asked softly.

"Well, yes. But all that happened before."

I didn't know if I should ask, but I had to know. "What happened before?"

"I don't usually talk about it."

"I'm so sorry. I didn't mean to pry. I completely understand you not wanting to talk about it."

Talitha shook her head. "No. I'm the one who is sorry. I wonder if I should have talked about it. Sometimes it feels like I'm carrying the weight of the world on my shoulders. Maybe I wouldn't feel like this if I had talked about it more."

I stared at her. "You? Carrying the weight of the world on your shoulders? No one would believe that. You seem like the lightest person imaginable."

She smiled sadly. "Good. Then I am a better actress than I always thought. I went to RADA, you know. I always wanted to be an actress." She shot me a sideways glance with a grin. "I have had tiny parts in a few films."

"What were you in?" I wondered if, without realizing, I had seen her on screen.

"I was an extra in *La Dolce Vita*." She grinned. "I don't think that counts. I had a small part in a film called *Return from the Ashes*, and another in one called *We Shall See*. And I met Anita filming *Barbarella*."

I looked blank. "Barbar what?"

She laughed. "*Barbarella*. It's a futuristic sci-fi film. It's coming out soon. Roger Vadim directed, and Jane Fonda's the star.

That's how we know her brother, Peter. We all became great friends, and Anita was in it. She was fantastic as the Black Queen. She stayed in costume all the time, it was hilarious. I think she thought she really was the Black Queen for a while. You'll see when it comes out. I, on the other hand, was not so genius. I was the girl smoking the pipe. Barely a word to say. I think I mustn't have been very good. Or…" She shrugged. "Maybe I was."

I didn't know what to say, but, it turned out, I didn't have to say anything.

"Confidence has never been my strong point, even though it seems the opposite."

I stopped and stared at her. "I believe you, but why? People gravitate to you. How can you not be confident?"

There was a silence for a while. I felt that Talitha was thinking about how much to tell me, how much to reveal.

"I was born in Indonesia during the war," she said. "My parents were Dutch. My mother was born in The Hague, and my father in Rotterdam. He was an artist, and they moved, long before I was born, to Java."

"Gosh, how alluring!" All I knew was that Java was very far away.

Talitha turned to me. "Do you know anything about the Dutch East Indies?" I shook my head, once again embarrassed.

"Don't worry. Nobody does." She started to sing, clasping her thumb with the fingers of the other hand, climbing thumb after thumb, switching hands, until the last verse when her hands fluttered down. "*Torentje, torentje, bussekruit, wat hangt er uit? Een dougen fluit. Een gouden fluit een gouden fluit met knopen, torentje is gebroken.*'" She laughed, her hands back down at her side. "That is my earliest memory. It's a children's rhyme. Turret, turret, gunpowder. What hangs outside? A golden flute. A golden flute with buttons. The turret breaks into pieces."

She sighed. "My mother used to sing that to me, in the camps. She would sing it throughout. It was the only thing that felt normal. It made me feel safe."

A shiver ran down my spine. I had presumed she wouldn't want to talk about it.

"I'm going to give you a history lesson," she said, as we walked down along the paths that crisscrossed the gardens, surrounded by freshly cut lawn. "I don't usually tell people. I try not to think about it, let alone talk about it, but…" She sighed. "Maybe it's time I did tell someone. Maybe it would do me good to talk about it."

I didn't say anything, a little frightened, and honored, that she would think of me as someone to confide in.

"The Dutch colonized Indonesia at the start of the seventeenth century. A Dutch trading company settled in a place called Batavia, which is now Jakarta, and quickly took control of all the islands. That was the Dutch East Indies. They made huge money for Holland. They traded mostly in cloves, pepper, cinnamon, tobacco and rubber. Over the centuries, more and more Dutch people moved there. My father had been living in Paris, working as a landscape artist, when he met my mother. They lived in Germany for a while, but so many people they knew had moved to the Dutch East Indies that they decided to start afresh.

"We lived in Java, in a small town with a sugar plantation. My father painted, my mother looked after me." She sighed. "I was a baby. I don't remember, but I heard the stories. How we were surrounded by nature, how we had a swimming pool. And then, when I was two years old, the Japanese invaded. Of course everyone knew the war was happening, but we were all so isolated, we never thought it would affect us. For a few weeks, nothing happened. Then, overnight, they took all the men. My father was swept up in the night. Within two weeks, they took everything. All our possessions, our house, everything we owned.

"They surrounded the whole island. There was no way to escape. No one knew what was happening, and no one knew of the cruelties that were waiting for us. They rounded up the women and children next, and took us to a prison camp in Bandung. We, the Dutch, were the first people to go. The second were the Indisch, the half Dutch, half Indonesian. Thankfully, we were allowed one small suitcase of personal possessions, and a mattress.

"At the first camp, there were about ninety people living in a house that was meant for one. Everyone was squashed together, and in a state of shock. There was little food. Half a cup of porridge a day, and sometimes some leaves. Once a week you would have a little bit of sugar. About a month later, we were put on a train and sent to another camp at Bogor. The train journey was over forty-eight hours, and we were given no food, no water, nothing. My mother was friends with a pregnant woman, and when she asked one of the Japanese guards if she could please have just some water, he shot her. In the head. In front of everyone. My mother was there. She saw. She never recovered."

Talitha showed no emotion as she told this story, her voice soft, as a lump formed in my throat.

"When we got to our final camp, we were put in these open barracks to sleep. At night, rats crawled all over you. Cholera broke out. There was one tap for fifteen hundred people. All the children had jobs. Some worked in the kitchen, others were in charge of getting rid of the bodies. They would put the bodies in wheelbarrows and take them to the graveyards. The littlest ones, me included, would try and find food. We were always starving. The Red Cross had sent boxes of food for us, but the Japanese buried them, hiding them underneath buildings. We would try and sneak out and find them. Three of my friends were caught in the kitchen at night, and they shot them."

I gasped. "Children? They shot children?"

"Yes. And they'd torture us terribly. We were made to stand in the hot sun for hours and hours every day, unable to move. Or they'd make us walk for miles. In the morning you had to line up, with all the Japanese guards standing in front of you, and we'd all have to bow. If you didn't do it correctly, or you didn't bow deeply enough, you would get punished. They would club you on the head, or beat the old women with a stick. With the children, they would stick fingers in our eyes. People can be so cruel."

"How did you get out?"

"Hiroshima. When the Americans dropped the bomb, the Japanese left. As horrific as it was, I will always be grateful. We woke up one day and everything was quiet. No one was there, all the Japanese had disappeared. The gates opened, and we all went running out. My mother went to find my father, and food."

"What happened then?"

"It took months, but we got back to Holland. They put us on these long train rides to the harbor and put us on Dutch ships."

There was a long silence as I tried to process.

"I don't understand." I stopped walking and turned to her. "Why doesn't anyone know about this?"

"It was war," she said simply. "The world was preoccupied with Nazi Germany."

"Your mother didn't die in the camp?"

"No, but it killed her nevertheless. She never fully recovered from the trauma, and died soon after. My father and I moved to London for a fresh start, and he fell in love with Poppet. That was when life got better again."

I think about that woman, Susie, and how she had said Talitha had never known trouble. What a cow, I thought, hating her with an unexpected and sweeping passion. Now I understood the moments when Talitha wasn't laughing, the sadness I sometimes saw in her eyes.

"How do you do it?" I asked. "How do you live your life and not let this pain take you down?"

She smiled. "I have a wonderful life. And when I get sad, or think about the past, or it all feels too much?" She shrugged. "I throw parties. I dance. I drink. I take drugs. I have sex. I laugh." She took my hands then, and together we danced across the lawn of La Mamounia as if we hadn't a care in the world, and much to my surprise, Talitha was able to laugh. "See?" she said. "Don't you feel better already?"

I didn't, and I worried for her. I could see the darkness in her, and had this terrible foreshadowing, but I didn't know then what it was, neither how to express it, nor how to stop it.

"Don't worry about me," she tried to reassure me. "I will be absolutely fine."

If only I could have believed her.

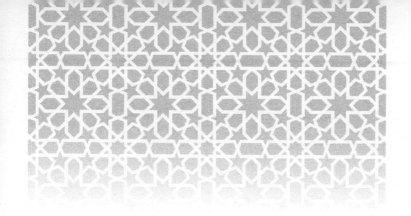

NINETEEN

I didn't sleep that night. I lay in bed, wide-awake, thinking about everything Talitha had told me, imagining the hell she had gone through, what she had to do to survive.

I wondered whether her desire for sensuality, for sexual pleasure, was just as much about intimacy and affection, the need to be held.

I thought about being separated from the people you love most in the world. Who did I love most in the world? I loved my father, of course, but we weren't close. I loved Robbie. Maybe Dottie. Who else?

It was the first time I realized how alone I was. I didn't have best friends since childhood, people who stood in as a surrogate family. I didn't really have anyone. It felt, lying in the dark, like I had a hollow pit inside me, and I wondered if it meant there was something wrong with me. Everyone had people they loved, surely. Why did I not feel a strong attachment to anyone other than my brother? Where were my own lifelong friends?

Perhaps I am making them now, I realized. Perhaps my whole life has been leading up to this moment, this place, these people. That Talitha trusted me with her story, honored me with her secrets, meant the world to me. It forged a bond between us, and I knew then that I had Talitha on my side, as part of my family; that even if I had no one else up to this point, I now had Talitha.

I slept very late. I was beginning to understand why you never saw anyone until late in the day. The smell of cooking woke me yet again, but this time, when I reached the kitchen, Eddie was sitting at the table, scowling as he read the papers, and Jimmy the chauffeur was standing at the stove, an apron tied around his waist, whistling as he cooked up sausages.

"Jimmy!" I felt like I was running into an old friend, relieved there was a friendly face to offset Eddie's grumpiness. "You made it!"

"Course I made it." He looked at me as if I were mad. "It's not exactly brain surgery, is it, driving from London to Morocco?" He laughed to prove he was joking, and I thought it best not to point out that it was normal for me to be worried, given how many drugs were hidden in the car.

"How's the silver bullet?"

"She's perfect," he said, and I smiled at how he had referred to the car as female. Of course she was, I thought to myself. She's sleek and sexy, and adept at hiding secrets. How else could the car be anything other than female?

"Eddie?" I went to sit at the table. "Are you okay?"

Jimmy turned from where he was frying, looked at Eddie,

who didn't look up from the papers, and clamped his lips tightly shut, giving an almost indiscernible shake of his head.

"What's going on?"

"I'm fine," said Eddie, but he got up and walked out of the kitchen.

I looked at Jimmy. "What is it? What's happened?"

"I can't say anything other than women troubles."

"Women troubles?" I was confused. "But Eddie's single, isn't he?"

"I can't say any more," he said. "Sausage?"

I declined, but Jimmy saw that I was practically salivating and slid two sausages on a plate in front of me.

I had just finished when I heard laughing from the courtyard. I put my knife and fork together on the plate just as Lissy walked in, giggling, and behind her, holding her hand as carefree as you like, was Dave Boland.

"Alright, Jim?" Dave kicked a chair out from under the small table and sat down. "Eddie's bangers, is it? I'll have a couple. Alright, Cece?" He nodded to me, but I just glared at him. Lissy bent down next to me, putting her lips close to my ear.

"Forgive him," she said. "I have."

I didn't want to forgive him, I didn't think I could forgive him, and catching sight of Jimmy's face, I was pretty certain he felt the same way. Jimmy's jaw was clenched as he slid the sausages onto a plate. Two for Dave, two for Lissy, none for himself. He banged the plates down on the table, untied his apron and slapped it down on the counter before storming out.

"Uh-oh," Dave said, his mouth full as he pulled Lissy down onto his lap. "I've gone and pissed off Jimmy. What do you think?" He stabbed a sausage with his fork, picked it up and examined it closely, turning the sausage over and over. "Do you think he and Eddie slipped some arsenic in here?" He laughed at his joke, but Lissy, sitting on his lap with one of his hands slipped between her legs, frowned, her lips tightening.

She stood up from his lap and walked over to the other side of the kitchen, leaning with her back against the wall, lighting up a cigarette. "Don't say that," she said. "That's not nice."

"You're right." He shrugged. "I'm sorry. Come here and give me a kiss."

To my surprise she did, and he pulled her back onto his lap, nuzzling her neck and making her squirm with laughter, before taking a big bite off the end of his speared sausage and then dropping the fork back on the plate with a loud clang.

"I want to go into the hills and find the pipe people Brian Jones worked with," Dave said. "Let's do it today. Cece? You should come, too. Have you been into the mountains yet?"

I thought about our picnic at the foot of the mountains and didn't know if this was a trick question. I caught Lissy's eye and she gave an almost imperceptible shake of her head. Dave hadn't heard about our picnic, hadn't heard about the scene afterward, didn't know that Lissy had stripped off her clothes and was well on her way to, at the very least, a three-some when I left.

"I haven't."

"It's gorgeous. You'll love it. Let's go off and get high and have a crazy, groovy day." It was hard to hate him in these moments. He seemed bright and happy and in love. He seemed like the sort of man you would want to spend time with. When I thought of him slugging Lissy—and it was hard not to think of that given her eye was still black-and-blue—it didn't make sense. It seemed impossible that this man would do that. It was so improbable that I started doubting it myself.

"You're such a sweet man," Lissy said, holding his face in both hands and planting a kiss on his lips. "I do love you."

He smiled at her, his eyes lit up with love. If Lissy could forgive him, shouldn't I, as well? "Good. Because I love you."

I went to the mountains with them. What a group we made, Dave in a straggly fur coat, yellow velvet flares and an embroidered pink-and-orange shirt that had huge balloon sleeves, Lissy in her striped stovepipe trousers, high-heeled suede boots, a see-through blouse, and me, in one of Talitha's floor-length kaftans.

The funny thing is, when I look at old photographs today, I see how glamorous we looked, how of the times, but back then I remember thinking we all looked a bit straggly, a bit dirty; Dave's hair always needed washing, and Lissy almost always had yesterday's mascara smudged under her eyes and stains on her clothes.

Dave thought Jimmy would drive us, but I knew how little Jimmy thought of Lissy and presumed he thought as little of Dave. Jimmy was nowhere to be found, which I thought smart. I got Abdel, one of the house boys, to find us a driver, and the three of us headed into the hills with Jamal.

We laughed all day. Lissy and Dave seemed so in love, so delighted to be together, that I felt a pang for Eddie. If he had seen them like this, it would have hurt him, for he would have known he would never, could never, stand a chance with her.

We found the Joujouka musicians, in a small village at the foot of the Atlas Mountains, who were delighted to meet Dave.

"Brian Jones!" He kept saying very slowly, and they repeated it, grinning toothlessly and nodding. "Brian Jones! Brian Jones!"

Dave was, I realized, a talented musician. He didn't just have a fantastic voice, the charisma to lead the band, he also knew how to play. And it seemed, he knew how to play anything.

"Has he played these pipes before?" I was watching as he

joined them, putting the pipe to his lips and blowing experimentally, laughing in delight as he produced sounds. Initially, just a few notes, but soon he was playing properly, harmonizing with the musicians, all of them delighted. Watching Dave perform was mesmerizing. I had loved him before I knew him, and now I knew why. Offstage, Dave was a mixed bag. He could be effervescent, fun, funny, bright, or, as I was discovering, dark, paranoid, angry. But onstage, he was a god. Even here, playing the pipes in a small stone hut in the middle of nowhere, you couldn't take your eyes off him.

Next to me, I was aware that Lissy was shifting around, bored.

"I don't care if they're master musicians," she whispered to me. "When will these fucking panpipes end?" She mimed a rope around her neck, her tongue lolling out her mouth as she bent her neck sideways. I snorted to try to hide my laughter, for it did feel like we had been sitting on the dusty floor of a hut, listening to the pan people, for a very, very long time.

She grabbed my hand and pulled me up, leading me out into the bright sunshine. We walked over to a low, flat rock nestled in between huge round cacti with ears like Mickey Mouse and she pulled her suede shoulder bag into her lap, sweeping aside the fringe and pulling out an opium pipe.

I knew now that opium was Lissy's drug of choice, and I wanted to belong, to be one of them, but it scared me. When she passed it to me, I shook my head, and, to my relief, she just shrugged and carried on smoking.

"The two of you seem so happy." What I meant to say, what I wanted to say, was *Will he hit you again? How do you know it won't happen again? Why do you put up with it?*

Lissy gave her signature grin, and it was the first time I noticed how her incisors were sharp. It gave her a wolfish smile, and although her beauty should have been marred by the imperfection, it somehow made her more attractive. And more dangerous. I understood that Lissy was tough in a way I could never be, tough in a way I couldn't understand.

"You're wondering why I am back with him, aren't you?"

I nodded.

"It would be so simple to just say that I love him, which I do, of course, but it's more than that. You have to understand where Dave came from. Because he sounds middle-class, everyone thinks he had an easier childhood, a more privileged upbringing, but it was so difficult. He was always brilliant, but wild, and his parents didn't know what to do with him. His father hated him, and his mother sided with his father. They gave up on him. He'd have terrible beatings when he was a child, and eventually, when he was fifteen, he came home one day and found the door locked, and all his things were in two suitcases on the doorstep."

"Jesus. That's awful." I thought of Linda kicking me out. But for the beatings, was my own childhood so different? Lissy didn't notice.

"I know. He lived with a mate for a while, and then ended up in a squat with a bunch of other wayward kids. Luckily, he always had music. That's the thing about the middle-class upbringing. He had piano and flute lessons for years. Music saved him. One of the other kids that moved into the squat was Kevin, and Dave came up with the idea of starting a band." She slid off the rock onto the dusty ground and leaned back against the rock, closing her eyes for a few minutes, lost in what I was beginning to recognize as an opium haze.

"When I look at Dave, I see a little boy lost. That's why I can't leave him. I'm his mummy. I'm the only woman he's ever trusted, so how could I abandon him?"

"But the hitting. Lissy, the black eye. How can you stay?"

"He feels so awful afterward. He's racked with guilt. He swears he'll never do it again."

"You know that's not true though."

Lissy let out a short laugh. "It's the triumph of hope over experience. It's not just that. Dave's fragile. He's not like the others. Eddie is strong, he can handle anything, but Dave isn't. He's moody, and difficult, and brilliant, but he's also child-like. His darkness isn't the whole of him. It's just one part. Sometimes you have to forgive the bad and focus on the good. There is so much more good than bad."

It sounded like an excuse to me, but I didn't know what else to say. How could I tell Lissy Ellery that she deserved more if she refused to believe it?

"You don't have to worry about me, you know. I give as good as I get. The time before last, he was the one left with the black eye."

"That's not really the point, is it?" I was frustrated. "I just think…you deserve, we all deserve, to be loved, and that doesn't involve, or shouldn't involve, anything physical."

"Yeah. I know," she said. And then she was in too much of a haze to say anything else.

When we got back to Sidi Mimoun, Lissy and Dave, in their opium haze, stripped off their clothes and climbed, giggling, into the large fountain in the main courtyard to cool off. I leaned over the edge, draping my arms over, my fingers trailing lines and circles, dancing in the cold water.

I listened to their cooing and murmuring, and wondered about love. When it would happen for me, how it would feel, and whether I would recognize it when it arrived.

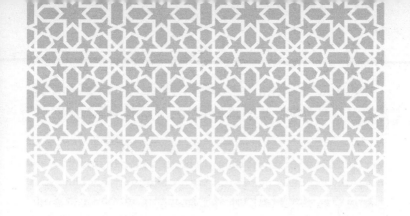

TWENTY

Sidi Mimoun was at its most beautiful in the early evening. The lanterns lining the pathways were lit, camphor flares in the garden, olive logs burning brightly in the firepits and fireplaces. The air smelled of jasmine and wood smoke, and Talitha came running down the great marble staircase to greet us, a velvet beaded beret on her head, harem pants tucked into white suede knee-high boots, a lavishly embroidered silk cape. As she ran down the steps, the cape opened to reveal a completely see-through mesh top with an intricately embroidered neckline, although, frankly, you didn't really notice the neckline. Her breasts were full and pear-shaped, exposed for all the world to see.

"Now *that*," said Dave appreciatively, "is what I call a good outfit."

"Darlings! Just in time!" said Talitha. "We're off to Café de Paris for drinks! Everyone's there! We've been waiting for you."

Dave made a face. "I don't want to go to one of these bloody Moroccan restaurants. You can't drink anything there."

Talitha laughed. "There are a few places you can drink in Marrakech. You'll be happy to hear the Café de Paris is one of them. And then we're going to Bill's for dinner."

"Bill?" Dave asked.

"Bill Willis. He never serves dinner before ten, so we'll have lots of time for drinking."

Just then, a crowd of people came down from the sunroom on the roof, which they called the minza because *minza* means *star* in Arabic. It had banquettes all around and a huge fireplace, and the glass room shone at night.

Eddie was there, in the rear, a scowl still on his face when he saw Lissy next to Dave, her fingers entwined with his, her head resting on his shoulder. Arndt Krupp and Hetti were also there, along with an American writer, Gore Vidal, and Ira Belline, a Russian whose accent I found hard to understand. There were others, so many others, whose names I didn't catch, many of whom were either drunk or high or some combination of the two. They were loud and raucous, as they ran around the courtyard chasing the peacocks who squawked and ran clumsily to get away.

A shout from the window upstairs made us all go silent. "Shut up!"

Giovanni, a handsome Italian man, started to laugh. "You shut the fuck up!" he shouted back, as everyone started jeering, but Talitha looked, suddenly, scared.

"Shh, shh," she said. "That's Paul. Let's go."

But before the doors had been opened, Paul had stomped into the courtyard, his face dark, his mood, it seemed, darker.

He made a beeline for Talitha, who, in all her splendor, shrank back from him.

"Get them out of here!" roared Paul, indifferent to the crowd in the courtyard. "I've had enough. Get rid of all the bloody freeloaders!"

"It's okay, everyone's leaving." Talitha tried to calm him down.

"These people are sucking the life out of everything. Just go. All of you." He was dark with fury as the gates finally opened and everyone, many of whom were laughing at him, taking the piss out of him, started to leave.

I was mortified. We had clearly outstayed our welcome. I had never seen Paul angry before and it scared me, but more than that I wanted to make him feel better.

"Come on." Lissy grabbed my hand and pulled me out the door. "It's okay. Ignore Paul. He gets like this. He's the most charming man in the world, until he's not. Talitha always says he's moody, but we won't let it spoil our evening. Talitha!" She turned, Talitha lingering in the courtyard, seemingly unsure as to whether or not to leave. "Come on! We're going to have a lovely night!"

She joined us, but the light in her eyes had dimmed. She tried to smile, but it seemed forced. Paul's shouting had affected her, and I went over to her and linked my arm through hers, squeezing her tight.

We walked along the narrow streets with our noisy, rambunctious group, but Talitha didn't speak.

"I'm so sorry," she said eventually. "When Paul gets in these moods, he explodes. I love him so very much, but I don't know what to do. It's getting worse."

She was confiding in me yet again, and once again I didn't know what to say.

"I'm worried about him," she murmured. "I know we all

do drugs, and I know I probably drink too much, but he does it differently from the rest of us. I do it socially, as part of the wonderful parties we hold, but Paul does it alone, in his room, and he's spending more and more time in his room. You know he's doing heroin?" She didn't wait for my reaction, nor did she look at me, for she might have seen the shock in my eyes, might have stopped talking. She paused, and I turned my head to see a tear running down her cheek. "It's the drugs talking. Not Paul. Paul loves me. I know he loves me, but more and more he seems angry. He seems angry with me."

"He loves you so much," I tried to reassure her. "I have never seen anyone look at their wife in the way he looks at you. I don't know what to say about the drugs, but I know you mustn't worry about him loving you."

Talitha nodded, but her mind was far away. We walked together in silence for the rest of the way. The terrace of the Café de Paris was filled with Europeans. Every glamorous expat was there, it seemed. Bill Willis, with his flashing green eyes and black hair, elegant skinny Yves Saint Laurent, and the avuncular Pierre Bergé, sitting with La Comtesse, who, I now knew was nicknamed Beignet, a childhood moniker that contrasted sharply with her whip-thin physique.

A buzz went around the room when Mohamed El Hayani joined us briefly, charming all of us as he broke into song, his voice sonorous and beautiful. A silence fell upon the terrace as his voice soared.

When he finished, everyone got to their feet and cheered, standing on chairs and demanding more, but he declined with a bashful smile.

"The song is 'Rahila,'" he said, his face flushed with pleasure. "Thank you."

I was introduced to Christopher Gibbs, an Englishman,

beautifully dressed, with a sophisticated charm that made me swoon.

"Call me Chrissie," he said. "All my favorite people do."

Dave was delighted to see him. "I love that man," he said. "He did my flat. It's fantastic. All tapestries, and kilims, and velvets. I love it. Cost a bloody fortune, but it's perfect. He's good people."

"Is he a decorator?" I turned to Eddie.

Eddie scrunched up his face, thinking. "Yes, and no. He's more than that. He's a fashion editor, an antiques dealer, a decorator. And a bloody good chap. He's what you might call a Renaissance man. He's also very la-di-da. An old Etonian, don't you know."

I didn't really know, but I nodded as if I did.

Stash de Rola was there, with a wild outfit of stripes and swirls, his black hair in an elaborately curled-under bob, with a matching fringe. He was wearing a large velvet hat, with a huge ostrich feather sticking out. Lissy kept playing with the ostrich feather, sticking it under her nose as if it were an orange mustache, making everyone laugh.

"He's a prince, you know," she whispered. "Isn't it funny that they may be royalty, or millionaires, but at the end of the day, they're just like us?" It was. It was a world away from everything I had ever known.

Aperitifs and bowls of olives and briouats, rolled fried pastries, and msemen, a sort of pancake stuffed with spiced onions, circulated. There was harcha, a semolina bread stuffed with herbs and cheese, and kefta, ground spiced lamb on wooden skewers. I took a small bite of everything, knowing we were going on for dinner, not wanting to spoil my appetite.

"My goodness." I looked around. "Anyone who's anyone truly is here, aren't they?" I was talking to myself, but Bill, nursing his ubiquitous Jack Daniel's, in a long robe with dark

kohl smudged under those startling green eyes, heard me and
turned toward me.

"*Chérie*, it's the Cipriani of Marrakech."

I didn't know about the Cipriani in New York, a hot spot
on Fifth Avenue and 59th. But I knew that the rich and the
beautiful were here, and that, however inadequate I felt, however much of a Dorset girl I was, in this crowd of rock stars
and hippies and hairdressers and fashion designers, I had never
before felt valued or loved, had never felt, until this time, truly
accepted. For the first time in my life, I felt completely and
utterly at home.

A young man came to sit down with us.

"Hello, Bill." He extended a hand to shake Bill's. "I'm
Alex. I'm staying with Nuno. Can we come to you for dinner tonight?"

Bill did not take his hand and instead gave him a wither-
ing look. "I'll tell you what, sugar. You go off and learn some
manners, and maybe, just maybe, I'll deign to take your hand."
And he turned away, back to me, with a roll of his eyes.

Talitha was laughing at the other end of the table, putting
on a very good show. If you didn't know she was still upset
about Paul shouting, worried about his taking heroin, you
wouldn't have known. She was as bright and sparkling as ever,
as Yves persuaded her to unwind the scarf she had wrapped
around her head. "Your hair is so beautiful," he said. "Let us
see you in your full beauty."

He stood behind her, unwinding the scarf for her, dancing
around her like a child as she clapped her hands and laughed,
shaking out that dark chestnut gleaming hair when he was
done.

I was sitting next to Pierre, who was gazing at Yves in delight, shaking his head in amazement.

He leaned over toward me. "She is magic," he said. "She is

the only one who brings out this child in him. He's very serious, Yves, except when he is with Talitha. She makes him
feel a childlike joy. You wait. She'll have him dancing on the
tables later."

"You're coming to Bill's?"

"Of course."

I was delighted. I liked Pierre. He was older than the rest of
us and seemed…paternal. Sensible. I felt like nothing could go
too terribly wrong if Pierre was around, and I couldn't shake
the sense that things were going to go terribly wrong, that if
Pierre wasn't with us, I was the only one who might be able
to stop it or fix it, that I was the only one sober and sensible
enough to stand in the way.

"Oy! Brion!" Dave called across the terrace. "Where's your
Dreamachine? I want to try it out."

"Join the back of the line," Brion shot back.

"Who is Brion and what is a dream machine?" I asked
Christopher, who was sitting next to me.

"That's Brion Gysin. He's a fabulous artist who lives in
Tangier. There's a whole other scene in Tangier. William Bur-
roughs, Paul Bowles. They're all there. Except when, occasionally, they're here. And a Dreamachine?" said Christopher,
turning his full attention on me. "It's a strobing machine that
makes you feel like you're tripping, without taking any drugs."

"Did someone say drugs?" Talitha called out. "Yes, please!
Who's got the drugs?"

"Darling," said Christopher. "We all know you prefer your
alcohol to drugs. Don't pretend."

Talitha feigned a pout.

"The expert speaks!" Bill extended an arm toward Christopher. "Honey, you're the only man I know who has amyl
nitrite for breakfast."

Everyone laughed good-naturedly, including Christopher.

"Bill, darling? Isn't it time for dinner? Are we allowed to come to your house yet?"

"We're starving!" everyone started chiming in. "Hungry! Feed us, Bill! Feed us!"

He got to his feet, slightly unsteady, and downed his drink in one. "Let's go." He extended an arm, and off we went.

We didn't get to Bill's riad, Dar Noujoum, until after ten. It was the first house I had been to other than our palace, and although it wasn't as huge or impressive, it was equally stunning and opulent.

The rooms were scented with sandalwood, huge suede poufs ready to sink onto, dozens of candles making the soft plaster of the tadelakt walls glow in the candlelight. The table was outside in the garden, beautifully set—white linens and silver cutlery, crystal glasses. The trees were woven with deer antlers and lights, which cast a magical glow over all of us.

"Why the hell didn't you lay extra places?" Bill spit suddenly at one of his maids, one of the few women, most of the servers being beautiful bronzed young men, bare chested, embroidered sarongs slung around their lithe hips.

She responded furiously in Arabic, stepping toward him with a barrage of harsh words, which I felt he deserved. I was shocked at how he could be so charming one second and so brutal the next.

"This is what he does." Talitha's voice in my ear soothed me as we sat at the exquisite table, piled high with fruit and nuts down the center. "He's mercurial, like Paul, only more so. Every creative genius I know is a bit like that. You don't get to have the brilliance without a few demons."

"What's that about demons and creative geniuses?" Yves, on Talitha's other side, leaned toward us.

"I was saying you rarely get one without the other."

"Are you saying I'm a demon, my darling?"

Talitha rested her head on his shoulder. "Not with me!"

"That's because you're a queen." He leaned back then, his eyes moving over her face as he thought.

"I was wrong about the scarf. You need a crown." Yves jumped up, a naughty grin on his face, and stood behind Talitha, gathering her mane of hair in his hands and piling it on her head, before letting it fall and walking over to the orange trees at the edge of the garden. Everyone watched him as he returned with branches of shiny green leaves, heavy with pale young oranges not yet ripe, but also a few small, bright, luscious ones, ready to be picked. Within seconds, he had Talitha's hair up again, this time weaving branches throughout as she made faces at everyone around the table, making us laugh. He plucked feathers from the ground, placing them in her hair, stepping back and making her turn her head so he could examine his artwork as we all clapped.

And, finally, he pulled some deer antlers from a tree and wove them in, twisting thin green vines around the antlers, tiny white flowers and unripe green oranges nestled in, with a brilliance that took my breath away.

Talitha was indeed a queen, in a magnificent crown of leaves, fruit and feather. She looked like a sprite emerging from the forest. Breathtaking.

Bill clearly loved Morocco. His house was furnished in haute Moroccan style, his clothes were Moroccan, his lovers were young Moroccan men. He said he had never loved anywhere nor felt as at home as he did the minute he arrived in Marrakech.

And yet, much to my surprise, the dinner he served was not Moroccan in the slightest. We started with a corn soup, with what he called biscuits as a side dish, but which seemed to me

to be more like a scone. I followed his lead and slathered it
with butter, and immediately realized the difference—I had
never eaten a scone as light or fluffy. It was delicious, not to
mention a welcome break. I found the Moroccan food delicious, and I welcomed the change. It was nice. It was nice to
eat something that reminded me of home.

After the soup was a cheese soufflé, and barbecued chicken
with coleslaw, with a huge chocolate cake for dessert.

"Habiba has outdone herself tonight," Talitha said. "This
is delicious. I need the chocolate cake recipe."

"Honey, you can have it anytime. These are my late mother's recipes. I taught Habiba well."

"Here's to Habiba!" Talitha raised her glass, as did we all.
"For learning to cook Bill's mother's delicious recipes!"

"To Habiba!" we echoed, as I whispered, "Who is Habiba?"

"Bill's chef," Talitha whispered back.

Yves leaned over. "He loves Morocco like no other. The
buildings. The clothes. The boys…" He grinned. "But there
is nothing that can ever replace the food of your childhood."

After dinner, when we had retired to the cushions on the
floor, sipping mint tea, smoking hookahs, a male server approached Bill and whispered in his ear.

"I have a surprise for you." Bill's eyes twinkled with mis-
chief as he got up and stalked off through the garden. He
emerged a few minutes later, with a shadowy figure behind
him.

"Look who's back from his travels!" he exclaimed, stepping aside to reveal a young man, maybe twenty or twenty-
one, with shoulder-length hair that he brushed back to reveal
large blue eyes framed in thick, dark lashes. He was beautiful.
He might have been the most beautiful boy I had ever seen.

He wore a loose shirt, open to his navel, his smooth tanned
body golden in the candlelight, and he stood still for a mo-

ment, soaking in our admiration, as if he was used to doing this, showing off what true male beauty was.

"Gerard!" Talitha, who had done her best to hide her sorrow ever since Paul shouted at everyone to leave, finally, authentically, lit up. They stood up and embraced, and started kissing, truly kissing, with tongues, as everyone cheered, and he cupped her breast before leaning his head down and began kissing between her cleavage.

He sat down at the place that had been squeezed in for him between Talitha and Yves.

"Where have you been?" Lissy, sitting opposite us, asked. "We've all missed you terribly."

"If I'd known you were here, I would have come back earlier." He winked at her.

"If I'd known you'd be away, I would never have bothered to come to Marrakech," she said, her Swedish accent and low, throaty voice making it sound like an invitation. Gerard blew her a kiss, and we laughed, but I looked at Dave's face and saw a shadow cross it.

"I've been in India," Gerard said. "Buying up treats for all my friends."

Treats? What kind of treats? I imagined this man bringing in a suitcase, opening it up to reveal a mountain of printed clothes, beaded headdresses and masks, handing them out like candy.

I gave a start. Of course. *Gerard*. Now I knew where I had heard his name. The wayward son of the Comtesse. The drug dealer. The one Bill had warned me not to fall in love with. I had no intention of falling in love with anyone, but I now understood what he meant. It wasn't just that Gerard was beautiful or that he gave everyone exactly what they wanted, but that he had an air of absolute confidence combined with an inherent insouciance; you knew he didn't care what anyone thought of him because he didn't have to. He had aristocratic privilege written all over him. I had thought the privileged were better than me. I had heard of schools like Eton, Harrow, Winchester, and knew, of course, about Oxford and Cambridge, but up until now, had never met anyone from that walk of life. But all the people I had met in Morocco, the royal, the wealthy, the aristocratic, were…normal. Other than the Comtesse, no one treated me as inadequate in any way, didn't talk down to me in the way I always presumed they would. In fact, if you weren't aware, half the time you wouldn't know.

But suddenly, in Gerard's gaze, I somehow feel inadequate. I still don't know if it was him or me. Or perhaps some combination of the two. Perhaps he picked up his manners from his mother.

"Ooh! Treats for me? How could I ever possibly thank you?" Lissy broke my reverie as Dave's face got darker. It felt almost as if she was goading him, and I didn't know why she was doing it.

Eddie was at the other end of the table, watching her, watching Dave, pain written all over his face, which he quickly masked when anyone spoke to him. I was heartbroken for him and relieved he was there. I knew that Eddie would stop at nothing to rescue Lissy, that she would be okay as long as Eddie was around.

I couldn't say the same about Talitha. Who would protect her?

Gerard took a swig of the wine and sat back in his chair, reaching into the pocket of his suede trousers. He brought out a plastic bag, filled with light brown pills, and tipped them into the palm of his hand, showing them to everyone.

"What is it? Is it acid? Is it an opium pill? Is it an upper? Is it a downer?" The table clamored, everyone shouting their best guesses across the table.

"I have all of the above," he said finally, "but this? This is something new. These are mandrakes."

"Mandrakes?" Dave spit. "Don't you mean *Mandrax*, mate? Jesus." He whistled to himself. "You'd think a fucking drug dealer would get it right."

Gerard shrugged good-naturedly. "It has a few names. Quaaludes. Ludes. Sopers. Mandies. I picked the one I liked best. It's all the same thing. Doesn't make any difference to me what you call it. It's still lovely."

"May I?" Talitha was the first to ask, and he bowed his head in assent before taking a pill and putting it in her mouth, holding his wineglass to her lips for her to swallow. "What does it do?"

"It's blissfully relaxing," he said, handing the rest of the pills around the table. "It's a sedative, so don't fall asleep. Once you push through the sleepiness, you'll lude out, man. And it's seriously groovy. Almost hypnotic. All your cares will disappear."

There was a murmur of excitement as the pills were passed around, everyone taking them at the same time. I hesitated, looking at the biscuit-y pill in my hand, and looked up to see Eddie watching me. He gave me the tiniest shake of his head, which I took to mean, *Don't do it if you don't want to.* I didn't know whether I wanted to or not. Or rather, I did want to, but after I saw what it did to everyone else first.

Gerard spotted me with the pill in my palm before I had a chance to hide it, to let him know I wasn't doing it.

"You won't want to miss out." He smiled, those blue eyes gazing into mine. "This might be the greatest drug I've ever taken, and best of all, it's completely legal. They're giving it out on prescription in America, as a sleeping pill. Everyone's prescribing it there. There's nothing to be worried about."

I had no reason not to believe him. If they were prescribing it in America, then it was safe. Then I would do it. I popped the pill and washed it down with wine.

Lissy appeared with a hand outstretched, but Gerard smiled and shook his head. He placed a Mandrax between his teeth and leaned toward her as she laughed. She snaked her tongue out toward Gerard's mouth, catching the pill. Once she had swallowed it, she came back in, as he pulled her toward him and kissed her.

I watched, mesmerized, before a huge crash made me jump. Dave was on the floor, having launched himself at the two of them in a rage. It seems a quick-thinking guest had pushed a chair in the way, and Dave had tripped over it and was now sprawled on the floor.

Gerard let go of Lissy and looked down at Dave, a sneer on his beautiful face. "Oh, look," he said. "Scrabbling in the dirt, where you belong."

"Fuck off, you fucking wanker," Dave spat, scrambling up and taking a swing at Gerard, who laughed as he dodged it.

"Is that the best you can do?" Gerard smirked before dismissing him with a light hand. "I suppose one can't expect more with such a poor education. What was it, kicked out of school at thirteen?" His voice dripped with derision, and I watched the shame and rage in Dave's eyes. He knew he wasn't a match for Gerard. This wasn't about Lissy, this was class warfare, and Gerard, who was a count already thanks to the death of his father, had won. To him, Dave Boland wasn't a rock star who commanded adoration and reverence—he was a commoner whose fame was irrelevant; he was outclassed.

Dave slunk off then, realizing there was nothing he could do, no one who would come to his aid.

"Come on, Lissy," he said, but she ignored him, wrapping

herself around Gerard and staring at Dave as he cursed at her and stumbled off into the darkness.

"Why are you even with him?" I heard Gerard say.

"I'm not right now, am I?" she purred, as she slipped into his arms.

I don't know what else anyone took that night. The one mandrake was enough for me. I was lulled into a deeply relaxed haze. I woke up in Bill Willis's garden, lying on cushions on the ground, beneath a jeweled bedspread, a brass tray on which sat a patterned ceramic pitcher filled with water, and a small brass pot of coffee.

I sat up, rubbing the sleep out of my eyes, trying to remember what happened the night before. I had snapshots, as if it was a dream, but couldn't remember the sum of the parts. I remember Gerard and Talitha passionately embracing, her leading him into Bill's house, away from the others. I remember Lissy flirting with everyone, Dave glowering darkly in the background, the fight with Gerard, all the while Eddie watching, waiting. I remember Bill going off with a young man, and seeing various drugs brought out during the night. Opium, cocaine, hash, with pipes and hookahs, and music and laughter, and everything lazy and dreamlike and then, finally, sleep.

The maid that Bill Willis had shouted at last night was picking her way around the garden, clearing up the debris. She didn't look at me. I didn't blame her. I felt ashamed at waking up in the bright morning sunlight in a relative stranger's garden. I wondered how many times this happened, this maid cleaning up the morning after, and I wondered if she was offended by our behavior in this devout Muslim country. Were I in her shoes, I thought, would I be offended? Would I feel disrespected? Would I judge all these Westerners who arrived and treated the town as if it were theirs, rules and regulations there to be flouted?

I knew from staying with the Gettys that the staff here would turn a blind eye, just as Talitha and Paul's staff did. They bowed and smiled and cleaned up, and procured and hid, and never showed a hint of resentment at being underappreciated, being taken for granted. They were part of the secrecy.

Who was I becoming? I wondered. I hadn't done any drugs other than the mandrake last night, and a little hash, but I was not the sort of girl to sleep on cushions on the floor; I was not the sort of girl who had to apologize. I had wanted to live, but I had not envisioned it looking like this.

I made my way out of Dar Noujoum and wound my way through the streets of Sidi Mimoun, back to the palace, back to those who were fast becoming the people I trusted, the people I cared about, the people who cared about me.

I heard them as soon as the huge gates were opened, as soon as I entered the main courtyard. The screaming was coming from the second floor, from one of the bedrooms. It was Lissy's voice shrieking,

"Don't be such a fucking lunatic, Dave! Nothing happened!"

I could hear Eddie, banging on the door. "Let me in, Lissy. Dave! Open the fucking door!" I went running up to try and help.

Then crash, bang, a roar of anger from Dave. "You fucking slut, Lissy. You're just a Swedish slut. You'll fucking sleep with anything, won't you. You'd be nothing without me. You're just a fucking junkie slut."

"Me, a junkie? Ha! That's rich coming from you! You've never met a drug you didn't love. Fuck off, Dave. Can you blame me for screwing other people when you're comatose most of the fucking time?"

There was a loud crack, and then a howl of pain from Dave,

just as Eddie sent the door crashing down and we burst into the bedroom to see Dave, passed out on the floor, his hand covered in blood, Lissy weeping, the first time I had seen her cry, as she tried to revive him.

"What happened?" Jimmy came running into the room, an apron tied around his waist. He had evidently been cooking again. "Jesus H. Christ." He knelt down and felt for a pulse before looking up at us. "He's passed out. Not dead. What happened to his hand?"

"I don't want to tell you." Lissy pouted, like a little girl.

"Don't be even more of a fucking idiot than you already are," said Jimmy, his voice flat but firm. "What happened?"

"He went to punch me." She looked at the floor, unable to look at any of us. "And I ducked. He punched the wall instead."

"Are you fucking serious?" Eddie went as white as a sheet as we all looked at Dave on the floor, his smashed-up hand covered in blood. "How hard would he have hit you? Lissy? He could have killed you."

"He wouldn't have killed me," she said flatly, but she knew, as we all knew, that a punch with that kind of force was a very serious punch indeed. "Should we call an ambulance?"

"It's quicker if I put him in the silver bullet and take him to hospital," said Jimmy, disdain dripping from his voice. He picked up Dave as if he were made of feathers and carried him downstairs. "Not that he fucking deserves it," he muttered to himself as he passed me outside.

"What do you think you're doing?" Eddie said, as Lissy started following.

"I'm going with him," she said.

"No, you're not. Not this time. Lissy? Do you understand what just happened? If you hadn't ducked, Dave would have killed you."

Lissy was in shock, I realized. Running around her room, grabbing her hat, her scarf, not looking at us. Eddie grabbed her arms and held her still, forced her to look at him, whereupon finally she collapsed in huge, heaving sobs. He held her tight as I backed out the room.

I could hear the opera coming from Paul's room, and knocked, quietly at first then harder, until he came to the door, naked but for a towel wrapped around his waist.

I blushed. "I'm so sorry. I can come back later."

"No, no. It's fine. Come in. We're just finishing."

He was back to his old, happy self, I was relieved to see, but when I walked in the room, there was a beautiful dark-haired woman lying in his bed, the bedspread covering her nakedness.

"Come along," Paul said to her. "I've got things to do. Cece, why don't you sit over there while I get dressed." My face was flaming again, and I tried to concentrate on the newspaper lying on his desk, pulling it toward me and pretending to read as a naked woman slipped behind me, unabashed by her nudity, pausing to say politely, "How do you do," before pulling on her clothes and kissing Paul goodbye.

Paul emerged from his dressing room a few minutes later, fully clothed, his glasses on, ready to do whatever he did in his room all day. Which now included, I was trying not to show my shock, sleeping with other women. Oh yes, I knew everyone was sleeping with everyone else, I was there at the start of the orgy the other night. But this felt more like traditional cheating. Did Talitha know that there was a beautiful, beautifully spoken naked Englishwoman in her husband's bed, I wondered? And where, in fact, *was* Talitha? I cast my mind back to the selection of snapshots from the night before. Could she have gone home with Gerard? Back to Villa Schiff? I didn't understand any of it. The two of them—Paul and Talitha—seemed to be deeply in love. I could see it in their eyes, in the way Paul looked at her, the way she brought him to life. I couldn't see how their open marriage, if that was what it was, could possibly lead to anything good. Talitha had already said that she had a tendency to be jealous. Would having lovers of her own make that jealousy disappear? And how could there be a happy ending with so many dangerous trysts?

I was embarrassed that I had disturbed Paul. "I can leave," I said. "I'm so sorry. I didn't realize you were in the middle of things."

He grinned, and I felt myself relax. "I wasn't in the middle. I was very much at the end. I'm glad for a break. I like talking to you, Cece. You're one of the few voices of reason here. And I know Talitha adores you. She was telling me that she feels safe with you, able to confide in you in a way she does with few people."

I swallowed the lump in my throat as I nodded.

"I'm glad you came into our lives, Cece. She needed someone like you. She needs a real friend. She is a magical woman, my wife, but she is not who everyone thinks she is. I know she's revealed some of her other side to you. I just wish she could see herself as I see her. Can you imagine? This beautiful, generous, spirited girl, who doesn't believe she's worth anything. She's terribly lonely, which is why she surrounds herself with all these people, but it doesn't help." He shook his head. "She believes that if not for me, no one would be interested in her. Isn't that the most ridiculous thing you've ever heard?"

I nodded. I couldn't say anything. I was so upset by what he was saying, how he was able to put into words everything I felt about Talitha, everything I saw, all the things I knew to be true, without knowing how to articulate them.

"She sparkles like no one else when she's around people. She puts on a wonderful show, but when she's alone, as you have seen, she can be depressed." He sighed. "She can go to really dark places. There are times when I don't know what to do for her. I don't know how to help."

"Do you…" I took a deep breath, unsure as to how honest I should be but trusting him, respecting the level of honesty he had just shared with me. "Do you think this helps? Other women?"

Paul shook his head. "Talitha doesn't mind about lovers. We both have lovers. She is very sexual, as am I. Yes, she can sometimes be jealous, but not really. She wouldn't want to change that, and neither would I. The monotony of monogamy. Argh." He shivered in mock horror. "All that I ask, all that I have ever asked, is that I know who she is with. If she has an affair with anybody, that's okay with me, as long as I know. Then everyone is happy."

"She seemed depressed last night. After we left."

"Yes. I'm sorry that I shouted. I just can't tolerate all the freeloaders all the time. I don't mean you," he was quick to reassure me. "But there are always people here, eating, drinking, partying. Most of them are passing through, few are real friends."

"Perhaps you can talk to Talitha privately? Come to some kind of compromise?"

He smiled sadly. "Do you think I haven't tried? It's why we can't ever stay in Marrakech too long. It's too wild for me. I love this house, but more madness happens here than anywhere else. Rome is where my children are. Rome always feels more settled. And of course, London."

"What can I do? How can I help?"

"Be there for Talitha. Support her. Help lift her up when she's down."

"Is she here?"

He shook his head. "She has gone away for the night with the good doctor."

"The good doctor?"

"Gerard. Everyone calls him the Candyman, but I prefer the good doctor. He—" he looked over at his opium jar "—prescribes for me. I don't trust him, and I'm not sure I like him. I think he's pretty evil actually, but I need him."

I thought about what Talitha had said, that Paul was dabbling in heroin, and I shuddered. I wasn't going to ask him about that.

"Where have they gone?"

"To Essaouira. It's on the coast. It's beautiful. You must go one day."

"And…the freeloaders. Do you want us to leave? I can speak to the others…"

"Absolutely not!" He put a hand up to stop me saying anything else on the subject. "First of all, you now work here. It's official, and secondly, I don't mind Lissy and the others being here. Talitha needs people, and everyone comes here to live out their fantasies. I understand it. God knows, I'm doing much the same thing, except, I think, my fantasies are changing. Right now I have a fantasy of a quiet life surrounded by books, art and music. But please, don't worry. As long as there aren't too many, it's fine."

"Did you hear the argument? Has someone told you about Dave?"

"No. I play my music loudly precisely to drown everyone out. I don't want to hear anyone or anything." He seemed disinterested, but I felt he ought to know.

"I'm just letting you know that Dave punched a wall and passed out. I think he may have broken his hand. Jimmy's taken him to hospital."

Paul shook his head with a laugh. "Bloody rock stars.

They're all like that. Actually…" He paused thoughtfully. "They're not all like that. I like that Mick Jagger. He's very bright. Very thoughtful. He's someone I can really talk to."

I was surprised.

"Now," Paul said, dropping the subject, "why don't you and I listen to some music. How much do you know about Wagner?"

"Absolutely nothing." I smiled.

"Good. There's nothing quite like Wagner. I shall be very interested in what you think. He is extraordinarily divisive. You either love him or hate him, but so often people hate him because they do too much too soon." He walked over to the record cupboard and pulled out an album, taking it to the turntable and putting it on. "I'm going to start you gently. This is the 'Wesendonck Lieder,' a set of five songs for women. He was writing *Tristan und Isolde* when he decided to set poems by Mathilde Wesendonck, the wife of one of his patrons, to music. To my mind, it is quite beautiful."

The music started playing, and within seconds, tears were running down my cheeks at the beauty of the opening bars, the beauty of the voice. Paul leaned back in his chair, smiling, before pouring himself a small drink and reaching for his opium pipe.

SOUTHERN CHEESE SOUFFLÉ

INGREDIENTS:

¼ cup Parmigiano Reggiano cheese, freshly grated

3 tablespoons unsalted butter

3 tablespoons gluten-free flour

1-¼ cups heavy cream

4 extra-large eggs, separated (room temperature)

3 extra-large egg whites (room temperature)

2 cups Jarlsberg cheese, shredded

2 tablespoons chives, minced (optional)

1-¼ teaspoons kosher salt

¼ teaspoon cream of tartar

METHOD:

Preheat the oven to 375°. Position rack in lower third of the oven. Butter a 1-½-quart soufflé dish and coat it with the Parmigiano.

In a medium saucepan, melt the butter. Stir in the flour to make a roux. Gradually whisk in the cream and bring to a low boil over moderate heat, whisking constantly. Reduce the heat to low and cook until very thick, about 3 minutes. Transfer the roux to a large bowl and let cool. Stir in the egg yolks, cheese, salt and chives.

Put the egg whites in the bowl of a stand mixer. Add the cream of tartar. Using the whipping attachment, beat the whites until firm peaks form. Fold in the whites until the streaks of white disappear.

Pour the mixture into the prepared dish. Bake for about 35 minutes, until the soufflé is golden brown and puffed. To test for doneness, insert a kitchen needle into the center. If it comes out wet, cook another 2 or 3 minutes.

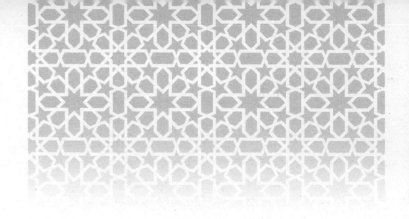

TWENTY-ONE

There was no one around that day save for the usual servants, and little to do. There had been so much drama, I was relieved to have something of a break. Sidi Mimoun was gorgeous when it was quiet. I wandered into the courtyard where Talitha had planted roses and spent some time deadheading them, ripping the rosehips off the bushes and plucking off the dried leaves, ignoring the thorns scratching up my fingers. It felt good to be connected to nature.

In the garden a large rattan chaise longue lay beneath a canvas canopy, and I settled there with a book, *Rosemary's Baby* by Ira Levin, trying to take my mind off Dave, off Lissy, off the worry of where they were and what they were doing. The birds were chirping above the faint sounds of opera coming from Paul's room. After a while, I fell asleep.

When I woke up, the sun had gone behind the clouds, and I shivered. I had no idea what time it was but heard conversation in the adjoining courtyard, where I found Lissy and Eddie, sitting at a small table by the fountain, heads together, deep in conversation.

"Thank God you're back! What's going on?"

"Dave's broken his hand," said Eddie. "They've put a plaster cast on it, but he had a bit of a breakdown at the hospital when he came to."

"A bit?" Lissy shot Eddie a look. "He went completely fucking nuts. He started tearing up the hospital. They ended up shooting him with tranquilizers and chaining him to the hospital bed."

Eddie grinned, shaking his head. "I have to give that mad fucker some respect. He managed to throw the IV out the fucking window."

"That's terrible. God. Wow. So where is he now? What's happening next?"

"I've spoken to our manager, and he's found a place that's a kind of retreat, out in the mountains, near Ourika Valley. Jimmy's driving him up there now and dropping him off. They specialize in giving people lots of rest and relaxation. I think he's better off there for now."

"What if he won't stay?"

Eddie laughed. "Oh, he'll stay. They've got these giant men who work there. It's one thing for Dave to take on Lissy, but he'd have to be off his rocker to take on one of those men. They're big, beefy bodyguards. Dave's little. Sorry." He shot Lissy a look, but she shrugged. "And when he comes out?"

Eddie looked at Lissy. "Let's cross that bridge when we come to it, shall we?" he said.

"I know I've said this before, but this time, I think this really is over." Lissy's hand, as she lit her cigarette, was trembling. "I know that if my reflexes hadn't been so quick, I'd be bread."

Eddie laughed. "Not bread. Toast."

"Pfft. I'm Swedish. I can't get everything right."

"Almost everything," Eddie said adoringly, shaking himself out of his reverie. "And yes, you would be toast. You definitely wouldn't be sitting here right now."

"What would I do without you?" Lissy was serious as she gazed at Eddie, her voice soft. She was a fighter and she was tough, but that afternoon, after all that had happened, I saw her vulnerability. Perhaps she had to be tough to protect herself from Dave, but with Eddie she could be fragile. She didn't have to have the walls up.

Eddie blushed and shrugged. Watching them together, I saw something beginning. That was the moment when Lissy started to look at Eddie in a completely different light.

Much has been written about Lissy Ellery and Eddie Allbright falling in love, but I was there right at the beginning, and I watched it happen. I knew already that Eddie would never raise a hand to Lissy or to anyone else, and I understood why and how she turned to him when everything became too much.

"I need to go and clear my head," Lissy said. "I'm going to walk the gardens at La Mamounia. Who wants to come?"

Eddie paused and then, with a tender nonchalance, said, "I'll come if you want."

"Cece?" She looked at me, but I shook my head. They needed this time together. I had no interest whatsoever in being a third wheel.

"I think I might go to the souk. I want to explore a bit more."

"See you later then." Lissy stood and gave me a tight hug, and the two of them walked off through the courtyard. I watched them go, Lissy in tight, hip-hugging low-slung flares and Chelsea boots, a crocheted top and large hat, Eddie, almost a foot taller than her, in red velvet pants and a flowing shirt, a matching hat of his own. They walked side by side, close, and I could feel his protectiveness as they walked, watched as he put a hand on the small of her back to guide her through the archway, saw how she looked up at him, a smile of thanks in her eyes. She didn't get this with Dave, I thought. With Dave, they made up a pair of naughty twins. Both of them troublemakers, both of them feisty, both of them trying to be the boss, terrified to let their guard down. They were competitive, daring each other to be the wildest, the most carefree, the winner. They were the same size. Yet Lissy was so clearly the stronger of the two.

Watching Lissy and Eddie, I realized how this made sense. Eddie was calm, he didn't like drama. Whatever craziness Lissy could get up to, Eddie would be a good foil. In turn she would draw him out, help him loosen up a little. They made a good couple, and more than that, they made a couple that felt right.

And he made excellent sausages.

I had yet to try his shepherd's pie.

I was walking out the door when Jimmy the chauffeur called to me.

"Where are you off to, all by yourself?" He walked down the stairs, no pinny round his waist, this time in a suit and tie.

I was off to the souk, thinking I would buy small gifts for people back home. I thought Robbie would get a kick out of some babouche slippers, and Dottie would love an embroidered scarf or a big straw hat. I'd seen some beautiful enamel hookahs, which John would probably like. Not that I had any idea where I stood with John. Here I was, having the time of my life, and I hadn't thought of him at all. I certainly hadn't had time to miss him, and doubted he missed me. Whatever the case, I felt I owed him. All of this, these amazing people, the strange turn my life had taken, was down to meeting John on the bus that night. I hadn't realized before then how life

can turn on a sixpence, and was pretty certain that the closest
I would ever have got to Dave Boland, Lissy Ellery or Eddie
Allbright before now would have been, if I was very lucky,
standing in line to get their autograph.

"I'm off to the souk." I looked Jimmy up and down. "Where
are you off to, then? The office?"

He winced a bit. "I tried all that Moroccan palaver but I
felt like a fool. I'm much happier in a suit and tie. No one
messes with you in a suit and tie. I'll come with you, shall I?"

"Oh no, it's fine. I'm just going to have a wander."

"Oh no, I'm coming with you." He was stern. "I'm not
having a young, impressionable girl walking round Morocco
by herself."

"It's perfectly safe," I said. "Look at Talitha. She goes and
buys food by herself every day."

"She knows her way around, and even then I don't think
that's safe. I wouldn't let my daughter walk around by herself,
and I'm not letting you walk around by yourself."

"You've got a daughter?" I was intrigued.

"I do. She's probably the same age as you. She's twenty-
two. Gillian's her name. She's a nurse."

"How lovely. You must be so proud. I had no idea you were
a family man! How on earth do you manage this crazy rock
and roll lifestyle with a wife and daughter?"

We walked out the gates and into the alleyway. I stopped
to pet two kittens that were playing in the doorway opposite.

"I didn't mention anything about a wife." He watched me
tickle the kittens under their chins. "I don't think there are many
women who would put up with this lifestyle. We're divorced.
She left me years ago." He shook his head. "Which is fine. I'm
not built to be a family man. I'm better off on my own."

"I'm sorry. Maybe you could find yourself a rock and roll
chick," I teased, standing up and continuing to make my way
down the alley. "Someone like Lissy."

He rolled his eyes. "God forbid!"

I laughed. "You don't like her, do you. It must be hard, doing so much for them when you feel like that."

"It's not that I don't like her, it's that… Well, I can't say too much. I work for Eddie, and my loyalty is to him. I worry about Lissy and Dave. He's a bad seed, that one. Too many drugs, and he doesn't have a strong constitution. He's going to be the death of this band, you mark my words. Lissy's not good for him. The two of them together are on self-destruct mode. That's what I don't like. I don't like watching them together, and I don't bleedin' like how he treats her, or how she treats him. I don't like what it does to Eddie, and the band. They've all worked too hard for it to come crashing down because one of them can't control his impulses."

"What do you think it is with Dave? Why does he do the things he does?"

"I think he's not well. In the head, you know? I've no doubt he's clever. He's got a good voice, and he's probably the most talented one in the band, but the circuiting's off in his brain. He can be fine, for a while. He can be funny, and generous, and great company. But just when you think you might have imagined everything, he'll go off on a bender, or have a fit about something. I tell you what though, fame's not good for him. I've watched him change, and it'll be the death of him."

I felt a shiver go down my spine and turned cold, even in the sunlit street. I stopped and looked at him.

"Do you mean that, Jimmy?"

He nodded. "I do. I think there's always been something a bit wrong with Dave. I once had a neighbor who was a manic-depressive. He could seem normal, until he wasn't. Dave's like that. He reminds me of my neighbor."

"But if he does have something like that, can't he be treated? Aren't there drugs that could cure him or at least help him manage it?"

Jimmy snorted. "Those aren't the kinds of drugs he's interested in. Although, he'll take anything on offer."

"Can't you do something? Can't their manager? Someone, somewhere, surely can get through to him."

"Nah. They can't. Everyone's tried. This is the worst it's been though. He's smashed up his hand good and proper, and all I keep thinking is thank the bleedin' Lord she ducked. Imagine if he'd landed that force on her face?"

I went quiet. I had thought the same. We had all thought the same.

"What do you think will happen?"

He paused and raised his eyes to the blue skies above. "I don't know, but I'm praying that something happens soon to fix him, or stop this. He's in that retreat now, and he was calm when I left him, but they'd shot him up with sedatives. God knows what he'll do if they don't keep a very close eye on him."

I felt a shiver of fear. "Should we be worried?"

"You? Not at all. Lissy? Yeah. The band? Probably."

"You're scaring me, Jimmy."

"Don't you worry your pretty little head about it. I'm right here. I won't let anything happen to any of you. Promise. You have my word."

I stopped then and solemnly held out my hand. "You have to shake on it," I said. "If you shake on it, you can never renege."

He laughed, and I was relieved. It was the first moment of levity on that walk.

"Alright," he said, and he shook my hand, and I have to say, as soon as I felt my hand in his, felt his strength and warmth, I knew we'd be alright.

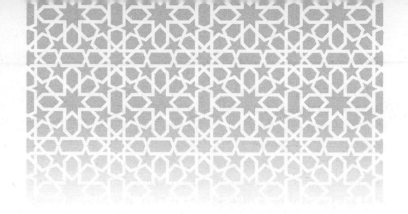

TWENTY-TWO

When Talitha heard about Dave, she came back. She planned a small picnic that night just for us, and I was relieved to have a small break from the madness, the constant throngs of people; I was beginning to understand, I think, how Paul felt about it all.

And, I was beginning to understand how the days were ordered here. The mornings were quiet, save for the workmen who were finishing off the zellige tiles and the tadelakt plaster.

Bill was never there in the morning, sleeping off copious amounts of alcohol and cocaine from the night before, but his foreman, Chérif, was always around, softly speaking in Arabic to the workers, explaining how things should be done.

"Morning, Chérif!" I'd sing, used to seeing him moving through the courtyards. "How are you today?"

"I am wonderful, Miss Cece," he always said. I once had the temerity to ask about Bill always being late and immediately regretted it, knowing I had made a mistake. Later, Chérif took me aside to explain.

"He is a great scholar," he said. "He is an artist. 'Chérif,' he said to me, 'go visit the Koutoubia Mosque to see what your grandparents did with their eyes.' I went there. And I discovered the perspective."

"What do you mean?"

"Before him it was rare to put tadelakt in a room. This was only used for hammams. He is an artist."

Bill was, indeed, an artist. A mercurial one. I knew that I did not want to make an enemy of Bill Willis. As much as he seemed to adore me, he could turn on a dime and could be brutal to those he didn't like.

"I forgive you, sugar." Bill would sip his ubiquitous Jack Daniel's. "We're in Morocco here, and taking our time is the essence of true craftsmanship. Who cares about time when we are creating such beauty? I'm bringing back a lost art. You only saw this work in the highest end palaces and mosques. Who, more than the Gettys, deserves to bring back a lost art?"

That night, later, I asked Talitha about the hammams, the Turkish baths, and she immediately said she would take me there the following afternoon.

I sat back, smiling. I would have gone anywhere with her, done anything. Every invitation gave me something to look forward to, a chance to get to know Talitha better, a chance to more fully envelop myself in her world.

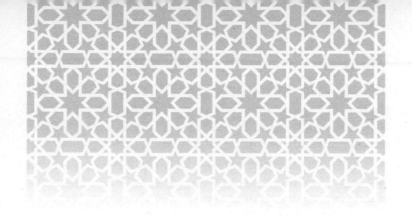

TWENTY-THREE

The hammams, or Turkish baths, had been around since the Ottoman Empire. They were a much-loved and crucial part of traditional Islamic life. Washing before prayer is part of everyone's life in Morocco, Talitha explained to me. After hearing about Dave, she had returned to the palace. Now, as we made our way through the streets, she explained our next adventure.

"We have to purify our bodies," she said. "God knows, mine needs purifying." She paused to laugh. "But it's more than that. It's unbelievably relaxing, and social. All the women meet at the hammam. Many of them don't have hot water, they don't have access to baths or showers like we do. This is their time to bathe, and meet friends, and get away from the daily chores. It's also a reminder of how fortunate *we* are." She squeezed my arm. "Lucky us, getting to spend time in this beautiful city,

welcomed by the Moroccans. I adore them, the most welcoming, wonderful people. They've made us so at home."

I thought about having no hot water. About stepping into
ice-cold baths, and I thought about feeling at home in Morocco. I understood what Talitha meant. There was a warmth
here, an easygoing, relaxed approach to life that allowed you
to shine, to truly be yourself. If you had told me, a month
ago, that I would feel more at home in Marrakech than anywhere in England, I would have laughed. And yet, it was true.

"Is the hammam…public?" I was nervous about stripping
off in front of other people.

She shot me a look. "Don't be scared. No one cares what
anyone looks like. I promise you no one's looking at us." I
found that hard to believe. Wherever we went, people stared at
Talitha. She couldn't hide her beauty or her magnetism. That
energy drew stares wherever she went. Even now, in a robe
with the hood pulled over her head, a bag containing sandals
and toiletries over her shoulder, everyone stared at her as we
made our way through the streets, men and women alike.

"What do we do?"

"You'll see." She grinned, taking my arm and stopping in
front of a low stone building, white walls and large arches, a
sign above the door: *Since 1562 Hammam Mouassine.*

"Here." She pulled me into an alleyway at the side and
dug around in her bag, pulling out a long, thin pipe made of
ivory and ornate silver, studded with jewels. It was an object
of beauty and danger, a pipe I now knew to be an opium pipe.
"This will make it even better."

She took the black tar-like opium out of a container and
put it in the bowl of the pipe, holding a flame until the gooey
substance was giving off smoke, and then she handed it to me.

I knew what to do.

Whatever she wanted.

★ ★ ★

Naked but for towels wrapped around ourselves and plastic sandals on our feet, we left the changing room for the steam rooms. Talitha giggled at my self-consciousness. Happily, it didn't last long. We were surrounded by naked women of all shapes and sizes, merrily chatting away with their friends as they headed to the steam rooms.

The opium started to hit about thirty minutes later. Everyone said that opium was a body high rather than a head high, and if that was true, I preferred the head high of kif. I didn't understand what the big fuss was with opium, or why Paul took it as much as he did before he progressed to heroin. Was I relaxed? Yes. Was I more relaxed than I would have been had we not taken any drugs at all? I will never know.

Most of the women around us carried buckets, their own toiletries and soap, but Talitha, who had brought the toiletries, had organized a private scrub, each of us having our own kessala. I had no idea what this meant, but imagined small ground kernels being massaged into my body, sloughing away all the dead skin, much like the facials Dottie and I sometimes gave ourselves at Warwickshire House, facials made of egg whites and porridge oats, that we massaged in and let dry before rinsing off with very hot water, then splashing with ice cold.

Talitha and I sat in the first steam room for a while, adjusting to the heat before moving to progressively hotter rooms. By the third room, as I sat on the wet tiled bench, I felt the sweat, first a few beads, then a trickle, then a flood pouring off my body.

Time passed slowly. I saw Talitha lying there with her eyes closed.

Two women came in, one for Talitha, one for me. She started to smear a liquid black soap all over my body, a soap Talitha explained was Moroccan soap.

"What do you think?" she called over from the other side of the steam room. "Isn't this delicious?"

"I've never had any kind of massage before. It's...strange. But nice."

"Never?" She was shocked, and I thought how much more shocked she would be if she saw the world from which I came. The small cottage in Evershot. My dad's slippers waiting by the fire. My stark shared bedroom in Warwickshire House, knickers and tights draped over the radiator. Oh, what a different world it was! And yet, her words from the other day came drifting back. Standing in the hot sun for hours and hours, terrified of guards sticking their fingers in her eyes. Beatings. Terror. Living in constant fear.

I knew which life I would rather have had, however much I wanted to be part of this one now.

The kessalas left us for a while, and I closed my eyes, lying on the hot tile. I opened them with surprise when I felt something tickling my leg. I looked down to see Talitha's hand moving up my thigh. Steam was swirling around as I looked at her, now standing next to me, looking into my eyes, waiting to see my reaction. I felt both confused and turned-on. Her touch was so soft as her hand moved higher and higher. I held my breath, unsure what was happening. My entire body felt like it was on fire as her small fingers traced their way up my inner thigh.

The door to the steam room opened, and the kessalas returned, chattering away, breaking the tension. Talitha giggled as if nothing had happened and returned to her own side of the steam room, leaving me trembling with uncertainty. I didn't know how far Talitha would have gone had they not come back in. I didn't know if she was seducing me, or playing with me to see my reaction.

And my own reaction shocked me. I hadn't known lust

until then, but suddenly I could feel it, every nerve and fiber tingling. I wanted the kessalas to leave, wanted it to be me and Talitha, wanted her hand to finish its journey. But the moment had gone.

The kessala started scrubbing my body, pausing only to show me the flaky layers of my dead skin on the glove, which I pretended to admire, all the while wishing it would stop. It wasn't unpleasant, but neither was it exactly comfortable, and certainly not the deliciously luxuriant cleanse I had imagined.

"Well?" said Talitha, when we were sipping sweet mint tea, getting ready to leave.

I wondered whether it had been the opium, whether I had imagined the whole thing.

"Well," I echoed, not knowing what to say, not knowing whether this was the opium, a dream or both.

That night was quiet. There were no parties at Sidi Mimoun, no hangers-on, no freeloaders, as Paul would say. Lissy, Eddie and Jimmy were supposed to be leaving in three days, but not, as planned, with me. I would be staying on, to watch over the workmen, watch over the house and feed the cats. I didn't know how I felt about staying on by myself. A part of me was frightened. I had never been alone, and although I knew everyone there was to know by that time, none of them were friends yet.

"Maybe I should bring you to Rome," Talitha said, wrapping her arms around me from behind and resting her chin on my shoulder. "I love having you around. You make me happy." She kissed me on the cheek, and I felt an explosion of joy in my chest. I had never had a friend like Talitha, had never known this kind of closeness with anyone. The British in me was reserved, cool, but it was impossible to stay reserved and cool around Talitha; her fire and warmth melted the steeliest of resolves.

The only person that didn't like Talitha, or so she told me, was Paul's father, Jean Paul Getty Senior. In my head, I thought of him as Old Paul, only because people who knew them from Rome referred to the old man as Big Paul.

Old Paul had not been impressed with Talitha, it seems. He liked Paul's first wife, Gail, very much. He had been estranged from all of them for years, but Gail had facilitated a reunion, and they had spent days together, during which time the old man had referred to them as "my little family." But Talitha was unable to charm him, and he was appalled at Paul's lifestyle here in Marrakech. He knew, I was told, about the drugs, the parties, the orgies, the drinking. He blamed Talitha for his son going off the rails. He didn't know, perhaps, that Paul's marriage to Gail wasn't broken up by Talitha, that Paul had been unhappy for years. This, his disappearing into his office, his mood swings, his depression may have been exacerbated by his drug and alcohol use, but it was there long before he met Talitha.

Years later, I ran into Gail in Rome, and introduced myself. We spent hours talking about Paul, about the Marrakech years, about the dream life that was so different from the way it looked to the outside world.

"He just stopped doing the things I wanted," she said, talking of her marriage to Paul, before she left him for the actor Lang Jeffries. "He had been warm, affectionate, but he started to lose interest in our marriage. It got very heavy. There was no lightness. I was much gayer. I loved going out, loved to dance. He slowly became a recluse, lost his vitality."

She might just have easily been talking of his marriage to Talitha. The reasons were different. With Gail, they had been living in Rome with their four children. Paul had taken a position running the Italian branch of his father's oil company, wearing a suit and tie every day, which he hated. He didn't want to be a businessman, he never wanted to be a business-man. But with Talitha, he retreated into alcohol, drugs, his classical music, his rare books and his art.

Those last few days at Sidi Mimoun, I barely saw him. I barely saw anyone other than Talitha. I think Dave breaking his hand, the potential for violence that we had barely man-aged to avoid, scared all of us a little. Things were quieter, then.

Eddie would call the retreat every afternoon for an update on Dave. He was sedated still, but calm. They were taper-ing him off the pain medication and he was doing as well as could be expected.

I didn't see Eddie and Lissy much. They were busy falling in love. I heard Lissy's laughter and watched them through the window as they continued to grow closer. It was no surprise at all to find them on the roof one day, Eddie lying on the cushions, Lissy straddling him, kissing him and holding his cheeks gently with her hands. I backed down the stairs quietly.

And I was glad. My experience with Talitha at the hammam had left me unsettled. I waited and hoped that something else would happen, that I would once again experience the ten-sion and anticipation, but Talitha was back to being my best friend again, and there was no hint of passion.

I would be lying if I said I wasn't disappointed. But I was also relieved. I wasn't the kind of woman who had these feel-ings for women. Surely this was all for the best.

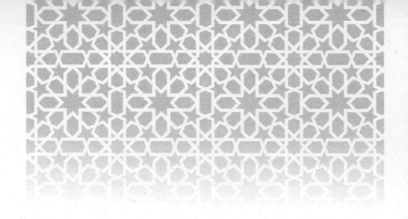

TWENTY-FOUR

"Let's have a quiet night tonight," Talitha said. "Let's cook."

I didn't cook. I had little reason to, had no idea how to make much other than a fried egg, but I happily joined her in the kitchen. She gave their old cook the afternoon off and seemed to know exactly what she was doing. Together, and much to my shocked delight, we produced a golden brown and perfectly crisp canard à l'orange.

We were dipping our fingers into the sauce, pronouncing it delicious, when we heard a deep "Bonsoir."

Talitha and I both turned to see Gerard in the doorway, lounging beautifully against the door frame, holding a bag out for Talitha.

"Oh, goodie!" She grabbed the bag, kissing him at the same time, and opened it, sniffing before swooning with pleasure. "Smell this!" She held the bag out to me.

"What is it?"

"The finest sativa you will ever have," said Gerard.

"Sativa?"

They both laughed. "How I love my innocent Cece," said Talitha, as I blushed. I didn't care that I didn't know what sativa was. I cared that I was loved. I cared that Talitha felt the same way about me as I felt about her.

I cared that Talitha said she loved me.

"Cannabis," drawled Gerard, but I already had my nose in the bag, already realized from the smell what it was.

"Gerard, you are a darling, thank you." Talitha turned to me. "I'm now going to make my world-famous chocolate cake. Actually, it's not really chocolate cake, it's hashish fudge. And…" She paused, with a small frown. "It's not really mine, it's Alice B. Toklas's recipe. Still, it's delicious, and you will love it. Thank you, darling, darling Gerard. Will you stay? You can't possibly leave until the cake is done."

Gerard was clearly not leaving. He was already sitting down at the small kitchen table, looking very much at home.

He brought out some white pills and shook them onto the table, bringing a razor blade out of his pocket. I watched, fascinated as he cut the pills and squashed them into a powder, chopping and chopping until it was as fine as icing sugar.

Talitha ignored him, whirling round the kitchen for a pestle and mortar, grinding cinnamon sticks and peppercorns, toasting coriander seeds and adding them to the mix, holding out a finger covered in paste for us to taste, Gerard first, who licked it off her finger and took her finger in his mouth, his eyes never leaving hers, and then, to my surprise, she did it again to me, this time putting her small finger in my mouth. She held my gaze, my cheeks flaming red, and I turned away.

I did lines of coke with both of them, ignoring the sour taste, the rancid drip in the back of my throat. It sobered us up enough to keep drinking. We turned the music up and smoked cigarettes, talking about the state of the world, how we were going to change it, how we, the youth of today, were the only ones who could.

We smoked and drank and talked, and as the afternoon slipped by, Gerard produced more and more drugs.

I ate the hashish fudge. I smoked the opium. I took the Mandrax. And I kept drinking.

We rolled the fudge into balls, laughing at the mess we made, and Gerard kept pulling Talitha onto his lap, his hands roaming all over her body. Finally, they sat, kissing, in front of me, and I was too far gone to be embarrassed, too far gone to remove myself.

Talitha put on "She's a Rainbow" by the Rolling Stones, and the two of them danced, Gerard twirling her round the kitchen and pulling her into his arms, as I stood and watched. Until he pulled me in, danced with me, spun me and dipped me as Talitha whooped with joy from the sidelines. I felt free, unencumbered, loose and sensual. I felt, for the first time, beautiful. When Gerard bent his head and put his lips on mine, when our tongues met and intertwined, when I felt a hand on my waist that was too small to be Gerard's, it didn't feel awkward or wrong, and I didn't feel embarrassed or ashamed. I didn't feel confused.

I felt like I belonged.

And it was everything I had never realized I wanted.

We broke apart, laughing and sighing, and pulled a large brass tray from the cabinets and stacked it with food.

We put the duck on the tray, with a plate of figs, of pastries, of oranges and olives and the hashish fudge. We carried vodka and champagne and bourbon, and followed Talitha up the wide marble staircase and into her bedroom. The bed was tucked behind carved stone pillars that soared to the high ceiling above. The bed itself was a tent, with thick white wool curtains lined with embroidered silks and velvets in the richest of colors. The bed's silks and velvets holding secrets that would never leave this room.

Gerard reclined on the bed, reaching for a nearby hookah, inviting us to join in.

We smoked and Gerard invited us to dance for him, and we did, Talitha lifting up silks from a chair, draping them around herself, around me, as she slid her hips in front of mine. She lifted my arms high in the air, bent her head and kissed me.

She untied the belt of my kimono and spun me slowly, unwrapping me, her tongue in my mouth each time I faced her.

"My gift," she whispered, as she pushed the kimono off my shoulders and pulled my underwear down, coming back up to kiss my breasts as I caressed her head, her hair, my body feeling as if it was one with hers.

She laid me back on the bed and kissed down my body until I felt myself melting into her, as Gerard watched, reaching out a hand to caress her, or me, until I didn't know whose hand was whose, whose mouth was whose, who was above, below, inside.

There were moments of sighing, soft breathing, quick breathing, moaning; moments where we laughed, paused, took more drugs, had more drinks. And finally, finally, as the soft light of dawn whispered its way into the room, we fell asleep, tangled up together, an arm here, a leg there, lips pressed against soft skin.

HASHISH FUDGE
BY ALICE B. TOKLAS

This is the food of Paradise—of Baudelaire's Artificial Paradises: It might provide an entertaining refreshment for a Ladies' Bridge Club or a chapter meeting of the DAR (Daughters of the American Revolution). In Morocco, it is thought to be good for warding off the common cold and in damp winter weather and is, indeed, more effective if taken with large quantities of hot mint tea. Euphoria and brilliant storms of laughter; ecstatic reveries and extensions of one's personality on several simultaneous planes are to be complacently expected. Almost anything Saint Theresa did, you can do better if you can bear to be ravished by *un évanouissement reveillé* (evanescent dream).

Take 1 teaspoon black peppercorns, 1 whole nutmeg, 4 average sticks of cinnamon, 1 teaspoon coriander. These should all be pulverized in a mortar. About a handful each of stoned dates, dried figs, shelled almonds and peanuts: chop these and mix them together. A bunch of cannabis sativa can be pulverized. This along with the spices should be dusted over the mixed fruit and nuts, kneaded together. About a cup of sugar dissolved in a big pat of butter. Rolled into a cake and cut into pieces or made into balls about the size of a walnut, it should be eaten with care. Two pieces are quite sufficient.

Obtaining the cannabis may present certain difficulties, but the variety known as cannabis sativa grows as a common weed, often unrecognized, everywhere in Europe, Asia and parts of Africa; besides being cultivated as a crop for the manufacture of rope. In the Americas, while often discouraged, its cousin, called cannabis indica, has been observed even in city window boxes. It should be picked and dried as soon as it has gone to seed and while the plant is still green.

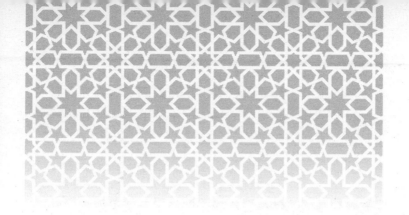

TWENTY-FIVE

I woke up coughing and spluttering, a black liquid streaming out of my mouth.

My eyesight was hazy and it felt like I was underwater. I knew people were in the room, but I just wanted to go back to sleep. When the coughing fit was over, I managed to focus on Jimmy, several Jimmys, his face swimming in front of me, looking both angry and frightened.

"Drink this," he said, pressing a spoon up against my mouth. I closed my eyes, wanting to drift back down to the lovely nothingness. Jimmy shook me, forced the spoon between my lips and tipped my head back. I reluctantly swallowed as something gritty slid down the back of my throat.

This time I wasn't coughing. Everything came back up. I vomited all over the bed.

"Good girl," said Jimmy. "One more."

I groaned and tried to go back to sleep, but he forced another spoon into my mouth, more liquid down my throat, then made me get up.

"You take her into the shower," he said to a hazy figure in the background. "Hold her under cold water until she's properly awake." Lissy stepped forward, guiding me into Talitha and Paul's bathroom.

She sat me on the tiled floor, my back against the mosaic step that surrounded the bath, and pulled a French jet hose off the wall, drenching me with ice-cold water as I yelped.

She didn't stop.

I was soaking, covered in goose bumps, my teeth chattering. Eventually, she turned the water off, grabbed a towel and wrapped me up, holding me close.

"Tack Gud," she kept murmuring. *"Tack Gud."*

"What are you saying?" I mumbled into her shoulder, still tired, but the drowsiness had dissipated.

"Thank God," Lissy said, standing back and looking at me before bursting into tears.

"What's going on? Why are you crying?"

Lissy wiped the tears off her face. "We thought you were dead, Cece. Do you not realize that you overdosed?"

"What?" I almost laughed, the very concept of me overdosing was ludicrous.

"Cece, Talitha got up this morning thinking you were asleep, and went to the market. Jimmy was the one who was worried. He said you're usually up early, and he didn't like the fact that he hadn't seen you. You weren't in your bed, so he looked for you, and finally, finally, he found you in Talitha's room. Cece, you were gray, and your lips and fingertips were turning blue. If Jimmy hadn't decided to look for you, you'd be dead. What did you do last night?"

"I don't know. I think everything." I was shocked into silence. Lissy gave me a reassuring hug before shaking her head.

"You're an innocent, Cece. It's different for us. We've been doing this for ages. I don't think you have the constitution, and certainly not for these kinds of drugs. Promise me you won't do this again?"

I saw, suddenly, a cut-up montage of scenes from the night before. White lines of fine powder disappearing up our noses, pills of different shapes and sizes, vodka, pipes, smoke, laughter, skin, caressing, mouths.

"Where's Talitha?"

"She's still out. She doesn't know. Look, we're all going back to England in a couple of days. I know Talitha asked if you'd stay and help out here in Morocco, but I don't know if that's a good idea. Jimmy wants to send you home today."

"No!" I almost shouted, my horror was so great. I knew that I would never be as happy anywhere else, that everywhere would pale in comparison. Even London, as groovy as it had become, wasn't a patch on Marrakech. I never wanted to leave.

Lissy sighed and shook her head. "I knew you'd say no to leaving today. But you are coming home with the rest of us the day after tomorrow. Let's go and get you dressed. I think you ought to get some food inside you." She shook her head. "I can't believe how close you came."

"What was that stuff Jimmy gave me?"

"Our miracle drug. Activated charcoal. This isn't the first time this has happened. Jimmy's had to rescue all of us at some point. I overdosed on bloody sleeping pills once, and Dave was so out of it he had no idea. Jimmy put his fingers down my throat to make me throw up."

"Really?" I felt better knowing that this wasn't unusual, I hadn't embarrassed myself in ways that were unrecoverable.

Still I had never felt quite so ashamed. I didn't know how I would ever be able to look Jimmy in the eye again.

"Really. We've all been there. We owe Jimmy everything."

Jimmy wasn't around for me to thank. I was lying on a daybed in one of the alcoves off the main salon, admiring the views of the Atlas Mountains glimpsed through a window, when Talitha came in.

"Cece!" She jumped on the bed and threw her arms around me. "Oh, my God! I just heard. Thank God you're okay. Oh, Cece. I feel terrible. I don't know what to say. This is all my fault."

I was relieved that there was no awkwardness between us, and no immediate acknowledgment of our affair.

"It's not your fault at all. I'm a grown-up. I just overdid it. Luckily I'm absolutely fine."

"I should never have let Gerard come over. Paul always says he's a bad seed. This wouldn't have happened if I hadn't allowed him to stay. I'm so sorry." Her face, normally shining, was creased with concern. I felt a deep urge to reassure her.

"It's fine, Talitha. Don't worry. Please. Let's just pretend it never happened."

I don't know what I meant by that. Was I talking about the drugs only? I remembered her kissing me, slipping the kimono off my shoulders, as if in a fever dream. I was filled with lust, regret, hope, fear and a terrible sense of foreboding. I was now aware of the danger. Not just of the drugs, but of all of it. The lifestyle, the exuberance, the parties. And Talitha.

It was all so confounding. I hadn't known real adult attraction until then. I shuddered with lust every time an image from the night before flitted through my mind. Talitha's tongue, her scent, her softness. I was so drawn to her, even though I didn't want to be, not in that way.

Now, of course, I can admit that I was in love with her.

Then, I only knew that I didn't want to leave her, that I felt a responsibility as her protector of sorts, and that even though I was asking her to pretend it never happened, another part of me wanted it to keep happening. It wasn't about sex. It was about comfort. And solace. And home. I wanted to become part of her. I wanted her to become part of me.

"I'm going to keep a better eye on you." She wagged a finger in my face. "I don't want anything to happen to you, ever."

"Okay." I gave in to her embrace, and out of the corner of my eye I caught sight of a figure walking slowly into the main salon. For a moment I thought it might be a hallucination. I closed my eyes, but when I opened them again he was still there.

What on earth was he doing *here*?

"Benji?" I jumped up, never happier to see his familiar ginger hair and freckles. "What on earth are you doing here?"

"Ducking and diving." He came over with a huge grin, allowing me to give him a big hug. "I'm joking. I'm not ducking and diving." He shot a look at Talitha, and I knew he wouldn't tell me the truth until we were alone together.

"I'm sorry. This is Talitha. This is her place."

Sweet Benji dropped his wide boy act for Talitha. "Goodness," he said, extending a hand to shake hers. "I've never seen anything quite like it. It's spectacularly beautiful. How do you do. I'm Benji. I'm an old friend of Claire's."

"Claire?" Talitha looked at me with a raised eyebrow, and I blushed.

"Everyone calls me Cece now," I explained to Benji.

"I can't call you Cece. I've spent my whole life calling you Claire. How am I supposed to change now?"

"It's fine," I mumbled. "You can call me Claire."

"Where are you staying?" Talitha asked. "When did you arrive? What are your plans?"

Benji laughed. "I'm staying at a riad owned by a friend of my father's. You may know them. Lord and Lady Comstock?"

"Of course I know them! But you can't stay there with old fuddy-duddies! You must come here instead! We have lots of guest rooms, and Cece will tell you that this is the place where everything happens." She shot me a look. "Mostly good, but sometimes bad. We love a redhead." She looked at his hair, and I suppressed a chuckle, for her husband's hair was also a dark red. "It's fun, fun, fun! Stay! You'll love it!"

I thought Benji would decline, but much to my surprise he thanked her, and before we knew it a man was walking through the courtyard with Benji's suitcases, putting him in the room next to mine.

"We'll have to celebrate tonight." Talitha clapped her hands, running off to find the cook. "Let's have a party on the terrace! But not you." She turned and gave me a stern look. "I mean, you can party, but not too hard." Then she left.

Benji sat on the bench outside his room and looked at me with a strange expression I couldn't read.

"What is it?" I asked, sitting next to him.

"I didn't understand, but now I do. She is entirely irresistible."

My cheeks flamed red. What did he know? How did he know? Did everyone know about the ménage à trois the night before?

Benji sighed. "Jimmy called me."

I stared at him, shocked. "Jimmy? How does Jimmy even know you?"

"We met at Robbie's birthday party, remember? Just before you all piled into the car, I got nervous about the crowd you were running with. I slipped Jimmy my phone number, and told him to call me if ever he needed anything. Specifically, what I meant was to call me if you were ever in trouble. He called me this morning."

"But…" I had so many questions, I didn't know where to start, so I began with the stupidest one. "How are you even here so quickly?"

"Our neighbor has a plane. I got him to fly me over."

I started to laugh. "Benji. Only you would have a neighbor who has a plane, who's able to fly you somewhere at a moment's notice."

"True. But even if I didn't have a neighbour with a plane, I would have found a way to get here. Jimmy's worried about you."

"What did he say?"

"That he thinks you're in too deep. He says that as glamorous and exciting as this world is, it's dangerous. Too many drugs, too much excitement. He's a good chap. I'm grateful that someone's looking out for you."

I loved that Benji was here, that he cared enough to drop everything and show up. I didn't need him though. I had grown up immeasurably and was proving to myself that I could make it alone in this world.

"Benji." I laid a hand on his arm. "I truly love seeing you, and it's wonderful that you dropped everything and came out, but it's not scary here. You'll see tonight. It's all rather wonderful. Have I overdone it a bit? Yes. But I don't intend to keep doing that. I had a scare last night, and I'm definitely going to avoid doing that again."

"I heard," Benji said. This time he wasn't laughing.

"I'm fine," I reassured him.

"But you almost weren't."

"What did Robbie say?"

"I didn't tell him I was coming. What I'd like to do is take you home with me."

My face fell. "I can't, Benji. Talitha and Paul have offered me a job, and I love it here. I'm going to stay. For the time being, at least."

Benji sighed deeply before leaning forward. "Claire, this is magical and wonderful, and everything a perfect holiday should be, but that's the thing about holidays. They don't last. They shouldn't last, because they'll always turn into something else if you stay."

"I'm not Claire anymore," I said sternly. "I'm Cece."

"Fine. Cece. I think you need to come home."

"I can't leave," I said.

"I understand how compelling this life is, how compelling her world is." He paused. "How compelling *she* is. But this isn't your life, Cl... Cece. You need to get back to your life."

I thought then of my walk with Talitha through the gardens of La Mamounia. Her unique combination of vulnerability and strength as she described her childhood, the pain and trauma that she had managed to put behind her to become this shining light, the center of every room. And I thought of the other Talitha, the one who linked her arm through mine as we walked the souk, who felt like the best friend I had never known I wanted, the best friend I hadn't missed, until I met her.

We were two motherless daughters who had found each other. Whatever happened last night between us... I wanted it to happen again, and I didn't. It felt messy and confusing and bewildering. I didn't know what it meant, if indeed, it meant anything at all. The only thing I knew for certain was that I had never met anyone like her. And she needed me. I knew she needed me.

I couldn't possibly leave.

"Maybe you're right." I decided to leave Benji's statement unanswered. "And maybe you're wrong. Everyone's leaving in a couple of days. Why don't you stay until then, and then we'll decide."

Benji looked relieved. "Okay," he said, "that sounds like a good plan."

"If we've only got a couple of days here, you have to come and see the souk. Why don't we go for a walk now, before dinner."

"I'd love to," he said, standing up and offering a hand to help me up.

Lovely Benji, I thought, walking through the courtyards and showing him where everything was, appreciating how he appreciated everything, how much he cared.

However much he tried to be one of the Krays, he was unfailingly a gentleman until the end.

The souks were entirely different with Benji. Walking through with Talitha I had been the willing student, Talitha the master. Now, with Benji, I was showing him things, explaining how it all worked, without realizing how much knowledge I had acquired.

I took him to the spice market, to show him the pyramids of bright yellow turmeric and red cayenne. I took him to the eucalyptus stand, and watched him laugh in delight as the eucalyptus crystal mixed with water and exploded his sinuses in pleasure. I was the one pulling him out of the way as the donkeys, horses, camels and goats clattered past. Night was falling as we made our way back through Djemaa El Fna. The scent of grilled lamb wafted through the square.

"It's a feast for the senses." Benji shook his head.

"It gets even better." I laughed, leading him back to the palace.

Benji got pulled in. Of course he got pulled in. One minute he was there, telling me he had come to take me home, the next he was sitting next to Talitha on the cushions, laughing with her under the glass ceiling on the roof, a million stars glittering like diamonds, candelabras lighting up the faces of all the people I had come to know and love.

But now I felt cautious around Talitha. More drawn to her

in some ways, naturally, but also more frightened of getting lost in her glow. I sat in the minza on the roof, and laughed and chatted, trying to quell the ripples of fear. There were hookahs everywhere, and I may have been smoking kif, but that was all I was planning to do that night. I did not want a repeat of the overdose.

Instead I eavesdropped. Lissy was charming Yves, telling him about a film part she had just been offered, attempting to persuade him to do the costumes. Christopher Gibbs was there, Bill Willis, La Comtesse. Her son, however, was not there. I was relieved.

I had no wish to see Gerard again.

Paul, who had been scarce that day, sat next to me.

"I heard that you had a scare this morning," he said softly. I saw real concern in his eyes. "I'm worried about you. This... lifestyle is not for everyone."

"I'm fine, Paul. Look at me!" I stood up. "I'm perfect!" And I twirled, looking down to see the upturned faces of people I now loved, their eyes shining in the candlelight.

"Dancing!" Talitha clapped her hands, and soon there was music, and, with her signature dirty laugh, Talitha pulled Benji up from the cushions and pulled him onto the low table, where she did an incredibly beautiful, sensual belly dance. Benji awkwardly tried to copy her, grinning, but I was pretty sure he couldn't wait for it to be over.

"How's Dave?" I asked Eddie, when the first course had been removed.

"He's doing well," he said. "I spoke to them today. They've stopped sedating him and apparently he's very calm. On his best behavior, which is a relief."

"What's your plan?" I couldn't help myself, I shot a look at Lissy, as Eddie laughed.

"Do you mean, how do I tell him that Lissy and I got together?"

"Well, that wasn't all I meant, but yes, that's certainly part of it."

He shrugged. "It's time for us to make some hard decisions about the future of the band. I wish Dave well, but I don't think any of us can do this anymore. I've spoken to Steve. As the manager, he makes the final decisions. He's going to fire Dave when we get back to London. The good news is, Nick Whitstone is looking for a new band."

My mind was blank. "Who?"

"He's the lead singer of Nick's Maestros?"

I had seen them on *Ready Steady Go!* and *Top of the Pops*. I knew exactly who they were. Nick Whitstone was darkly charismatic, and handsome. He would be perfect.

I frowned. "What happens to Nick's Maestros without Nick?"

"They become The Maestros?" He laughed. "Don't tell anyone though. Not until it's a done deal."

Jimmy appeared in the sunroom, making his way over to us. He leaned down and whispered something in Eddie's ear, and Eddie put down his drink.

"Fuck," he said. "You're joking, aren't you?"

Jimmy said something else, low. It was Jimmy's form of whispering, but I heard him. Eddie nodded, and Jimmy left.

"Is everything okay?"

"It will be." He picked up his glass and downed the bourbon in one, reaching for the wine in the middle of the table and drinking that. "It never fucking rains," he said, raising his glass. "Cheers."

"Cheers." I drank my own glass. I wanted to know what they had been talking about, but I knew it wasn't my place to ask.

As usual, there was a mountain of food—spiced lamb and wood-grilled chicken, aubergine and salads, breads and couscous. My desire to eat everything in sight, a compulsion that had fueled my growing up under Linda's critical eye, had disappeared in this wondrous place. Perhaps it was the drugs. Perhaps it was feeling fully accepted. But I no longer had an empty hole inside that needed to be filled. I kept catching Benji's eye, who would grin at me from across the table, shaking his head. I knew he understood why I couldn't go home.

After the main courses, came the mahjoun, and the sweets, and the pastries, and the opium pipes, and then the entertainers. The dancers, the magicians, the acrobats.

My life, I thought, lying back looking at the stars through the glass roof, will never be as *alive* as it is right now. There was Benji, entranced by Talitha, entranced by it all; there was Bill Willis, drinking his body weight in Jack Daniel's, there was Christopher Gibbs, charming everyone around him, there were Yves and Pierre, sitting with La Comtesse, who had barely eaten anything, had instead chain-smoked Sobranie cigarettes throughout the meal. There was Paul, who smiled at the end of the table, pretending to be interested, before drifting away back to his room. There were Lissy and Eddie, no longer keeping their budding romance a secret, cuddling up together on the cushions.

"This is perfection," Benji said to me, unable to stop smiling, although whether it was because he was stoned or happy I couldn't tell.

"It looks like it, doesn't it," I said. But looks, I thought to myself, with more than a hint of irony, weren't everything. Not by a very long shot.

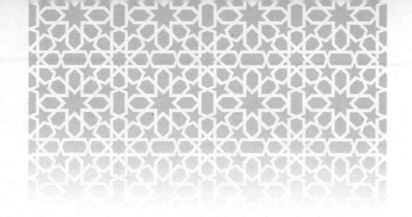

TWENTY-SIX

I went out for an early morning walk by myself, before anyone was awake, before the souk was even open. I was aware that I was avoiding everyone, and that in itself scared me. I had been so entranced, so in love with the extraordinary bubble that was the Morocco I was experiencing through Talitha's eyes, I didn't understand why suddenly I had the urge to be alone, to escape.

The only person I wanted to see, the thought of whom was enough to eventually get me out of bed, was Benji. Benji wasn't Morocco. Benji was safety, and comfort, and certainty. Benji was *home*, the only one I wanted to spend time with. It wasn't that I was any less drawn to Talitha. If anything, I was more drawn to her, but it came with a tinge of fear. I understood now the trouble I could get into; I understood that excitement came with risk, that perhaps all of them had been right when they had called me innocent, teased me about not being able to keep up with them.

They were right. I could keep up with them as long as the lifestyle remained an idea. Once it became a reality, once I attempted to dive into it headfirst, into all their life had to offer, it almost killed me. I had no wish for that to happen again. However sophisticated I thought I was, however much I believed I had reinvented myself, they had all seen beyond Cece to Claire. That's why they called me an innocent. They were right.

I felt such a fool.

Eventually, I returned to the room, bathed and dressed, then walked through the various courtyards and salons, looking for Benji. I didn't see a soul other than the workmen and the houseboys, sweeping the leaves and debris out of the courtyards, cleaning out the fireplaces and setting orange wood in for the fires to be lit that night.

Paul, I thought, hearing classical music drifting across the courtyard. He'll know where everyone is. I made my way to his room, hoping I wasn't interrupting again. I was relieved when he called for me to come in as soon as I had knocked, more relieved to see that it was early enough in the day that he was not off his face on drugs, but drinking coffee and in a good mood.

"Paul! I'm so sorry to disturb you but I can't find anyone. Do you by any chance know where Benji is?"

I was glad that I had caught Paul alone. I felt in need of some steadiness and comfort.

"Ah. The delightful Cece. Come in, come in. Have a seat. Your nice young man, Benji." Paul's eyes twinkled.

"He's not my nice young man," I protested. "He is a nice young man though. Just not mine."

Paul didn't respond, just grinned.

"I know what you're thinking. You're thinking the lady doth protest too much," I quoted Paul's words back to him, not knowing at the time that they were, in fact, Shakespeare. I had heard him say the same thing to Talitha a few days ago, and was gratified to now see him roar with laughter.

"You have been paying attention, little Cece, haven't you. Have you read *Hamlet*?"

I shook my head. The only Shakespeare I had read was at school, *Twelfth Night* and *A Midsummer Night's Dream*.

"Would you like to? I have a copy here somewhere. Shall I find it for you?"

"I would love that, but I probably won't be able to start reading it until everyone's gone and I get some time to myself."

"Ah…" Paul sat back in his chair. "I was rather wondering about that. Given what happened the other night, we would all completely understand if you decided not to stay."

I wondered whether he was referring to my night of passion with Talitha and Gerard, or my overdose. I wondered if it mattered. I felt as if I had disappointed them all. I had never been good at hiding my feelings, and my face fell.

"Oh, my dear. I didn't mean to upset you. It is entirely up to you. I think both Talitha and I are a little concerned that this is all too much for you."

I felt the tears well up in my eyes and tried to blink them away, but it was no use. I didn't feel like beautiful Cece, sitting there in Paul's room. I felt like Claire, who was being told she wasn't good enough, she didn't fit in, she didn't have a right to any of this. Before I could help it, a tear escaped and trickled down my cheek.

"Oh, Cece." Paul came to sit next to me and put a comforting arm around my shoulders. "I didn't mean to make you cry. If it means that much to you…"

"No, it's okay," I tried to reassure him. "It's not that. It's…" I stopped. I didn't really know what it was, perhaps a mixture of disappointment, rejection and relief.

I tried to find the words, and turned my head to look at Paul. "I don't want to let you down," I said.

"It's not me you have to worry about," he replied. "And whatever you decide will be the right decision. Take your time. There's no rush. How does that sound?"

I nodded and swallowed my tears. That was what I needed to hear.

I didn't see Benji for the rest of that day. I didn't see anyone. I walked the gardens at La Mamounia by myself to sort through my feelings, find a sense of equilibrium again in this peaceful oasis.

On the way back, a man with two gold teeth whispered at me from a corner. "Hashish?" he whistled, between his teeth. "You want kif?"

Yes. I wanted kif. I gave him money and floated through the souk, back to the house. By the time I got back, it was cocktail hour, and I no longer cared about anything.

I made my way up to the roof, where a crowd of people were already sitting, drinking, getting stoned. They were having an intense conversation about astral projection and existing on other planes, about the possibilities the universe offered once you were able to expand your consciousness.

Seeing Benji among them was a massive comfort. Whatever else might happen here in Marrakech, as long as Benji was around, I knew I would be okay. His face lit up when he saw me, and I thought back to all those years I had adored him. I wondered, for a fleeting second, whether the tables might be turned?

Benji moved over on his cushion, making space for me, and I sat down next to him, grateful for his solidity and familiarity.

"Are you okay?"

I nodded, tempted for a second to tell him everything. What had happened with Talitha, my confusion. I opened my mouth to speak, but something caught my eye, a figure appearing on the rooftop that put my senses on high alert. He was shrouded in darkness, and I was so stoned, it took me a while to realize who it was.

"Dave!"

I don't know if I called out a greeting or a warning. I do know that Lissy and Eddie, who had been curled up together opposite us, jumped apart, as if they had been stung, as Dave launched toward them, letting out a cry that sounded like a wounded animal.

"What the fuck?" Eddie scrambled to get up as Dave ran toward him. Suddenly Dave was on the floor. He had tripped over Benji's leg and was sprawled on the ground.

He picked himself up, shadows dancing on his face as he loomed forward, but this time, Benji leaped up and held him back. "You fucking traitor," he spat at Eddie. "I should have known."

"Dave," Eddie said. He stayed sitting, his voice calm. "What are you doing here? You're supposed to be at the retreat."

"Fuck the retreat," he spat. "Fuck you. And fuck you." He looked at Lissy.

"Now, now," Benji said.

"She's a fucking slag."

"That's enough," said Benji, struggling to contain Dave. He looked around the table. "I could do with some help here."

"Where the fuck is Jimmy?" Eddie muttered, looking around the terrace, but Jimmy was nowhere to be seen.

Christopher got up, and Bill, who was more than a little

unsteady on his feet, and two young men from Rome who had shown up that evening. They all helped Dave down the stairs. We heard him continuing to shout even when he'd reached the courtyard.

"I don't know what to do." Talitha looked worried. "Shall I call the retreat?"

Eddie sank his head in his hands. "Shit. This was exactly what I didn't want to happen. I knew he'd left. They let Jimmy know earlier. They'd stopped sedating him thinking that he was finally stable, but that wily little fucker was just pretending. He waited for everyone to go to bed before escaping. I should have known he'd do this. When Jimmy told me they'd phoned to say he'd disappeared, I sent him out to look for him. I was worried he'd just show up. Christ. What a nightmare."

Talitha laid a hand on his arm. "Let me deal with it. We'll be fine. I can put him in a guest room and we can lock him in, if you feel unsafe. Why don't we do that, and we can deal with it in the morning?"

Eddie looked grateful. "You would do that?"

"What else can we do? We can't just send him away. I can phone the retreat and see if they have someone to pick him up, but if they can't, we'll keep him safe until tomorrow."

"Thank you, Talitha." Both Eddie and Lissy looked relieved.

I decided to go to bed soon after that. I didn't have the energy or the wherewithal to stay up all night, to have another crazy drug-filled night. The kif had made me sleepy, I was coming off the adrenaline high of Dave Boland bursting in, and all I could think about was being safely tucked up between crisp, cool sheets.

To my horror, as we were walking through the salon, I glimpsed Gerard sitting on one of the chairs by himself. I didn't want to see him again, but there he was, and there was no avoiding him. Benji was with me, walking me to my room. I saw no choice but to introduce them, praying Gerard wouldn't mention the other night.

"I'm off to bed. An early night," I said quickly, hoping to cut the conversation short.

"I should be doing the same," said Gerard. "I just have to drop something off."

"You know Talitha is upstairs on the roof?"

"Oh, it's not Talitha I'm looking for. Do you by any chance know where Jimmy is?"

"I haven't seen him. I'm so sorry."

"It's nice to meet you," said Benji, who would never have said that had he known anything about Gerard.

Benji walked me to my room. I turned and saw the locked door to Dave's room, and all was quiet. I hoped he was asleep. I hoped he was peaceful, that it would all be better by daylight.

I looked at Benji in the moonlight. "You get it, don't you. The magic of Marrakech, of Sidi Mimoun. The magic of Talitha and Paul, of this world. You understand why I want to stay."

Benji sighed. "Of course I get it. How could I not? Talitha casts a spell that bewitches everyone. But..." He paused. "I still don't think you should stay. There's too much drama here. Too much unpredictability. I know some of these people, and I know something of this world. It never ends well. Cla... Cece. I think you need to come home."

"I know." I stood on my tiptoes and did something I dreamed of doing as a ten-year-old, a twelve-year-old, a six-teen-year-old. I kissed Benji on the lips. When I pulled away, he looked startled.

"Thank you for taking care of me," I said quietly, walking into my bedroom and closing the door before I could do anything I might regret.

★ ★ ★

I woke up once in the early hours of the morning. I heard a noise, the sound of a door opening, and went to the window, opening the shutters quietly, peering out. The sun was coming up. I watched bleary-eyed as Jimmy let himself into Dave's room and emerged a few seconds later, propping Dave up, Dave's arm draped around Jimmy's neck, stoned out of his mind. As they walked, Dave's foot kicked one of the lanterns, which tipped over onto the mud, the glass making a sharp cracking sound which neither of them noticed as Jimmy dragged Dave across the mosaic tile. Good, I remember thinking to myself. Jimmy takes care of everything. He must have given Dave something to calm him down before returning him to the retreat. I went back to sleep, unburdened.

When I woke up again, I felt decent. I had only smoked some kif, eaten a little mahjoun. I wasn't hungover, was ready for the dawn of a new day, excited that Benji was here. He had taken my thoughts away from Talitha, and my passion for her, my guilt, my concerns about what the other night meant had diminished.

Who was I, anyway, that felt the need to look after a woman I barely knew? Talitha was a grown-up; it wasn't my responsibility, and she was more than capable of looking after herself. Benji was the exact distraction I needed, and I had never been more grateful to him. I loved being the teacher with Benji and decided to show him more of Marrakech today, astounded that for the first time in my life, I seemed to be more worldly than he.

Perhaps I would take him to Yves and Pierre's house. They were living at Dar El Hanch, House of the Serpent, which I hadn't yet seen but heard was sweet and, naturally, beautifully decorated. Perhaps I would take him to visit Bill Willis, or to the infamous Villa Schiff to see La Comtesse, for I hadn't yet seen the famous gardens there.

I threw a robe on and walked out, inhaling the orange blossom and jacaranda, realizing that I *could* do this; I could stay here. Maybe I was more of an innocent than the others, but I wanted to be in Marrakech; I had never known who I was before now, had never felt as much my own *self*. Everyone was leaving, which left me bereft and a little relieved. There would be no more temptations or mistakes. I would deal with the loneliness.

Despite what had happened with Talitha, despite my confusion about it, I knew we could all put it behind us and establish a respectful working relationship. The pros far outweighed the cons.

The thing about loneliness is that you don't often know how lonely you are until you find the people, or the circumstances, that make you feel whole. The loss of my mother had left such a void, but now I felt it growing smaller. I was learning that I was enough. I didn't have to lose weight or iron my hair to be accepted. Paul and Talitha, Lissy and Eddie saw who I truly was, and that made me realize, for the first time, that I was lovable.

Would I still feel that way once everyone had left? Mostly, despite the craziness, despite trying to tell myself it would be a relief, I knew that deep down I wanted things to stay much the same. I didn't want Talitha and Paul to go back to Rome, nor did I want Lissy and Eddie, my new family, to go back to London. I didn't want Jimmy to leave, this lovely man who felt like my protector. In a strange way, I didn't even want Dave to leave. I wanted everything to stay the same.

I made my way through the guest courtyard, under the giant arch and into the main courtyard, thinking I would perhaps attempt to make Eddie's sausages myself. Out of the corner of my eye, I saw something that felt...wrong.

I have replayed this moment many, many times, and still don't understand how it took me a while to decipher what I was looking at.

There were so many colors there, you see. The mosaic that Bill Willis had installed, the hand-painted wooden doors and shutters, the intricate carvings, the stained glass windows. There were the pillows, and the beds, and the palm fronds, and the ferns, and the pepper trees, and the banana leaves and the jacaranda above. The green floor tiles, and the purple blossom, and the turquoise and gold of the peacocks that were strutting around. The orange and brown of the tabby cat that had adopted Talitha. A flash of blue, that, out of the corner of my eye, I somehow knew, didn't belong.

I turned my head before the dread had settled in.

In the large fountain, in the middle of the main courtyard, floating facedown, his embroidered shirt billowing around him in the water, barefoot, was Dave Boland.

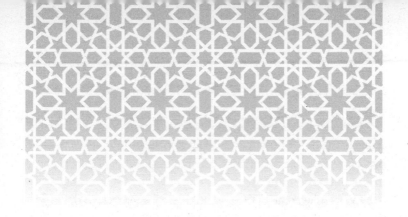

TWENTY-SEVEN

The shock was so great that it is hard for me to describe the next few days. The press descended upon Marrakech, setting up camp in the alley outside the riads. Thank the Lord for those high walls and those thick doors. On Paul's instruction, Si Mohammed refused to allow entry for anyone unless they were expected. Various friends showed up to see how we were faring, shouldering their way through the crowd of photographers, heads down, hoods on, slipping through the tiniest crack, the most that Si Mohammed allowed.

As for us, we huddled together in the main salon, trying to find comfort in the endless sweet mint tea and mahjoun, in each other, but there was little comfort to be found.

The police had come, and the coroner. They ruled Dave's death a suicide. Lissy, who struggled between love and relief that she had got away, screamed at the coroner when he said that.

"It wasn't suicide!" she shouted. "I know him. He would never." Eddie tried to put his arms around her, tried to lead her away, but she shook him off. He stepped back, wounded, unsure of what to do next.

"Do you hear me?" she repeated, stepping toward the coroner, who was Moroccan, who didn't understand exactly what she was saying but understood the emotion. He bowed his head and said the few English words he knew. "Sorry. Sorry."

I found Lissy alone on the roof. She was curled up at the end of one of the banquettes, hugging her knees, holding a cigarette, her face turned to the wall. I sat next to her and put a hand on her back to let her know she wasn't alone.

I didn't know what else to do.

She turned and buried herself in my arms, my thin cotton shirt collecting her tears. We sat like that for a long time, until the rising and falling of her body slowed down, her sobs subsiding, and she pulled away, her face blotchy and tear streaked.

"This is my fault." Her voice was flat and broken. "If it wasn't for me, Dave would still be alive."

I laid a hand on her arm. "Lissy, don't. This isn't your fault."

"Of course it is. If I hadn't been with Eddie, this would never have happened. I can't believe it. I just… How can Dave be dead?"

We sat in silence for a while. There was nothing I could say to make it better, so I sat, smoking cigarettes with her, grateful for the mint tea Talitha had sent up. There was something I couldn't quite understand, not quite a thought, more of a whisper at the back of my mind, something that wanted to be known, but I wouldn't let the whisper be heard.

I believed that Dave was volatile and unstable. Unpredictable. These days we would say he had mental health issues. These days, he might have been medicated to even out his mood swings, his paranoia. But was that paranoia and rage enough to commit suicide? Perhaps. There were other pieces of the puzzle that didn't seem to quite fit together, but I accepted that someone like Dave could so easily have wanted to disappear. And perhaps, this was his ultimate punishment. To take his own life so Lissy would never be able to fully enjoy hers, for of course he would have known she would blame herself.

What demons he had, Dave Boland. The world knew none of it. I had known none of it when he was a poster on my wall. With his angelic blond curls and pretty boy looks, he seemed to be the perfect man; a mix of rock and roll, and boy next door. Oh, how little I knew back then.

Benji appeared on the roof, walking toward us slowly, carefully.

"I just wanted to check that you were both okay," he said. "Can I get you anything?"

I was about to say that we were fine, when Lissy said, "Vodka."

Benji turned to go and get vodka, as gratitude washed over me. This gorgeous, glamorous life had become so dark so suddenly that I needed stability.

Watching him walk away, I also realized how much security his background gave him. He may have tried to hide it with his cod cockney accent, but he couldn't hide that he fit in here; he fit in with millionaires, and rock stars, and old Etonians, and fashion designers, and shopgirls, and drug dealers, and European countesses whom no one had ever heard of, and young counts of no account.

He fit in with everyone because he was brought up believing he was born into superiority. And that, combined with his inherent humility and desire to have come from the diametric opposite of the background from which he came, gave him a comfort in his skin and a desire to please that made him welcome everywhere.

His red hair and freckles, the grin that lit up his face, his way of putting everyone he met instantly at ease, helped.

Talitha came up later and joined us on the roof, followed by Eddie, Benji and Paul. Lissy pulled herself together, and for a few hours that evening it was almost as if it hadn't happened. We talked, and drank, and smoked, and ate mahjoun, but no one touched anything heavier. Dave's death had shaken us into a new awareness.

Or so I thought.

"Can you go and see how Talitha is doing?" Paul whispered to me at one point. "I'm worried about her. She has already experienced so many terrible things."

I walked over and sat down next to Talitha, who was chatting quietly with Benji. "Are you okay?" I asked. "I'm so sorry this happened in your house. I can't imagine how that feels."

She leaned forward, out of Benji's earshot, her mouth close to my ear. "Do you think it really was suicide?" Her voice was low.

I leaned back a little, thinking, then leaned forward, my voice a whisper. "Do you?"

What I had realized about Talitha, you see, was that her intuition was second to none. She had an extraordinary empathy, an emotional intelligence, and I was curious to see what she thought, without any prompting from me.

She shook her head. "No. He had so many problems, but I don't think he would have committed suicide."

"So…do you think it was an accidental overdose?"

Talitha widened her eyes. "Or could it have been something else? Could he have been…pushed?"

"Talitha!" I sat back, as the whisper in my head got louder and I forced it away. "Are you saying what I think you're saying?"

"No. Ignore me. It's just… I'm trying to find answers, I suppose. We'll probably never know for sure. I hated the way he treated Lissy, but that poor man. What a terrible way to end. And in the fountain! My God. It's unimaginable."

"How will you ever be able to look at that fountain again?" How would I, I wondered. I had been through that court-yard numerous times since seeing Dave floating there, and each time I had averted my eyes, keeping them firmly focused on the tile, the peacocks, the palm trees; anything but the fountain.

"I've called a shaman," she said. "He's coming tomorrow morning to cleanse the energy here. I feel it, don't you? It feels heavy, and sad. It's not that we shouldn't feel sad, but I'm terrified of the walls holding on to bad juju. We're flying him in from Peru. He has rituals he performs to change the energy. God knows, I couldn't bear for this wonderful place to hold on to the sadness we all feel right now."

"I think that's a perfect idea," I said, but I was thinking about what Talitha had said about Dave, and whether he knew what he was doing, whether he might have been helped, or guided, toward a situation he didn't realize would end in the way it did.

Lissy didn't go near Eddie that night. I understood, but I'm not sure that Eddie did. He drank himself into oblivion, speaking to no one, eventually falling asleep on the banquette. Lissy stayed on the roof, smoking cigarettes and reading the book that Paul had given her for solace, *A Grief Observed*, by C. S. Lewis.

"It is a beautiful book," Paul said, handing it to her. I presumed he had drifted away to his room for good, to listen to music and read, but in fact he had gone to find something to try and help ease Lissy's pain.

It seemed to help. She opened the book immediately, and barely spoke for the rest of the night. From time to time she would command us all to fall silent and listen as she read a paragraph that resonated.

She looked up at one point, with a frown. "Where's Jimmy?" she asked.

And the whisper exploded into a shout inside my head. Was it a dream? Was it real? If it was real, I had seen Jimmy this morning, when I was half-asleep. Carrying Dave. Dave couldn't walk by himself, I realized. There is no way Dave Boland could have got himself into that fountain. He had to be lifted into it. Or dropped into it.

A cold shiver ran down my spine as I got up.

"I'll go and find him."

I scurried down the stairs to what had been Dave's room, my heart pounding. Outside, the lantern was still lying down. I picked it up, remembering the sharp crack where a stone had broken the glass. There it was. The broken glass. With shaking hands, I righted the lantern on the tile and went to look for Jimmy.

I found him eventually, in one of the small courtyards, dark sunglasses shielding his eyes, smoking as he sat as still as a stone, gazing into the distance.

He didn't move as I pulled up a chair and cleared my throat. I had thought Jimmy was one of the good guys. My protector. Had I been wrong?

"Jimmy. I… I need to ask you something about Dave."

He turned his head slowly until he faced me, though I couldn't see a thing through his sunglasses. He said nothing.

"I had what I thought was a dream last night. Well, not last night, the early hours of this morning. I thought I had had a dream where I saw you coming out of Dave's room, sort of carrying, dragging Dave through the courtyard…" I went silent, waiting.

"The thing is," I said eventually, when Jimmy said nothing. "It wasn't a dream. I thought it must have been, but it wasn't."

Jimmy sighed deeply, pulling the last drag of his cigarette out before grinding it viciously to nothing in the ashtray. I watched, feeling a shiver of fear.

"It was a dream," he said quietly.

"That's what I thought at first," I said. "But Dave caught a lantern when you were dragging him out, and it fell over. I just went to check because I knew that if it was a dream, the lantern would be fine, but the lantern was tipped over and cracked. So the thing is, I know it wasn't a dream. And I know Dave couldn't have got into that fountain by himself." I looked at the ground as I said that last bit, my voice almost a whisper.

Jimmy leaned forward, his elbows on the table, his voice soft. "Cece, I like you. You're one of the good ones. You're going to leave this period of time behind and go off and have a good life. You'll get married, and have children, and all of this will soon feel like it happened to someone else."

"I know, but that doesn't make it right."

Jimmy sighed again. "Would you agree that, given Dave's liking for a bit of violence, especially with women, Dave would have killed Lissy if he could?"

I nodded.

"And would you agree that, knowing what he knew, Dave would have killed Eddie if he could?"

I thought for a second and reluctantly nodded. I believed that Dave, out of his mind on drugs, rage coursing through him, was capable of anything.

"What I did, if in fact I did anything at all, and I am not

admitting anything, but if I did…appear in your dream, it would have been to save two lives. Lissy's and Eddie's. I'm paid to protect them. I would do anything to protect them including lay down my own life."

"You would take another life?" My voice was a whisper.

"I'm ex-army, Cece. I've taken many lives." Jimmy stood then and kissed the top of my head, as if the conversation was over. "You're a good girl, and you're going to have a good life. Like I said, it was all a dream."

"But wha—"

He squatted then, on his haunches, took his sunglasses off, and his eyes were as hard as coal, all the warmth in them now gone. His voice was low and firm.

"No buts. No ifs. Dave Boland was one of the bad ones. You saw what he did to Lissy. You have no idea what he was capable of. Which is irrelevant. You had a dream and now you are going to forget about it. Am I clear? Do you understand me?"

I swallowed hard, a buzzing in my ears, and I nodded.

There was nothing else to do.

I would tell myself for years that I didn't know for sure. Even if Jimmy hadn't helped Dave to the fountain, or drugged him, or done anything, I saw how fragile Dave was. He would have died anyway, the state he was in. That's what I kept telling myself. That was how I got through that first night, and that is how I got through the rest of those nights when I woke up in a cold sweat, remembering, the weight of this knowledge sometimes unbearable.

He would have died anyway. I told myself that story so many times, I believed it.

The next morning, the papers arrived. Dave's death was front-page news on all of them, from the *Sun* to the *Times*. Broadsheet and tabloid, all of them shouted the headlines in bold black type: DAVE BOLAND DEAD; DEAD IN FOUNTAIN; ROCK STAR FOUND DEAD; BOLAND DROWNED WHILE 'DRUNK AND DRUGGED.'

Reading the headlines made it real, again. I went in and out of grief and shock. I would think I was fine, and for a few minutes I would be able to focus on something else, but it always came back to the image of Dave in the fountain. The image of Jimmy helping Dave out of his room. I pushed the images aside as I sat by myself in an alcove, reading the papers, terrified of seeing my name, of somehow being associated with this, but no one knew about me. Lissy and Eddie were mentioned, photographs of them walking through Djemaa El Fna had somehow been snapped, and of course Talitha and Paul. But not me.

Benji came and found me, to inform me that a private flight had been arranged back to the UK.

"Your friend with a plane?"

"No. Eddie's manager has organized it. We're all flying back tonight."

I nodded. There was no fight left in me. I hadn't wanted to leave Talitha or Morocco, but Dave's death had changed everything. I couldn't walk through the courtyard without seeing Dave's lifeless body floating in the water. Suddenly, in the space of twenty-four hours, the prospect of staying here alone, my friends gone, was unfathomable.

Suddenly, all I wanted was the security of home. Even if I had no idea where home would be.

TWENTY-EIGHT

As soon as Talitha put her arms around me, I started to sob.

"It's okay," she said, rubbing my back. "We'll see each other again. I'll be back in London soon and in the meantime, I'll write."

I pulled away feeling as if my heart was going to break. She looked at her hands then, gold serpent rings on every finger, and pulled one off, holding it out to me. "Take it until we see each other again. That way I know you'll always have a part of me with you." I put the ring on my right hand, and it fit perfectly.

Paul extended his arms, that impossibly charming smile breaking my heart.

"Little Cece." He held me tight. "You have been an absolute pleasure and delight. I am so sorry you won't be staying, but of course I understand. You are welcome here any time you like."

As soon as we piled into the car to head to the airport, my tears started again. I knew why I was crying. It wasn't only because of the shock, because of Dave's death. It was because this magical time had ended so horrifically.

I understood that our lives would never again intertwine in the way they had. I was not a rock groupie, nor was I particularly cool. What I was, was a country mouse from Dorset who had stepped into a role and found, ultimately, that the script wasn't right for her.

On the plane, Benji and I sat together, behind Lissy and Eddie. All of us were quiet. Lissy laid her head on Eddie's shoulder, and he put an arm around her, holding her tight. Benji read the papers, and I looked out the window, wondering if and when I would ever see Talitha and Paul again.

We had managed to skirt the press waiting in the cobblestone lanes in the medina, but we weren't able to avoid the scrum waiting for us at Heathrow. Lissy pulled her hat down low, square sunglasses covering up most of her face.

"Lissy!" shouted the photographers as if they knew her. "What happened? Was it you who found Dave?"

"Lissy! How do you feel? Are you okay?"

"Lissy! Is it true that you and Eddie are a couple? Is that why Dave killed himself?"

Everyone knew, it seemed, that Lissy and Eddie had become a couple. I still don't know how they knew. Someone must have tipped them off. It could have been anyone. For all I know, it may even have been their manager. Who was it that said there is no such thing as bad publicity? It was no coincidence that the Wide-Eyed Boys reached the number one slot that week with "Anna's Light," a song that had been released months prior and hadn't cracked the top twenty.

I believe it was Gerard. It seemed like the kind of snake-in-the-grass thing that he would do. That was the thing with Marrakech back then. We were such a small, closely woven crowd; everyone knew everything about everyone else. He would have known that we were leaving, and it would have taken nothing to find out when. He had Talitha under his spell. However dangerous she knew him to be, she also found Gerard as compelling and magnetic as the rest of us found her.

"Wait." Benji put a hand on my arm and held me back once we were off the plane. He pulled me to one side, by the window, and there we stood for almost an hour. By the time we started walking through the airport, the press had followed Lissy and Eddie to the parking lot where Jimmy was waiting. No one was left to photograph us, and I was relieved at avoiding Jimmy. I didn't want to see him ever again.

"How did you know to do that?" I asked him.

"I know a few things about life," Benji said, and I found myself laughing for the first time in what felt like ages.

"What?" he asked.

"Sorry. It's just, the minute we land in London, you've abandoned your real accent again and you're back to your best Michael Caine impersonation."

Benji looked shocked. "I didn't even realize I was doing it."

"Well, you are. It's funny. But you know you don't have to pretend to be anyone else with me."

"You're right. I'm sorry."

"No need to apologize. It's sweet." And I realized it was. I was surprised to see Benji blush.

"What are you going to do now?" he asked, as we walked out of baggage claim and looked for the car and driver Benji had organized. "About a job and all that. Are you going to go back to Dorset?"

"Not Dorset. I can't go back."

"Linda too much?"

"Linda too much. I'm supposed to be finding a flat with Dottie, but…" I trailed off. I loved Dottie, but I now felt like a completely different person than I'd been a few weeks ago. Sharing a flat with Dottie meant trying to be the person I used to be. I had no idea how I would tell her, but I knew I was forever changed. I was no longer the sort of person who could sit up all night giggling over magazines, or moon over pop stars.

Benji turned slightly pink again. "Do you… I mean, if you want, you're welcome to stay in my flat for a bit. Just while you find a job again. It's not much. I've got a tiny spare room, but I don't mind moving into it. You can have my bedroom."

I had heard about Benji's flat from my brother. It was in Shepherd Market, in Mayfair, and many was the time Robbie had slept over. Unsurprisingly, Benji's family kept a London pad, a grand mansion in Curzon Street, but Benji, in his bid to be a man of the people, bought a flat above Linley Gill, the chemist. The red phone box on the corner was littered with taped pieces of paper with phone numbers for ladies of the night, many of whom congregated on that same street corner, most of whom were known to Benji but, as Robbie said, "not in that way." On particularly cold nights, Benji would buy the ladies of the night a cup of tea and a sandwich, making sure they were okay.

"D'you know, he's been offered freebies more than once," Robbie told me, wide-eyed.

"No! He hasn't accepted, has he?"

"Of course not! I think it's all part of his family's noblesse oblige. He's such a good chap, Benji. Salt of the earth."

He was indeed. And here he was, offering me a place to stay. I immediately accepted. Dottie would be upset, but I would make it up to her. I wasn't sure how, but I would try.

★ ★ ★

I hadn't been to Shepherd Market before. As the car was driving along, Benji told me about its history, how the land was bought and developed by Edward Shepherd, where the original May Fair took place.

"Gosh!" I felt stupid. "Mayfair! Of course!"

"I know. I didn't realize it, either. The original May Fair happened on the first May bank holiday every year, from the 1200s. It was put on by the hospital of St. James, and continued through to the 1800s, but the locals were getting very unhappy."

"Why on earth would they be unhappy about a lovely fair?"

"It had become an agricultural fair, and there was an awful lot of drinking and gambling going on, which, inevitably, led to brawling. Some of the local gentry had started to build big houses in the area…"

"Like your family?" I nudged him.

"Well, yes." He was a little bashful. "My family was one of them. And all of them were very unhappy about it. Mr. Shepherd bought this land so they could keep the fair going in a contained spot."

"Is there still a fair?"

"No, but there are a few fruit and veg stalls, and flowers. I love it because it feels like a country village in the heart of London."

"And it's steps from your parents' just in case you get into trouble."

"Oh, Bean, my parents are the last people I'm going to go and see if I get into trouble. It would have to be really bad for me to do that!" He grinned, as did I. It had been ages since he called me Bean. It made me feel even closer to him than I already did, aware of the years of history between us, that we had known each other forever and ever.

The car turned off Park Lane, and back in time, navigating through crooked streets and old-fashioned shops, pubs with window boxes spilling over with clouds of blue lobelia and pink petunias. Past the Mayfair Florist, past the Punchbowl, we pulled up outside the chemist and I followed Benji up the narrow staircase to the flat.

The funny thing about Benji, I realized, as soon as I stepped into the flat, was that he did such a good job of his wide boy act, you didn't expect his taste to be sophisticated; you certainly would not have expected a flat above a chemist in a less than salubrious part of London to be filled with exquisite art, bronze busts of his predecessors, Chinese black lacquer coffee tables and oversize velvet sofas with Indian embroideries draped over the back.

"Benji!" I gasped, taking in the crystal chandelier. "This is delightful!"

He flushed with pleasure. "Do you like it? My mother gave me a bunch of furniture from the country house, but I like to think I've added my own touch."

"It's lovely. It's quite grand, but also so comfortable." I ran over and jumped on the sofa, sinking in. "Yes! It's just as comfortable as it looks! Benji, I'm quite happy taking the box room. You don't have to give me your bedroom."

He wouldn't hear of it. Within the hour I was firmly installed in his bedroom, its walls covered in a green tartan in a nod to his Scottish ancestry, my Moroccan kaftans and shirts hanging in his closet.

That night, we went to The Iron Duke for a drink. With a gin and tonic in hand, we chatted easily back and forth. It was a relief to be home. Even though I hadn't been in this particular part of town, in this particular pub, everything felt familiar. I knew England. I knew English culture. And while I didn't know who anyone was in this pub, I thought it fairly safe to assume there probably weren't any drug dealers there. There certainly weren't any rock stars. I felt myself relax.

"I have an idea for you if you're willing to hear," Benji said eventually.

"Is it working in a shop?" He laughed, knowing my heart wasn't in it.

"I could talk to my friend who's got a gallery here in Mayfair. I ran into him just before I came to Morocco and he was looking for a gallery assistant. I don't know that it's terribly exciting, but he needs someone pretty with a lovely personality to welcome people that come in and show them around."

I gave Benji a sly look, thinking back to the night I hoped he would kiss me, the night I ran off. What a different girl I was now. "Do you think I'm pretty with a lovely personality, then?"

He blushed. "I'd say you're very pretty, and if I'm pushed, I'll have to admit that your personality's not bad, either."

I felt a warmth spread throughout my body. "But I don't know anything about art. How could I show them around?"

"Oh, don't worry about that. He'll teach you everything you need to know. Rosalind, the girl who works there now, got married a while ago and she's having a baby. She's staying until he finds someone and she's going to train them up."

"Gosh, Benji. It sounds fantastic."

"I'll arrange it for tomorrow, shall I?"

I nodded, marveling at my brother being right about Benji. He knew everyone, and he knew how to make things happen.

On the way home, we passed a woman standing by herself on the corner of Shepherd Market. There was a chill in the air, and she huddled against the wall, burying her chin in the fur collar of her jacket, puffing on a cigarette. Every time she exhaled, you could see her breath intermingling with the smoke.

She had on a miniskirt and high boots, and I wondered

whether she was waiting for someone. She glanced over and saw us.

"Alright, Benji?"

"Alright, Eileen?" He was back to Michael Caine. "How's business tonight?"

She rolled her eyes. "You know what it's like when it gets chilly. They all go back to their wives. I might call it a night myself in a bit."

I almost gasped. It was the first time I had knowingly been this close to what we now call a sex worker, and the biggest shock was that I would never have known.

"Can I get you anything? Cuppa tea?"

"No, you're alright, love. I just came back from the caff."

"You take care of yourself, Eileen, you hear?"

"You, too, Benji." She nodded at me. "Nice to see you've got yourself a nice girl, at last," she said.

"Oh, this is Cl… Cece. She's my friend's sister."

Eileen winked. "That's what they all say."

The next day, I went to the gallery in Aldford Street. I met Leonard, the art dealer, and Rosalind, who immediately took me under her wing. By the end of the afternoon I'd not only got the job, Rosalind had suggested I take her place in the flat she had previously shared with two other girls in Deanery Street.

Marrakech was already beginning to feel like a dream. I bought the paper at the newsagent on the corner, and this time Lissy and Eddie were plastered all over it. Again, it was like reading about rock stars I didn't know, as if it was a life I had never been a part of at all.

Except for the gold serpent ring I wore on the third finger of my right hand.

"Talitha," I whispered, flattening my fingers and looking at the ring.

★ ★ ★

I loved my new job. There were quiet times when I could bring a paperback to work and lose myself for a while. The ring of the doorbell alerted me to any potential customers, and I'd hide the book and stand up to greet them.

At Rosalind's suggestion, I went to the library and checked out a stack of art books. In the evenings I would research the artists so I could pretend to know what I was talking about.

"Isn't it amazing how it seems to move?" I'd stand in front of Bridget Riley's *Fall*, the undulating black and white lines making me dizzy. I'd explain to them about op art, that these abstract works were designed to create optical illusions. The more I read, the more I wanted to learn. It was the first time I had a glimpse of what it might be like to be passionate about your work, and I wanted more.

Leonard didn't speak to me much, but he came in one morning and placed a box of chocolates on my desk.

"This is to thank you," he said.

My cheeks turned red. "What for?"

"We just sold the Bridget Riley for an unprecedented amount. The Lloyd-Joneses were rather impressed with your knowledge. Play your cards right, young lady, and you'll be taking over this gallery soon!" He winked at me and walked off as I popped an orange cream into my mouth.

The following week, on a quiet day, the phone rang.

"Leonard Brilley Gallery. How may I help you?"

"Cece?" I heard.

"Speaking."

"Cece! It's John."

John who? I thought, immediately feeling guilty as I realized. John! My almost but not quite boyfriend.

"John!" I injected an enthusiasm into my voice that I didn't feel. "Goodness! It's been a while!"

"Well, yes. I did rather think you might try and phone from Marrakech, but, on the other hand, I completely understand why you didn't. God, how awful about Dave Boland. You must have been through the mill. Are you okay?"

"I am. How did you find me?"

"It took a little bit of investigation, but Robert Fraser said he heard someone called Cece had just started round the corner at Leonard Brilley's, back from Marrakech. A lucky break. Would you like to have supper on Friday?"

"That would be lovely. Thank you." I gave him the address of the flat in Deanery Street and put down the phone, wondering why I wasn't excited in the least, wondering how it would feel to see him again.

That night, I had a drink with Benji. I had drinks with him most nights. I think the fact that we had been in Marrakech together, that we had shared the experience, the terrible experience at the end, made me feel closer to him.

At least, that's what I told myself.

Benji was the only person I wanted to be with. It wasn't just that he was there when Dave stormed onto the roof, and there when Dave was found in the fountain, but he was there for some of the good, as well. He was charmed by Talitha. He understood that the grief I was feeling wasn't just about the terrible tragedy of Dave, but about something more. I think he may have understood in a way that I didn't even understand myself.

"The thing is," he said that night, at the Red Lion, over a pint of lager and a gin and tonic for me, "I'm not sure it's possible to know Talitha without falling a little in love with her."

I found myself blushing, and looked away.

"She's the sort of person who casts a spell over everyone," he said. "Men and women alike. You somehow become brighter, funnier, just better, in her gaze. What a magical time they provide for everyone there."

I looked back at him. "You get it. You got it. That's exactly it."

"I do. And, for all the magic, it is also shockingly hedonistic and indulgent. It's not sustainable. You know that, don't you? It's all going to end in tears. She's an enchantress, I get it. I spent hardly any time with her, but I saw it. I can only imagine the loss that you must be feeling right now, being back in London."

I nodded and swallowed the lump in my throat. There was nothing else to say. I just hoped she was okay. She had written to me. Yesterday morning there was another letter from Talitha.

Darling Cece. Rome isn't nearly as much fun as Sidi Mimoun! We just had Groovy Bob come to stay and he says he's hearing wonderful things about you at your gallery. Oh, Cece! I am as proud as a mother watching her baby chick take flight. Look at you! I love and miss you, but am so happy you sound like you are doing well. I would love to hear from you. Please write! I love you. T xxx

I hadn't responded to any of her letters. I kept telling myself I would, but suddenly it would be days, and I would forget, and then another letter would arrive. It felt like she needed me, but she was in their apartment in Rome, in the Piazza d'Aracoeli, and I was in London, finding my feet.

What could I do even if she did need me? Benji's words echoed through my head. Hedonistic and indulgent. I knew he disapproved. And I knew he wanted to keep me safe.

I didn't respond.

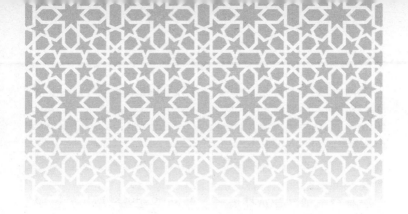

TWENTY-NINE

I was surprised at how nice it was to see John, and unsurprised that I felt no physical attraction to him whatsoever. It was like running into a nice friend, one you can enjoy for a few hours, knowing you probably won't see them again for ages.

He took me to The Casserole, on the King's Road, opposite Paultons Square. The restaurant was dark and cozy, and filled with bright young things. We sat in a booth, and the red plaster walls and patterned carpet reminded me a little of Marrakech, and gave me a pang of loneliness. No, I told myself. Don't miss it and regret not being there now. Think how lucky you are to have ever experienced anything like that. Don't focus on the fountain and the tragedy, focus on the splendor and the magic and the people you met, and the fantasy world you were able to enjoy, just for a little while.

And be grateful that it was just for a little while. Had it gone on much longer, perhaps I, like Dave, would not have survived it. I did, after all, have a very close call. Had Jimmy not noticed that my routine was broken, that I was not up as I usually was, it is entirely possible that I would not be here, either.

I couldn't think about that too much.

Sitting across from John in The Casserole, pretending to be hungry when I had no appetite at all, I kept asking myself whether any of it really happened.

John was as lovely as he had always been. Except I no longer found myself falling for his charm. He was trying to get his new band on *Ready Steady Go!*, and asking me lots of questions about my holiday. He wanted to know all about Marrakech and, particularly, what exactly happened with Dave.

"But you were there." He leaned forward. "I'm dying to know everything! I can't believe I didn't come with you."

"I really don't know," I lied. "I think he had a bit of a meltdown, and went off to a retreat somewhere, but… Honestly, I think he was pretty unstable."

"I know he beat Lissy horribly. That's the rumor in the industry at least. In some of those pictures of Lissy walking through the airport, it looked like she had a black eye behind those sunglasses."

I shrugged. I didn't want to reveal anything more. John was charming and chatty, but I was tense, unwilling to give anything away, to reveal anything I might regret. As we were leaving he asked if I wanted to come back to his place.

"I can't," I said, which wasn't what I meant. What I meant was *I don't want to.*

"You know this is one of Mick's favorite restaurants," John said, as we were leaving. "I saw him here last week with David Bailey."

I didn't say anything. Three weeks ago, I was awestruck by

all the people John knew, even more awestruck at the prospect of breathing the same airspace.

I was no longer interested. I knew now what the rock and roll lifestyle entailed. As alluring as it was, it carried a darkness that could pull you under.

So no, I wasn't going to go back to John's. In fact, I knew I would be declining the next dinner invitation. If, in fact, there ever was another dinner invitation.

Which there was not.

THIRTY

LONDON, 1971

I peered through the gates of the Queen's house, aka the Rossetti house, on Cheyne Walk. The blue plaque by the door read: *Dante Gabriel Rossetti 1828–1882 and Algernon Charles Swinburne 1837–1909 lived here.*

By then I knew a little more about the Rossetti house and understood why it was so special to Paul. Rossetti, together with the other members of the Pre-Raphaelite Brotherhood, were the hippies' Victorian precursors. They were bound across generations by romantic idealism, free love and, unexpectedly, hallucinogenic drugs, much of which fueled their beautiful art.

Rossetti's wife and muse, love of his life, the artist Lizzie Siddal, suffered years of ill health and died of a laudanum overdose in 1862. Rossetti was struck with grief when he moved in to the house on Cheyne Walk. He was addicted to chloral, a Victorian narcotic, and drank it in quantities that disturbed his friends. He died a recluse in 1882.

Of course Paul fell in love with the idea of this house, in much the way, I thought, he fell in love with the idea of Talitha. Both were the embodiment of a romantic ideal. I wondered later if the house held a sense of foreboding for him. Did he ever think twice about the history it held?

As I strolled down Cheyne Walk, I thought about the people who now lived there. Rumor had it that Mick Jagger and his new wife Bianca were here, as were Keith Richards and Anita Pallenberg, and Eddie Allbright and Lissy Ellery. I wondered if I would run into any of them. I took my time walking up the street, trying to see into the windows, trying to spot Lissy or Eddie, but I saw no one.

I still wore Talitha's ring every day. Benji was trying to persuade me to add another ring, this to the third finger of my left hand, but I wasn't ready. He proposed properly, on bended knee, at Claridge's, and then promised to propose on the first of every month until I said yes.

Each time I would kiss him and tell him not yet. Not yet.

I hadn't written to Talitha, but still, all these years on, her letters kept coming. All of them filled with her exuberance, humor, fragility and love. Even though I read and reread those letters over and over, I never responded. I was becoming settled in my new life, it was going well, and a part of me knew that I couldn't be friends with Talitha part-time. She was all or nothing for me, and if I opened the door, I would be sucked back in. I couldn't take that chance.

I had been promoted to Leonard's assistant, and was spending my evenings studying for a degree in Art History. Benji and I stopped talking about Sidi Mimoun. There were other things to think about, our future to focus on, so when the phone rang at work, the receptionist calling out that it was someone for me, I was entirely unprepared.

I walked to the back of the room and picked up the heavy black receiver.

"Hello?"

"Cece!" A familiar dirty laugh echoed. "Do you know who this is?"

Her voice jolted me back in time. I knew immediately, all the memories flooding back. I almost dropped the phone, my heart pounding. "Talitha?" My voice came out in a whisper of disbelief.

"Yes, darling! Can you believe how long it's been! I'm back in London, living at Cheyne Walk and dying to see you. Did you get my letters?"

How to explain to her that I read them, reread them, and reread them again. I read them so many times that I had to eventually gather them up and put them away in a box so the paper didn't disintegrate.

Today, I have no doubt that I loved Talitha. Which is why I couldn't write back. I loved the life I had built, and I loved Benji. I didn't trust myself around Talitha, didn't know where I would or would not draw the line. Her letters were all that was left of a secret life I otherwise refused to revisit.

Until now.

"I got your letters." I didn't explain why I couldn't write back, but I didn't have to, Talitha's words tumbling over themselves in her excitement.

"Please say you'll come for tea. It's a bit chaotic. The workers are here, putting in modern central heating, and there's a lovely Italian family who look after everything for me, so we can have some proper time together. It will be so lovely to see you. I'm dying for you to meet the baby."

I had read they had a baby. Tara Gabriel Galaxy Gramophone Getty. Benji had looked stunned when I told him. I figured the gramophone bit must have come from Paul, the rest was, surely, pure Talitha.

"No," Benji said. "Apparently the Tara is after poor Tara Browne." Of course. I remembered John talking about Tara Browne all those years before. I remembered his shop on the King's Road, Dandie Fashions. I knew Talitha and Paul were friends with him, as well. How like Talitha to remember her friend in such a loving way.

"I'd love to come for tea," I found myself saying, desperate to see Talitha now that I was hearing her voice.

"Darling Cece!" Talitha pulled me inside as if no time had passed at all. Her hair was shorter now, fashioned in a trendy, feathered cut that suited her. She wore a fitted dress that flared out, and long leather boots. She had moved on from the Marrakech kaftans and harem pants, but had she moved on from anything else, I wondered? Had she moved on from drugs? I looked at her pupils, and thought them dilated.

Had she moved on from me?

"Oh! How did we let so much time go by?" She linked her arm through mine, just as she had in the old days, leading me through the foyer. As soon as I laid eyes on her, I knew I still loved her, would always love her.

I allowed myself to be given a tour of the house. Decorators were painting the paneling, and raising heavy dark curtains over the windows.

"I love it." She laughed. "But my stepmother is horrified. She used to visit the house in the thirties as a child, and remembered it as being very light and bright, but this is much more me." She gestured around at the dark, cozy rooms.

We went to the salon, where an Italian woman brought Tara

down, a chubby three-year-old, to say hello. He was gorgeous, and Talitha quite clearly adored him, showering him with kisses as he giggled, before the nanny took him out for his tea.

Talitha curled up on the sofa. "Oh, Cece. I'm so relieved to be back in London. I should have come back years ago."

"Where have you been? In Rome all this time? My God, there's so much to catch up on. And Marrakech! How is Sidi Mimoun?"

She shrugged. "I've hardly been there at all for the last couple of years. Can you imagine? We bought a huge villa on the coast at Palo, twenty miles north of Rome. The Posta Vecchia. Quite beautiful, but it's all been too much. The parties, the drugs." She took a breath. "I've stopped doing everything. I'm totally clean. Well, apart from the pills the doctor prescribes, but I need those for depression." She let out a genuine laugh. "God, Cece. Me! Depressed! Isn't that crazy? I'm terrified of everything. I'm terrified of growing old, and I've become terrified of this crazy life. No more drugs. No more madness. I'm a mother now. I can't live the life I was living before. Sometimes it gets me very down, and the pills help."

"I'm sorry you've been down." I looked at her and realized this was what was different. Talitha always had another side, but back then she knew how to keep it hidden. This time, it was clear to me that life was hard for her. Despite everything, life would always be hard.

"And Paul? How is Paul?" I had heard rumors that they were separated, but I refused to believe them.

She shook her head, sadness in her eyes again, and confirmed that the rumors were true. "It's not good. He's not good. I don't know, Cece. I'm praying he gets better and gives up all the drugs. Maybe then we could have another go of it. But…perhaps it's too late." She looked at me, her expression dark. "I blame myself. I introduced him to all my crazy friends, and got him into this. The drugs. The heroin. Before me, he just liked a drink, and I was the one who introduced him to all his bad habits. And now..." She trailed off. "I had to come back to London. I had to get away from Rome, and Marrakech. This feels like the only place where it might be possible for me to find my sanity."

"But it can't be over between the two of you. I know how much you love him."

"I do," she said. "I just don't know. I don't know what's going to happen. He has someone else, but..." She shrugged. "We've both had someone elses, for a long time. This feels different though. More permanent. He's installed me here, this house is for me and the baby, but I'm scared."

I looked at her. Scared? But before I had a chance to ask what she meant, she kept talking.

"He comes over. Paul's living with his mistress in Rome, and comes to see us here in London. This was our compromise, our way to keep everyone happy."

And yet, she did not feel happy. Her joie de vivre was muted. It felt as if she was trying to be in a great mood, rather than actually being in a great mood.

We chatted easily for hours. Talitha was lively and funny, but I felt her loneliness, her desperation for company. I worried about her health. She said she was having thyroid problems. I wondered whether her depression was linked to that or whether it was something more serious. She had said she was clean, but was she? I didn't know what to believe.

"I'm going to Rome this weekend," she said, as I was getting ready to leave. "Cece!" Her face lit up. "Why don't you come? I'm leaving the baby and going to see Paul. I don't want to be alone, and you and I would have such fun together! Please say you'll come! I'll show you all the best places in Rome!"

I was so tempted, but I knew I couldn't go. If I went, there was no telling who I would be by the end of the weekend. I didn't want anything to shatter my newfound life, and I knew the pull of Talitha was too strong for me. Even after a few hours in her company, I could feel myself falling under her spell.

"I don't think I can," I said. "I wish I had more notice."

Talitha pouted. "Oh, please come! I'll buy you a plane ticket and you can stay with me. It won't cost anything!"

"It's not that," I tried to explain. "I have an engagement party on Saturday, and... I just can't."

Talitha nodded, her eyes filled with sadness.

"Don't be sad," I said. "We'll see each other lots when you're back. Now that you're in London it will be easy!" But my words were empty.

We hugged for a long time, squeezing each other tight.

"We'll see each other all the time!" she said, when we pulled apart. "Just like this." She linked her arm through mine as she walked me to the front door. "Quietly. You and me, curled up on a sofa, drinking tea and catching up. You have always been the balm for my soul, Cece. No one has ever understood me like you."

When I left, halfway down the path I turned around. She was still standing in the doorway, watching me, her face stricken. I stopped and went back to her, taking her hands. "Talitha? Are you alright?"

She nodded, but once I turned and reached the gate, I felt a small hand on my shoulder. She was standing there, with tears in her eyes, shaking her head.

"No," she said. "I'm not alright."

"You'll be fine," I said with conviction, as I hugged her again, opened the gate, and closed it behind me without looking back.

★ ★ ★

Later that night, in bed with Benji, he asked about my day. I told him I saw Talitha and that I was worried about her. I told him she had invited me to Rome, and I had declined.

"Good," Benji said. "That was the right thing to do."

I realized that I had meant to give her back her ring but had forgotten. It would give us an excuse to see each other again, I thought. I didn't trust myself to go to Rome, but I did want to see her again. The thrill, or confusion, or whatever it was that prevented me from writing back to her all these years, was gone. We could be friends now. Or sisters. Soul sisters. Everything was clear. I wasn't under her spell in quite the same way, but I loved her. I would always love her. And now I knew I could have her in my life, on my terms.

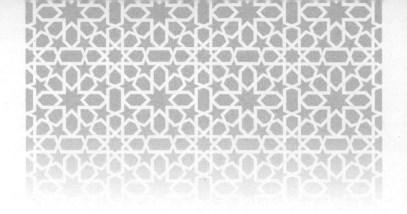

THIRTY-ONE

It was a beautiful Sunday afternoon. Benji and I had driven out to Henley-on-Thames to see Robbie and his wife, Susan. My brother had bought an old rectory on the water, and this was the first time we were seeing it. Four of us decided to go. Benji and me, with our friends Mark and Lisa. Mark had a Ford Anglia, and we piled in, with T-Rex playing on the eight-track he'd had installed in the walnut dashboard.

"That's amazing!" said Benji. "I had no idea you could do that to a dashboard on a Ford."

You can do anything to a walnut dashboard, I thought, remembering the silver bullet, and the hidden drug compartments all over the car.

"What?" Benji looked at me.

"What, *what?*" I asked.

"Why do you have that secret smile on your face?"

"What secret smile?"

"That smile that says you're remembering something from the past."

Should I tell them, I thought? Why not. All of the secrets had been put to rest. I was friends with Talitha again, and this time, it felt normal. There were no orgies, no parties, no drugs, no sex. At least not in my life. Nothing to be afraid of.

"Okay. I was thinking of the silver bullet. It was a Bentley owned by Eddie Allbright."

"I know that car," said Mark. "Now, that was a very special car."

"With," I added, from the back seat, "hidden compartments all over it, including in the walnut dashboard."

I could tell Mark didn't believe me. "A likely story. And how," said Mark, "could you possibly know a thing like that?"

"She's been around a bit, my girlfriend," Benji said, grinning. "She knows a thing or two."

"Would you believe me if I told you I once went to Morocco in the back of the silver bullet?"

"Would you believe me if I told you I once went to the moon with John Lennon?" shot Mark.

I could see Benji was fighting the urge to laugh.

"I might do, actually," I said. "It's not outside the realm of possibility."

"Oh, look!" piped up Lisa, looking out the window. "We're almost there! Look! You can see the river. Isn't it gorgeous?"

I didn't bother letting Mark know the truth. It was another life, and it didn't really matter whether they believed me or not. It was probably better that they didn't. I was the quintessential good girl, on my way to getting a degree in art history, with a boyfriend who adored me and who, in turn, I adored.

This was another life, the only vestige that remained being

Talitha, but even Talitha wasn't the Talitha of Marrakech. This was Talitha as a mother, as a grown-up, as someone trying to trade chaos for peace. That's what I told myself when I remembered her face, her voice, her words: *No. I'm not alright.*

We drove through Henley, and on to the little village of Hurley. Past the Olde Bell Inn, down the twisty, country lane, until we reached the rectory. Robbie and Susan were standing on the doorstep, waving furiously, proud to show off their new home.

"Robbie!" I leaped into his arms. It had been ages since I'd seen him, and when I went to give Susan a hug, I noticed a small bump.

"Is there…are you…?" I looked at Susan's sparkling eyes, then down at her belly.

"Yes." Robbie nodded, taking Susan's hand. "We're having a baby!"

"Oh, Robbie! Susan! Congratulations!" I hugged them both, and all six of us went inside to see their new house, including the baby's room, which already had a mobile waiting, even though Susan was only four months along.

"I couldn't resist," she said. "I saw it in a shop in London. I know it's bad luck to buy this early, but it was perfect. I was worried it wouldn't be there when the baby's born."

"It's not bad luck," I said. "People like you don't have bad luck."

"I'm the only one who has bad luck." Benji came up behind me. "I've been asking you to marry me for almost four years and you keep saying not yet. If that's not bad luck, I don't know what is."

"That's not bad luck," I said. "That's just, impatient luck."

Benji rolled his eyes. "Robbie? Can you talk to your sister? Get some sense into her head. I won't wait around forever."

"Let's not talk about this now," I said. "I'm starving."

★ ★ ★

We had a picnic on the lawn—Shippam's paste sandwiches, hard-boiled eggs, boiled ham and piccalilli—then walked through a gate to find ourselves on the banks of the Thames. Weeping willows dripped into the water as old barges made their way past.

"Oh!" I clapped my hands. "This is gorgeous!"

"It gets better," said Robbie, leading us up a little path to an old boathouse in which sat a beautifully polished motor launch. "Isn't she amazing?" Robbie sighed. "She came with the house!"

It was a day I would never forget. Discovering I was going to be an aunt, a picnic, a walk by the river, a proper English tea with homemade scones. At the end of the day, Robbie and Susan invited all of us to stay the night so we could drink champagne and celebrate the baby with them, and we accepted.

Later that evening, much later, Benji, who had been watching TV with Robbie, walked into the kitchen, his face pale.

"I've got some bad news." He sat down next to me and took my hands.

"What? What is it? You're scaring me." I had no idea what it could be, but my first thought was my dad. Had he had a heart attack? Was he dead? I couldn't imagine anything worse.

"No, no. It's not family. Everyone's fine." He took a deep breath. "I've just seen the news. It's Talitha." He shook his head with a long sigh. "I'm so sorry, darling, but Talitha is dead. She was found in Rome. An overdose of alcohol and barbiturates."

And the bottom spun out of my world.

I have read many different versions of what happened to Talitha that weekend in the years since she died. Some versions say she went to Rome in a bid to reconcile with Paul.

She had had divorce papers drawn up, but then asked her lawyers not to send them. They sent them anyway.

The first reports had her overdosing on alcohol and barbiturates. Later, that was changed to heroin. Did that explain her dilated pupils when I saw her in London?

Some versions have Talitha attempting to seduce a reluctant Paul, before taking a huge dose of heroin when she was spurned. Paul is said to have left the apartment for several hours and, when he returned, presumed she was asleep. Eventually, at around four thirty in the morning, he called Dado Ruspoli to come and help revive her. They tried to make her throw up, but she was comatose. At seven in the morning, they got through to an American doctor, who visited the apartment but couldn't revive her. He called an ambulance, and she died on her way to hospital.

The fine in Italy for possession of heroin at that time was seven years imprisonment. Allegedly Paul paid the coroner $25,000 to keep heroin off the death certificate, claiming instead it was an overdose of barbiturates.

To this day, I don't think anyone knows the real story. The versions I heard never quite made sense to me. Then again, the story everyone heard about Dave Boland, the one that made the press, didn't make sense to a lot of people, either.

I remember how proud Talitha was when she said she had kicked everything that wasn't prescribed, how she was finally clean.

As I say, it didn't make sense.

This is what made sense. That I survived. That I still had her ring. That I would remember her, and the impact she had on all of us, for the rest of my life. And that on August 1, when Benji came up behind me in the kitchen as I was washing up, sinking to one knee and asking if I would marry him, I said yes.

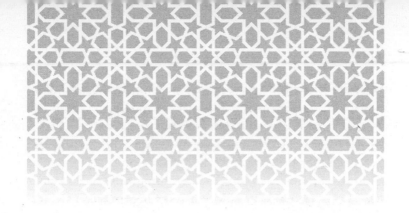

THIRTY-TWO
PRESENT DAY

My daughter sits back, staring at me, shaking her head. We are both exhausted. I have tried not to think about this for so many years, have pushed these memories to one side, but in revealing this part of my life to my daughter, I have set something free. Already I feel lighter. This story is part of who I am. I should never have pushed it to a corner of an attic.

I should have gone to Rome that weekend. I knew Talitha wasn't alright; she told me she wasn't alright. I eschewed my self-appointed responsibilities as her protector because I was too scared. And perhaps because I knew I might be dragged down with her.

I look at my daughter. "Do you have anything to say?" I am nervous suddenly. Will she understand that those were different times? Is she able to hear the story without judgment? Will she understand what it was like to emerge from the repression of the fifties, and how revolutionary it was, as a woman, to enjoy sex just for the sake of the pleasure?

Will she ever be able to look at me in the same way again?

"Mum!" She grins, and I relax. "Who would have thought you had it in you! My God! I always suspected you had a bit of a past, what artist doesn't, but I never expected this. It's incredible. How have you managed to keep this a secret all these years?"

My entire body exhales with relief.

"It wasn't intentional. It was, well, I think—more than anything—it was enormously painful. The pointlessness of Talitha's death. It was easier to not think about it, to pretend it never happened. To this day I believe she might not have died had I been a proper friend and gone to Rome with her."

"You were a proper friend," my daughter reassures me. "You had a responsibility to take care of yourself. What happened to Paul?"

"He went on to have a wonderful life. I would see him from time to time, at his place in the country. We'd have tea and he'd make me watch cricket. He became completely passionate about cricket." I laughed. "He and your father got on very well."

Tally looks at me. "Did Dad know about everything?"

I smile. "He knew how much I loved Talitha, and how terrible I felt about her death. He respected my wish for privacy. He never asked more about that one night, and I never volunteered."

Tally puts her hands over her ears. "I get it. I don't want to know any more, either. But I am impressed. Truly. And," she says, and laughs, "I had no idea Dad was known as Benji. That's so funny."

"I know. It was such a long time ago. He went back to being

Ben soon after we were married. I think he finally wanted to be a grown-up."

Tally looks at her watch. "Oh, shit. I have to go."

"Why such a hurry?"

"Polly's coming over."

"Polly?"

"The girl who wants me to come to Ibiza. She's borrowing an easel. Damn. I'm going to be late." She leans over and kisses me. "I'll call you later. And thank you, Mum. For sharing that incredible story with me. I knew I was named after Talitha Getty, but I never thought to ask more. I thought you just liked the name." She chuckles to herself. "I'll never look at you in the same way again."

I spend the rest of that day unpacking Morocco, welcoming back items I haven't thought of for many years, walking around the house and placing them, with pleasure, next to my sculptures, on my bookshelves, on side tables and on shelves.

Now, next to my bird sculptures, sit woven Amazigh baskets in shades of orange and brown; lanterns and fabrics and carvings fill my living room, jewel-colored tea glasses on a silver tray on my kitchen counter. Everywhere I look, I see a piece of Morocco.

Everywhere I look, I see a piece of Talitha.

And finally, after all these years, it makes my heart sing again, just as it did all those years ago when I first discovered Marrakech.

I don't hear from Tally for a few days, which is unusual. I worry that something in my story may have disturbed her so, rather than pick up the phone, I walk over to her house. I love the fact that, in a world full of Farrow & Ball Old White, hers is the only home on the street with a purple front door. That's my girl, I think. There's the artist in you.

Her footsteps clatter down the stairs. "Mum! Oh, God! I kept meaning to phone you. I'm so sorry, I've been so busy."

Good, I think. Tally is never busy. Tally has far too much free time on her hands.

"Busy doing what?"

"Come upstairs with me. I'm finishing packing. I'm doing it. I leave—" She pauses on the stairs and looks at her watch. "I leave in about twenty-five minutes. Polly's picking me up in an Uber and we're going to the airport."

I cannot hide my smile of delight. "Is it presumptuous of me to think, or to hope, that I may have had something to do with your sudden change of heart?"

"No. It's *all* because of you. I couldn't stop thinking about your story, and more, about how you went for it, you seized all that life had to offer. Not that I'm planning on orgies and drugs in Ibiza—"

"Unless you're very lucky," I couldn't help but interject, with a wink.

"Well, yes. But, the point is, I realized I'm not seizing life at all. I'm saying no to everything. Why not just say yes, and see what happens?"

"Oh, Tally!" I put my arms around her and give her a squeeze. I am so proud of her. This is all I ever wanted for my family; that they should always say yes, always seize the moment.

"Oh, and… I've got something for you."

"For me? What is it?"

"It's downstairs. Wait here."

I sit on the bed and look at Tally's packed suitcase. Her clothes are simple. Loose linen tops and simple cotton trousers. A small unzipped bag of jewelry. I pry off the gold serpent ring and slip it into the bag. She'll find it when she's in Ibiza, and she'll know what it means. I don't need to carry a piece of Talitha on my hand anymore. She resides in my heart. I hope the ring brings Tally luck.

Tally comes back holding an eight-by-ten-inch canvas. She turns it around and shyly puts it in my hand. It is a water-color-and-ink sketch, quite beautiful, of Talitha and Paul, as beautiful as they ever were, on the rooftop of the Pleasure Palace. Finally, for the first time in decades, I am able to look at them, to look at my daughter, without shame, without guilt and without regret. I do not wish any of it away. A tear runs down my cheek and I kiss my daughter, thanking her for such a priceless gift. I have seized all that Talitha and Paul had to give, all that life had to offer. And I have lived.

Now, it is my daughter's turn.

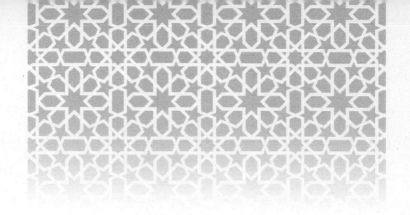

EPILOGUE

I thought I would never see anyone from those Marrakech days again, but I was wrong. I once ran into, of all people, Pierre and Yves. We had gone to Paris for our anniversary, which was an enormous treat. It was, I think, our twenty-fifth wedding anniversary. Silver. I was enjoying mild success as a potter on a very local level, and I loved it. I went to my little studio every day, and hand-coiled vases, and bowls and, eventually, sculptures.

I never thought of selling them. In the beginning, each time we went to someone's house for dinner, I brought them a bowl or a vase. Our closest friends were building quite the collection. Those early pieces were heavy, glazed in blues and greens, but as time went on I started to make simpler pieces out of porcelain, keeping them white, occasionally with splashes of colour that were, unconsciously I think, reminiscent of Bill Willis's tile palettes.

Our friends Gillian and Rob owned a gallery on Haverstock Hill, and when I started doing the sculptures, they came over for dinner and fell madly in love with an abstract bird sculpture I had made. Gillian immediately asked if she could buy it, then asked if I had enough for an exhibition. I didn't, but three months later, I did. It was extraordinary to think that anyone wanted my work. I was a bag of nerves on opening night, convinced that no one would come, or the only people to come would be our friends, who would then feel obligated to buy, out of pity, perhaps. But the opposite happened. The *Ham & High* had interviewed me the week before, and the gallery was packed. Of course, all our friends were there, but so were many others, drinking their warm white wine and picking at the canapés that were passed around.

By the end of the night, everything had sold. That was the beginning of the successful years. For our twenty-fifth anniversary, Ben had two pendants made, small replicas of that first abstract bird I had made, the first piece I had sold to Gillian. One was silver, and one was gold, they were about two inches high, the silver one with sapphire eyes, the gold one with ruby eyes.

He gave me the bird pendants for our anniversary, wrapped together with tickets to Paris. I felt so thoroughly spoiled, staying at the George V, spending hours and hours at the Rodin Museum, the Musée d'Orsay, the Louvre. We were having a quiet celebratory dinner at La Coupole, oysters and champagne, when a buzz went around the room. I looked over, and there were Yves and Pierre, exactly the same as they had been all those years ago. We were all older, grayer, but as I watched them make their way through the restaurant, diners standing up and applauding Yves, who had become a national treasure

in France, the years dropped away. I remembered him dancing with Talitha, weaving branches and berries through her
magnificent hair.

Ben turned to me. "Aren't you going to say hello?"

I didn't know whether I should or not. I doubted they
would even remember me. I once read an interview with one
of the old crew, Jane Ormsby-Gore, whose husband, Michael
Rainey, owned Hung on You, one of the cool clothes shops
from that time. I didn't know her, but I remember hearing
about her, knew that she was friends with all the same people.
She has gone on to become a celebrated designer, and during the interview she was asked about those times. She said,
"You know what they say—'if you remember the sixties, you
weren't there.'"

I didn't want the embarrassment of trying to remind Pierre
and Yves of who I was and how I knew them. But as they
walked past our table, Yves in the front, leading the way, gra-
ciously bowing his head at the applause, Pierre happened to
catch my eye. I thought I saw a flicker of recognition.

They carried on to their table, and I felt a mix of excitement, disappointment and grief. Being in their aura was an
instant jolt back to the past, and for a few minutes, there she
was again, in my head. Talitha.

We were finishing our coffees when Pierre appeared at
our table.

"It's Cece, isn't it."

I couldn't keep the delight from spreading across my face.
We hugged and Pierre kissed both my cheeks.

He joined us for a while. Of course, we talked about Talitha.
Her joie de vivre and magnetism. Pierre looked off into the
distance, nodding, before looking back at me. "People like
Talitha, Rudolf, and Yves have the same flair, the same percep-
tion of life. For these people, the rest of the world is square."

★ ★ ★

They said that Dave had committed suicide. They found enormous quantities of Mandrax in his system, and, combined with alcohol, they think it was deliberate, given his state of turmoil. Much the same happened to Brian Jones, who was found, just like Dave, fully clothed and dead, in 1969 in the swimming pool of his country house, Cotchford Farm, in Sussex, which had previously belonged to A. A. Milne, the beloved author of *Winnie-the-Pooh*.

How ironic, I remember thinking, that Dave had so wanted to emulate the Rolling Stones. When all was said and done, Brian Jones ended up emulating him.

Which wasn't all they had in common. To this day Brian Jones's death is suspicious, with many people believing it to have been murder, some believing that Brian's chauffeur/minder/babysitter Tom Keylock had something to do with it.

I have waited all these years for someone to question Dave Boland's death, but no one has in any meaningful way. Stories have come out of his final days, how he had a psychotic break, how he was likely bipolar. He was an abuser, of women, alcohol, drugs. He was also brilliant, but tales of his brilliance have faded; tales of his abuse have not.

But I know differently. I will never forget seeing Gerard in the main salon, and him asking where Jimmy was. And I will never forget seeing Jimmy go into Dave's room in the early hours of the morning he died, nor the conversation we had the following morning. Jimmy was Eddie's protector. He would have done anything to keep Eddie safe. He would have done anything for Eddie. Much later, I remembered something that had previously escaped me. That night, when Jimmy made his way up to our dinner on the roof to tell Eddie that Dave had escaped the retreat, he had whispered something to Dave.

"I'll take care of it."

And he did. My guess is that he met Gerard, the good doc-

tor, the evil doctor, the Candyman, the bad seed, and Gerard
sold him, I suspect, a huge amount of Mandrax, for that was
what was found in Dave's system. Mandrax and alcohol. A
lethal combination. How and where would Dave have gotten
Mandrax in a guarded retreat in the Atlas Mountains? I saw
Jimmy go into Dave's room. It would have taken nothing to
ply Dave with enough drugs and alcohol, to induce an overdose, before helping him out, as he was slipping into uncon-
sciousness, tipping him into a fountain.

I have never spoken of this to anyone. There is no way to
prove it, and what would be the point. I will never condone
what Jimmy did. Despite the abuse, despite the erratic, unpredictability of Dave Boland, he was a musical genius, and the
Wide-Eyed Boys would not have existed without him. Nor
would they have survived with him. I truly think Dave would
have ended up killing Eddie, or Lissy. Or both. As I say, it
doesn't make it right, what happened to him, but it happened,
and it was years ago, and even if I had gone to the authorities
at the time, who could have proven anything?

Dave's death was not the end of the band but, in fact, the
beginning. Nick Whitstone took the reins, and while he wasn't
as big a personality, nor was he as big a liability. The greatest
surprise, I think, was how good a songwriter he was, particularly teamed with Eddie. A year after he joined the band, a
year after Dave's death, the Wide-Eyed Boys had their biggest hit to date, "Perfect Life," a song Nick and Eddie had
written together.

Even today, they are still one of the biggest bands in the
world. I tell my daughters I used to know Eddie Allbright,
and they laughed at me. They didn't believe me. He is a rock
legend. How could their little old mum, their Hampstead-
dwelling, ceramic-obsessed, very boring mother possibly have
known Eddie Allbright?

"Yeah, yeah," they would say, rolling their eyes. "Of *course* you did. You probably knew the Rolling Stones, too, didn't you, Mum?" How they would laugh. Not that they even know who Brian Jones was. It was before their time. Eddie Allbright, on the other hand? They wouldn't believe me. They have never believed me.

"Oh, yes," added Tally. "Don't forget the Beatles, too. You must have known the Beatles!" I didn't say that I once stood next to Paul McCartney at the Ad Lib.

That's what Tally used to say, before she discovered the artifacts from a life gone by hiding in the attic, waiting for me to be strong enough, waiting for enough time to pass, waiting to be rediscovered.

Life was too big, too strong, too bright. Of course it was going to burn out, taking casualties with it. Dave first, then Talitha, then Gerard. He died a few months after Talitha. A heroin overdose. He was found in the upstairs bedroom at Villa Schiff, by his mother. There was little else written about it. I felt relieved that he was gone, and upset at such a tragedy befalling his mother. I had always felt that Gerard brought nothing with him but trouble. I was sad for La Comtesse, Beignet, who so clearly adored her son, but the world was better without him in it.

As for the rest of us, we survived. Those that are still alive today are dealing with bad backs, failing memories, the aches and pains that come with old age. I kept in touch with Paul, having tea with him from time to time while he was still living in Cheyne Walk. He became a recluse after Talitha died, but welcomed visits from people he trusted, and particularly, people who had known Talitha at her most vibrant. His bad luck continued for a while, with his son, Little Paul, kidnapped in 1973, returned missing an ear, which his kidnappers had mailed to the family to show they were serious. Oh, what tragedies that poor man endured, but by the end, he had constructed a life for himself that he loved.

By the time he died in 2003, he was Sir Paul Getty KBE, philanthropist, cricket enthusiast, bookbinder, opera lover and, finally, a British citizen.

Lissy and Eddie got married in Saint-Tropez, three years after Marrakech. I never socialized with them again. I ran into Lissy, once, at Annabel's, when Annabel's was a cozy, elegant basement club, like the best private party you had ever been to. She was there with Marianne Faithfull, and we all reminisced about how she, Eddie and I had hopped into the silver bullet and gone to Marrakech, thinking that Marianne and Mick would be there.

Lissy had four children with Eddie. They bought a huge house in Suffolk, the quintessential seventies rock star house, complete with sunken living room, shag carpets, and a sixteenth-century barn turned state-of-the-art recording studio. They had everything. I remember reading articles about them, so happy that theirs was a relationship that worked, that they had defied the odds and managed to find happiness. And then, when the children were still small, she had an affair with a young man, which resulted in his death. It was a disaster, and Eddie had had enough. I watched an interview with him on *Parkinson* once, and when he was asked about Lissy, about what had gone wrong, he shook his head, laughing. "Chaos," he said. "There was so much chaos."

He was right. There was so much chaos. There was so much magic, and beauty, and laughter, and joy, and darkness, and hedonism, but above all, chaos. Of course it was unsustainable. But for that short period of time, back in the late nineteen sixties, we learned what it was to be truly alive.

★ ★ ★ ★ ★

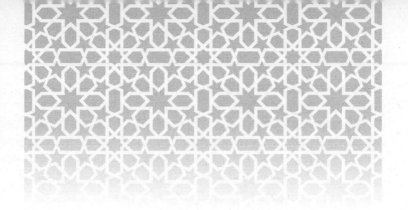

ACKNOWLEDGMENTS

A huge thank-you to the people who were willing to help or advise, in particular Philip Armstrong-Dampier, my dear friend Hajji Mohammed Ait Bouskri, Jose Fonseca, Zoe Craymer, Katie Taylor, Richard Cyzer, and Jane Hazel Wade for her wonderful stories of Bourne & Hollingsworth and Warwickshire House.

All the people who were gracious, or perhaps brave, enough to speak of those times, whether in person or in various articles and books, particularly the late Christopher Gibbs, Nicolette Meeres, Suzi Wyss and Prince Stash Klossowski de Rola.

Sam Taylor for so much, including the ultra-exclusive Rock House Writing Retreat, and Adrian Borra for the fabulous London pad.

Dave & Brandi Briggs, Jennifer O'Reilly and Russ & Jodi Hardin welcomed us back home with generosity, grace and love.

Enormous gratitude and love to Robert Carey for always giving me excellent advice, both professional and personal.

My early readers, particularly Laura Dave, Sarah Easley, Kristin Fine, Fiona Garland, Navida Greifenberger, Salima Saxton, Sade Strehlke, Julian Vogel.

My writer tribe, especially Jenna Blum, Laura Dave, Christina Baker-Kline, Jean Hanff Korelitz, Sarah McCoy, Dani Shapiro.

My editor John Glynn, whose brilliant idea it was to point me in the direction of historical fiction, and the entire impressive team at Hanover Square Press: Margaret Marbury, Peter Joseph, Randy Chan, Eden Church, Heather Connor, Hodan Ismail, Lindsey Reeder, Sara Watson, Amanda Roberts and Tamara Shifman.

My agent Jonny Geller, and his equally wonderful team at Curtis Brown, especially Sophie Storey, Viola Hayden and Ciara Finan.

My girls (some of whom have already been mentioned): Annie Woolf, Lisa Sewards, Dina Fleischmann, Lucy Krupenye, Sharon Gitelle, Sophie Pollman, Vanessa Morris, and my NC Mamas: Daniela Taplin Lundberg, Cat O'Neal, Brenda Battista, Holly Parmelee, Sarah Wynter, Maya Frey, Jill Connick, Kendra Seth, Kim Quinn and Carey Lowell.

Above all else, always, Beloved. And our children. Max, Henri, Harry, Tabs, Nate & Jasper.

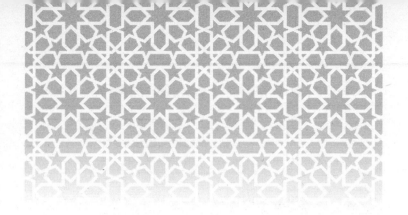

BIBLIOGRAPHY

Andersen, Christopher. *Mick: The Wild Life and Mad Genius of Jagger*. Simon & Schuster, 2012.

Beaton, Cecil. *Beaton in the Sixties. More Unexpurgated Diaries*. Alfred A. Knopf, 2004.

Beaton, Cecil. *The Unexpurgated Beaton: The Cecil Beaton Diaries as He Wrote Them, 1970–1980*. Knopf, 2007.

Beaton, Cecil. *The Unexpurgated Beaton: The Cecil Beaton Diaries, as They Were Written*. Weidenfeld & Nicolson, 2002.

Benaïm, Laurence. *Yves Saint Laurent: A Biography*. Rizzoli Ex Libris, 2019.

Bergé, Pierre. *Letters to Yves*. Editions Jardin Majorelle, 2010.

Boyd, Jenny. *Jennifer Juniper: A journey beyond the muse.* Urbane Publications, 2020.

Faithfull, Marianne. *Faithfull: An Autobiography.* Cooper Square Press, 2000.

Foulkes, Nick. "Sex, Drugs & Moroccan Roll." *The Rake.* July 2020. therake.com.

Fox, Charles. *Kidnapped: The Tragic Life of J. Paul Getty III.* Picador, 2018.

Gaignault, Fabrice. *Égéries Sixties.* Fayard, 2006.

Geiger, John. *Nothing is True Everything is Permitted: The Life of Brion Gysin.* Red Wheel Weiser, 2005.

Gibbs, Christopher. "A Magician from Memphis." *The Wall Street Journal.* 27 September 2012. wsj.com.

Grandchamp, Sibylle. "Bill Willis, l'esthète de Marrakech." *Vanity Fair.* 19 September 2014. vanityfair.fr.

Greenfield, Robert. *A Day in the Life: One Family, the Beautiful People, and the End of the Sixties.* Da Capo Press, 2009.

Hopkins, John. *The Tangier Diaries, 1962–1979.* Cadmus Editions, 1998.

Howard, Paul. *I Read the News Today, Oh Boy: The short and gilded life of Tara Browne, the man who inspired The Beatles' greatest song.* Pan Macmillan, 2016.

Jackson, Laura. *Brian Jones: The untold life and mysterious death of a rock legend.* Hachette UK, 2011.

Kavanagh, Julie. *Rudolf Nureyev: The Life.* Penguin UK, 2013.

Leary, Timothy, Ralph Metzner, and Ram Dass. *The Psychedelic Experience: A Manual Based on the Tibetan Book of the Dead.* Vol. 1. Carol Publishing Corporation, 1964.

Lenzner, Robert. *The Great Getty: The Life and Loves of J. Paul Getty—Richest Man in the World.* Signet, 1985.

Lewis, Randy. "How Peter Fonda's LSD trip with the Beatles produced a classic John Lennon lyric." *Los Angeles Times*. 17 August 2019. latimes.com.

Mayne, Peter. *A Year in Marrakesh*. Eland, 2002.

McEvoy, Marian. *Bill Willis*. Jardin Majorelle, 2011.

Miles, Barry. *In the sixties*. Le Castor Astral, 2018.

Millar, Peter. *Marrakech Express*. Arcadia Books, 2014.

Miller, Russell. *The House of Getty*. Bloomsbury Publishing, 2011.

Neville, Richard. *Hippie Hippie Shake*. Gerald Duckworth & Co., 2010.

Oldham, Andrew Loog. *2Stoned*. Random House, 2012.

Pearson, John. *All the Money in the World*. William Collins, 2017.

Peck, Carola. *Mariga and Her Friends*. Hannon Press, 1997.

Perry, George, ed. *London in the Sixties*. Pavilion, 2001.

Petkanas, Christopher. *Loulou & Yves: The Untold Story of Loulou de La Falaise and the House of Saint Laurent*. St. Martin's Press, 2018.

Pignatelli, Princess Luciana. *The Beautiful People's Beauty Book*. Bantam Books, 1972.

Pinnock, Tom. "Try on, tune in, drop out: the story of Granny Takes A Trip and London's psychedelic tailors." *Uncut Magazine*. 5 January 2018. uncut.co.uk.

Rawlings, Terry. *Brian Jones: Who Killed Christopher Robin?. The Truth Behind the Murder of a Rolling Stone*. Helter Skelter, 2005.

Rawlings, Terry, Keith Badman, and Andrew Neil. *Good Times Bad Times: The Definitive Diary of the Rolling Stones, 1960–1969*. Cherry Red Books, 1997.

Rawsthorn, Alice. *Yves Saint Laurent: A Biography*. HarperCollins, 1996.

Richards, Keith, and James Fox. *Life: Keith Richards.* Weidenfeld & Nicolson, 2010.

Rogerson, Barnaby, and Stephen Lavington, ed. *Marrakech, The Red City: The City Through Writers' Eyes.* Eland & Sickle Moon Books, 2003.

Sanchez, Tony. *Up and Down with The Rolling Stones—My Rollercoaster Ride with Keith Richards.* Kings Road Publishing, 2010.

Schonberg, Harold C. "History's last castrato is heard again." *The New York Times.* 1984. nytimes.com.

Vyner, Harriet. *Groovy Bob: The Life and Times of Robert Fraser.* Faber & Faber, 1999.

Wells, Simon. *She's a Rainbow: The Extraordinary Life of Anita Pallenberg: The Black Queen.* Omnibus Press, 2020.

Wyss, Susi. *Susi Wyss: Guess Who is the Happiest Girl in Town.* Edition Patrick Frey, 2018.